THE GIRL
IN THE BOX

Books 1-3 Box Set

ALONE
UNTOUCHED
SOULLESS

Robert J. Crane

Alone
Untouched
Soulless
The Girl in the Box, Books 1-3
Robert J. Crane
Copyright © 2012 - 2018 Ostiagard Press
All Rights Reserved.

1st Edition

BOOK I
ALONE

1

When I woke up, there were two men in my house. As alarming as that would be for most girls, for me it's doubly so; no one but Mom and I are allowed in our house. No one. That's rule number one.

I sensed them creeping around in the living room as my body shot to instant wakefulness. It probably sounds weird, but I could hear them breathing and an unfamiliar scent filled the air, something brisk and fresh, that brought with it a chill that crept into my room. They did not speak.

I rolled off my bed, making much less noise than either of them. I crouched and crept to the doorway of my room, which was open. It was dark; dark enough for me to tell they were having trouble seeing because one of them brushed the coffee table, causing a glass to clatter. A muffled curse made its way to my ears as I huddled against the wall and slid to my feet. We had an alarm, but based on the fact that a deafening klaxon wasn't blaring, I could only assume they must have somehow circumvented it.

I didn't know what they were looking for, but I'm a seventeen-year-old girl (eighteen in a month, and I guess I'd say woman, but I don't feel like one – is that weird?) and there were two strange men in my home, so I guessed their motives were not pure.

How did they get in? The front door is always locked – see rule number one. I peeked around the doorframe and saw them. The one that hit the coffee table looked to be in his forties, had a few extra pounds, and I could tell, even in the dark, that he had less hair than he wished he did.

The other one was younger, I guessed late twenties, and his back was turned to me. They were both wearing suits with dark jackets, and the older guy had shoes that squeaked. Most people wouldn't notice, but right then I was hyperaware. He put a foot down on the linoleum in the kitchen and when he went to take another step there was a subtle sound, the squeal of rubber soles that caused those little hairs on my arm to stand up.

I weigh a hundred and thirty-seven pounds and stand five foot four. The old one was over six feet, the younger a little taller than me. The young one held his hands in front of him, probably because his eyes still hadn't adjusted.

What do you do in a situation like this? I couldn't run; I'm not allowed to leave the house. That's rule number two, courtesy of Mom. So when she's at work, I'm at home. When she gets home from work, I'm at home.

I don't leave the house, ever.

The two of them edged their way around. The old fat one stepped on a soda can and swore again. I was suddenly thankful for my pitiful housekeeping efforts of late. I saw the younger one heading toward me, and wondered what to do. Can't leave. I reached to my right and felt the press of an eskrima stick in my hand, leaning against the old record player. I picked it up and transferred it to my left hand while my right went back to searching for its companion.

Eskrima sticks are batons, each about two feet in length. I could fight with one alone, if I had to, but I'm better with two. Mom started teaching me martial arts when I was six. I'm only allowed to watch an hour of TV a day, and that's if I do all my chores, all my studies, and I've behaved myself. The eskrima sticks are part of my studies. Two hours of martial arts every single day, no exceptions.

The young guy peered through the door and didn't see me. I was huddled against the wall, motionless, crouching at waist level for him. He swiveled when I moved but before he got a chance to react, I brought the eskrima stick up into his groin. I didn't know him or what he was here for, so I didn't swing with full force, but it still ruined his day. Just like Mom taught me.

He let out a scream and I rose, driving the point of my shoulder into his solar plexus – that's the place in your stomach where if you get hit, you'd say you got the wind knocked out of you. Wheezing and gasping, it sounded like he was going to get sick on me. Mom says that happens sometimes, so I moved out of the way as he fell to his knees. An eskrima stick to the back of the head put his lights out. As he fell, I caught a faint whiff of a pleasant scent – sweet yet pungent, cologne of some sort I guessed. It was unlike anything I'd ever smelled before. I liked it.

A stream of curses reached my ears from Oldie in the living room, and I saw his hand come through the door, so I reached out and made a connection with his wrist – with one of the sticks, of course. Just a tap. He yanked it back with a grunt of pain. I flung myself through the door, leading with a front kick that he blocked with the same hand I had just whacked, and he grunted again before trying to counter with a punch.

He was pretty far away, so I let him follow through. I didn't think he could see me, and he was as slow as a glacier compared to Mom. She practiced with me every day, and still beat the hell out of me during practice. You'd think after training with the woman for twelve years I'd have figured out how to beat her, but no...

Oldie took another swing and I sidestepped, my feet carrying me into the kitchen. I brought the eskrima stick overhand and cracked him on the head as I let out a little giggle. I couldn't help it, really. Day after day it was study, study, study, practice, practice, maybe watch a little TV, wonder why I'm not as good at fighting as Mom, and then one day you wake up and there are two men in the house. And I'm beating them both senseless without giving it my full effort.

What does it say about me that I haven't seen a living human being other than Mom in twelve years and my first instinct is to knock them unconscious?

I'd worry more about it, but Mom's been gone for over a

week – coincidence that these guys show up now? Mom comes home every day after work. Set your watch by her: with only an occasional exception, she was home at 5:34.

But I haven't seen her in a week. I thought about leaving, but what if it's a test? There was an alarm, after all; she could have been monitoring, and then I'd fail the test – and that would be bad. We'll define "bad" later.

After I giggled, Oldie whirled away from me. I pursued, and to the old guy's credit, he dodged pretty well. Of course, I was holding back. Not sure why. Mom would have been pissed that I wasn't attacking full out. I landed another eskrima on his chin and he staggered back and caught hold of the curtain in the dinette, yanking them off the wall anchors as he fell.

And thus violated rule number three: don't open the curtains or look out the windows. Most of them in the front of the house have heavy dressers and furniture blocking them, and all of them have bars on the exterior. The ones in the rear open to a backyard that has a fence eight feet tall all the way around and lots of old trees that pretty much blot out any view of the sun.

Don't think I'm a perfect goody-goody – I've snuck a look out back lots of times. My conclusion – it's a big, bright world out there. Really damned bright, in fact. Blinding.

I would have kept after him, but when the curtains fell the daylight streamed in and I couldn't see anything for a few seconds. When my eyes recovered I found the old guy throwing the curtains off himself and he came up with a gun in his hand. I guess I shouldn't have taken it easy on him.

The first shot would have gotten me in the face if I hadn't already been moving. I dodged behind the couch as the shot rang out. Then another and another. They were loud but not deafening. The microwave in the kitchen took the first two; the next three hit the sofa and I heard the muffled impacts as stuffing flew through the air. I was crawling my ass off, heading for the door. I dodged under the coffee table, the one Oldie had hit on his way in, rolled onto my back and put my feet and hands on the underside of the glass.

I saw him emerge from behind the sofa and knew my time

was limited. His gun was pointed at me, so I flung the table at him with my hands and feet. Kinda ugly, but it knocked him off balance as the glass shattered in his face and I heard the gun skitter from his hand back toward the dinette.

I didn't take any chances; I was on my feet in a second and sprinting toward the front door. He got the gun back as I was making my escape and I heard three more shots impact behind me as I slammed the door to the porch. I reached down and hit the outside lock – I know it sounds weird, but I locked them in my own house. Locked them in, and me out.

For those of you keeping score:

Rule # 1 – Mom and I are the only ones allowed in our house.

Rule # 2 – I am never to leave the house.

Rule # 3 – Never open the curtains or look outside.

Sorry, Mom, I thought. *We're just breaking your rules all to hell today.* I heard the gunfire again and I ran, dodging out the front door of the porch. I'd seen this space a thousand times as Mom was leaving, but never what lay beyond it. My hand flew to the knob that opened the door that led to the outside world.

If it had been up to me, I might have wanted to reflect on what a momentous day this was, going outside for the first time in twelve years; on violating so many rules, the first three big ones, all in a five-minute period. As it was, the sound of gunshots chased me into the light of day.

The cold hit me as I ran out, breath frosting as it hit the air. Fortunately, I'm always fully dressed – down to having on gloves all the time. That's rule four – always fully dressed, always long sleeves and pants, and always have your gloves on. I've asked why and Mom has declined to explain, answering with a simple, terse, "Because I said so."

I guess it was in case I ever had to run.

My eyes scanned the landscape of the suburban street in front of me. Even though the sky was covered in clouds, it was bright. The smell of the air crept up my nose along with the cold, and it felt like the inside of my nostrils froze. It was beyond crisp, and it almost hurt when I inhaled it. The frigidness bit at me even through my turtleneck sweater, and I found myself wishing for a coat. The wind blew down the road in front of me – rows of ordinary houses, idyllic and snow covered, trees in the front yards, draped in a blanket of winter white.

I slipped on the front walk and felt my heart kick me in the chest in a sensation of gut-punching fear. My hand caught me and I bounced back to my feet. *So that's ice?* I thought. Until now I had only seen it on TV and in the freezer. There was a black sedan in the driveway that looked like something I'd seen on a Buick commercial.

My hand brushed against it as I ran down the driveway and stopped at the end. I heard the sound of more gunshots and ducked behind the car. Clinking noises came from behind me as the shots bounced off their vehicle. Now what?

As if to answer my question a red SUV skidded to a stop in front of me. A small line of muddy snow splattered past me as the passenger door opened. Inside was a guy. Dark brown hair hung around his shoulders and his skin was tanned; I was not too flustered or in too much of a hurry to realize that he was not bad looking. His eyes broke the distance between us as he stared me down. His black coat ruffled from the open door and I heard his voice, raised to a pitch, and he spoke – something that should have sounded like a command, but was so gentle it came off as an invitation.

"Get in."

2

I looked back and saw Oldie coming around the edge of the car. He had the gun up and pointed, and was almost to me. My only thought was – *Damn, he's slow.* I blasted him with a roundhouse kick, minding my footing, and made solid contact, kicking his arm aside. I stepped in and delivered an elbow to his midsection, bringing my hand around with a perfect twist to pull the gun from his grasp. With a last effort I brought my knee up to his gut and then dropped him with an elbow to the back of the head.

He landed on all fours and grabbed at my foot, so I whipped him in the top of the head with his own gun, sending him facedown into the slush on the driveway. I turned back to the handsome man in the SUV and pointed the gun at him.

"Still want me to get in? Now it's on my terms."

His hands rose in surrender and a slight smile twisted the corner of his mouth. "Yes."

I got in and shut the door. "Where to?" I kept the gun pointed at him.

Brown eyes stared back at me, the color of the dark cherrywood our kitchen table was made of. "Where would you like to go?"

"Away."

His lips turned into a full-blown smile. He stomped on the pedal and we started moving. I'd seen a car move on TV, but it was nothing like the real thing. I felt the acceleration push me back into the comfortable seat. The whole car smelled good, with an aroma I couldn't define but that reminded me very vaguely of the times Mother would bring home flowers on special occasions.

My eyes stayed on him, even as we turned a corner. I darted a look out the window and then back to him. He kept that same faint smile but he watched the road. Houses passed us on either side in a blur of colors overwhelmed by the white of the snow. We shot through an intersection and the traffic light made me stare. I turned back to him. "What's your name?"

He looked over at me for a flicker before turning back to the road. "Reed."

I nodded. It was a nice name. I was suddenly conscious of the fact that Mom must surely have had a rule against talking to strangers, but we never discussed what to do if you're driven out of the house by men with guns. My hand ached where I had landed on it after my slip. "I'm…Sienna."

"Nice to meet you, Sienna." He moved one of his hands off the wheel and proffered it to me.

I shook it. "Thank you." It was the first time I had been out of my house since I was five years old. I hadn't talked to another human being besides Mom for that long. I wondered if this was how people talked? Had conversations?

"Where should we go?" His hands gripped the steering wheel tight, and I could see the knuckles of his darker skin turn white from the pressure.

My head was still spinning from all that had happened in the last ten minutes, but I had an idea. "Somewhere public. With lots of people. A grocery store."

"Fair enough."

We rode in silence. I studied him, looking at the lines of his face. He couldn't have been much older than me. Other than through TV, I hadn't seen another living soul in years except Mom. When your only human experience in life is through the TV, it warps your sense of reality. The people on TV are so flawless that you don't see the little blemishes on the skin; the little mole below his eye, the freckles that barely showed on his cheek.

We pulled into a parking lot and I marveled at the size of the sign out front. I stepped out of the car and the bite of the chill hit me. My black turtleneck didn't do much to protect me against the deep freeze that was the outdoors. I knew it had to be cold outside from the draft through the windows at home, but I didn't know it was this cold. My leather gloves felt like they weren't even there and the clouds covered the sky above, bathing the scene before me in a dull light.

The melted snow under my feet in the parking lot surprised me. Now that I wasn't having to run, I took my time, listening to the oozing, splashing sound it made as I brought my shoes down into it, then felt the cold of the icy slush go into my socks. I cringed. Not exactly how I pictured my first time out of the house: I assumed I would run barefoot through a meadow, with the sun shining bright above, the warmth on my skin, bright colored flowers and green fields around me. Silly, clichéd, I know. But that's what I wanted.

If I ever could have gotten out of the house.

We walked to the front doors and they parted for us. An involuntary grin split my face. Very cool.

Reed laughed. "Never seen an automatic door before?"

"Nope." I stared at them, almost afraid that if I took my eyes away they'd vanish and I'd be back in the house, alone and dreaming.

"Come on." His hand wrapped around my upper arm with a gentle pressure and I felt a slight tingle as he guided me inside – not pushy or demanding, but with…care. I could feel the warmth of his hand through my sweater and the weight of the gun in the front waistband of my jeans. The heated air of the store blew down on me as I walked through the entry, a pleasant feeling to counteract the chill.

We stopped inside and the smell of roasting chicken hit my nose. My mouth started to water; Mom hadn't shopped for at least a week before she disappeared. Last night I picked at the remainder of what was in the fridge. It was a little desperate; I was over ramen noodles and ketchup.

A big counter of clear glass stretched across the wall of the store. I could see a huge selection of meats and cheeses waiting inside it. My eyes wandered to the big freezers with boxes and bags of food, and I felt like I was going to start drooling. There were booths arranged near the deli counter – like a restaurant right there in the store.

"You hungry?" Reed's eyes found mine and I nodded. "I'll buy you lunch."

I stopped him. "Why are you being so nice to me? It's not like you pick up strangers on the side of the road every day who have someone pointing a gun at them." I paused. "Or do you?"

He blinked. "It's not a usual thing. But you have to understand…there are a lot of people looking for you."

"For me?" A doubt caused me to shiver. I hadn't believed he was someone driving by my house at random, but having the gun made me feel like I was still in control when I went with him. Still, it worried me when he confirmed what I suspected.

"Yes, you." He looked to either side. "Let me get you something to eat. I doubt you have any money."

"I don't."

He bought one of the big chickens that came in a cardboard box. I ate without consideration for how it looked, and he watched.

"Who are you?" I asked him between bites.

"Reed."

"Smartass." I glared at him, but it lacked intensity. I had a hard time being mad at someone who was feeding me.

He shrugged. "It's true."

"Beyond that."

"Someone who's concerned about you." His face grew serious. "There are dangerous people after you, Sienna."

"How do you know?" I sighed. "Beyond the obvious fact that they shot at me."

He hesitated. "Those guys…the young one's name is Zack Davis; the older one is Kurt Hannegan." He must have seen me stiffen in surprise, because he leaned back from the table. "I wasn't sitting outside your house by coincidence."

I felt the flush of blood running to my cheeks. "Are you with them? Are you one of them?"

"No." He shook his head, hot with indignation. "I'm not.

But there are worse things after you than those two."

"Who are they?" I asked. "Who are you?"

He placed his palms on the table. "That's not the question you should be asking."

"Oh?" My eyes narrowed. "What question should I be asking?"

"The question you should ask is 'What am I?'" His eyes darted left and right. "Do you think it's normal for a mother to lock her child in a house and not let her out for years? Even in your limited experience, that can't seem quite right—"

"Mom said it was for my own good—"

"I bet," he interrupted. His face barely concealed disdain. "Putting that aside, I know your mother disappeared—"

"How do you know that?" My fingernails dug into the soft wood surface of the table, leaving marks. "Do you know where she is?"

"No. But she goes missing and suddenly you have a host of people after you?" He wasn't smiling. "You realize that's not coincidence."

"I do. I'm not stupid."

"Didn't say you were. I—" He stopped midsentence and his eyes widened as he looked past me. I turned my head to follow his gaze as Oldie walked in through the sliding doors with a thin young guy at his side – the guy I had hit in the groin earlier. He was limping. And he was hot.

"How did they find me?" I turned to Reed, and he wore a stricken look.

"Some sort of tracking device, maybe," he murmured, sliding out of the booth. "Let's get out of here."

"Nuh uh. I want answers." My hand slid to my waistband. Mom had taught me the basics of how to use a gun, though I had never fired one. Tough to practice shooting live rounds in the house.

His eyes almost exploded out of his skull. "Are you crazy?" His voice was just above a whisper, but it was delivered with the force of a shout.

"I bet they know about my mom."

I started to advance on them, but he brushed against my

arm. I looked to his eyes, and they were wide with fear – for me. "You don't know what they're willing to do." He tugged on my arm. "Please. Let's leave before they see you."

The gears were grinding in my head. I'd been left alone for a week, and these guys came for me, armed. Mom was missing and I didn't know where she was. Lots of questions. I looked back at him and a hint of pleading was obvious in his brown eyes. Seeing the world on TV was different than seeing it like this. And for some reason I couldn't define, I trusted him – a little. "All right. Let's go."

We watched as the young man (so tempted to call him Hottie) and Oldie split up, each headed in a different direction to search the store. We waited until Oldie had walked down an aisle and Hottie had his back turned before making our move. We walked out the entrance door and into the parking lot, and Reed's pace quickened. The snow sloshed beneath us and the cold bored into gaps in my clothing that I didn't know were there.

As we approached his car, I looked up. The sun was still hiding behind the clouds; I had yet to see it. I looked over my shoulder. The two stooges weren't following us. I turned to Reed to make a wisecrack and stopped, my mouth agape.

A monstrous hand with long, pointed fingernails was wrapped around Reed's throat. His olive skin was turning purple and there was no sound coming from his mouth, which was open. His eyes were locked on me and his hands were wrapped around an arm that looked bigger than my torso. My eyes followed the arm to a man, at least a foot taller than me, built thick and muscled like a pro bodybuilder.

His head was huge, hair tangled and matted, dark with streaks of gray running through and it almost covered his brow. Furrowed above his black eyes were two eyebrows that were shaped like knife blades. His sideburns rolled down into a scraggly and unkempt beard that ran around his mouth.

Oh God, his mouth.

Pointed teeth. I've never seen anything like them – and his lips upturned in a cruel smile, his tongue lashing back and forth, not quite concealed by his incisors.

"Hello, little doll," he growled in a voice barely audible above the wind as he crept toward me. "My name is Wolfe. I've come to collect you."

3

I felt fear creep through me; the sudden sickness for home that told me that I wasn't sure I was ready to be out in the world. It only lasted a few seconds, and then I brought down my right hand in a hammerblow against the weakest part of Wolfe's wrist.

And it bounced off.

Wolfe didn't even grunt in acknowledgment of my attack. He reached for me with his other hand – and I have to give him credit: he was *fast*.

I was faster. I swept in below his arm and rammed my head into his solar plexus. Not my ideal choice, but I was a little off balance and I didn't want him to get ahold of my neck. I slammed my forehead into his stomach, straightening my spine. I'd broken boards like this training with Mother, and it's not without discomfort.

He didn't react. My head felt like I had hit a wall where it should have been soft tissue. I spun to slide under his arm to get behind him, but the pain from my failed headbutt slowed me. He grabbed me around my turtleneck and lifted me off my feet as if he were picking up a head of lettuce one-handed. I felt the blood pooling in my brain, fighting to get out through the veins he had squeezed shut.

"Hey!" A voice drew my attention and Wolfe's. I was still struggling, but two men in their twenties approached wearing heavy coats and jeans. "What are you doing?" Their faces were contorted with rage and the one that was speaking pointed at Wolfe. "You can't treat a girl that way! Drop her!"

Wolfe acted as though he did not hear them and the two of them rushed at him. I saw it coming through the haze that was beginning to cloud my vision, even if they didn't. Wolfe flung Reed into the side of a car and he ricocheted off, coming to rest in a pile on the ground. I would have worried about him if I wasn't too busy trying to free myself to take a breath.

Wolfe turned his body so that his left hand, the one he wasn't choking me with, could deal with them. His backhand sent the first flying a good six feet in the air and he landed with a crack on the asphalt almost fifteen feet away. It was so loud when he landed that it even caught my attention, and by this point sparkles of light were filling my eyes.

The second guy couldn't stop fast enough. Wolfe's hand lanced out, wrapping around the man's throat, but I could tell his grip was less merciful because the guy's eyes were bugging out of his head and Wolfe's fingernails had dug into his skin. Blood dripped down Wolfe's fingers, mixing with the spots in my vision. I hammered the bigger man's hands and wrists, searching for leverage, but I couldn't reach anything of importance.

By then things were so hazy it felt like I wasn't even in my body anymore. My hands relaxed and I stared into Wolfe's eyes, which were giant pools of black; no white, no iris, just black. I watched his hand relax and the Good Samaritan who tried to come to my rescue fell limp from his grasp. Blood was pooling in the snow and the man's eyes were open and lifeless. *Maybe if he'd had a gun.* The thought drifted into my mind.

A little shock ran through my brain. I had a gun.

My hand sprang to my waistband. I pulled the gun and brought it up as Wolfe licked the man's blood from his fingers. His eyes ran back to me as I pulled the trigger.

The shot hit him in the eyebrow and his hands flew to his face, releasing me. A howl as loud as an explosion threatened to overcome the sound of the blood rushing back to my head. I landed and my legs buckled. I fell to all fours, gun still clenched in my hand. I pulled up and shot at him twice more, this time aiming at his legs. My brain was sluggish, but when I looked to confirm that I hit him, all I saw was a thin black cylinder a little less than an inch long sticking out of the surface of his pants.

A dart was sticking out of his leg. Not a bullet wound. Damnation.

I raised the gun to shoot him again but his paw of a hand slapped it away. It skidded across the parking lot and under a car.

"Little doll," he breathed in my ear. I lifted my head up to see those great black eyes staring at me, but they were different, unfocused. "That's not a fair toy for playtime. What have you done to Wolfe?"

I might have responded if I'd had my wits about me, but his chokehold had deprived me of both oxygen and blood to the brain, and I was so dizzy I felt I might vomit. And if I did, I was aiming for him. Asshole. I was sucking down air greedily, large breaths so cold they hurt my lungs. It didn't seem to be helping. The spots were still clouding my vision. His eyes still stared at me.

"Back away from her!" I heard a voice from behind, but I was too gone to turn my head. Everything was spinning.

"New playmates are not part of our game," Wolfe breathed in my ear as he staggered to his feet. At least, I think he did. I saw his boots running through the snow, away from me.

I felt my head tilt back and my hair landed in the slush on the ground. I stared up into two faces – the men from my house. Oldie's swollen nose overshadowed his other features. They were both talking, but I couldn't hear a word by then.

The spots in my vision clouded everything out, and the spinning in my head worsened until it felt like I fell down, through the snow and slush and mud, through the concrete and asphalt of the parking lot, down into the ground. My vision darkened and blotted out the sky and faces above me.

4

I awoke in a small room surrounded by sleek metal walls that reminded me of a stainless steel refrigerator, save for one that was made of glass and mirrored. If I went by my TV experiences, it was a one-way, and someone was watching me from the other side. The walls were paneled into squared segments that were two feet by two feet each, allowing the door to be disguised so I couldn't see the way out.

I lay on a hospital-style bed in the middle of the room. I had a moment of panic until I realized that my hands and feet were unbound. I sat up and dangled my legs over the edge of the table, then blinked down at them. I wore the same shoes that I had on when I was attacked. My gloves, sweater and jeans all seemed undisturbed. My hand jumped to my throat, checking where Wolfe had grasped me. Bandages covered my neck.

I walked to the mirrored wall, staring at myself. My brown hair highlighted my pale face. My blue eyes turned greenish toward the iris and my skin showed nary a freckle. Strange what twelve years with no sunlight will do to you. My nose was not quite pointed, but long enough to make me self-conscious. I wasn't sure what to think of my height or weight – it's hard to compare yourself solely to people on TV.

My fingers found the ends of the bandages wrapped around my neck and I pulled on them, gently at first, and then harder as they began to unwind. They were wrapped three layers deep, with only spots of crimson showing on the first layer, then heavier as I peeled them back until the last layer of gauze was covered in dried blood. I looked to my neck in the mirror and smiled. The skin was flawless.

"Impressive, isn't it?" A voice from behind caused me to turn, bandages already forgotten and hands at my sides, clenched and ready to move into a defensive position. The speaker was a stately woman in her forties, with bright red hair that showed not a streak of gray, bound into a tight ponytail. She wore a black jacket and pants that gave her the look of a businesswoman – not quite severe, but hardly casual. Her arms were folded in front of her and she wore only the thinnest hint of a smile. "You're Sienna Nealon." It was not a question.

She took a step toward me and the door behind her closed with a soft click. "You've been out for about a day and the wounds around your throat are gone."

"I heal fast." My words came out more acidic than I had intended. "Where's Reed?"

"He beat a hasty retreat after my men scared off Wolfe." Her eyes showed the first trace of amusement. "You should get better friends."

I studied her as she slowly cut the distance between us. "Can't say I wouldn't have done the same if I'd been mobile at the time."

She bowed her head and the smile became more than a hint. "That would have been a mistake. Because there's no one that can help you as much as we can." Her eyes rose to meet mine.

I laughed. Loud. "I haven't even heard who YOU are and now you're talking about a WE."

Her smile didn't dim a bit. "My name is Ariadne Fraser. I'm Chief of Operations for the proverbial 'we' – which in this case is called the Directorate."

My right hand found its way back to my neck and kneaded the new skin against the leather of my glove. "And what exactly is the Directorate?"

"We identify and assist meta-humans like yourself."

I felt my head spin, and I doubted it had anything to do with my recent injury. "What's a meta-human?"

She blushed. "A meta-human is someone like you – who has powers beyond that of a normal human."

"I have no idea what you're talking about."

"Your strength is far above a normal human's, my men tell me." She pointed at my neck. "I saw your wounds when they brought you in. Gouges like that don't heal in a day, and they leave scars. I'm sure you have other abilities as well. If you'd allow us to do some testing, we could help you—"

"And if I don't want your help?" I set my jaw and could feel my teeth clench. I didn't know where I could go, other than home – and I'd have a hell of a time finding it.

It was as if she could sense the uncertainty beneath my facade. "And where would you go?"

"Home. Where I was before your men broke in and forced me to kick their asses. Did you know one of them shot at me?"

Her elegant face crumpled in a frown. "Which one?"

"I don't know names. The old one."

Her frown deepened. "Kurt Hannegan. It was only a tranquilizer pistol—"

"Yeah, I found that out after I took it away from him, cranked a few rounds into Wolfe and he didn't die."

She took another step forward, reaching the bed I had awakened on. "Kurt and Zack were ordered to bring you here. Although I would have preferred that it had gone more smoothly—"

"Smoothly? They shot up my house and drove me out into the world, where a huge mutant squeezed my neck until my head nearly popped off!"

She grimaced. "I realize that it was your first exposure to the outside world in several years, and I wish—"

"Yeah, well, if wishes were horses I wouldn't need a ride home."

She straightened. "You can't possibly be thinking of going home now. Not with Wolfe hunting you."

I glared at her. "I was doing just fine until your keystone cops broke into my house. Hell, I was doing just fine after they drove me out – and how do I know that this Wolfe guy isn't one of yours?"

"He is not—" she emphasized every syllable, ire running over her words—"one of *ours*. He is a monster, a killer by any definition, the type of threat we guard against. You must have seen – he killed two strangers in the parking lot."

Self-consciously, my hand played across my neck. Those men had been trying to help me, and they didn't even know me. "I saw it."

"You think we were involved in that?"

"Lady – Ariadne – whatever your name is, I don't know you. All I know is that my mom has been missing for a week, that your guys shot up my house—"

"With tranquilizer darts."

"—and then I meet one guy who says he wants to help me and another that grabs me by the throat and throttles me. Then I get brought here. I don't know any of you, I don't trust any of you, and I really just want to know where my mom is." The smallest dab of real emotion escaped me in my last words.

"I can help you with that – with finding her."

I paused in my tirade. "Do you know where she is?"

Ariadne deflated. "No. But we can search, and we have more resources to help with that than you do by yourself."

I smirked. "I'm sure you'd do that out of the kindness of your hearts."

"We're here to help meta-humans like yourself." Her fingers met and interlaced.

"And what do you want from me in return?"

She hesitated. "Nothing difficult. We'd like to run some tests—"

"Cut me open and prod my innards?"

"Nothing like that. We don't know what kind of meta-human you are."

I rubbed my eyes in fatigue and disbelief. "You keep calling me a meta-human. What is that?"

She straightened, portraying a certain pretentiousness as she lectured to me, the ignorant teenager. "Meta is from the Greek, meaning—"

"Beyond human. Yes, I know that." Her face fell and I was suddenly glad of the endless hours of study Mother had forced on me just for a chance to needle this woman who I'd known for less than five minutes but who already grated on me. "You were saying 'meta-humans' as though there are a lot of us."

Ariadne took a few steps away from the table and faced the mirror. I could still see her expression, and she looked up, as if she were recalling something. "There are six billion people in the world. By our estimates, less than three thousand are meta-human." She turned to face me. "Meta-humans have powers, skills and abilities beyond those of normal humans. Superior strength, speed and dexterity are usually signs of meta-human abilities."

"Is that all? Faster, stronger, more nimble?"

She shook her head. "Those are standard. Every meta-human has other, more unique abilities that manifest around age eighteen and are often hereditary."

Something clicked for me. "My mom was meta-human?"

A flash of surprise entered Ariadne's face. "Yes, she was - or is, depending on what's happened to her – meta-human, but we have no idea what type."

"How do you know about my mom?" My fists were clenched. I kept my eyes focused on her, trying to detect any hint she was lying.

"Your mother is a legend in our field," Ariadne replied. "She worked with the Agency – a precursor to the Directorate. It was the U.S. government's first attempt to monitor and control meta-human activity. She was a field agent, one of the best. She racked up an impressive string of captures of hostile meta-humans." Her expression softened. "She saved a lot of lives – human and meta."

"But she left?"

"The Agency was destroyed by a group of meta-human terrorists. Apparently she escaped before that happened, though it was assumed she hadn't survived the attack."

Understanding dawned on me. "You think she was involved?"

"She was with the Agency for ten years and disappeared at the same time it was destroyed? She must have been pregnant with you at the time, based on your age. So she disappears off the grid for over eighteen years if she's innocent?" Ariadne shrugged. "Maybe she was and she took the opportunity presented by the attack to escape to protect you. It is a dangerous line of work, trying to keep meta-humans under control."

"So you're with the government?"

"The Agency was. That's why they were found and destroyed. The Directorate is…not so encumbered." She smiled.

"Shady. So you want to test me?" I asked with more than a hint of suspicion. "Why?"

"There are different types of meta-humans. Let me start with some history. You've heard myths of giants, fairy tales, things like that? Meta-humans have been around as long as humanity, and humans described their abilities in ways that spread to become legend. For example, Wolfe." She took a deep breath. "He used to walk on all fours – I guess it's his preferred manner of movement; he looks—"

"Like a dog – or a wolf," I interrupted.

"Right, except he's one of three brothers, and – going by the word of a meta-human that's been alive for several thousand years – the three used to be guards for a Greek meta-human so vicious that he was known as Death. The brothers were called a three-headed dog at some point…"

"Three-headed dog…" I blinked. "…Cerberus?"

She cringed. "Appalling, isn't it? That's what several thousand years of folklore will do to the accuracy of a story. But according to our files, which only go back a century or so, he's killed hundreds, so he seems like the sort of hellhound that would guard the escape from the underworld, I suppose."

"And I'm like him in some way?" I felt a pang of disgust as I visualized the teeth of Wolfe.

Her voice became soothing, almost reassuring. "Like I said, there are different types of meta-humans. Wolfe is a creature who has built up a horrible legend, and he's lived for thousands and thousands of years. His proclivities for murder and torture are the stuff of serial killer stories." Her cringe turned to disgust. "He's a very powerful meta, but his homicidal tendencies put him on the fringe. I doubt you're anything like him." She shuddered. "I don't think anyone is – except maybe his brothers."

I tried to imagine three of them. One was plenty.

"About the testing process," she said. Her eyes bored into mine and I could tell she was trying to be caring or warm. It wasn't working. "We just want to help you find out what you are. If we had ill intentions, you would have woken up strapped to the table and the testing would have already been done. We're not here to hurt you or force you to do something against your will. We're here to help."

I thought about what she said. When I was unconscious, they could have violated me any way they wanted. Point in their favor, but I wasn't going to trust them that easy. "Noted."

"I don't expect you to make an immediate decision." She turned and indicated the place in the wall where she had entered. "Now that we've talked, you're free to explore our campus and give it some thought. I've had quarters prepared for you; you can stay with us if you'd like."

I stared her down. "And if I don't like?"

She shrugged again. "Then you can leave. But I'd ask you to give it a day of thought first. Meet some of our people – including the meta-humans – and see what they have to say. With your mother missing, I doubt there's anyone else that could help you make your way through what must be a strange transition. Or protect you from others who would wish you harm."

I stuck my chin out in defiance. "What about Reed?"

"I don't know who he is or what his agenda is." I couldn't tell if she was lying or not. Damn.

"And how did you find me?"

I caught the strain of hesitation in her face. "We'd heard Wolfe was in the Minneapolis area, tracking the daughter of Sierra – your mother – so I sent Zack and Kurt to follow him. He led us to your house."

"Then why didn't he come charging in before your boys did?" My arms folded in front of me.

"They…sidelined him," she replied. "Shot him with darts

that knocked him out while they entered your house to roust you."

"I see." I pursed my lips. "I'll stay – for a day. To…make up my mind."

A wan smile cracked her lips. "All I ask is that you give us a chance – to win your trust."

I returned her smile as she left, but as I turned my back on the one-sided mirror I felt it fade from my lips as I pondered her story about how they found me. I played back in my mind the expression on her face, the tone of her words as she told it. I considered how her eyes moved, darting back and forth.

That time, I knew she was lying.

5

The snow stretched across the horizon. The Directorate facility was isolated and surrounded by rolling fields bordered by forests. The woods had evergreen trees as well as the seasonal ones that had lost their leaves. The winter had left the grounds settled under a couple feet of snow.

I sat on a bench behind the dormitory building. The Directorate campus was huge, dozens of buildings strung together by a web of interconnected paths that had been plowed and salted. After being shown to my room, I explored the closet and grabbed the heavy coat and gloves they had left and headed outside. After all, I had not spent any time outdoors in several years, and I took this, my first opportunity, to really look at and feel the snow.

I smiled as the wind swept over me, stinging my cheeks and chilling my nose. I felt the cold creeping between my toes in the thin boots I wore. The air was fresh; fresher than anything I could recall ever smelling, with just a hint of smoke from somewhere in the distance. I couldn't hear anything but the blowing of the wind. It was enough to make me forget that I couldn't go home and that even if I did, Mom wasn't there.

A memory sparked to mind, of us downstairs. Our house was old, with a basement that had concrete block walls, and pipes hanging everywhere. Mom had turned the largest part of it into a workout room, with mats on the floor for practicing martial arts. She had weapons hanging on the wall, and every day we'd practice for a few hours. She was good; she taught me everything I know.

And now she's gone.

I heard the footfalls behind me and turned. It was Oldie, Kurt Hannegan and his younger partner, Hottie. Zack, I remembered Ariadne calling him. They were both wearing their dark suits with black ties and looking solemn. In the light I could see them a little better. Kurt's nose was swollen from where I had hit him. Looking at Zack reaffirmed my suspicion that he was not hard on the eyes, and had sandy blond hair and a tanned face.

I had already gotten a look at Kurt when he was coming at me in the house. Big around the midsection, the waistband of his pants sticking out to wrap around his outstretched belly, giving him the look of a penguin. His face bore the scars of a long-ago bout with acne, and the little hair that remained on top of his head was thin and combed over from the bushy brambles that wrapped the sides of his skull. If he could wear a fedora, his baldness might be passable.

They both lurked just out of arm's reach. Zack looked at me and smiled, far more warmly than I deserved since a day ago I had hit him in the groin so hard I was surprised he was still walking. I felt a little tingle and looked away, straight at Kurt. Oldie glared, giving me a wary look you might reserve for a criminal offender.

"Nice to see you boys are up and walking," I said with a sarcasm that I couldn't get rid of, no matter how hard I tried. All right, I'll admit it – I didn't try very hard. But at least in Zack's case, I felt bad about it.

Zack spoke first, looking back at Kurt, almost for reassurance. "Yeah, you pack a mean punch with that baton." His eyes were brown, but I saw some humor in them. The forgiving sort? I pegged him for a sucker. One day out in the big, bad world and I could already spot them.

"Yeah, she's a real champ in the dark with a baton," Kurt shot back. "Step into the ring and lace up a pair of boxing gloves and we'll see what kind of fighter she is."

I smiled at him, a kind of dazzling, annoying, faux smile that probably set off his bullshit detector. He wasn't a sucker.

"It wouldn't matter if it were drunken boxing, muay thai, kickboxing or just straight up, 'Marquess of Queensbury rules', because I could flatten your fat ass with any of those styles." I turned my head away to hide my smile but listened for footsteps in case he took umbrage and tried to sucker punch me. Even if he did, I would have bet I could still beat his ass.

Kurt's snort of indignation was drowned out by a chuckle and low whistle from Zack. The big man recovered. "I don't beat up little girls."

"You certainly don't succeed at it, but you try – and when that doesn't work out, you shoot at them until they take your gun away." I turned back in time to watch his face contort at my goad. My faux smile had turned real, an impish grin rooted in my deep amusement at twisting his tail. His little piggy tail.

Zack laughed again, a wheezing cackle that made him stoop to slap a knee. Kurt's face was ashen. "They don't pay me enough to deal with your meta crap. They should have sent M-Squad after you; I'm not a retriever—"

I smiled at him. "You should add that to the list of things you're not – a retriever, thin, a good shot, attractive, young, virile—"

He turned and stormed off in a perfect impression of countless divas I'd seen on TV over the years. I saluted his back as he walked down the path. "Don't forget 'possessed of a sense of humor' or 'gracious loser'!" He threw up a finger behind him as he continued his walk. "Oh! And 'witty'! You're not witty!"

"Damn," Zack said in mild consternation as he watched Kurt walk away. "I'm gonna have to soothe his wounded pride later." He turned back to me. "You really do pack a mean punch. Sienna, right?"

My smile went from mean-spirited to as pleasant as I could muster and I wasn't quite sure why. I guess there was no point in being wicked to everyone, especially not when Zack was trying to be nice. Besides, I'd already proven I could drop him to the ground if need be. "That's right. Sienna Nealon. You're Zack…?"

"Davis." He smiled. "You taken a tour of the grounds yet?"

I shook my head. "Saw the dormitory and the big building over there—" I waved in the direction that Kurt was heading—"that I woke up in."

"Yeah, that's our headquarters. But there's other stuff, too, like a gym, a garage and a firing range."

"A gym?" I cocked an eyebrow at that. The desire to work out was stronger than I would have guessed. I'd gone the week since Mom left without following the routine.

He shook his head, eyes wide. "I guess I shouldn't be amazed, but I kind of am. We brought you in less than twenty-four hours ago and I had to hold a jacket around your neck to keep you from bleeding to death. And now you're fine and looking for a place to work out." He pointed down a path and started walking. I fell into step beside him.

"You're not meta-human?"

He shook his head. "Just a normal guy. I work with them a lot, like M-Squad – they're all metas, and normally they'd be the ones that would have come to get you, not Kurt and me, but they're down in South America doing…something."

"Ooh, ominous."

He laughed. "Not supposed to be. They're probably bringing in another meta, but I'm not exactly in the loop, so I don't know for sure. That's what they do though; bring in new metas that we identify, or bring down ones that are causing trouble."

I eyed him. "And what I did yesterday, would that fit your definition of 'causing trouble?'"

He laughed again. "Nah, I would've fought back too if strangers broke into my house. We were supposed to bring you in quiet, and you metas don't typically do anything quiet if it's against your will. Kurt told 'em that, but Old Man Winter said to tranq you and be done with it."

I stopped walking. "Old Man Winter?"

He stopped and his tanned face adopted a pinched "I-shouldn't-have-said-that" look. "Ahh, I mean…damn. The boss."

"I thought Ariadne was the boss?"

He shook his head. "Ariadne's in charge, mostly, but she's not the big cheese. Old Man Winter…we call him that because…you know, some people say 'The Old Man' and he's kinda up there in the years, but he's…I dunno, cold. Like he never shows emotion. Never smiles, never gets angry."

"So you call him Old Man Winter. He got a name?"

"Erich Winter."

I laughed. "That explains it."

"Yeah. He's a good boss, just…"

"Cold."

"Right."

"So how long have you been with the Directorate?" I cast a sidelong glance at him as we walked. Ahead of us loomed a building that matched every other in the complex. Gray concrete walls, squat and blocky with a section that extended well above the rest of the building. Glass doors marked the entryway, but like all the others I had seen, it was unlabeled.

"Couple years. They got me coming out of the U of M."

"University of Minnesota?"

"Yeah. You gotta be close to college age. Were you thinking about going?"

I laughed. "You know my background, right?" He nodded. "Mom wasn't big on the idea of me leaving the house. Ever. Said it was dangerous."

His face turned serious. "She was right, you know. She kept you quiet all these years; now it's a rush to get ahold of you. Wolfe and whoever he works for – they're rounding up every meta they can lay hands on – and if Sierra Nealon's daughter is in play, it was going to be a mad dash to get to you first."

"What about the guy who saved me from you?" I looked at him as I asked the question, trying to see if he was as bad a liar as Ariadne. "His name was Reed. Do you know him?"

He shook his head with perfect sincerity. "I hadn't seen him before, but this isn't just a two-sided game. There's a lot of factions out there trying to get metas on their side."

"How did you know where to find me?" I eyed him and gave him a little smile. *So this is what it's like to play a man.*

29

Kinda easy.

"I just go where I'm told." His smile was knowing. *Damn. Maybe it's not so easy.* "So, are you going to let Ariadne run her tests?" His voice quavered a little bit and I knew that it wasn't him asking this question.

I sighed, mostly for effect. Maybe it was because I'd never had the company of a man anytime in memory, but I was enjoying myself so much I almost forgot that I didn't have any friends, just a suspicious number of desirous and questionable "allies." "Maybe," I replied. "I'm still thinking about it."

"Tough choice, I guess." He sounded sincere. Maybe he was. "Your whole world gets turned upside down and you're left without anyone to rely on. Gotta figure out who's telling the truth."

I flashed him a tight smile, and I felt my heart beat faster than it should have after such a short walk. "Or figure out if nobody's telling the truth. You all have fantastic stories of meta-humans with amazing abilities, but so far the closest thing I've seen to the truth of that is a grubby mountain of a man that looks like he could have stumbled out of a pack of wolves."

Zack grinned. "It does sound kind of crazy."

"You're all saying that there are people with superpowers, and that I have one but no one can tell me what it is unless you 'test me.'" I rolled my eyes. "Forgive me for not jumping to sign up for that medical experiment."

His smile faded. "But…you realize how strong you are compared to a normal human, right?" He stopped as we neared the entrance to the gymnasium. "You realize how much more powerful you are?"

I started to suppress my instinctive reply but I was a half second too slow. "I don't know what to think. I don't know where to go. And I have no idea who to trust." *And I don't have any idea why I told him that.*

He kept his distance and his hands slid into his pockets. I almost felt like he was doing it to avoid patting me on the shoulder or something. He took a step back to the concrete bench sitting in the shadow of the entry and did a double take as he looked down at it. "I can't help you fix all those problems. But maybe I can give you one answer." He pointed to the bench. "See this?"

"I may be meta-human, but I'm not blind."

His face twisted with a touch of condescension. "Nobody but Ariadne and Old Man Winter call them meta-humans. M-Squad just says 'metas' and it's kinda stuck for everybody." He leaned down and tried to push the bench. "It's a few hundred pounds, easy." His eyes glimmered with mischief. "Why don't you try lifting it?"

My stomach made a noise and I hoped only I could hear it. I walked over to him and studied the bench. It was concrete, with a nice pattern around the legs to give it some aesthetics. And Zack was right: it looked like it weighed quite a bit.

I reached down and grabbed hold by the edges. I cringed and counted down from three in my head and lifted with everything I had.

It flew off the ground and swung up, almost popping me in the mouth before I stopped it. I could feel the weight of it, but it wasn't that significant. I swung it around and hoisted it over my shoulder, holding it with one hand. "Wow."

"You never lifted anything like this before? Never tested your strength?" Zack kept his distance. I think he saw me lift it a little too aggressively and assumed (rightly) that I may be able to lift it, but I couldn't necessarily control it.

I shrugged, almost dropping the bench from my shoulder. I caught it and laughed. "What in our house would I have lifted?" I worked to keep a smile plastered on my face in spite of a sudden disquiet within as a memory of my hand pounding against metal, drawing blood, flashed through my mind.

"Odds are that your powers didn't manifest until recently anyway," he said with a shrug. "You might not have been able to do this a month ago. Metas I've talked to say it onsets over a few weeks or months…you just start getting faster, stronger, more agile than you used to be." My eyes glazed over for a moment as another memory floated to the top of mind. Zack looked at me with a quizzical expression. "What?"

I blinked. This one wasn't so bad. "A couple weeks ago, Mom and I were in the basement, sparring like usual. We trained martial arts a couple hours a day, and I've never been able to lay a hand on her. She's super fast, like a blur, and she always dodges. Always encouraging, you know – 'Keep it up, that's good, you came close there…'. But that time, a couple weeks ago, I thought she was a little slow and I dodged one of her kicks and tagged her in the ribs."

Zack nodded. "Ariadne and Old Man Winter said your mother was one of the most powerful metas in her generation. That's pretty good if you got a hand on her like that."

"Yeah…" I gazed off into the distance.

"What is it?" His brown eyes were rimmed with concern. Not an act, I think.

My eyes snapped back into focus and landed on him before I flicked my gaze away again. "Nothing…well…after I hit Mom, I was all flushed with victory. I took a step back; point scored, you know…formalities of sparring. I dropped my guard when I went back to my ready stance. She didn't even hesitate – she planted one on my jaw that knocked me off my feet and blurred my vision."

Zack physically recoiled and his eyes got wide. "That…that's horrible."

I felt the wind run through me and clamp down on my heart, pushing it into my throat. "No, it was good." I wiped any trace of emotion from my face. "She was trying to teach me not to ever let my guard down because it can cost you." The pain in my chest swelled as I pictured Mom's expression after she struck me down – fire blazing in her eyes; that look of spite and revenge all rolled into one as she looked down on me.

My mind raced, trying to think of something to ask Zack to change the subject. "You said my mom was one of the most powerful metas in her generation? So not all metas are the same, power-wise?"

"Yeah, there's a scale – some metas are stronger than others." He looked up at the bench still balanced on my shoulder. "That's why Ariadne wants to test you. Even without knowing what your other powers are, knowing your strength could give some insight into what kind of meta you are."

"Hm." I whipped the bench as if to smash it against the ground and noted the panicked look in Zack's eyes as he flinched and brought his hands in front of his face. I stopped it a few inches from the walk and gingerly placed it back where it had started and shot him a dazzling smile. "Fraidy cat."

He looked at me, eyes wide. "I couldn't tell you without testing, but seeing the way you handled that bench, I think you're right up there with your mom on the meta power scale."

I looked down. "I don't know about that. I fought back against Wolfe and he shook off my attacks and grabbed me like I was nothing."

"Yeah, but Wolfe is a freak of nature. Most metas don't live for thousands of years. He has."

"I don't doubt that, but he manhandled me. His strength was incredible; I couldn't fight back at all." I felt the bile rise in my mouth as I said that. Mom had always dominated me, but she'd never completely crushed me the way Wolfe had. It made me sick – and angry.

"He's THE top of the scale for power and he has millenia of experience fighting. He'd give M-Squad a run for their money, and they're all way up on the scale, and there's four of them." He shook his head. "I want you to promise me something."

I looked up at him and felt a tremble. "What?"

"You ever run across Wolfe again, do what the rest of us do – run like hell. He's a beast. And he will kill you."

6

Zack showed me around the grounds and after we walked through more buildings and met more people than I could possibly remember, he took me to a four story brick building, a perfect square but with windows spaced every five feet on each floor. There were entrances at each corner. We walked into one of them to find the interior indicated it was a much older building than most of the others.

Yellowed corridors ran around the perimeter. They looked as though they might have been white when the building was built, but they had yellowed through time and use to the color of a boiled egg's yolk. The center of the structure looked to be one giant chamber and around the edge of the building a variety of labs were open to viewing by glass walls. "It's the science labs," Zack said.

"So this is where they cut me open?" I looked at him with a raised eyebrow.

"Not quite." A voice from behind made me turn. A small man with glasses and a white lab coat covering a shirt and tie came in behind us and stomped his feet. His hand came up to brush some snow off his shoulder and I saw no rings or jewelry on thin, delicate fingers that matched with his gaunt figure. He had zero hair on his head, not so much as an eyebrow, and wore the hipster-chic black rimmed glasses that seemed popular nowadays based on how many people wore them on TV. I think they look stupid, but in his case it might have been a clueless fashion decision.

"This is Dr. Ron Sessions," Zack said with an introductory wave. "He's our chief science guru."

Dr. Sessions took a couple of strides toward me. "Is this Ms. Nealon?"

I looked from Zack to the doctor. "I'm Sienna, yeah."

His eyes lit up, and it was a calculating stare. "Ariadne sent me to look for you and here you are, in my humble halls."

"She wanted you to talk to me about the testing?"

He nodded a bit too eagerly. "Wanted me to explain the basics of it. It's a thorough process, so it could take a little while to go through and answer any questions you might have. Do you have some time now?"

I felt a gravitational pull toward the door I had come in through. "I'm kind of tired. Why don't we talk about it tomorrow?" I threw a thumb at the darkening skies outside. "It's close to sundown; been a long day, you know."

His hairless eyebrow scooted down his face. "It's four o'clock."

"Yeah," I said with an air of excuse-making. "But I nearly got strangled to death yesterday and it took a lot out of me. I'll stop by and talk with you tomorrow."

I threw a look at Zack, and I could tell he knew I was lying. "I can show you to the cafeteria if you want. You should probably eat before you sleep."

"Nah." I waved him off. "I'm just going to head back to the dorm. Thanks, though."

He froze next to the doctor, who was still squinting at me. "All right. See you around."

I gave them both a last wave and pushed my way out the door. I didn't run across the campus, but I definitely walked faster than normal. I wasn't used to the cold wind that whipped over the grounds as sundown approached. It felt like it was cutting right through me.

I walked into my dorm room and flipped on the lights. It wasn't huge, but bigger than I would have expected. It had a full bathroom, a queen sized bed, small refrigerator, a desk and a walk-in closet. Some thoughtful person had even left a pen and paper on the stand next to the bed, in case I wanted to write a letter home to no one.

I checked the fridge and found a half dozen bottled waters. I pulled one out, broke the seal on it and dumped it down the sink in the bathroom. I washed out and refilled the water bottle from the tap. Can't be too careful.

I took a sip of water as I looked around the room. I didn't know much about video surveillance, but there were a half-dozen places they could have put a camera. The good news is that it was on the ground floor and there were big windows, so if they came for me in the middle of the night I could send a chair out the glass and follow behind. I had a reasonable amount of confidence that I could run faster than any of them. Hopefully fast enough to escape into the trees if need be.

I sat down on the bed and realized for the first time just how tense I was. My shoulder muscles were crying out for relief; I'd been walking around ready for someone (Wolfe) to come jumping out at me. I rubbed my neck with one hand while I held the bottle with the other.

The bedspread was dark navy, the only splash of color in a room that was a dim beige. It was so generic and stark, totally lacking in décor, it had to have been done by a guy. No woman could abide anything this plain and boring. I thought about how straightforward and businesslike Ariadne's wardrobe was and conceded that maybe she could have done it. But no one with any taste.

I found it hard to believe how much things had changed for me in the last couple days. My mind went once more to Reed, and I found myself wondering if he was okay. I thought about those brown eyes, and they hung in front of me. I lay back on the bed and they still lingered; and a few moments after I lay my head on the pillow, I fell into a deep sleep.

7

I knew I was dreaming. It was weird, but I could feel it, the darkness of the room just fading away as I slipped off to unconsciousness. Streaks of light from outside the window shot through my field of vision and a sensation of falling was replaced with a feeling of weightlessness, like the moment before you step down a stair in a dream and your heart catches and you wake.

Except I didn't wake. I saw Reed again, those brown eyes staring, searching for me. The haze around me began to lighten. Splashes of color entered the world around me and I realized Reed was coming into focus, details adding in front of my eyes. He looked at me with confusion. "Sienna? Where are we?"

I felt a chill and looked down. There were two figures at my feet. A face stared back at me with dead eyes. "I think we're in the parking lot of the grocery store where Wolfe found us."

He looked at me with practiced skepticism. "What's going on here?"

I shrugged. "I don't know."

He looked at the body at my feet. "I remember going to sleep…but this isn't like any dream I've ever had. In a dream, you can't pick your words, and ridiculous things happen. Like a man with a platter of cheese slices comes wandering through, and it seems totally normal until you wake up." He eyed me with an air of uncertainty. "Right?"

"I've never dreamed about a man with cheese slices."

"But you know what I mean? This really happened, right?" He looked down at the body. "I remember this guy's face."

Remembering the two men who died here – trying to help me – took the thought of laughter away. "What happened to you? I woke up at the headquarters for those two clowns who broke into my house."

Reed flinched. "Yeah, I saw them get you. I had to bail. Wolfe messed me up pretty bad or I might have tried to fight them off."

I narrowed my eyes as I looked at him. "Are you a meta too?"

His hands fell to his waist. "Yeah."

"So what can you do? What's your…power?"

"The basics. Stronger than most. Nothing compared to that Wolfe guy, but I can tip over a car if I have to. I heal fast, of course. Some other stuff. Nothing major." He looked down, eyes avoiding mine.

"Uh huh. So why didn't you square with me when we were talking in the store?"

"It's your first day out in the world, you're running to escape from some guys who are shooting at you, and I get to break the news to you that you're a superhuman. Yeah," he said with sarcasm, "that wouldn't have sent you running away from me."

"It might not have." I thought about it for a minute. "Yeah, it probably would have before I met Wolfe. Where are you now?"

He shied away from my look again. "You're at their base?" He hesitated. "With those guys…from…"

"The Directorate. It's what they call themselves."

"Yeah. You're with them?"

"Not 'with them' like we're on the same team, but yeah. They want to run tests on me. Tell me what I am. Where are you?"

"Can't tell you." He cringed as he said it. "Sorry. I don't trust them."

I looked at him in annoyance. "I'm not staying here forever. I'm trying to decide if I want to let them figure things out for me before I leave. How am I supposed to find you if you won't tell me where you are?"

He finally looked me in the eye. "Seems like you've found a way to contact me. So talk to me again when you've escaped."

I threw my hands in the air. "Where am I supposed to go?"

He started to fade, getting hazy again, like there were gaps in his skin replaced by darkness. "Anywhere. Just get away from them."

I woke up with a start.

8

I sat up in bed and looked around. I hadn't even bothered to crawl under the covers. The red face of the digital clock on the dresser told me it was after midnight. I reached over and found the bottle of water I filled earlier. I picked it up, took it to the bathroom and dumped it out again. Just in case they snuck in while I was sleeping. Paranoia, thy name is Sienna.

After I filled it from the tap and drank two bottles, I laid back down on the bed. I was almost positive I had just talked to Reed in a dream. I went to sleep thinking of him and I dreamed of him. But he was right. What happened there was not like a regular dream. All the weirdness and surreal atmosphere of a dream was gone; it felt like we'd had a conversation in the waking world, but with a hazy backdrop.

Could I touch people's dreams? Was I a telepath, a mind reader? My thoughts raced while I thought about the possibilities. I'd never read a mind, so it probably wasn't that; unless it hadn't fully manifested as a power yet. Or maybe it was just limited to dreaming.

I thought about Mom as I lay there. Thought about when she used to get home, and how we'd eat dinner and talk about...I dunno, whatever. Training, mostly. TV shows, sometimes.

The world outside? Never. Rule #5. We don't talk about the outside world. It doesn't exist, for conversational purposes. We stay inside the house. The four walls that defined my life.

I thought about Mom and her rules and I wondered if maybe I could dream and talk to her, see where she was. I set the water bottle aside and lay back, this time crawling beneath the covers. I thought about her, about the smell of the chicken soup she used to heat up out of the can with the TV going in the background as we sat on the couch and talked. I recalled watching her walk out the door in the morning, and hoping that she'd open the outside door to the porch before the inside door to the house had shut, so I could catch just a glimpse of the outside world (she never did).

Then I thought of the times I'd disobeyed her. The times I'd let her down. I shuddered. The times she punished me.

The last time.

Somewhere in that succession of thoughts I drifted off again, and I woke to the sound of distant voices and a raging hunger. I blinked the bleariness out of my eyes and felt my skin covered in a cold sweat. My dreams this time had definitely not brought me to Mom. Light streamed in from a gray sky outside, peeking in through the blinds.

I padded into the bathroom and stripped off my clothing, which was sticking to my body. I thought for a moment about the idea of the Directorate watching me and I sighed, a deep, uncaring sound as I looked around the bathroom. I felt truly disgusting; there was still residual mud and grit in my hair from the parking lot two days ago when Wolfe had dropped me, even though someone had tried to clean it.

I sighed again and with a shrug I decided that I wanted a shower more than I wanted to worry about someone spying on me in the bathroom.

The hot water felt great, renewing me as it washed over my skin. Little flecks of dried blood that had caught in my sweater from the fight with Wolfe flaked off and swirled down the drain. I stayed in there longer than was necessary to get clean; the shower has long been my place for rejuvenation, the only spot where I could get privacy from Mom. The only place I'm allowed to shed my gloves, my shirt and all else.

I stepped onto the rug and took a moment to appreciate

the warmth of the dormitory bathroom. Even in a house as buttoned up as ours had been, drafts ran through it with alarming regularity. I could always tell what season it was by how cold I was when I got out of the shower. The bathroom here was perfectly insulated, though, and as I felt the soft squish of the plush bathmat between my toes there was a touch of that feeling of unfamiliarity again. It was as though I were so far outside my comfortable life that I almost couldn't recognize the actions I was taking as my own; like they were those of a stranger I was watching on TV.

I stepped out into my room wearing a towel and pulled open the closet to find a half dozen outfits. I took a look at the clothes I had discarded – dirty, disgusting and a little bloody. I wanted to put them back on, but it would undo the shower. Instead I picked out a black turtleneck and a pair of jeans and put them on, unsurprised to find that they fit me perfectly. I was only going to the cafeteria, but I grabbed the coat I had worn yesterday and slipped on my gloves, the only part of my ensemble not completely caked with filth. Rule #4. Old habits die hard.

The dormitory building was large and seemed to contain quite a few people. I guessed they were all metas like me, retrieved at some point or another by the Directorate. They seemed to be keeping to themselves, didn't meet my eyes in the corridors, which caused concern for me. Some of them hung together in small groups, and I could feel them looking when my back was turned.

I remembered seeing a sign for the cafeteria somewhere near the entrance I had used yesterday, so I walked the corridors looking for it. When I found one, I followed it to a large, open space with a hundred or more tables. Glass windows stretched from floor to ceiling of a two story-high space, looking out onto the snowy grounds. One wall opened up into a long serving line with a variety of different foods sitting out in a self-serve style, from Jell-O to meatloaf. A digital clock hung overhead, announcing that it was almost noon.

I passed through the line without difficulty; there was no cash register at the end, so I just walked off through the ever-increasing crowd and found a table by myself next to the window and sat down, ready to eat.

I was attacking the meatloaf when Ariadne sat down across from me. She wore an overly friendly look that put me on an annoyed footing made worse by some of my food choices. The coffee was not going well with the meatloaf. How was I supposed to know that? Mom never let me have coffee and people on TV drank it with everything. Bleh. Meatloaf tasted different than I expected, too.

Ariadne must have sensed my disquiet because I did not acknowledge her after she sat down. "Good morning," she said, breaking the silence. "Actually," she continued, smile widening, "I suppose I should say—"

"If the next words out of your mouth are 'Good afternoon,' I promise it won't be for you."

She blinked in slight shock. "Didn't—"

"Sleep well? No." My eyes narrowed as I lied. "Something about the thought of having a load of tests run didn't sit well with me."

"Does that mean you've decided against the testing?" Did I detect a note of disappointment in her voice?

"Didn't say that. I haven't decided yet. Either way, I'm not enthused about them."

"Ah." She nodded. "Perhaps we can help change your opinion. I've been asked to bring you to see the Director."

"Erich Winter?"

"Yes."

"Great." I slid aside the tray with the coffee and gawdawful meatloaf. "I'd like to ask him some questions anyway. Shall we?"

The priceless look of uncertainty on her face gave way to a forced confidence as she led me downstairs to an underground tunnel leading to the headquarters building a few hundred yards away. "No need to walk through the snow if we don't have to," she said. I had wondered why she wasn't wearing a coat. She wore instead another colorless business suit, not the same as the one she'd had on when I met her but not different enough for me to care.

We emerged from the tunnel into the basement of the

headquarters building and climbed a staircase to the fourth floor. I looked out the window as we walked down the corridor. The sky was still covered in clouds. I sighed. I had yet to see the sun.

We paused before a set of heavy wooden double doors. Ariadne knocked so softly I wondered if it was even possible to hear it inside. There was no answer but a moment later a click came from the handle and the door swung open to admit us. Ariadne gestured for me to go first but I shook my head and pointed for her to enter. She shrugged and did. I followed her a moment later.

The office was big, with a heavy stone desk standing in the middle of the room. It looked like a slab of flat rock that someone had propped up on two supporting blocks and used as a table, and it stretched about six feet across. There was no sign of paper on it anywhere, just a tablet computer. A lone painting of a winter landscape hung from the wall on the left hand side and two chairs were set before the desk for audiences.

Old Man Winter had opened the door, but by the time I was inside he'd already returned to his chair and sat down. He was tall, probably at least six foot five. His hair was close cropped on the sides and deep furrows were carved in the lines of his brow. His face was long, his eyes were sunken; bags hung beneath them, giving him a look of a man well over sixty and possibly over seventy. He was not thin but neither was he fat – he had a look of muscle and power that belied his years.

And his eyes were an icy, icy blue, and fixed with a stare that sent a deep chill through me.

"This is Sienna," Ariadne said to him, as though I could be anyone else. The only sign that he heard her was a slow, short nod, during which he never broke eye contact with me. I stared back, unwilling to be the first to look away. This was a game, I thought.

Ariadne said nothing and neither did he. He didn't blink, didn't look away, until finally my eyes were burning and I had to close them. He did not smile when I looked at him again, but I caught the thinnest suggestion of upward movement on his lips.

"Sienna is still considering whether or not to go through with the testing," Ariadne informed him. He sat stock still in his chair behind the desk and continued to stare me down. I like to think a lesser person would be intimidated by his constant eye contact. I was annoyed. "She has questions for you."

His gray eyebrows rose as if he were asking a question of his own. He waved his hand at me in a vague gesture that I took as a sign to proceed with my inquiries.

I stared back at him, trying my utmost not to blink. "Do you know what happened to my mother?"

He shook his head slowly, breaking eye contact for the first time since I entered the room. "No." His voice carried an obvious Germanic accent, even in the brief response. He raised his hand toward me once more, indicating to ask my next question.

I tried my hardest not to glare, but I probably failed. "Who would know?"

This time the eyebrow rose only a hint and he glanced toward Ariadne, who answered for him. "We have a variety of different sources of gathering information, including sending some of our agents to question people under the guise of being police officers investigating her disappearance. I have a report that you can read, but here's the gist: your mother has been working as an MRI technician at Hennepin County Medical Center for the last fourteen years under an assumed name—"

"So she's really not Sierra Nealon?" I asked without surprise.

Ariadne's fake smile held more patience than irony. "She is. She's been working under the name Brittany Eccleston. She has friends and co-workers, a pretty well established life built around her work – and none of them that we questioned knew she had a daughter." Ariadne hesitated. "She's had a reasonably active social life, dinners with friends, though not much indication that she's done any dating—"

"Did she ever mention any men? Your father, for instance?" Old Man Winter spoke up, his voice at a low

9

"Excuse me?" Ariadne stared back at me open-mouthed. "Did getting strangled cause you brain damage? Don't you think that your house would be the first place Wolfe would try to re-acquire you?"

"Re-acquire?" I scoffed. "He didn't acquire me in the first place."

She looked at me with something short of astonishment. "He damned near did – if it hadn't been for our agents showing up when they did—"

"No," I said with a vehement shake of my head. Old Man Winter hadn't shown the slightest reaction to our entire exchange. "By the time your boys showed up I had pumped Wolfe so full of tranquilizer darts he'd have had a hell of a time fighting off a grasshopper, let alone carry me away."

"Wolfe jumped a ten foot tall fence to escape from Kurt and Zack," she said, her jaw clenching. "Maybe you missed that too, since you were unconscious in a pool of your own blood when it happened."

I rolled my eyes. I am a teenager; might as well fight like a one. "I want to go home – not permanently, but I have some personal effects I'd like to retrieve." I turned an irritable gaze from Ariadne to Old Man Winter.

He stared back, still unblinking.

"No," Ariadne said. "You're far too valuable to risk Wolfe getting his hands on you. We have no idea who he works for, if he works for anybody – or what he wants with you, but it's nothing good."

"Ah ha!" I crowed. "So you *do* intend to keep me here against my will!"

"No," came the quiet, accented voice of Old Man Winter. "If you want things from your home, perhaps we can come to an agreement."

I looked at him. "I'm listening."

He turned to Ariadne, who spoke in his stead. "We send agents to retrieve whatever you want and bring it back here. In exchange, you do the tests."

I thought about it for a minute. "Counter-offer – and be assured, I'm not really offering so much as telling you what I'll accept. You send your agents to the house to confirm it's clear and I go in and get what I want and need, and we leave in five minutes or less. I do the testing after."

"Are you suicidal?" Ariadne looked at me in amazement. "You know Wolfe will be there somewhere, watching. At least if we're going to engage in this madness, let's wait until M-Squad returns—"

Old Man Winter cut her off, soft voice firm. "They will not be back for some time. We will send agents – ten should suffice to scout and keep a perimeter." He looked back to me. "Your terms are acceptable. Dr. Sessions will test you when you return."

"No cutting," I said to him, finding that this time his expression hinted at amusement, "nothing invasive, my hands will be free at all times, and don't expect me to drink anything."

He nodded once more and she bit back her response but shot him a look that indicated great displeasure. "Very well." With a curt nod of her head that reminded me of a bow of submission, she backed toward the door. I followed her and cast a last look at Old Man Winter before I left. He stared back, unapologetic, watching, surveying, who knew what for.

The door closed with a soft click and Ariadne rounded on me. I could tell by the fire in her eyes that she was preparing to unload. "Stick it," I told her. "Call me when your boys are ready to leave." I didn't bother to look back to see what reaction my words had caused. Well, maybe a little peek. Not sure why antagonizing her was so enjoyable; it wasn't like she'd done anything to wrong me.

I was sitting on my bed a few hours later when I heard a knock on the door. When I opened it, Zack was waiting with a dour look. "Ready to get killed?" His expression did not show any hint of lightness.

I smiled, trying to lighten his mood. "I thought you guys were going to sweep the house and the area first to make sure Wolfe isn't around?"

He gave me a kind of exasperated shrug with a marked exhalation. "Kurt and I get to sit in the car with you until we get the all-clear, but let's not fool ourselves. If Wolfe's strategy is to not be seen, he won't be seen – until it's too late. If his strategy is to take one of our guys and squeeze him until he lies and says it's all clear, then that's what he'll do and we still won't see him until it's too late." His eyes blazed. "Wolfe is the most dangerous meta I've heard of and it's insane that we're going into this without M-Squad for backup."

"Have you guys run across him before?"

"Nope," Zack said without emotion. "But one of our other branches did, and it ended bloody. Just like every other story in his file."

I scoffed. "He's not some invisible boogeyman. He has weaknesses, and he can't be everywhere at once. Maybe he's watching my house, maybe he's not." I stared him down as another possibility occurred to me. "Why couldn't he be here, watching the Directorate campus?"

Zack's hand crept up to his face, covering his eyes as he rubbed the bridge of his nose. "I don't know that he's not, but I know we stand a better chance of taking him here than in the middle of a South Minneapolis neighborhood. What could possibly be in your house that's so damned important that you're willing to risk your life and ours?"

I didn't answer him. He shook his head and gestured for me to follow him, which I did. The truth was, I didn't need anything from my house. When we got there, I was going to load up as many weapons as I could carry from the basement, but I didn't really need any of them. And it's not like any of my clothes were so amazing that I couldn't live without them; nor personal items, none of it.

I wanted to go back because I thought Wolfe would be there.

I hated the way I felt after our last fight, that sick feeling in the pit of my stomach thinking about it – about how he beat me down, made me fear him. I wanted to run into him. This time I'd be ready. Mobility and agility were my weapons. I couldn't beat him for strength, but I moved faster than him last time and if I hadn't rammed my head into the iron wall of muscle that was his stomach…I think I could take him. I wanted to. I was faster than him, I knew it. Not by much, but enough. I just had to aim for the weak points – eyes, groin, kidneys.

At least it would be better than sitting around the Directorate for tests I didn't really want to do, waiting for a mom who probably wasn't going to show up.

I followed Zack to an underground parking garage where I found ten guys, all dressed in suits, carrying rifles and shotguns. Kurt was standing there waiting and he greeted me with a scowl and a grunt that bordered on rude. I waved coquettishly with a big, fake smile. "I should get a gun too," I said as Zack and I walked up to their car.

"No," they both chorused. I shrugged; I hadn't expected them to say yes and I didn't press the point. If I was facing off against Wolfe and needed one, I'd take it from an agent. When Wolfe showed, I knew I was going to have to move fast; I didn't want any of these guys to die, after all.

We drove to a gate that opened for us, the entrance to the Directorate compound, which was surrounded by a high brick wall. I counted three security cameras without difficulty and I had a suspicion that those were for show; I would have bet the real cameras were much smaller.

We drove down straight roads in a convoy, empty fields of rolling hills on either side. After about twenty minutes we hit a major highway and followed it for another twenty minutes until we hit a suburban area replete with malls, stores and retail outlets. Another few minutes and we exited a freeway into an area of older homes that looked familiar. I couldn't be sure, but I thought it was the same cross street where Reed and I entered the freeway a couple days before.

A few streets later I found myself staring at the front of a house that should have looked familiar, since I lived in it, but didn't because I hadn't seen the exterior in over a decade except while fleeing from it in a rush.

"We'll wait here until we get the all-clear," Zack told me, leaning over the seat to talk to me. A few of the cars parked in front of us emptied and the agents were all wearing full length coats to conceal their weapons. They streamed across the street in a mass.

"Um," I said with amusement, "shouldn't we have parked a few streets away if we're afraid Wolfe is watching the house?"

"Wow, you've outsmarted us. It must be our first day on the job," Kurt answered with a snotty air of aggravation. "We are a few streets away. They're going to walk the three blocks to get to your place."

I looked at the house I had thought was mine. I tried to reconcile the facade with the brief glimpse I had gotten of my home as I fled into Reed's car days earlier. I shook my head. They were all snow covered, blotting out differences between them. I gave up and looked at Zack, who was shaking his head at his partner.

We sat in silence for the next few minutes. Tempted as I was to make smartass comments to annoy Kurt to the point where he'd get out of the car, I restrained myself (not sure how). We waited, tension filling the air as mundane reports from the agents came across their radios. Staticky "all clear" calls came through over and over. Zack had unplugged his microphone so it piped out over a speaker.

I gnawed on one of my fingernails as I listened. The voices didn't sound unhappy, just clipped and professional. I wondered if Wolfe would show up, if he was even looking for me here. I mean, he couldn't just hang around my house all day, every day waiting for me to show up, could he?

I thought about those black, soulless eyes and suppressed a shudder. He could. He would. I had to act fast here, get him before he got to anybody else. My ears focused on the radio, waiting for the first hint of any trouble.

"Found something in the basement," came the voice over the speaker. I felt myself tense. If it wasn't Wolfe, I could bet I knew what they found. "It's…ugh…well, it's not Wolfe. All clear."

"All clear," came another voice in agreement. "That's the whole house."

"You haven't sent anybody here since the day I left?" I asked Zack, who was staring into space, concentrating.

"No." His head gave a quick shake. "You ready?"

"Yeah," I replied. "Is our driver going to give us curbside service or do we have to walk from here?" I looked at Kurt and the flash of a scowl was my reward.

"One of these days, little Miss Daisy, you and I are going to go head to head," he growled as he threw the car in gear and stomped on the accelerator.

"And I shall look forward to that day with greatest anticipation," I said in a mocking southern accent, "if for no other reason than I'll get to watch your head cave in from finally meeting one stronger."

He said nothing else as we turned and flew down an alley, almost taking out a garbage can. His next turn was almost as violent and I didn't get a chance to ask whether he was scared and pissed or just a bad driver, because he came to a screeching halt and the wheel hit the curb.

"Settle down," Zack told him, wide-eyed.

"I'll settle down when we're out of here."

"Only if you can find a nice fella who'll take you," I quipped.

"Oh, how quaint, a gay joke," Kurt said without turning back. "I'm married."

"Actually it was my way of calling you a little girl. What's his name?"

"Haha. To a woman."

"Shocking! Because no reasonable man would have you?"

"Can it, please." Zack turned to me. "We're here. Let's hurry and get the hell out."

"Sure," I said as I slid over and opened the door, stepping out onto the curb covered in a half foot of snow. He parked this way intentionally. Ass. "Just trying to express my happiness for your pissy partner that he could find someone to put up with his menstrual cycles." That wicked feeling of glee buoyed itself in my soul again as I stepped onto the sidewalk. I ignored Kurt, who made a rude gesture at me from behind the trunk and made no move to join us.

Zack followed me up the driveway, which had a thin layer of snow over it. I wondered if Mom used to shovel it herself after a snowstorm? No…she was always dressed nice before she went to work. Flurries fell around me and I found myself sticking out my tongue, trying to catch one.

Zack watched me with a small smile of amusement that evaporated after a few seconds. "We're in a hurry, remember?"

My goofy grin faded. "Right."

There was an agent at the door of the porch, hands buried inside his coat. I stepped past him with a sarcastic salute and he rolled his eyes and smiled. Now there was a man with a sense of humor. The screens and windows of the porch were all boarded up and covered – so that when Mom left in the morning, I couldn't see outside.

It was dark as we stepped into the entry. The lights were on, but they didn't cast much light compared to even the cloudy sky outside. I looked around the living room. Everything was where we left it, upturned furniture and all. There were a few darts sticking out of the walls, and a couple of the agents were chuckling over them.

I smiled as I passed them and brushed into my room. A few articles of clothing were on the bed, not where I left them, since the last thing I did before I left was sleep and then whoop the hell out of Zack and Kurt.

I felt Zack edge up behind me. "If your men didn't move these clothes around, someone else has been here," I told him.

He had the radio plugged back in and I saw his fingers move to touch his ear. "Did anyone move any clothes in this room?" He paused for a moment, waiting for responses, then looked back at me and shook his head. "Guess he's been here."

"Or someone has," I replied.

He handed me a black duffel bag that he'd had slung over his shoulder. "Get what you came for and let's go."

I threw some clothes in the bag at random, then tossed in my eskrima sticks after retrieving them from where I left them behind the couch in the living room. As I picked them up I half-smiled, half-frowned as I remembered leaving them behind while I crawled away from Kurt as he fired his dart gun at me.

"Is that it?" Zack's voice almost cracked with the sound of his nerves. "Can we go yet?"

"Just a few more things," I said as I headed toward the door to the basement. My hand froze for a moment at the handle, then I slowly turned it. "Anyone down there?" I asked as I hovered in the doorjamb, waiting for Zack's answer.

He shot a look at the other agents in the room. "Not right now."

The white plaster of the living room walls gave way to concrete block at the entry to the basement. The staircase made an abrupt turn to the left ahead, following the foundation of the house. The steps were an old, unvarnished wood, and the only illumination was the single light overhead. I used to walk down these steps several times per day, but it was the last time I came up them that was giving me pause.

I reached the landing and turned, most of my thoughts about Wolfe forgotten. I knew he wasn't down here. The smell of old sweat, blood and other foulness filled the air.

I looked back at Zack and saw him scrunch his nose in displeasure at the aroma. "Did your mother kill someone down here?"

I didn't blink. "No. But not for lack of trying."

He laughed, and I continued down the last few steps and felt the concrete underfoot. Even though there was a thick sole on the boots I was wearing, my mind filled in the sensation from the thousands of times I had trod these floors barefoot while Mom was away, giving my feet a ghostly feel of the familiar chill. It crept up my legs, infusing my body, and I felt an involuntary tremor run through me.

The smell was worse down here, and my eyes wandered over our assorted weapons, hanging from hooks on the far wall. Katanas, nunchucks, scythe, rapiers and so many more. Mats covered the floors in the middle of the room and pipes crisscrossed the ceiling overhead from the exposed beams of the floor above. A slight clinking could be heard from overhead, as well as soft footsteps of the agents treading upstairs.

A couple of buried windows provided a little bit of light in the back, but they were covered by a film of white, providing enough opacity that it was impossible to distinguish anything through them. For illumination there were three naked bulbs swinging from the ceiling. In the far corner I could see the faint outline of a blocky shape in the shadows and the tremor got a little worse; I shook for a second.

I had halted in place and I felt Zack's hand brush my shoulder. I looked back in slight surprise and found his eyes looking into mine. My goodness, they were pretty. "Hurry up, okay?" His face was all sincerity, so I shook off my reverie and pushed myself to cross the mats to the far wall. I pulled a katana off the hooks and slid it into the loops of the bag, then threw a pair of sais and a dagger into it as well.

Zack watched me with wide eyes and a look of abject absurdity. "If you wanted weapons, we had plenty back at the Directorate…"

"Just figured I'd get them while I'm here," I replied. "Besides, Kurt's not too keen on me being armed."

"I'm not that excited about it either," he admitted with a wry grin. "But that's because I've felt what you can do with those sticks."

"In fairness, you did break into my house."

"Yeah, I…" His words trailed off as he looked into the corner. "What is that?" He started across the mats to join me on the far wall, but I met him halfway.

"Nothing. I'm done, we can go."

"No, wait." He was peering into the darkness.

"It's really nothing. You were worried about Wolfe, weren't you?" I plastered a smile on my face. "We should go."

"Just a minute." He reached up and grasped one of the overhead lights, pointing it toward the corner. He took a step closer and I withheld any additional protests and felt myself brace internally. I turned away and shut my eyes, facing the stairs and took a couple steps in that direction. There was an agonizing and sudden tightness in my belly. "What…is…this?" Zack's voice was low, but rising with each syllable, incredulous. I heard the squeak of hinges behind me, then retching from Zack, then a firm declaration. "Oh my God. Oh my God."

I squeezed my eyes shut tighter.

"OH. MY. GOD!" The last declaration was the most frightening, but it was nothing compared to the sound that followed it.

"I'm not a god, but it's always nice to get a compliment." I opened my eyes to find twin pools of blackness staring into mine from just a few feet away as he descended the stairwell. "Hello, little doll," Wolfe breathed. "Time to play."

chills through me, "Wolfe's amusement is running low…Wolfe is bleeding…and Wolfe doesn't like bleeding…a few drops of his blood is of more worth than this entire, stinking gutter trash city…"

I chanced to look down at my handiwork on his ankle, but what was there could scarcely be described as bleeding. A few drops no bigger than the head of a pin dotted the mat where he was standing. His grin had faded, replaced by a look of savagery that brought back the fear of our first encounter full force. I was face to face with a seemingly unkillable menace – what was I supposed to do now? Run for the stairs? He'd catch me on the turn.

My breathing had become ragged, not from exertion but from fear. I put myself in this situation because I was sure I could beat him. Now I was almost sure I couldn't. Unless…

I lunged forward before he made another move, holding my sword at maximum extension and aiming for his eye. I might not be able to break his skin, but the eyes were always a weak point…

Once more I felt the blade stop as though it hit an immovable object. I opened my eyes (I hadn't realized I closed them when I lunged – Mother would have been very upset with me) and saw his hand wrapped around my katana, the tip stopped only inches from his right eye. I pushed it harder, and watched as a thin trickle of red ran down his wrist. He yanked the blade down to his chest level and pulled it toward him. I let it go, but not before he had pulled me off balance and brought me within his reach.

This close to him, I had a revelation. Where a normal person would have fingernails, he had claws. They jutted out an inch or so above the ends of his fingers, black, with a pointed tip that looked sharp. They seemed to extend as I watched them.

I tried to stagger back but he seized my right arm and his claws raked into the skin, shredding through my sleeve. I pulled away and fell down, rolling to my feet and slipping away just in time to avoid a slash. I felt my back bump into the wall and realized he had cornered me. I reached up by instinct and grabbed for a weapon, pulling down a dagger and holding it in front of me as he leaped forward and slammed into me, driving me into the wall.

I opened my eyes and I felt like I'd lost a few seconds. My head spun from the impact. Wolfe was big; I would have bet he weighed well over three hundred pounds. I took a sharp intake of breath and realized he had been laying across me; that he had actually broken through the concrete block of the basement wall by driving my body into it. The powdered dust from the destruction hung in the air like a haze over me as I lolled in some twilight form of consciousness.

I tried to move my arms but failed. There was a long shadow stretching to the ceiling above me and it reached down with a pointed hand and grasped me, once more, around the neck, hauling me into the air. I knew my feet were dangling below me, but I couldn't feel them. I looked into those black eyes and my view expanded a little, like a camera when it zooms out, and I realized his face was contorted with rage.

"Look what you did to Wolfe, little doll." He shook me, hanging in the air as I was, and twisted my neck so that my eyes rolled toward his midsection. The knife I had pulled from the wall and stuck out to stop him was buried in his gut and a steady stream of blood had soaked his shirt. I would have smiled, but I wasn't really in a position to.

His hand wasn't choking me this time, just dangling me in place. I realized later that I must have been concussed when he smashed me through the wall; had some bones broken, probably my spine as well, because the feeling in my extremities was missing.

"Wolfe is tired of the way you play." He pulled me closer to him and I felt his nose run along my neck, heard the faint sound of sniffing. "I don't think you can move now…" The ominous way he said it turned my stomach. "Now Wolfe can play with you his way…without any interruptions—"

Before I could find out what that meant (though I had a disgusting theory) a flash of light seared my eyes and something rocked Wolfe from behind. He dropped me and I fell to my side, curled up. Upon impact, I lay there for a moment, unmoving, then realized I could now feel my arms, my legs and everything else. And they all hurt. Another flash of light lit the room and I sat up, nursing a half dozen cuts and some agonizing pain in my back and neck.

Kurt Hannegan stood at the bottom of the stairs, eyes blazing, what was left of his hair in disarray. In his hands was a shining silver gun unlike any I'd seen before, with a series of three cylindrical barrels that were smoking. "Can you move?"

I nodded, blanching from the pain that filled me.

"Then go!" He jerked a thumb toward the stairs as he pointed the weapon at Wolfe once more and fired. The barrels emitted a beam of pure white and Wolfe's body shook, pushing him from his side to his back. His nose twitched and his eyes, though glossy, looked at me with inarticulate rage. His hand slid from where it lay to grasp me around the ankle, just barely holding it.

"Little doll…"

I ripped my ankle from his grasp and brought it down hard on his face. Then again. When I lifted my foot, I saw him smiling. He tried to roll to his side but failed.

"GET MOVING!" Hannegan fired twice in rapid succession, his blasts rolling Wolfe to a facedown position.

I staggered over to Zack, whose eyes were shut, his face a bloody mess. "We have to get him out of here," I said to Kurt.

"Dammit," I heard Hannegan mutter under his breath. The gun went off twice more when my back was turned and I shot a look back to Wolfe, who was fighting to get back to his feet. "I'm running out of juice for this thing!"

I reached down to Zack and wrapped an arm under his chest and pulled. Lifting him was only marginally more difficult than walking by myself was at this point. Unfortunately, walking by myself was quite the challenge. I made for the staircase, supporting him as I climbed. I heard the gun discharge twice more, then some swearing from Kurt, and heavy footfalls on the stairs behind me as I turned the corner and entered the living room.

I staggered past the sofa, pausing for a beat as I saw two dead Directorate agents in the living room, one with a look of shock on his face, the other missing his head. I stepped over another body on the porch, this one missing at least one arm. Another was splayed out under the tree in the front yard as though he were napping in the snow. I almost slipped at the same spot as last time I left the house, but recovered.

I opened the door to the backseat and threw Zack in, then hobbled to the front just as Kurt cleared the driveway. He slid into the driver's seat and was already starting the car as he slammed the door. His foot was on the accelerator before it was in gear, causing a loud thump as the car rocked and the tires slipped on the snowy pavement.

I looked back at the house. Wolfe staggered out the front door, clutching his ribs, and broke into a run as we shot down the street.

"He's gaining on us!" I shouted as I looked back, watching Wolfe streak along behind us, loping on all fours. Like a dog.

Kurt took the corner so fast we slid until the wheels caught and took off again. I heard a screeching noise and turned to see Wolfe dig his claws into the trunk. Little bits of metal flaked off as if they were paper. I looked through the rear window and saw those black eyes staring back at me, the mouth of the demon upturned in a grin. I couldn't take my eyes off him. He was keeping pace with the car, barely, trying to use his claws to secure a hold to grab on.

Kurt floored it as we shot through another intersection, then turned to get on the freeway. Wolfe's hands fell free of the trunk, but he kept running behind us, still watching me. He maintained his pace all the way to the top of the onramp, at which point Kurt put the accelerator to the floor and I saw Wolfe's black eyes recede in the distance as we made our escape.

11

As the car sped down the interstate, I stole a look at the speedometer. Kurt was doing close to a hundred as I slipped into the back seat and knelt on the floorboard next to Zack. One of my gloved hands held his head while the other wiped the blood from his face. It flowed from his nose, which was broken. The rest of his handsome face seemed unharmed and his eyes fluttered open.

"What happened?" he asked, woozy.

"Wolfe," I replied.

"Oh. Did we win?"

I heard a snort from Kurt in the front seat. "Do you feel like you won, kid?"

He turned his face to look at the back of Kurt's head. "I'm still alive, so yeah. Kinda." His hand crept up to his nose and held it, stemming the bleeding. He sat up, his eyeballs rolling. "What about the other guys?" He looked at Kurt, who made no move but to stiffen and keep focused on the road.

Zack turned to me. His eyes met mine and I had to look away. "I don't think there any survivors," I said, looking down.

"How did we get away?" His voice carried a dreamlike quality.

Kurt harrumphed in the front seat. I shot a glare at him. "Your partner shot Wolfe with some kind of epic blaster weapon that kept him down while I carried you out. Why weren't all your guys carrying those?"

Kurt didn't deign to look back. "Because that's the only one we had."

I looked back to see Zack studying me. "You're hurt," he said.

"You too."

"Lean forward." He gently pushed me toward the front seat. "Your shirt is bloody in the back."

He started to lift my sweater but my hand brushed his away. "I'm fine," I assured him. "Wolfe rammed me into the wall but I'm already healing."

"I should check." Concern lit his slender face and warm eyes. I stared a moment too long, got embarrassed and looked away again. Damn.

I ran my gloved hand down my back and felt a half dozen places where it hurt, but wasn't agonizing. Then my hands moved to my front and I found some broken ribs and cringed. "I'm fine," I said as he started to lean toward me. "Really. I'll be back to a hundred percent before you know it."

"Must be nice," Kurt spat. "I know a few guys that wish they had that ability right now."

"Kurt…" Zack started.

"What?" Kurt's tone was acid in reply, and he shot a look of pure malice at me. "Miss High And Mighty Little Meta got them killed. Is that too deep for you, Zack? Are you too busy staring into her eyes to realize that there are eight of our guys dead because of her?"

"Shut up!" Zack answered for me, but I was smoldering on the inside. I couldn't deny the truth of what he was saying, but it didn't make it sting any less. They were dead because of me.

"We didn't walk out of there with whatever it was she went for," Kurt went on, voice breaking like a man on the edge. "What did you need to get from your house that was SO important, little girl, that you'd risk meeting up with Wolfe to get it?"

I opened my mouth to speak but no words came out. I stuttered for a minute before Kurt cut me off.

"I see. Well, I'm glad it was so important that it was worth another shot at you—"

"Maybe it was the other way around," I said, turning to meet his accusation. "Maybe I wanted another shot at him."

Everyone froze. Kurt looked down at me with an almost total lack of understanding. A look of knowing had dawned across Zack's face while Ariadne appeared stricken at the window. Old Man Winter, as per usual, kept his expression neutral through either long practice or a complete lack of emotional attachment to the situation. I suspected the former, but I didn't know him well enough to be sure.

It felt like the air had stagnated, as though everybody had paused and no one was taking any breaths; as though I had tossed out a grenade in the middle of the room and we were just waiting for it to explode.

"You did it on purpose." Kurt was the first to recover. "You didn't go back for anything; you went there so you could take a crack at Wolfe, and you threw away eight of our guys in the process, you—!" He lunged at me, screaming unintelligibly, and Zack caught him midway, struggling to control his partner's bulk as Kurt pushed toward me.

I continued to stare at the blood in my glove. It was a few drops; nothing compared to what was on my hands.

"Get him out of here, Davis!" Ariadne's shout crackled through the air. "Hannegan, get yourself under control!"

I turned to look at Kurt, whose face was purple with outrage. Zack was no longer restraining him, but he still held a protective arm out between me and Kurt. I didn't need it. Beaten, wounded, internally bleeding and I could still have broken him into tiny pieces, then everyone else in the room one by one. Sweet gesture, though.

"Zack," Ariadne called out to him. "Go to medical. You look like Hannegan drove over you."

They walked out together, Kurt storming and Zack following a few paces behind. Zack turned back to meet my eyes at the door and mouthed the word "Later" before he closed it. If Kurt had said it, I would have considered it a weak threat. With Zack, I knew it was a promise – of a conversation that I didn't want to have. Ever. I sighed and turned back to Ariadne and Old Man Winter.

Ariadne seemed to be struggling for words and I recalled our last conversation and my suggestive insult. "We are...glad to see you made it through this episode in one piece. Dr. Sessions is all set to begin your—" she paused for a moment—"non-invasive testing tomorrow morning."

I stood up and started to leave, but something stopped me and I turned back to face Old Man Winter, who was still looking at me with that damned eerie stare. "You knew Wolfe would cut through your agents, didn't you?"

"That's a ridiculous assertion," Ariadne said from behind him. If he was insulted, he didn't show any more umbrage to it than anything else I'd said. "If we'd known this was going to happen we wouldn't have sent anyone, especially not you."

"Not what I asked," I replied. "And you're not who I asked. You offered to just send your agents because you didn't want to endanger me. So my question stands – you knew he would cut through them, yes? Not you, Ariadne." I pointed at her. "He overruled you."

Old Man Winter gazed back at me. "If Wolfe was there, it was certain that he would cut through any agents we sent."

I felt my mouth dry out at the words he spoke, and my voice quivered, just a little, as I whispered my next question. "Then why did you let us go?"

"Enough." Ariadne's words cut off his quiet reply, and she surged forward from her place behind him, putting a hand on my elbow and trying to escort me out the door. I restrained my impulse to flatten her. "You wanted to go, we helped you in exchange for your consent to test you—"

"No." I shook her hand off with almost no effort. "I need to know." I looked back at Old Man Winter, and he did not shy from my gaze. He held his hand up to stay Ariadne.

"Because you demanded it," he said with slow, measured words. "And you are more important to us than a hundred agents."

The blue eyes forced a chill in me as he answered, and they followed me unceasing as Ariadne led me from the room. This time I did not resist her.

12

I parted from Ariadne after a muttered curse under my breath, leaving her with a shocked look (again). She lanced back with a scathing reminder about the testing, set for early tomorrow, at which point I left. If I could blame my antisocial behavior on Asperger's like some ridiculous TV character I would, but the truth is that I was trying my hardest not to think about the lives I had cost in my attempt to face off with Wolfe. And I was still struggling with who I could trust.

Old Man Winter had said I was more valuable to them than a hundred agents, but the question I had to ask was 'why?' I walked back to the dormitories using the above ground route, and when I walked out the doors of the headquarters building the icy sting of the wind lanced my cheeks.

I smelled that familiar scent hanging in the air again, that of a real wood fire, just like Mom used to build sometimes in our fireplace at home. We would actually make s'mores on it, like people in movies do when they're camping, and one time she got mad at me for breaking the rules and stuck my hand in the fire. True story. It had healed by the next day, but it hurt like hell, the flesh nearly peeling off the bone. That time was for the audacity to ask about how people lived in the outside world, breaking rule #5. Oops.

My eyes looked over the grounds and I found myself wondering what this place looked like in the middle of summer. Then my thoughts went back to the faces of those agents, in the garage when I met them, and I wondered what they did on a normal day, when they weren't escorting me to my house. Some of them had families, wives, kids. I didn't know a single one of their names.

It was only about four in the afternoon, but it was already getting dark. The haze of clouds hanging overhead was only making it worse. Still no sign of the sun, just like if I'd never left home. The wind was bitter, bad enough that even I didn't want to stay out for very long. After being cooped up inside for a decade, you'd think I'd want to spend as much time outside as possible – and I did, but there were limits, and apparently they were at three degrees Fahrenheit.

I entered the dormitory building to find people going about their business in the hallways, passing me with the occasional nod. I wondered if these people – metas, I thought – knew the agents that got killed. I wondered if they worked here or if they were just here for study, like me. I wondered what their lives were like, their stories, and if any of them missed their parents.

I opened the door to my room and didn't even bother to do a thorough check before I lay down. I grabbed a bottle of water from the fridge, twisted the cap and drank it without replacing it from the tap. Who cares? What were they going to do, poison me? Bring it on. I was at their mercy – I didn't trust them, but it wasn't like I had anywhere else to go.

Except I thought about Reed again, and about how I dreamed of him. I wondered if I could do it again. I put the water aside and lay down, thinking of him. I remembered his brown eyes, his hair framing his tan face, and I drifted off.

It felt like I lingered in the dark for hours before he showed up, fading into view a little at a time. He looked around and saw me, a look of unsurprise on his face.

"Hi." I waved, feeling more than a little stupid.

He lowered his head and shook it in something akin to deep disappointment. "You stirred up a hell of a hornet's nest."

I blinked at him, and wondered for a second why I would be blinking when my eyes were closed and I was asleep. "What do you mean?"

"I mean your showdown with Wolfe."

I looked away. "Yeah, I know. I got people killed."

"It's not that!" Reed said, incredulous. "Directorate agents die all the time. Whatever you did when you fought Wolfe, he's lost it. He's over the edge now."

"He wasn't before?"

Reed exploded. "This is no joking matter! He was going to capture you before, when he was following his employer's orders. Now he's lost it and they're panicking because he's gone rogue. He wants to kill you."

"How do you know that?" Little tingles of suspicion started inside me; my stomach churned, hinting at a feeling of betrayal.

"The people I work with have spies inside the group he was working for. You *really* pissed him off. What did you do?"

I shrugged, numb at the revelation. "Made him bleed."

Disappointed, Reed's hand found its way to his face. "Why did you go back to where you knew he could be?"

I clenched my jaw and felt pain, and thought about whether I must have been doing it in my sleep. "Because I didn't want to just sit here and stew in my fear of him. If you sit around and think about how much you're afraid of something, it just makes it worse. I didn't think he was that bad…I thought I could beat him." I lowered my head. "I was wrong."

"You *wanted* to face off with Wolfe?" He shook his head. "That's madness. You need to stay where you are, let the Directorate protect you."

"The Directorate can't protect me. He went through their agents like they were made of whipped cream."

"It doesn't matter, Sienna. I don't think he can touch you so long as you stay there."

"I don't want to stay here any more," I said. "I'm ready to leave and join you."

He shook his head again. "Sorry, but you can't do that. I can't protect you right now, not from Wolfe. Soon, but not right now."

"I just…" I crinkled my eyes, closing them as tight as I

could. "I just want to get out of here. Out of town. Away from everything and everyone." I took a breath. "I read a book about towns in western South Dakota, and it had pictures; they were gorgeous, green and mountainous. I want to see mountains, Reed, and beaches, and anything but this gawdawful snow. It's so dim and dark all the time and I hate it…"

"This is not a problem you can run away from," he said with a look of sadness. "Wolfe is relentless."

"He doesn't know where I am now, and he can't know where I am from here on if I'm careful. My mom dodged these people for years. He's not a psychic and he's not infallible."

"You don't know Wolfe. He's lived for thousands of years and he uses time to his advantage. You're right: you'd likely make it out of the Minneapolis area, maybe even out of the state and the country, but he'd track you down eventually."

He wore a look of pity and I felt something sharp inside that woke up my defenses. I didn't know Reed any better than the Directorate people. I composed myself, pasting a smile that was as fake as any I'd ever worn. "Fine. All right."

"I can tell you're hurting…"

"You don't know anything about me," I snapped. Not sure where that came from, but I had a suspicion.

"Not much, but I can tell you're blaming yourself for what happened to those Directorate agents."

"I have to go," I replied, as brusque as I could make it. "I have to wake up. They're going to test me in the morning."

"Just make sure you—" His words faded as I struggled and forced my way out of the dream. I didn't wonder until later what he was going to say.

13

I woke up just after one in the morning. Except for a few minor aches, my injuries from the battle with Wolfe had healed themselves without much sign of anything odd. I realized I had gone to bed without dinner and that I hadn't eaten much lunch the day before either. I left my dormitory room (always fully dressed, remember?) and wandered the halls. I didn't hold much hope that the cafeteria would be open at this hour, but I doubted I would have a problem stealing some food.

Besides, was it really stealing? They would have given it to me if they'd been open. I came through the entrance to the cafeteria and found a few lights on, scattered throughout the place. Spotlights outside the massive windows showed snow was lightly falling outside. The smell of cleaning solutions hung in the air and when coupled with the dimness it gave the place the vague sense of what I'd imagine a hospital to feel like.

A lone figure was sitting in the corner where the two glass walls met, staring out into the dark. I crept up quietly until I got close enough to realize it was Zack, then started to tiptoe away. I didn't want to talk to anyone, least of all him.

"I can see your reflection," he called out. He turned, revealing a series of bandages over his nose with a piece of metal over it to hold it in place for healing. "I figured you'd be hungry sooner or later."

"Yeah," I replied. "Hungry and tired, so I think I'll just get something and go…"

"Why don't you sit down?" His eyes didn't let me retreat. They were watching me and I felt almost as helpless as when Wolfe's black eyes were on me. I felt myself lower into the seat opposite him and he stared back at me as I did. I had the nasty feeling I knew what was coming next, but like a scene in a horror movie you don't want to watch but can't look away from, I was stuck in place.

"I want to talk about the basement." He was still watching me. I didn't like it. I hated it. I despise feeling trapped, and trapped I was. I hoped this would be quick – I hoped it was already over, actually, that maybe he didn't see as much as I thought he had, that he'd not bothered to report it to Ariadne or Old Man Winter, and definitely not Kurt.

"About the fight with Wolfe?" I tried to keep the hope out of my voice.

"You know that's not what I mean. Before him. What I saw…" His voice trailed off.

I remained silent. In a failed effort to be casual, I focused really, really hard on my left middle fingernail and started counting backward from one hundred.

"Sienna?" He repeated my name twice more in a bid to get my attention.

"I don't want to talk about this." My voice was quiet, but firm. Maybe a hint of a crack.

"You need to talk to somebody about it."

"No, I don't." I could feel myself get defensive, pissed. "I'm pretty much a full grown woman at this point, and I can make my own decisions about what I want to talk about and don't, and this falls into the territory of 'don't'."

"You were locked in a house for over ten years and you never escaped? With your mother gone to work all day, every day?" He shook his head. "I've been asking myself since we met how a mother could keep a kid in check that long, even if they were the most passive, easygoing person on the face of the planet—"

"I gather you're saying I'm not—"

"—let alone a stubborn, willful child that probably resisted from day one, just bucking for freedom any which way she could—"

I pursed my lips. "You make me sound like a wild horse."

"Let's go with that analogy," he said, nodding, which broke our eye contact. "How does someone domesticate a horse?"

"They break it," I said with a hint of defiance. "Do I look broken to you?"

"Looks don't mean a thing. She did break you, didn't she?"

I blew air out my lips and stared out the window at the snowfall. "I broke rules all the time," I said in a tone of forceful denial. "She wasn't home during the day, and I could do anything I wanted—"

"Except leave the house."

The wind outside kicked up and the snow started falling sideways. I hadn't seen that before. "No, I didn't leave the house, but I looked outside plenty of times."

He leaned across the table, making a bid to recapture my attention from the snow drifts that I allowed to distract me. "When she caught you breaking the rules, how did she punish you?"

I was stronger than him – I could have knocked him out and broken through a window and been gone. Gone from the Directorate and gone from this state and gone from my sorry little example of a stunted life. Tomorrow I could be living somewhere else and no one would catch me.

It was funny, because the cafeteria was hundreds of feet long and hundreds of feet wide, and the nearest table was ten steps away, and yet I felt like I was trapped in an enclosed space; it was just like…

"Yeah." My acknowledgment came out in a voice of surrender. "That was how."

In the corner of our basement stands a box. Made of hardened steel plates an inch thick, welded together, it's a little over six feet tall, about two feet wide and two feet deep, when it stands long-end up. It opens like a coffin, along the longest plane. There's a sliding door on that side, about two inches tall and four inches wide, just enough to see out of – or into – the box. There are hinges on one side and a heavy locking peg on the other.

I knew when Zack saw it that he would figure it out. But it

was worse when he opened it.

"She didn't let you out to…do your business?"

I shook my head. But he already knew the answer to that, because the smell inside it was horrific; it made the whole basement stink of rot when it was open.

"How long did she leave you in there?" His eyes still appeared unreactive.

I laughed, a dark, humorless bark that rumbled through me, keeping my emotions in check behind a facade of false bravado. "Which time? There were so many. As you mentioned, I am somewhat stubborn and defiant. I was in there at least once a week. Usually for smarting off; Mom didn't like that much."

"How long?"

I shrugged. "An hour or two, most of the time – with the door closed on the front, so it was completely dark. And that, honestly, wasn't so bad. It was the times when I was in there for days, those were the ones when it was bad—" The times when my stomach screamed at me because it was sick of nothing but the water that was piped in from a reservoir by a small tube. The times when I started to get lightheaded and had to sit down, where I just felt weak and near dead by the time she let me out.

If she let me out.

He grimaced, the first sign of emotion I'd seen from him since the conversation began. "What about the longest time?"

I paused, and an insane sounding laugh bubbled out of my mouth. I felt a stupid, pasted-on grin stretching my face. "A week, I think."

His voice had grown quiet, but it was undergirded by a curiosity. "When was that?"

Silence owned me, but just for a beat. "Let's see. After I ate something and showered, I lay down to sleep – you know, horizontally, because trying to sleep curled up in a ball inside it sucks, just FYI – and I woke up and you and Kurt were in my house. So…a few days ago."

This time the silence was stunned. "She left you…after locking you in?"

I nodded, hoping he wouldn't ask the dark, piteous question I'd been asking myself lately. "And I haven't seen her since."

14

That ended Zack's questions, thank God. He said some more things after that, but I missed pretty much all of it. My head was buzzing and I couldn't focus. I forgot that I was hungry and as soon as I could get away from him I did, leaving him in the cafeteria. He extracted a promise from me that we would talk more soon, and I didn't argue because I didn't have the energy.

Ever been in a fight that gets really emotional, and you may have been feeling absolutely wonderful five minutes earlier but suddenly you're just exhausted? That was me; all my energy was shot and I dragged myself back to my dormitory. I crashed on my bed, but I didn't fall asleep. Instead I thought about Mom again; of the last time I saw her, when she shut the door on me, even as I was screaming, hammering my palms against the steel and begging her not to – and then she peered at me through the little sliding door, her eyes looking into mine, and she said something different than the hundreds of other times she'd put me in.

"Whatever you may think, I do this all for your own good." I wasn't in a position to pay attention at the time (I was as distressed when I went into the box as a cat being dunked in water – I've seen it on TV) but her look was different than usual. Less spiteful. Less vengeful. Less pissed. I might have seen a trace of sadness in her eyes, though I didn't recognize it at the time.

Then she shut the little door and left me in the darkness.

I thought about her again, concentrating hard, trying to focus on her as I drifted off to sleep. I awoke the next morning, an alarm going off beside the bed. I hadn't set it, but it was blaring. I looked at the clock and realized it was timed so I didn't miss my appointment with Dr. Sessions. Someone from the Directorate must have done it, fearing (probably rightly) that I didn't much care if I made them wait. Probably Ariadne. That bitch.

I thought about blowing it off, but the truth is I was curious. After all, they kept telling me I was meta-human, and I believed it, but I wondered what other abilities I might have. I was hoping for flight, because that would be cool.

When I got to Dr. Sessions's office, he was sitting behind his desk, looking at something. When he heard me enter he turned and pushed his glasses back up his nose and looked through them at me. "There you are." He began nodding and picked up a tablet computer that sat next to the laptop on the desk. "Have a seat; I need to have you fill out this questionnaire before we begin…" He handed me a clipboard and pen, then turned to walk away. I gave him a quick smile of thanks, which caused him to back away. I sighed internally. Even when I wasn't trying to, I could drive people away from me.

The questionnaire took an annoyingly long time and asked some invasive personal questions ("How many sexual encounters have you had in the last seven days? Two weeks? Month? Six months? Year? Five years?") Not like it was a difficult one, since until a few days ago I'd had zero human contact outside of Mom.

There were other ones that delved into health history, how I was feeling, when was the date of my last physical ("Never!" I printed in big, bold letters), when I first noticed a difference in my abilities – and on it went for a hundred and fifty questions, covering both the important ("Do you have any known allergies?") to the mundane ("When was your last bowel movement?"). I thought about scrawling "None of your damned business" but ultimately I just answered the questions – almost all – truthfully.

The last question – "Describe in detail any unusual abilities or skills" – gave me pause. Part of me wanted to know more, to find out what kind of meta I was. Okay, all of me wanted to know. But that was tempered by the fact that I had only been here for three days and still had zero idea of who (if anyone) I could trust. If I told them I suspected I could use my dreams to communicate with others, would that be considered some kind of power or a sign that I was slipping in the sanity department? I believed I could talk to Reed through my dreams, but it was too weird to consider normal and as yet too unconfirmed for me to know with certainty I could do it. After all, it could have been his power, not mine.

I answered the question, "Superior Strength, Speed, Agility and Intelligence" (no, I didn't put a smiley next to the intelligence part) and left any other suspicions off. As I had filled out the form, the doctor had milled around the lab, adjusting various pieces of equipment, humming as he skittered about.

He noticed me after a minute or so, and favored me with a smile as he approached. "We're going to do some physical tests next, then I'll give you this – a standard, multiple choice I.Q. test – and we'll see how you do."

For the next three hours, he put me through my paces. I thought maybe I had pissed him off in some way, because he was not kind in his efforts to "test" me. I ran on a treadmill at the highest setting for a long time, well past the point where I was bored and into the realm of thinking of casting myself into the place where the tread meets the plastic at the back, hoping to end my life with the added benefit that perhaps the running would stop as well. It couldn't have been an ordinary treadmill because I swear I had to be running at fifty miles an hour.

He made me breathe into a machine (to test my lung capacity), had me lift weights (I cursed him because there was no measure of how much they weighed and he refused to tell me) and hit a punching bag. Then he handed me rubber balls and had me throw them at a target on a wall at full strength, which I did (until I turned all three of them into pancakes).

"It would have been easier if you would have taken your

gloves off," he said, looking over his glasses at me.

"Sorry, Doc. Rule number four."

A look of confusion swept over his face. He led me over to a table in the corner. "One last thing." He bade me to sit.

"The intelligence test?"

"Two more things. First—" He reached onto the table and picked up a needle along with a strip of rubber. "I need blood."

My eyes narrowed. "I would suggest trying your local blood bank, because you'll get none from me."

He didn't smile. "In order to analyze—"

"Test what you have, Doc," I said in a voice that I hoped didn't allow for argument, "if none of that pans out, we'll talk about a blood draw in the future."

He stood there for a moment, looking like he was a broken robot, his head shaking in a twitchy fashion while he tried to come up with a response. He must have failed, because he never said anything, just tossed the I.Q. test on the table and shuffled away.

I attacked the test with a certain frustration. It was easy, and I used the pen provided to violently circle my answers on the multiple choice form. As I did, thoughts of the agents I had gotten killed kept running through my head. Zack had worked with all of them. He didn't seem that bent out of shape by the fact they were dead.

Kurt did. That was an honest reaction. Hannegan had already disliked me; now he hated me. I circled answer D, responding to a question about square roots, bringing the pen around to give it an extra loop, and nearly tore through the paper. Whoops. Gotta be careful with super strength, I guess.

But Zack? He was more concerned about things that happened to me (an almost total stranger) instead of worrying about his co-workers being dead because of me. I came to the conclusion that he had to be planted. Like Ariadne, he was restraining his emotions, putting them in the backseat to focus on the job at hand. Had to be.

Which meant Ariadne and Old Man Winter probably told him to get close to me, because he was the nearest to my age of all their people. And hot. H-O-T. Ariadne may be dumb, but I doubted she was blind enough to miss that little fact. And Old Man Winter himself said I was more important than a hundred of their agents.

That was a harrowing boost to the ego, let me tell you. There wasn't much on the I.Q. test about history, which was a shame because it was one of my best subjects. It wasn't the first time in history someone's life had been prioritized over another's. Not even close. But when I heard him say it, it started to worry me about the Directorate.

It got me wondering if they were some sort of racial superiority group, focused on putting meta-humans into a power position. Or maybe Old Man Winter was just that screwed up in his priorities, that he could cast a hundred human lives aside without losing any sleep over it.

Or maybe he was losing sleep over it. It wasn't like I knew him well enough to tell.

I finished the last question and looked around for the doc, but he was gone. He must have walked out while I was focused on the test. I left it on the table and walked out of the lab, heading out into the cold air thinking I might finally get that meal I had been craving since last night. A blast of windblown snow hit me in the face as I left the lab and hiked across the campus. I marveled at how smooth it looked.

I found the cafeteria crammed for breakfast. In fact, based on the size of the room there had to be at least a couple hundred people in there. I had only visited in off-peak times so to see it full was quite the surprise. There were men in suits scattered through the room, as well as other men and women dressed in work attire of various sorts, and a smattering of people I assumed were metas dressed in casual clothes, jeans, t-shirts, most of them younger than the folks dressed professionally.

As I walked to where the line formed to get food, my stomach rumbled. It coincided with a hush falling over the cafeteria – a slow, steady lowering of the volume level. I got a tray and began filling it. I was hungry, and not for broccoli. As I worked my way to the end of the line I started to overhear murmurings from both the workers behind the counter and people talking in the rest of the cafeteria.

"...that's her..."

"...got all those agents killed..."

"...heard some crazed meta named Wolfe is hunting her..."

"...she did it on purpose..."

"...eight of them dead, almost got Kurt and Zack too..."

"...crazy bitch."

The last one caught my attention, but I restrained myself before I whipped around to confront whoever had said it. I realized my hearing had not gotten sensitive, that most of the people were speaking loud enough for me to hear them. Which meant they were looking for a reaction. My eyes scanned the crowd as I left the line with my tray. The professionally dressed people looked away. About ninety percent of the folks in casual dress did likewise if they saw me look at them; a quick, furtive glance here and there if they got "caught."

But a few of the men in suits – the agents – were speckled throughout the crowd, and their looks were hard, hiding behind furrowed brows and cold eyes. And a small contingent of the casually dressed – the metas – were glaring and not bothering to hide it. They were all concentrated around one table.

I stared back at them, defiant. Yeah, I screwed up. But good luck getting me to admit it in public. I didn't bat an eye as their ringleader, a young guy probably only a few years older than me, gave me the stare-down right back. He had short dark hair and a nose that rounded a little at the end. The look of spite in his eyes overpowered his other features, turning what might otherwise have been a nice smile into something that looked more like a downward facing crescent moon.

I saw a small table empty in the far corner where the two windowed walls met each other – maybe the last unoccupied table in the place. Not a friendly face in sight, just a lot of people shunning me and a few more that were clearly pissed. Perfect. I pondered just carrying my tray out the door and back to my room where I could eat in comfortable solitude, but something in me resisted it.

I'd been alone for years. Locked away, trapped, whatever. It didn't bother me if I had to eat by myself. In a lot of ways, especially right now, doing that would have been the easiest choice. But still, my brain resisted the notion, urging me to not let these people get to me, to not run away and hide.

So when I picked my path to the empty table I made sure it went right past the group of metas that were scowling me down.

I waited to see if they would speak as I approached. I even pondered being a real ass and inviting myself to sit down in one of the empty seats at their table, but decided against it. I may not have been looking to make friends, but I didn't want to actively cultivate enemies if I didn't have to.

I just wanted to…confront them. Just a bit.

I almost didn't get my wish. They kept silent and a few even broke off their glares as I approached. I returned each hostile look in kind, until finally I rested my eyes once more on the young man: the ringleader, judging by the vibe I was getting off him. He didn't look away. He was waiting to see if I'd flinch.

I didn't. But neither did he. He stood up as I passed. Damn. Thought I was gonna make it by.

"Hey," he called out. "Friends of mine got killed on your stupid errand."

"I'm sorry about your friends," I said with an astounding level of calm for the tension I was feeling inside. I think I meant it.

"'Sorry' doesn't bring them back." His glare was piercing.

"Neither does anything else I can do." The acerbic edge to my statement was probably what pissed him off. "Unless I have some amazing powers of resurrection I have yet to discover."

His look got angrier, thanks to narrowed eyes and a snarl on his lips. "They stuck their necks out for you."

"Far be it from me to suggest otherwise. But they also died doing the jobs that they took on, that Old Man Winter sent them to do. They knew there was a risk Wolfe could be there." I had stopped my forward motion and waited for Mr.

Angry to reply. Might as well get this out of the way, and if I was lucky I could get the entire cafeteria off my back in one move.

"So you're one of the self-superior metas that gives the rest of us a bad name." His arms were folded across his body. "Don't really care if a bunch of humans die, so long as you get what you want."

I had a feeling that one was going to sting later but for now I pushed it aside and focused on my reply. "That's not what I said."

His chin jutted out. "But it's what you meant."

"Oh, is your power to read minds? No? Then don't tell me what I meant." I looked back at him with a gut full of defiance. I'd likely be blaming myself again later for the deaths, but I wasn't going to let him burn me with it; not now. "If I could do it all over again, I wouldn't have gone back. But I can't and I have to live with what happened. And you can take your rage and fire it up your ass."

He didn't say anything, but his jaw hardened and his nostrils flared. I realized that the pretense of standing there if I wasn't looking for a fight was pretty flimsy, so I made my way to the table. I sat down and looked out the window, trying to ignore all the stares from behind me.

A figure came up from behind a few minutes later and slid the chair out without asking. I was ready to gripe when I looked up. "Oh, it's you."

Zack sat down. "What are you doing here?" He cast an almost furtive look around. People were still staring. "It's not the most comfortable environment to be eating your lunch in, is it?"

I took another forkful of beef and chewed it while I pondered my response. "You mean because everyone in the room hates me?"

"That's not true," he said. "I don't hate you."

"Kudos to you for being the only one." I feigned applause for a couple beats before reaching down with my fork and spearing a bite of stray roast with unnecessary force. "So this is what being the school outcast would have felt like. I didn't really miss much being locked away all these years." My voice quavered and came out much lower. "Not that it matters."

"It doesn't matter if anybody likes you?" His voice carried a hint of skepticism.

"Nope. I've lived my entire life without the approval of any of these people. I suspect I can live the rest of it the same." I stabbed another piece of beef. "Especially considering how short it's likely to be."

"We can protect you from Wolfe if you stay," he said, his tone soothing.

"Oh boy," I said with mock enthusiasm. "I can spend the rest of my life wandering the halls of this place, feeling useless and listless and trapped, just like when I was at home – except here I'm surrounded by people who hate me." As if to punctuate my statement, I pushed my tray away. I was done.

"At least nobody here will lock you in a metal box for days at a time," he replied, a touch defensive.

"My entire life is boxes." I twirled the fork before setting it down on my discarded plate. "First I was trapped in my house or in the box; now I'm trapped on your campus. Most people are trapped in their towns, or their jobs, or their way of life. We go through life in our little boxes until we find ourselves in the last one, buried in the ground."

My tone was rueful, and I didn't care how general I was being. I was in a foul, depressive mood. I suspected that this guy, the only one in my life to ever show an interest in me (other than Reed, I guess), was doing it to spy on me for his boss, and I found myself longing for the simplicity of my house, where at least I knew where I stood. Act out, Mom gets pissed and I get stuck in the box. Simple.

He pushed back from the table. "That's a bit—"

"'A bit' what? Accurate? Morbid?" I laughed. "It's a bit irrelevant. I'll stay here, milking the security of your Directorate for all it's worth, because I've got nowhere else to go and there's no way I can beat Wolfe. So I'll wait, and bide my time, and hope that when your much vaunted M-Squad comes back they can find a way to kill him so I can at least have the luxury of deciding where I want to go and what I want to do with the rest of my life."

"It doesn't have to be this way." His voice was soft, almost lost in the din of the cafeteria conversations. "You could work with us here, build a life at the Directorate."

"And what? Join M-Squad? Be a test subject? Hang out like all these other metas, waiting for – what? I don't even know what they do here!" My hand gesticulated toward the table of metas that had accosted me earlier. "Part of me just wants to go home. And the rest of me…" My voice cracked.

"What?" He leaned forward but kept his hands far from mine. I could see the intensity in his eyes, the concern, and it just pissed me off all the more because I was so sure it was fake and I wanted it to be real, more than anything. "What do you want?"

I froze, and I knew in that moment I was on the brink of tears. *Suck it up*, I told myself. I took a moment to compose my emotions, shoving them into the back of my mind. I'm tough. I made the decision not to let even an ounce of feeling into my voice. "I don't know." It came out more brittle than I would have hoped, but it still sounded strong. "And it doesn't matter right now, because my only priority is survival." He nodded almost sadly as I stood up. "Everything else comes later."

I left the cafeteria, head in a spin. I waited around my room for a while, not really sure what to do. There was a flatscreen TV hanging from the wall, but I didn't see a point in watching anything. I didn't really miss it that much after not watching for a few days.

I settled on going to the gym, which I did in spite of the fact that Dr. Sessions had paired me with the treadmill from hell earlier. I stuck with a recumbent bike for my self-directed cardio, and whaled on a heavybag that a trainer assured me was made especially for metas (she told me this with a very friendly attitude until someone came up and whispered to her, at which point her disposition matched the weather outside). So I hit the heavybag even harder, punishing it for every bad decision I'd made lately, imagining the face of that guy in the cafeteria as I belted it another one, then wished I could pound Wolfe like I was pounding it. Unfortunately, Wolfe hit back.

After I finished I went back to my room and showered. I checked the time and found that it was mid-afternoon. I hung around a little longer. Someone had left me an e-reader. After reading for an hour or so I realized it was basically the same as a book but more convenient, and the novelty wore off. I've read lots of books.

At four thirty I decided I could get dinner and that it'd be early enough to dodge most of the crowd at the cafeteria. Besides, the sun would be down by 5:30, so I might as well be ready to sleep when it got dark. I decided I'd try and dream of Mom or Reed again. Probably Mom, since I wanted to prove I could contact others in their dreams and I'd talked to Reed twice already.

The cafeteria was near empty, and I snaked as much food as I could, keeping a careful watch on what went on my plate. It's not that I thought the workers would do something evil; it's just I've seen enough on TV detailing what wait staff do to the food of people they don't like to make me paranoid. It adds another dimension to being hated.

The dinner was chicken, and it was good. I managed to creep out of the dining hall just as it started to get busy. A few poisonous looks and some stage-whispered comments that lacked originality were my reward for lingering too long. A hall clock told me it was 5:45. The sun, which I still hadn't seen, was either down or the cloud cover it was hiding behind was thick, because it was dark outside.

I paused by a window in the corridor outside my room and stared across the grounds. What would Mom think of all this? I wondered. Where was she? Why did she leave? I swallowed hard. What caused her to flee? Was she in trouble?

Was it me?

The smells of dinner filled my nose as the volume of the crowd in the cafeteria was on a steady rise, so loud now I could hear them from where I was on the other side of the building. Most of the professionals had gone home for the day, but the casually dressed metas passed me in the hall, on their way to evening meal. Their conversations were excited, those of people among friends, and they dropped off when they saw me.

I realized I had been staring out the window at a lamp for the last five minutes. Going to the gym to work out again didn't appeal to me, and I had a feeling Dr. Sessions wouldn't be getting back with my results this evening. I thought of Mom again and knew that what I wanted was to go to sleep and try to dream of her.

I walked down the hall to my door and opened the handle. It wasn't locked, because I didn't have a key for it. Since everyone hated me, I supposed I should get a key, so that no one could sneak into my room while I was away.

I closed the door and flipped the light switch and realized that I was, by far, too late, because not only had someone snuck in while I was at dinner, but they had stayed to wait for me.

"Hello, little doll," came the whispered, throaty voice of Wolfe, towering above me. His hand came down and grabbed me around the neck while I was still too stunned to react. "Wolfe has been waiting for you." He pulled me close to him and I felt his hot, stinking breath on my face, then felt the warm wetness of his tongue licking my cheek. "It's time to play."

15

However I might have responded, speech was not possible with his hand squeezing my larynx. His black eyes were bulging out and his smile was a grin that revealed his spiked teeth. I felt them brush against the side of my head as he pulled me close and took a long breath through his nose, inhaling on my hair.

"Wolfe has missed you twice, little doll, but now we can be together and play the way we're supposed to. Then, whatever's left of you when Wolfe is done…" I felt his breath drift down to my neck as he embraced me and his teeth slightly bit into my shoulder – enough to puncture the cloth of my turtleneck and the skin but not enough to cause a deep wound – and a little sucking sound followed for about a second. "…*they* can have. That will make them happy. And you…will make Wolfe happy first." A half-insane titter of glee came from him and I heard the smacking of his lips.

I made a guttural sound of choking and he loosened his grip as he moved me in front of him, enough so I could take a breath but not much more. I could already feel the pins and needles in my feet and I tried not to jerk too much for fear of breaking my own neck. I must not have been the first person he'd placed in a chokehold because he'd learned to grip low enough on the neck that he didn't cut off all circulation.

"Pl…pl…" I couldn't get a word out.

He turned me around in his hand so that he was behind

me. I could feel his body pressed against me, as though it were an iron wall at my back. My feet touched the floor again but his grip assured me that if I tried anything out of line, I wouldn't survive until the agents came to my rescue. Not that they would at this point. Not after what I did. I was alone here.

"Pl…please…" I rasped through the barest opening he gave me to speak.

I could hear a moan of pleasure. "Yessss, little doll. Begging is good play. Pleading is fun." His other hand crept around my waist and I felt a shudder of revulsion when it came to rest on my belly and one of his claws raked through my clothing, giving me another superficial laceration.

I felt a twinge of pain, sharp despite the shallowness of the cut, and I felt the trickle of blood start to run down my abdomen under my sweater. His finger ran to his mouth and I heard the sucking sound again followed by another little moan of pleasure that made me ill. "I can taste everything about you in your blood. Your fears. Your doubts…every exquisite little part of you…this will be satisfying for both of us…" His hand slid around my belly again and I grunted, my fear for my life momentarily outweighed by a rising sense of disgust.

"H-how…" The words stumbled out as my mind sought out any delay I could find. "How did you find me?"

His grip tightened and once more I found myself in a battle to breathe. "It's not your place to speak or ask questions. You are to be silent except for the occasional moan or scream." His fingers dug into the cut he had made in my stomach and it suddenly wasn't superficial anymore. I would have screamed, but he had a choking grip on my neck, as though he anticipated it.

"I'll tell you," I heard him say through the searing agony in my guts. "You shouldn't have left all those agents lying around when you ran from Wolfe last time…two of them were alive, you know…and very helpful, after Wolfe spent some time playing with them…very helpful…and tasty. They were no little dolls, but they made a fine distraction until I could get my hands around you…and in you…" He stabbed his finger back into me and I wanted to scream but was out of air. Lights blurred my vision and the edges of everything in the world smoothed out. A flash of light blinded me.

I felt a spasming shock of pain, lighter somehow than what was going on in my guts but still painful, and I felt his grip loosen. Another flash, another shock and his hand slipped from my neck. My hands found their way to my belly to staunch the bleeding. It felt like he had torn loose my intestines and I crumpled into a pile on the floor just trying to catch my breath. My eyes made their way up to an astounding sight.

The windows had exploded inward and men in black tactical vests swarmed the room, guns firing all around me. The one in front that was a little too small for his tactical equipment was blasting away with the same type of weapon I had seen Kurt use at my house. With a shock I realized it was Hannegan, his gear tight on his massive frame. Wolfe seemed to be resisting the weapon even more fiercely this time, shrugging off the shots. Shotguns were going off in cascading blasts of thunder in front of me, the muzzle flashes lighting the room.

A scream from Wolfe seemed to stop time and I saw a blur of motion from his hands as he lunged forward. Kurt went flying, hitting the wall and bouncing off, landing in a heap on three of his fellows. He was lucky; Wolfe had punched him rather than using his claws.

The next hit from Wolfe was a slash and it caught two guys with shotguns that had closed on him. One of them lost his head, literally, while the other started gushing blood from the chest. Wolfe lashed out with a kick in the other direction and I heard it make contact with a Directorate agent standing above me, just out of my field of vision. There was a sickening crunch of flesh and bone drawing and breaking, then a desperate sucking sound that tapered off after three breaths; it was audible to me only because he landed less than a foot to my right. I dared not look at the dying agent for fear of who it might be.

My hand clutched at my wounded stomach and I tried to get up on all fours but failed, lying prone on the ground. I saw another body hit the floor in front of me and realized that there was only one pair of feet still standing and it was the booted set belonging to Wolfe. I raised my head to look up at him as he stopped in front of me. He looked down with a twisted anticipation that made me feel nausea that had little to do with the fact that I was nearly gutted.

"Now…" he breathed, lifting me into the air, twisting my torso and wrenching a scream from my lips. "Before we were so rudely interrupted…" His finger hovered in front of my eyes and he twisted me around and laid me facedown on the bed. The pressure of his hands around my neck hurt as his claws pricked through my sweater and drew blood. I felt him standing above me even though my face was buried in the bed. I screamed again but it was so muffled by the mattress that it didn't even sound that loud in my head.

He wrenched me around, twisting my midsection once more and then forcibly placing an arm over my upper body, anchoring me in place. "Much better," he said in a whisper. "Now I can hear you scream."

I'm ashamed to say that the next sound I made was more of a whimper. At least if I screamed defiance I could have vented some emotion in his direction. As it was, the panic was so rooted in me that I had no idea what I could do about it. He was invincible, I was wounded, everything hurt. I'd watched a whole army of trained agents go up against him and lose. What could I do? He rolled me to the right and then left, enjoying the squealing sounds I made from the pain in my stomach when he moved me. I was crying from the agony; it was horrific and I just wanted it to end.

The bedspread was slick with blood by this point, and he pushed me again. I caught a glimpse of a notebook and pen as he climbed up onto the bed and straddled me, looking down, one hand at his side and the other being used to completely manhandle me. I flopped about, offering little resistance. The pain was so bad I felt like I'd been cut in half. The best I could do was let him flip me again and maintain enough presence of mind to let my hand go to the pen on the nightstand, grasping hold of it.

"Grr…uckle…" I made a pathetic kind of gurgling noise

that was about 90% from the pain that was starting to dull as I verged on passing out and about 10% from being unable to articulate the terror, agony and rage that flooded through me with the adrenaline.

"Tsk-tsk, little doll…I told you, your place is not to talk…it takes Wolfe out of the moment…"

I made another gurgling sound as I tried to speak. I wish I could say I had some witty remark in mind, but I was far beyond that point. I was just trying to get him to hold up for a moment, to get him to listen to me.

It worked. "What's that, little doll?" He leaned in close, tongue running along my cheek. "We're destined to be interrupted any time, so perhaps Wolfe should finish now? Or perhaps carrying you away will heighten the anticipation for later?" His free hand pawed my chest, bringing a fresh wave of nausea as he took liberties with me that no one had ever taken before.

"Not…like…this…!" I spat a mouthful of blood in his face, causing him to recoil as I brought the pen up and around, driving it into his ear. His hand was already moving to wipe off the spit when the pen made contact. I didn't have much strength left, but I used it all and aimed it perfectly. It sunk in and he tore off a scream that sounded like the world was ending in front of my face; then he hauled off and backhanded me so hard I flopped off the bed, landing on the floor facedown.

"BITCH!" His fury was white-hot and I could hear him above me. At this point I was immobile, unable to move anything but my hands, which had found their way to my stomach wound. "I'm going to finish you now, and I'm not even going to be nice, little doll. There won't be anything left when I'm done with you—"

His hands seized me on the shoulders and he rubbed my face into the carpet hard enough that my nose broke. I felt him clutching at me, scratching and cutting as he used his claws to hack at the waistband of my pants – then I heard another horrific cracking noise and it took me a minute to realize that the sound wasn't made by him hitting me but by someone else hitting him.

A blast of chill ran through the room from the window and I could have sworn that there was a winter storm even though a few minutes earlier it had only been cloudy. A gust blew in a circle and I realized my door was open. The breath of frost licked at me and the feeling of a deep chill ran up my spine, causing me to wonder if it was from the blood loss. The cold wind carried its own smell, unique, but a subtle reminder of the walks I had taken around the grounds in the last few days.

I used the last of my strength to roll to my back and realized I was surrounded by the prostrate bodies of the agents that had stormed the room. My eyes moved to Wolfe, on one knee, still impossibly tall, but faced down by a dark figure that stood between him and me. Wolfe was breathing in fits and crimson ran down the side of his face in a dark stream from his ear. "Jotun," he said in a low voice. "You're still alive after all these centuries."

"Only just," came the quiet voice of Old Man Winter. His height was not quite that of Wolfe when the beast was standing, but seemed like a giant from my perspective. "The millenia have been kinder to you than to me, I'm afraid."

"Let me have the girl," Wolfe said, dragging himself to his feet. "You can have the little doll back when I'm done, but I have to…have to…finish…I can even leave her alive when I'm done…at least a little…"

"I think not," Old Man Winter said without pause. "I have another squad of agents on the way, and you know that with my help…" He let his words trail off.

"I'm not done with her." Wolfe's voice was infused with a kind of mania that chilled me worse than the freezing air. He stomped his foot and I heard a snap that I suspected was the sound of his foot finding a Directorate agent's neck as it landed. "I won't stop until I have her, 'til we…play." The last words came out in a twisted, lyrical note that would have filled me with disgust if I weren't completely wrecked.

"You are done with her," Old Man Winter said as the chill intensified, both from his words and from a howling tempest of cold winds. "You will not seek her here again unless you wish to face me…and as old as I am now, you and I both know that although one may survive a confrontation between the two of us, the survivor would never be the same…"

I thought I saw a brief tremor from Wolfe, but it faded as his eyes flickered and the most horrifying creature I could ever imagine bounded out the window. I heard the crushing of snow for a few footfalls, saw Old Man Winter turn to face me with those ice blue eyes, and then it was as if my brain blissfully proclaimed me safe, because I lowered myself back down and passed out.

16

When I woke up, things were hazy and a small woman was hovering over me in a lab coat. She flashed me a quick smile as I blinked at her. "Don't try and sit up yet," she said, brushing a lock of black hair out of her eyes as she leaned over me. I obeyed her, mostly because I didn't feel as if I could move. I looked down to see my clothes replaced with a hospital gown.

The memory of Wolfe's attack cut through the haze and I felt nausea set in below the pain in my stomach. I started to gag as I recalled every sickening detail of what he tried to do to me and I began to retch. Searing pain raced through my abdomen.

"Whoa!" The woman grasped me under my shoulders, helping me turn. I threw up over the edge of the table, unable to control my reaction. A disgusting feeling of being violated seeped into me and I retched again. I wanted to shower, to scrub my skin until it bled. I grimaced from the pain in my stomach that was made worse by my heaving. "You need to settle down. That maniac nearly pulled out your intestines and that'll slow anyone down, even a fast-healing meta like yourself."

I coughed. "Who are you?"

She wrapped a stethoscope around her neck before answering. "Dr. Isabella Perugini. I'm the resident M.D. here in the medical unit."

I blanched as she turned and injected a needle in an IV that ran to my arm. "Where's Dr. Sessions?"

She snorted. "The lab rat is where he belongs – playing with test tubes and beakers."

The haze of pain began to lift. It was still there; I just didn't notice it as much. "So he doesn't treat patients?"

"No." She turned back to me, a clipboard in her hands. "I've treated you both times you've come through my doors. Want some medical advice?"

"Will it stop the pain?"

"Not immediately, but it could prevent it in the future." She turned serious. "Stop facing off with this Wolfe character, will you? I'm sick of having blood all over my floor."

"Send some of it to your pal Dr. Sessions; he's jonesing for it."

"First of all, it's not all yours," she said with a nod to a half dozen figures on beds down a line from me. The agents that tried to rescue me from Wolfe. "Second, if he wants it, Ron's welcome to come over here with a mop; I suspect the janitorial department is getting quite sick of cleaning up these sorts of messes."

"Did someone say my name?" I looked as far as I could toward the doorway and saw Dr. Sessions silhouetted in the frame.

"Yeah," I said in a ragged whisper. "I was just telling Dr. Perugini that she should save you some of my excess blood since it's everywhere."

"Yes," he said with excitement, "that would be marvelous."

"Ron," Dr. Perugini said in acknowledgment, with a tone that indicated some impatience. "Why are you darkening my door?"

"I came to give Ms. Nealon her test results." His face twitched and he pushed the glasses back up into position on his nose. "Quite interesting."

"Of course it escapes your notice she's near dead," Perugini muttered under her breath, sparking a quizzical look from Sessions. She opened her arms wide. "By all means, deliver your test results."

"So what am I?" I said without preamble.

"No idea," he replied as he crossed the floor and halted at my bedside. "You defy immediate classification." A smile of delight colored his pasty features. "Truly bizarre."

"He's a sweet talker, that one," I said to Dr. Perugini, who snorted again, this time in amusement. "Why is that bizarre?"

"I've analyzed hundreds of meta-humans," he went on, "and most fall into common types – a half-dozen or so groupings depending on the special powers they exhibit. Some tend more toward incredible physical attributes, some have energy projection capabilities or—"

"Perhaps speak to the girl in English," Dr. Perugini interrupted.

"No need for that," he corrected her. "I gave her an intelligence test as well; I could be having this discussion in Latin and she'd pick up the essential points. The simple fact is—"

"I defy classification," I interrupted, my words calm, coming out over the foul, acidic taste in my mouth from my recent bout of vomiting. "Even among the bizarre, I'm bizarre."

A phone rang across the medical unit and Dr. Perugini gave Dr. Sessions a thinly lidded glare before striding away to answer it. He kept his distance, as though he were uncomfortable stepping any closer. Instead he stared at me in a way that, had any other man done it right now, would likely have set me to vomiting again. I stared back at him. "What?"

"Your physical strength is high above a normal meta's, so you should be manifesting soon, if you haven't already. No unique abilities to report yet?" I felt zero compunction about lying, but was relieved that Dr. Perugini had stepped away; I suspected she would see through my untruth; Dr. Sessions didn't have a prayer.

"No. Nothing unusual."

He turned back to his clipboard. "Well, that's fine…it's normal that you wouldn't be experiencing anything yet. But as time goes by, additional abilities will materialize." He looked down at the blood pooled at his feet. "And I'll, uh…" He pulled a small test tube out of his coat pocket and stooped down, scraping it across the tile floor, forcing a small amount into the vial before putting a rubber stopper on it. Dr. Perugini rounded the corner just in time to see him and threw up her hands in silent exasperation.

He stood up, failing to notice her behind him. "I'll get this analyzed and maybe it'll give us some ideas of what you are." He turned and started when he saw Dr. Perugini, then shuffled around her as she glared at him.

"He has the bedside manner of a goat," she said with a hint of a European accent. "But not the common sense nor tact. That—" she pointed to the phone behind her—"was Ariadne. She and Old Man Winter are coming down to see you now that you're awake."

"Did they already know I was awake when they called?" I asked. I could believe Dr. Sessions would wander over and not know that I was unconscious; I'd be shocked if Ariadne and Old Man Winter weren't spying on me.

She stared back at me, her dark eyes cool and unflinching. "Yes." She turned away, grabbing a clipboard off a nearby shelf. "You're going to need to start eating again soon. I don't want to strain your digestive tract until I'm sure it's fully healed, so I'll be giving you another ultrasound in a couple hours to confirm you mend as fast as I suspect you do. After that, dinner will be served."

"I'm not hungry," I said. The brush with Wolfe made me wonder if I'd ever be able to eat again without heaving.

"That's okay," she replied without looking up from her clipboard. "I'm not feeding you yet."

The medical unit was a long room, probably as long as my house but narrower, with curtains separating individual beds and a private room at the far end with an oversized door for rolling gurneys in. Every surface was the same flat metal that I'd seen in the room I'd woken up in when I'd first arrived at the Directorate, broken up by glass windows that looked out into a hallway that matched the distinct look of the headquarters building.

The sharp odor of disinfectants wrinkled my nose as I took it in for the first time, almost giving me another reason to gag. I could hear the low beeps of monitoring equipment in the background and the faint hum of all the machinery. I counted the number of occupied beds I could see from where I lay. Less than a half dozen. "How do you handle so many at one time?" I asked.

"I don't," she said, a slight tremble in her voice. "I had to triage, and Old Man Winter demanded I treat you first."

"But I can survive more than any of them."

"I know," she said with a nod, not looking up from her clipboard. "And once I had established your wounds were not of the life-threatening variety, I moved on to the next critical patient."

"How many of them died?" The words were like ashes in my mouth. Bitter.

A moment of silence passed between us. "Five."

I did not respond to her statement, and she didn't speak either. The doors on the far side of the medical unit opened to admit Ariadne, who looked drawn, her severe suit wrinkled as though she had slept in it. Old Man Winter followed a pace behind her, his age less obvious today, I thought – or was that because I knew he wasn't what he appeared?

"Hello," Ariadne said. I didn't bother to glare. She took this as an invitation to move closer, and hovered over my bed. "How are you feeling?"

"Like I've been kicked, punched, gutted, slapped and stomped on," I said without much feeling. "So basically like you look all the time." I couldn't stop myself. Ouch.

Her jaw dropped only a little, and she recovered quickly. I think she was getting used to my barbs. Good. Old Man Winter stood a few feet behind her, watching me, but did not speak.

Ariadne looked chastened, but began again. "We've been keeping updated on your progress through Dr. Perugini. She's most impressed with your healing abilities, which rate very high on the meta-human scale."

"That's coming in handy more often than I would have hoped," I replied. "I take it Wolfe breaking into your dormitory building came as a surprise for you, too?"

Ariadne folded her arms and shook her head. "We

102

shouldn't have taken Kurt's report that all our agents at your house were dead at face value; we should have verified to make sure nothing was left behind that could be traced back to us. But at the time we viewed sending a recovery team for the bodies as too great a risk for fear that Wolfe would somehow track them back to us."

I pictured the oversized Wolfe driving a car, following a convoy of agents, then had an idle thought wondering what kind of vehicle he would drive. The image of him crammed behind the wheel of a Volkswagon bug popped into my head and in spite of all the emotional turmoil I had to stifle the urge to laugh, which was overtaken by the feeling of sickness again when I thought of him.

"Are you okay?" Ariadne looked at me with a concern that I would have found touching if I trusted her in the slightest. As it was, she spurred my instinct to aim at her if I felt the urge to vomit again.

"I'll be fine." I waved her off. "You didn't come down here to talk to me about my abilities, did you?"

"No," Ariadne replied after a moment's pause. "We came to talk to you about security. Yours."

I felt hollow, a complete lack of emotion. "What about it? Do you want me to leave?"

"No, no." Ariadne shook her head with emphasis. "Now that Wolfe has found our location, though, it changes things. We want to keep you away from the outbuildings and here in the headquarters, where we have the greatest chance to be able to protect you from him."

I wasn't stunned. I wasn't even surprised. But I did feel a clutch of fear at the thought of not being able to see the sky, cloudy though it was, or feel the frigid winter air on my cheeks. Funny, since I'd only just felt it over the last few days, that I was already addicted and unwanting to give it up. "So you don't want me to leave the building…at all? Is that right?"

Ariadne shared an uncertain look with Old Man Winter, who nodded. "Just for the time being," she said, returning her gaze to me. "Until we can resolve this Wolfe situation."

I laughed, that scornful noise I make when I'm not really

finding something funny but I want to show my disdain for what's been said. "He's wiped out everything you've sent after him, including your security here on your campus. What, exactly, is going to resolve this 'Wolfe situation'?"

"M-Squad will be returning from special assignment down in the Andes Mountains as soon as we can get in contact with them. Once they return," Ariadne continued, "we have full confidence they'll be able to take Wolfe out of play. Or," she said with another backward look at Old Man Winter, "at least contain him."

"Contain him?" I scoffed again. "The people I've talked to—"

"Meaning Zack," Ariadne interrupted.

I ignored her and continued. "—seem to think that he's one of the strongest metas on the planet. Is that accurate?"

Ariadne exchanged an uncomfortable look with Old Man Winter. And by uncomfortable, I mean on her end. He looked placid as ever. "He is one of the strongest, yes," she said. "But that doesn't mean he can't be stopped."

"That's funny," I said with a calm I didn't feel. "Because Dr. Sessions told me I was a super strong meta, and I can't make much of a dent in him, unless you count when I stuck a pen in his ear."

"A clever strategy, by the way," Ariadne added.

"A desperate one that bought me all of thirty seconds before he reaffirmed his desire to rape and kill me," I raged back at her.

"It bought you enough time to allow us to intervene," she said in a voice that was overly complimentary.

"Allowed him to intervene, you mean." I pointed at Old Man Winter. "Wolfe called you Jotun – a Nordic frost giant." He nodded at me with a ponderous, slow dip of his head but did not speak. "You've faced Wolfe before?" He nodded again. "But you both survived. And Wolfe has been alive for thousands of years?"

Old Man Winter nodded again and broke his silence once more. "He has. A cannier foe there is not; he has survived living on the razor's edge all these years and always among people that are the world's most dangerous. What does it say about him to be able to live millenia in such conditions?"

My heart sank. "That he's dangerous. Worse than anything you can throw at him."

Old Man Winter nodded, once more fixated on my eyes. "In order to protect you, we must keep you in this building. Do you understand?"

Unbidden, a memory of the door of the box closing came to me, and I felt a momentary urge to fight, to argue, to struggle out of my bed and scream at him in defiance. Then the pain in my stomach surged as I moved, and another, hotter emotion came over me, a disgust and humiliation at the thought of Wolfe manhandling me in my room in the dormitory, of his hands all over me, his finger inside my guts, ripping me up…and I almost gagged. "Yes," I said simply, swirling emotions batted to the side.

"Good," Ariadne said with undisguised relief. "I was worried that you might be headstrong and try to resist good sense."

I felt weak, drained. "Glad I could allay your misperceptions." I laid my head on the pillow behind me, not bothering to look at Ariadne or Old Man Winter any longer.

She hesitated. "There will be agents surrounding the medical unit. They're on constant watch, especially after what happened to the agents at your house and the way Wolfe was able to breach security in the dorm. If you need anything – food, books, entertainment – just ask." She smiled, as if she could sense that although I wasn't shooting any venom her way it wasn't because I didn't want to.

She and Old Man Winter left, but only after he gave me another long, hard stare. After they left, Dr. Perugini took a moment to record my vitals, fluffed my pillow with a matronly cluck, and then, with an admonishment to call out if I needed anything, walked to her office and shut the door.

The curtains were up between me and the rest of the patients, and from where I was sitting I could see the backs of agents through the windows, stationed outside the doors of the medical unit, and I heard a healthy cough from behind one of the curtains, telling me there were more behind the partitions. Yet still, I felt alone. Again.

I thought back to what Ariadne had said about expecting a different reaction from me at the thought of being in lockdown. I wondered for just a moment what I must look like to them, how my actions must appear; then I dismissed it and realized I only cared a little. I still didn't trust them. They would protect me now, but for reasons that were their own; reasons that were still unclear to me, but almost certainly involved using me and my powers, whatever they were, for their own ends.

I looked across the unit and found the wall there to be made of reflective metal that allowed me to see a distorted picture of my face. Bruises dotted my cheeks and wrapped around both eyes. There was crusted blood under my nose, and it looked misshapen. My eyes were haunted, the look of someone who had the spirit battered out of them.

The overhead lights went out, dimming the room, and my reflection was shrouded in shadow. It was nighttime; I knew it even though there were no windows.

I heard a door close heavily at the far end of the ward, and it brought me back again to the sound of the box when Mother would slam it shut. "Keep your fingers out of the way," she'd snarl just before she closed it. Then the little clicks followed as she worked the pin in place to lock it. She always shut the little viewing slit last, usually after saying something reassuring or taunting through it, and the light would go out from the world and I'd be alone in the dark, all by myself.

Confinement or Wolfe. I knew which I feared more.

17

I don't know when I fell asleep but I know that when I did my head was still swirling with thoughts about Wolfe and the fight, if you could call it that. I drifted into a darkness that had little to do with my physical surroundings. I felt myself swallowed in that surreal, faded world that had been present both times I had talked to Reed in my dreams. But this time, somehow, it was different.

The world around me swirled in a sort of rough clarity; as it came into view I recognized the surroundings. Little lights hanging above, soft blue mats on the ground below, and blurred concrete at the edges of my vision gave rise to the realization that I was in my basement. I looked into the corner and sure enough, there it was – the box – peeking out of the darkness, its flat edges visible in the low light of my dream.

"Little doll…" The growling voice sent an involuntary twitch through my body, stiffening my spine and causing me to raise my guard. It did not a whit of good. Wolfe sprung at me from out of the darkness by the box, bounding at me, leaping from all fours. I was paralyzed, unable to move as he crossed the divide between us. I blanched away from the impending hit, throwing all the training Mother had given me right out of the nearest window.

Wolfe sailed toward me, then passed through me as though I were as insubstantial as the air we were breathing. He came to rest without touching the wall, pivoted and came back at me, passing through once more. An angry, perplexed expression darkened his already vicious features, and he bore the look of a man denied his fondest wish. He drew once more to his full height and looked at me with suspicion, keeping his distance and watching me, eyes wary and calculating.

"A dream walker…this is not real…" His voice was low and gravelly, and even though he couldn't touch or hurt me, his words sent a very real chill of fear through my guts in the same place where his finger had ripped into my abdomen.

"What's a dream walker? Is that what this is? What I am?" I put aside my fear, desperate for answers.

He ignored me. "You caught the Wolfe while he's sleeping. Very tricky. You're hiding, sneaking around behind the Directorate's walls, counting on the Jotun to protect you from Wolfe?" His feral smile returned. "Why don't you come out and play? It could be so fun."

"Gee, I wonder why I don't want to face a psychopathic lunatic like you," I snapped at him. Hot anger boiled in me. "You're unhinged."

"Come out and play, little doll." The smile was worse, a nasty, stomach-turning reminder of what he'd tried to do with me; *to* me. "The Wolfe just wants to play."

"Are you stupid? Or are you deaf from where I stabbed you in the ear?" He flinched. I saw it and it gave me a moment of hope. "I'm not coming out. I'm going to stay here, because I have zero desire to be your plaything and die a horrible death after you do God knows what to me."

"You won't die, little doll," his voice rasped. "That wasn't a nice way to play, stabbing Wolfe in the ear. It makes him think about you every time the pain flares. But Wolfe won't kill you, oh no, not yet. Not until they say so, because they want the little doll oh-so-bad."

"Who are *they*…and what do they want me for?" I looked down at him, on all fours, as though he were ready to spring at me again.

"Ah, ah, ah." He shook his head. "I'll tell you if you come out and play."

"I'm not leaving this place," I told him. "Not a chance."

He sighed, a deep, throaty sound. "Wolfe knew you'd say that. But you don't understand…see, Wolfe *has* to have the little doll. Not just for his…masters…but for himself." His eyes looked at me suggestively, leering in a way that would have induced more nausea if I hadn't been transfixed with fear at his words. "So now Wolfe has to be persuasive. Now Wolfe has to convince the little doll to come out of her dollhouse."

My voice cracked. "What…what are you going to do?"

"If Wolfe didn't know better, he would guess that you don't care about people, since you let all those little toy agents get slaughtered at your house." He ran his tongue over his incisors. "But Wolfe thinks maybe you just wanted to play so bad that you didn't think about what would happen to them. But what if Wolfe started playing with others? Would you like that? Would it make you happy or sad to know that other people were getting played with…because of you?" The last bit crossed the realm from suggestive to disgusting as he stood upright and ran a hand down his own chest, raking himself with his claws.

When I said nothing, he continued. "Here's what will happen. Wolfe is going to go out and find a nice family…and he's going to play with them. Mommy, Daddy, little kids. And then he's going to find another. And another. Until the little doll comes out. And if the police try and stop him, well…he'll play with them too, won't he? And we'll just keep going…through this whole rotten city…" His tone turned predatory and savage. "…until the little doll comes out to play."

His grin was surreal now, like the quality of everything else in the dream, but it was growing and expanding, taking over, and I realized I wanted to be away from it, away from him, away from myself. I snapped awake in the medical unit, not even fading back to consciousness like I had with Reed but experiencing a sudden, brutal awakening as though I had missed a step coming down the stairs and tumbled. My breaths were ragged.

I stared into the dark and thought about what Wolfe had said. It had been real, I was sure of it now. I talked to him in my dreams. I was sure of another thing too. His threat to kill others – he *would* carry it out. Carry it out – and love every minute of it. I looked around and saw the curtains still drawn, soft breathing of a few wounded agents coming from the other side of it. Wolfe was going to kill until I came out and faced him. He wouldn't stop until he had me.

And there wasn't a soul that could stop him.

18

I heard a click at the far end of the medical unit and started, my eyes darting to the door of Dr. Perugini's office where she stood silhouetted in the dimness. She stretched her hands above her head and yawned. "I saw you wake up." She took a long, meandering walk toward me. "Trouble sleeping?"

My hands clutched the sheets, my palms sweaty and sticky. In spite of the warm, comfortable air in the room, I felt a trickle of sweat run down my spine underneath my cloth gown. The bitter taste in my mouth became synonymous with the fear I felt every time I came across Wolfe, and the thudding of my heart was so loud in my ears I was amazed I could hear the doctor. "Yes. Just a…nightmare."

She nodded and stifled another yawn as she snapped on a pair of latex gloves. "Let's check your injury."

"Don't you mean injuries?" I said it with a bitterness that welled up deep inside; a cutting edge of irony that reflected my inner turmoil at the fact that since I left my house I'd been severely beaten twice. Far worse than any punishment Mother had ever levied.

"No," Dr. Perugini said with an odd tone, and reached to the end table behind me, clicking on a lamp and coming back with a mirror. She put it in front of me and I looked at the face within.

There were no visible cuts, marks or bruises. My dark hair and pale skin, my big eyes and pointed nose all looked back at me, a contrast to how I had looked only a few hours before. The only sign that something was different were the bags under my eyes. I looked tired.

"So you see," she said, returning the mirror to the nightstand, "there's only one wound left." She lifted my gown to reveal gauze and bandages on my lower abdomen, around my belly button. "He ripped through the skin and pushed through your peritineum, perforating your intestines." Her brown eyes looked at me, almost as though she were lecturing. "If you were human, it would have taken a surgeon who could work miracles to keep you from dying. All I had to do was give you time to heal yourself."

She peeled back the medical tape securing the bandage to reveal red, scabby tissue beneath, roughly the size of a quarter. She plucked at the pink, sensitive skin around the edges, eliciting a hiss of pain from me. "Be grateful you're alive," she admonished, throwing the bandages in the garbage can and taping a fresh piece of gauze onto the smaller wound, then pushing on my stomach to either side of it. "Any pain here?"

"No." I looked at her hands as she pushed again and this time I cringed, not entirely from the pain. I watched her gloved hands pressing on my skin and had a remembrance, like a flashback in a TV show.

Mom had been sitting on the sofa, not even changed out of her work clothes yet, her dark hair tucked back in a ponytail. She was pretty, I thought, and all I had to compare her to were the actresses on TV. I got my dark hair from her, but her features had always seemed more chiseled than mine, making her look statuesque. Her complexion was darker than mine; not surprising since she did go outside more than I did. Her eyes were green rather than the cool blue of mine.

Her head was resting on the back of the sofa, her eyes lolling a bit, but she focused on me when I approached her. I had in my hand the calculus book that I had been studying from on the kitchen table, my assigned space for working. If I didn't work there, I got in trouble. Needless to say, I only worked in my room when Mom wasn't home.

"Finished your test?" Mom said, looking up at me with

indifference. She reached out and took the paper I handed her. She leaned over the end of the couch and pulled the teacher's edition of the book from her bag. She always took them with her so I couldn't cheat by looking up the answers. Nor did we have an internet connection for me to cheat with.

She browsed through it. Her dark eyebrow rose at one point as she chewed on the end of her pen. I stood back, in my sweatpants and t-shirt, the heat of nervous anticipation on my cheeks as I waited to hear the result. She reached the bottom of the paper and looked up at me, still impassive.

"Flawless," she pronounced with a curt nod. "I think you could do a better job of showing your work, however, so keep that in mind next time." She gave me a half smile, the highest mark of affection offered in our house. "You can watch one hour of television, then we do our evening training session."

I let out a squeak of happiness at her pronouncement of TV privileges (I was fourteen, what do you want from me?) followed by the slightest sigh of disappointment at the news of an impending workout. That was the end of her half-smile.

"You think I'm too harsh, but you don't know." Her eyes narrowed and her lips were a thin line. All traces of prettiness vanished in a hard look that drove terror straight through me. "You don't know what's out there."

Her hand pointed toward the front door and I stifled any word of argument I might have given – something along the lines of, "You're right, but only because you won't let me outside…"

She went on. "You can't ever get soft. You can't ever get weak. It's a dangerous world out there, filled with people who want to give nothing but harm to a little girl like you." She stood up and tossed the TV remote on the couch, never looking away as she brushed past me, taking particular care not to touch, and went into her bedroom.

I longed for a hug, affirmation, something. I lowered myself to the couch. All the little words of approval were washed away in the heat of her anger, light as it was. I didn't pay much attention to the TV that night for the hour I watched it, instead thinking about my life and how much I wanted someone to just hold me.

"I expect you'll be up to full strength again within a day," Dr. Perugini spoke, jarring me back to the here and now.

"Good to know," I mouthed more by instinct than from processing the words she'd spoken. She fussed about for a few more minutes, then admonished me to "get some rest" and retreated back to her office, shut the door and turned off the light. I don't know why I wasted my time letting my head get clouded with that stupid memory of Mom when I had Wolfe to think about. His threat.

I had let the doctor distract me for a few minutes while I should have been pondering whether to tell Ariadne and Old Man Winter about my dream. I couldn't blame myself too much, because honestly, I didn't want to think about it. Didn't want to consider the idea that Wolfe might be out there right now, killing people because of me.

I repeated to myself that it was just a dream. Then again. Then five more times. I really wanted this "dream walking" to not be a power but a delusion. I kept repeating it to myself until I fell back to sleep, blissfully uninterrupted by any more horrific visions of Wolfe.

The next morning when I awoke the medical unit was still quiet. I lifted my gown and checked my wound; it was gone. I bent at the waist to sit up and felt no discomfort. I stood, letting my feet touch the cold floor. It didn't bother me.

A hiss came from my left and the door to the unit opened, revealing Ariadne, a key card in one hand, newspaper in the other. "Glad to see you're awake," she said with a perfunctory smile. "We've prepared accommodations in the basement, but first we have to go speak with…" She hesitated.

"Old Man Winter?" I said with a nasty smile in return.

She blanched. "I wouldn't call him that to his face."

"Think he'd get mad at me?" My smile got worse, I could feel it.

"I wouldn't care to find out," she said without further comment. "You should know something."

I froze. "What?"

She threw the newspaper onto the tray by the bed, and underneath the banner was the headline "Family of Five Slaughtered in South Minneapolis". A photo of a home not unlike mine sat underneath the blaring headline. Police tape blocked the entire scene and there were at least a dozen officers in the photograph.

My hands went to my mouth, covering it, pushing the words back in before they could come out. I halted, tried to regain control before speaking. My eyes flew up to Ariadne. Hers were fixed on mine, watching to see my reaction. When I said nothing, she spoke.

"We think it's Wolfe."

19

I sat across from Old Man Winter in his office, Ariadne standing behind him as always. There was no trace of warmth within these four walls and the day outside looked to be the gloomiest I'd seen thus far. There was a hint of light that told me where the sun had to be, hiding behind a cloud, but the bastard just didn't want to show himself. Ariadne had led me up here after letting me read the article, the gist of which was that another five people were dead because of me.

I clutched the newspaper in my hand and tossed it on Old Man Winter's desk. "Why did you tell me this? Wouldn't it have been more helpful to you if you hid it from me?"

Ariadne shook her head. "You'd find out eventually."

Old Man Winter studied me as he always did. "By telling you, we hope to gain your trust. To let you know that we aren't hiding anything from you; that it is all out in the open."

A roiling torrent of emotion bubbled beneath the calmest exterior I could produce…so probably not all that calm. "Why do you want my trust?"

Ariadne fixated on me. "To let us protect you from Wolfe. We need to keep you safe."

"How can we even be sure it's him?" I hoped it wasn't. I hoped I was wrong, that five more bodies weren't added to the pile of corpses I was responsible for in the week since I'd left home. The number of people dead because of me outweighed the number of people I'd met.

Old Man Winter nudged open a file folder and pulled out a glossy 8x10 photograph, sliding it across the desk to me. I picked it up and stared at it: a photo of a wall. Two bodies were visible at the bottom edge of the shot, a woman and what I thought might have been a little girl; she was almost cropped out of the frame. There were words scrawled on the wall, in a dark crimson that almost looked black: *Waiting for a little doll to come out and play.*

I felt sick all over again, but in a different way.

"There are more," Old Man Winter said in his devastating, quiet timbre. "At least two other houses last night, five more victims. They were not discovered in time to make the morning paper."

A small, plaintive cry of despair escaped my lips. "More?" I croaked. Numbness replaced the sick feeling. "How many more can there be?"

Ariadne looked at me with a pained expression. "Will you let us protect you?"

My mouth was dry. "Who's going to protect all those people out there from Wolfe?"

"We can't protect everybody," Ariadne replied. "All we can do is keep you safe. Will you let us?"

I felt a twinge in my belly where Wolfe had clawed into me. "If I do, how long does this go on?"

"We're trying to make contact with M-Squad, trying to get them back here sooner, but…" Ariadne trailed off.

"Still out of contact," I finished for her, not really hearing my own words. "What are the odds that they can take Wolfe, anyway?"

"I would bet on them," Ariadne said with a slight smile. "They'll sort out Wolfe when they get back. We just need you to endure until they get here. It will get worse before we can make it better."

I leaned back in the chair opposite Old Man Winter. "So I just sit back and let these people die, family by family, to save my own skin?"

An air of silence hung in the office, colder than the air around us. "Would you rather go and face him?" Old Man Winter said. "Would you care to taste what he has in mind for you?"

"They say I'm strong." I spoke fast, words bubbling up from emotional depths, fear and hatred of Wolfe fueling me in equal measure. "Stronger than most metas; and Wolfe is afraid of you – between the two of us, maybe a few others, couldn't we…maybe we could…"

For the first time since I'd known him, Old Man Winter hung his head in obvious defeat. "I cannot win a fight with Wolfe; my earlier efforts at fending him off were purest bluffery. I have not a quarter of the strength I had when last we fought, and he has grown stronger, more canny and more experienced. He would," Old Man Winter said with resignation, "destroy me in mere moments, and you shortly thereafter, along with any other metas we brought along." His head came up, and the cold blue eyes held an aura of sadness.

Ariadne spoke, her words coming almost as low as his. "You are the strongest meta left on the campus at present. Only one other is even close. Not enough to take Wolfe."

"No," he said, shaking his head again, "M-Squad has all the strength of the Directorate and it is in them that our hope lies."

"So we just sit back, hide, and watch as he kills three or four families a night until M-Squad comes back?" My voice was raw. I thought back to my encounters with Wolfe and wondered again if there was any way I could beat him myself. I thought about the pen in his ear and wondered at any other weak points he might have; eyes, mouth…his bones felt unbreakable, but with enough force they could surely be destroyed. The only question would be what could deliver enough force. "There has to be a way to beat him."

"Would you suggest shooting him?" Ariadne asked.

"No," I said with a shake of the head. "Guns don't even break the skin. The tranquilizer darts, though. Maybe if we loaded him up with those darts…"

"Based on what we've seen, one of his powers seems to be to adapt to attacks – the shock cannon that Kurt hit him with was less effective each successive time it was used, to the point where he shrugged it off when he attacked us here." She cast a sidelong glance at Old Man Winter. "We suspect his resistance to bullets is something that has developed over time; it's doubtful that the darts or the toxin would be as effective this time around."

"He has always been uncannily adaptable to changing situations," Old Man Winter said, "and has lived through battles that have killed lesser metas by the hundreds. There is a reason that Wolfe and his brothers lived for thousands of years."

"There has to be a way to beat him," I said with urgency. "Something. Some weapon in your arsenal that you haven't tried yet, like that shock cannon…something that can just buy us a few minutes."

"I'm sorry," Ariadne said, voice gentle. "There's nothing. We've bluffed him well enough that he seems to be steering well clear of the Directorate, but until M-Squad returns, it is only a bluff. We need to keep you here, protect you, until we can work out this situation. It's the only course we have available."

My voice cracked. "Unless I give myself up."

"Ridiculous," Ariadne replied. "You know what he would do to you. Do you really want to go through that?"

"No," I answered. "But neither do I want to keep sacrificing others, watching bodies pile up and families get destroyed because I'm too scared to face Wolfe."

"Give us a little more time," Ariadne said in a pleading tone. "Let us get M-Squad back. Once they're here, we can take care of Wolfe."

I put my hands in front of my face and started doing the mental arithmetic. Two dead in the parking lot outside the grocery store. Eight at my house when I wanted to face Wolfe the first time. Eight more when he attacked the Directorate campus. Ten last night, none of whom I'd even met. Almost thirty dead at the hands of Wolfe, every single one of them because they stood between me and that maniac. How many would it take? What if I left town? Like Zack said, he might eventually find me, but how many people would he kill in the interim? Hundreds? Thousands? Would he eventually just burn the city to the ground?

The fear choked me again. I wasn't as afraid of dying as I was of what Wolfe was going to do to me first. I had caught a sample of his idea of play and the thought of uninterrupted time with him doing what he liked was enough to make me sick again. He would violate me in ways that I couldn't imagine, based on my limited experience in the world and with men. In a way, my naïveté probably spared me from being even more fearful. Or maybe the fear of the unknown made it worse.

I looked back to Ariadne and Old Man Winter, who were looking at me, waiting for a response. I wanted to be brave. Part of me wanted to fight him again, to knock him down, to make him fear me the way I feared him.

But my hands felt weak. They shook. I couldn't beat him, I knew that. I didn't want him to touch me, didn't want to smell his disgusting, rotten breath or feel his claws caressing my skin and drawing blood, didn't want to feel him rubbing and pushing against me again. I choked on my cowardice and justified it in my head – I didn't want to be near him again. Ever.

All I wanted was to go home, back to the simple world of Mom, and when I was bad, the box. Nobody but me got hurt there. Nobody died.

But Mom was gone. My house was forfeit; it was Wolfe's domain now, he owned it, and every thought I had of it from now on would be tainted by the memory of how he beat me, broke me in that basement in a way my mother and the box never had. I had nothing left but the Directorate, and no one to trust but these two people that I didn't even know.

I looked from Old Man Winter to Ariadne, each in turn. Winter was brooding and quiet while Ariadne was waiting with patient expectation. I choked on my words, but finally they came out, filling my ears with the sound of my cowardice, drawing a nod from Winter and a smile from Ariadne.

"You win."

20

Two days and twenty-eight dead bodies later, I wished I hadn't listened to my fear. I had been stewing in a basement room of Headquarters, walls made of reinforced concrete and plated with steel or some other metal that didn't bend when I punched it out of fury or frustration or sheer pitying despair. I punched it a lot.

Ariadne had done everything in her power to make me comfortable in my oversized room. I had my own bathroom, they'd brought in a bed from one of the dormitories that felt like it was cushioned with air – not that I'd been sleeping, but I lay down on it a lot while I watched the news.

They'd brought me a big TV and it was tied in to all the networks. I flipped back and forth between three different local channels and the national news stations depending on who was on commercial. Having never been able to watch TV for more than an hour a day, news was never on my to-watch list. I always caught a smattering over Mom's shoulder at night while I studied at the table, but I much preferred sitcoms and dramas over news.

I found myself glued to the goings-on. One network proclaimed: "Minneapolis: City Under Siege" while another network decried that Minneapolis was "In the Grip of Terror." The third was speculating on the source of the violence and assigning blame politically.

The local stations were somewhat less objective as the anchors seemed to be in fear for their lives. It was hard not to feel for them the same way I'd feel for characters on the TV shows I watched – sitcoms had the ability to bring me to tears, which I always hid from Mom. She would roll her eyes and make snide comments about "weakness."

As I watched the news hour after hour, as the days ticked by, I felt nothing but weak. I wished I'd told Ariadne and Old Man Winter to stick their offer of safety in a warm and uncomfortable place. I stared at the walls as the news showed photos of the latest victims, trying to avoid the looks on the faces of the family in the picture. They were all smiling, but it felt like they were silently accusing me of dooming them to death. This one was a family with a dark haired father, a blond haired mother and two little blond girls. All staring at the photographer with happy smiles on their faces.

Now dead. Because of me. Because of my cowardice.

The door slid open and the agent outside stuck his head in. "Visitor, miss." He said it without a wasted syllable or any emotion. After two days and a half dozen such messages, I was beginning to suspect that the agents assigned to guard me had very clear memories of their fellows who died at my house, and what they had died for. There was not a drop of the milk of human kindness in any of the men I had interacted with while in this place. The only friendly face was Ariadne's, and she had dropped in for conversations twice now – ones which I had kept civil by virtue of not wanting them to end prematurely.

After twelve years alone and one week in the company of others, I found myself not wanting to go back to alone.

I was sitting on the bed, t-shirt and pajama pants on, in violation at last of Mom's fourth rule, the only one that I had been following lately, the one that demanded I remain fully dressed, down to my gloves and shoes at all times, ready to move. (When she wasn't home I frequently took my shoes and my gloves off, among other things, which led to punishments if I wasn't quick enough on the days she'd arrive unexpectedly early).

I had been enjoying the feel of the soft bed against my skin, something in great contrast to the marked discomfort I felt on the inside from what I was watching. Self-consciousness came over me as I realized I wasn't dressed for visitors, then tried not to care.

I jumped to my feet as the door slid open again to admit a familiar face. Zack walked in wearing a leather jacket, his hair tousled, and gave me a smile. I breathed a sigh of relief; I hadn't seen him since Wolfe attacked the Directorate. Then I felt a stir of embarrassment for my attire; I would have preferred to greet him in something more presentable. Or presentable at all, really. I stood in place, unmoving, the bed between us. His arm was immobilized in a sling and his face was flecked with cuts. A bandage still covered his nose but otherwise he looked fine.

"How are you holding up?" he asked after he'd seated himself at the table in the corner of the room. I sat across from him, reminded of the last time we had talked like this, in the cafeteria a few days earlier.

"Me?" I asked, breaking through the dark clouds of emotion. "I'm fine, physically. You still look wrecked, though."

He raised an eyebrow. "Physically, huh? Yeah, I look pretty rough. Us humans don't heal as quick as you metas. I wasn't asking about how you're doing physically, I can see you're fine." He sat back and winced as he bumped the back of the chair with his elbow. "How are you holding up…in other areas?"

"You mean emotionally?" Two days of beating the hell out of myself for my cowardice left me without the strength to lie. "I feel like crap. Lower than low." My voice came out so matter-of-factly, Zack blinked in disbelief. "I feel like I've sacrificed the lives of everyone who's died so I can save my own ass."

His disbelieving expression spread from a cocked eyebrow to the downturned corners of his mouth. "Do you think you can beat him?"

"No, I don't think I can beat him." The sterile air of the room washed through my nose as I took a breath. "I don't think I can even come close."

"Then why try?" He looked at me with incredulity. "You

made the smart play. Wolfe's a psycho killer; he's lived way longer than any of us; he'll outlive us all unless M-Squad can kill him. You're crazy if you don't let us protect you."

"How long?" I asked, the emotion breaking into my voice. "How long do I keep watching them report person after person dead? How long can I hide behind you guys? Don't you think at some point Wolfe will get tired of slaughtering innocent people and come back here for another round?" I stared at my hands, pressed palm down on the cold surface of the metal table. Everything in this place had the feel of sterility, of having never been lived in.

"Old Man Winter doesn't think that'll happen."

"Then Old Man Winter's crazy." I pulled my hands up and folded them. "Wolfe loves to kill and he loves pain. He'll come back here sooner or later, when he gets tired of the slaughter. He'll go through the dormitory building before you drive him off again, or try to get through HQ – he'll find me eventually, and all that's going to be different is how many people he kills between now and that day." The quiet certitude of that thought filled me, and I watched Zack's expression deteriorate as he pondered it.

"It's not gonna happen like that. M-Squad is coming back. You've never met them: they are the toughest metas you can imagine. They'll set a trap for Wolfe and they'll punch his ticket. That's if the Minneapolis cops don't get him first."

"He'll go through them like a boat through water."

"Yeah, in ones and twos – but they'll be deploying in big numbers and call in state and FBI for a case like this." Zack's eyes were animated. "My degree is in criminal justice. Once they get a taste of him, they may even call in the National Guard. Mark my words, this town's about to get too hot for Wolfe. He'll either bail or—"

"Decide it's not worth the trouble waging a campaign of terror and turn right back to attacking the Directorate." I stared him down. "And we're back to the same place – how many die before he gets me?"

Zack almost seemed to retreat. "He's not some invincible god creature. He's just damned strong and canny." Suspicion clouded his features. "You almost sound like you've given up. You eager to get raped to death by him?"

"That's so stupid I'm not going to dignify it with a response," I shot back. "But he seems unstoppable! So the alternatives are run and hide somewhere else – which lets him slaughter a whole bunch more people so I can get away or keep hiding here, which again leads to the slaughter of more people and eventually me. Or I could just get it over with now."

My fingers crept up to my face, lending it support. I was more tired than I was willing to acknowledge. "The idea of him slaughtering more people is wearing on me. It's wearing on my mind. My conscience. What did any of them do to deserve this?"

"Deserve doesn't have much to do with it," Zack said in a gentle tone. "What did you do to deserve having this psycho want to gut you?"

I paused before answering, and a steady flash of images rolled before my eyes, of all the times I'd ended up in the box, all the little crimes I'd perpetrated, all the little acts of defiance against Mom. All the punishments, all the times I was bad. "I don't know," I mumbled, lying.

"Listen…" He paused. "Old Man Winter is sending me to South America with a couple other guys to track down M-Squad. Figure I'm going to be gone for a few days because we don't know exactly where they are. While I'm gone…" He paused again and his eyes bored into mine. "Please don't do anything crazy, like go after Wolfe." He thought for a second and amended, "Again."

I sat very still, fighting not to make a sound. When I answered him, it was as bold a lie as I thought I could get away with. "I don't think they'd let me out at this point."

His voice hinted that his disbelief at my last answer had carried over to this one. "I don't think you're the sort to ask permission after you've made a decision. Which is why I'm asking you…" A hint of pleading entered his tone. "Please let me get M-Squad. Just hold on until I get back."

The earlier picture of the family from the news, their accusing eyes, shot through me. "People are dying."

"I know." He nodded and bowed his head in a sort of

solemnity. "And I really, really don't want you to be one of them. Old Man Winter says there's a reason…something about you had Wolfe's employer pull out all the stops and send him instead of anybody else. He says it means you're important…maybe even vital…to what's going to happen in the future."

At that moment I would have happily given up everything I had, including my so-called powers, whatever they might be, in exchange for a destiny that included me living a normal life where I never had to worry about people dying for me. Maybe a boyfriend, eventually a husband, a house I could leave at will, a job, friends…minor things. "I could stand to be a little less important at this point," I said with muted interest. I was so down I didn't even care much what that meant.

"I don't want to see you get killed." Zack lowered his head to try and meet my eyes. I didn't look away from him, but I didn't have much energy left. "You've had a rough life so far, and I'd hate to see you get taken out before you had a chance to actually live it."

"Live it?" I echoed. "How?"

"Have you ever been to a movie in the theater?" He stared back at me, slight smile lightening his face. "Or been out to a restaurant and then to a club? Done any dancing? Been to a concert? Gone to the mall? Comedy show? Theater? Been to Valley Fair?" I shook my head after each question, remembering commercials I'd seen, things I'd put on a list in a diary that had been under my bed for years, something I'd outgrown.

Actually, something I'd put aside because Mom thought it was too close to breaking rule #5: no talking about the outside world. "No," I said.

"They're all things I think you'd enjoy," he went on. "I need you to hang on…just a little longer…til I get M-Squad, and they take care of Wolfe." He said it with a reassuring smile. I could feel his confidence and I knew he believed to his depths that M-Squad could take Wolfe. I was less sure, but it didn't matter. He believed it totally. "Will you promise me you'll wait?"

I didn't know what to say. I felt the pressure of his eyes on me, so calm and reassuring, looking at me in a way I had rarely seen. "I…I…" I stuttered.

Caring. That's what his eyes were. And I realized again how good looking he was. And older. And I tried to keep in mind that he was spying for Ariadne and Old Man Winter, but that thought faded when I looked into his deep brown eyes. "I…I promise."

"Attagirl." He stood, extending a hand to help me up. I humored him and took it, feeling a little dazed. I kept focused on him and watched his eyes swim for a moment, and he let go of my hand. "I should…uh…get going." He took a step and seemed to trip, then cast a look back at me to see if I noticed. "Felt a little lightheaded there for a second." His smile turned to a grin. "Must be the effect of being around you." He walked to the door and knocked on it, then left when it slid open, sending me back one last smile.

I groaned when he left, mostly from the last cheesy line he'd said, but also from the fact that he'd extracted the promise from me that he had. My fingers tingled with pleasure from the feel of his touch on my hand and left me wondering about all the things in the world that I'd never experienced – but less about the ones he had mentioned…and more about the ones he hadn't.

21

Three more days, one hundred and thirty-two more dead. I was well past the point of sick and into the realm of deathly numb, if such a thing existed. If I had any doubt that I was the world's worst person, it was dissolved when some unnamed individual slid a note under my door that I found first thing in the morning. I didn't bother to ask the guards how it got there. It read:

People are dying by the hundreds and you're hiding. If he comes back here, you won't find much help from any of us because everyone here pretty much hates you and we're all rooting for him to turn you inside out.

Ariadne hadn't stopped by in several days and the guards hadn't initiated any conversations, so my only human contact was when a cafeteria worker brought me meals three times per day. It was always the same person, a middle-aged woman who didn't have anything to say. At all. I caught her scowling at me when she thought I wasn't looking. Based on her attitude, I had to guess the letter was on target.

The crisis in Minneapolis had gotten so bad that there were police and SWAT teams on constant call. Helicopters circled, watching for any sign. Wolfe had progressed from only slaughtering people in their homes to killing people in public places as he moved between potential victims – he had been caught on several automated cameras. When four houses in a row in one of the western suburbs was hit it started a louder clamor; previously Wolfe had restricted himself to working in Minneapolis proper.

Since then he had jumped around, but the police always seemed to be a couple steps behind him, at least according to the news. Hundreds of witnesses reported seeing him, even just a flash in passing, and the police were overwhelmed because at the slightest hint of a noise people were calling 911 for help; as a result, instances of violent crime were up 142% (again, according to the news) and tons more were going unnoticed. As one reporter put it, "It's a good time to get away with murder in Minneapolis because, amidst all the other bodies, who's going to investigate one more?"

All my fault. Every last one of them.

I was still glued to the TV, watching every update, every bit of breaking news that really wasn't breaking, every police press conference, every release of another victim's name. I felt more powerless than at any time prior in my life, worse than any occasion I'd been locked away. When I was prisoner in my own home I never had to worry my actions would cause harm to anyone or anything – except maybe Mom's feelings, if she had any.

I was waiting, hoping to hear that M-Squad had returned or that Wolfe had been run over by a garbage truck (maybe that would kill him) or anything – anything to break the twenty-four hour press of guilt.

And then I did.

"Breaking news," I heard an anchorperson say for the one millionth time in the last few days. I was lying on the floor. It wasn't as soft as the bed but I didn't feel like I deserved the bed right now. "We go live now to Winston Haines, who is in a chopper above Southdale Mall, where Edina police have cornered the suspect in the slayings that have gripped the Twin Cities in a wave of terror."

I stood and moved closer to the TV. The angle changed to look down on a parking lot, where a lone figure raced across the pavement. My heart stopped, along with my breath.

It was Wolfe.

I watched as he hurdled a car, running flat out from three police cruisers and a SWAT van that were behind him. Two more cruisers cut him off and boxed him in. Cops opened doors and I saw them fire right away, not even bothering to say anything. It was a smart move on their part, but I had to wonder if it would be enough.

Wolfe went down to a knee under the sheer volume of gunfire. The reporter was blathering on about civil rights but I silently cheered the cops on, hoping that they would put him down like the rabid dog he was.

And maybe it would be over. And I could get out of here. And go…anywhere else. Somewhere that I wouldn't have to think about any of this.

The SWAT van popped open and black-suited team members swarmed toward Wolfe, who was now on all fours, and a moment of silence prevailed as the reporter shut up. They surrounded him and I hoped that maybe the bullets they had shot him with had more power than the shotgun rounds I'd seen him shrug off. They pointed their guns at him point blank, and then one of them stepped in, handcuffs at the ready, going slow, amazed that Wolfe was still alive and moving after the hail of bullets that had been thrown at him.

As he started to reach for Wolfe's hand to place the cuffs on, I flinched away. It was an involuntary response born of the realization that something terrible was about to happen. When I blinked my eyes open a second later, it was already done. Wolfe was in motion, his claws raking through body armor, sending cops flying through the air just as he had when he assaulted the Directorate.

They didn't shift the camera away from the scene, which surprised me, especially when the blood started to flow. Wolfe swept through the SWAT team in less than ten seconds, and their Kevlar vests and riot helmets did nothing to stop his slashes and punches.

When he was finished with the SWAT team, he started on the cops from the cars that had surrounded him. The first few kept shooting, dodging him in futile efforts to escape his grasp. He used his teeth when he got hold of them. The last few ran, each in a different direction, and the camera followed him as he bounded after them. I didn't watch nature programs very often, but I'd seen lions take down wounded gazelles, and it was disgusting to watch.

The reporter provided commentary on the horrors of what we were seeing as Wolfe finished the last police officer with a rough decapitation, holding the man's head up in the air, facing toward the helicopter. He then pointed right at the camera, and it zoomed in to the point where every detail of his horrible face was visible, his teeth, his black eyes and even the blood dripping from his claws as he pointed.

At me. I could feel it. He was pointing at me. He hoped I was watching. Maybe he *knew* I was watching.

He mouthed words. "We don't know quite what he's saying…" The reporter's voice was sheer astonishment. But he was wrong. I knew exactly what he was saying. And I didn't even have to be that good at reading lips to figure it out; just had to have heard the repetitive taunting from him, with that same sadistic look, the one that I knew contained not one ounce of insincerity.

"Little doll…come out and play."

22

Wolfe bolted into the mall at the approach of another half dozen cop cars; probably not because he couldn't take them all out and then some, but because he had other things on his agenda. The news reported later that he'd cut his way through the patrons of the stores, leaving another thirty or so dead, a few others wounded before he bolted out an exit and disappeared.

At this point I was ill enough that I flipped off the TV. Watching wasn't helping. A reminder that I'd had a hand in the deaths of another sixty or more people, people who had families, parents, kids – that didn't help me at all. It didn't help me want to keep my promise to Zack, anyway.

I stared at the stainless steel walls for the next hour. I resolved not the smash the TV to pieces, no matter how much I wanted to vent my frustration. I went to the bathroom and took a long, hot shower, but not as long as I wanted because I kept thinking about all the people dead right now that wouldn't ever again get to experience the simple pleasure of something as basic as a hot shower on a cold day. Or shopping malls. Or theaters…or anything that Zack had listed off. Ever again.

Or a hug from someone who loved them.

I had been ready to turn off the water and get out when I started shaking with emotion at that thought. I heard someone say once that it wasn't possible to miss what you never had. But if that was true, why did I want someone to love me, to hold me, just once?

It took me almost twenty minutes to compose myself, and when I stepped out my dinner was waiting for me, along with an unpleasant surprise.

"I brought your food," Kurt Hannegan said with a sneer. "No one else wanted anything to do with you." He had been almost to the door to leave and had turned back just to toss the shot at me.

"I'm not hungry."

"I guess it's hard to work up an appetite when all you do is sit by while people die because of you." He paused at the door for a beat, then turned to knock on it so the guard would let him out.

"Wait," I called to him. My voice must have sounded as lifeless to him as it did to me, because he listened.

"What?" The air of impatience surrounded him as if, insult now delivered, he couldn't wait to get away from me.

"I don't want anybody to die," I said in a voice that sounded smaller to me than I could have imagined when I formed the words.

"It's a little late for that now," he snarled. "Hell, it was too late the day after you goaded Old Man Winter into sending us back to your house."

"I need your help," I said to him.

He laughed. "You've had my help before and all it got was a bunch of my buddies dead—"

"I want to go to Wolfe. Myself." He raised a stunned eyebrow. "I don't want anybody else to die. I need to get out of here so I can go to Wolfe; so I can end this." I held up my hands at my sides. "So I can give him what he wants."

Hannegan hesitated, regarding me with suspicion. "You playing games with me?"

"No," I said, returning to the lifeless voice. "I just want this to be over."

"Yeah," he said, suddenly incensed, "and get my ass fired for helping you commit suicide." His eyes narrowed. "But I tell you what…your guard changes at seven A.M. If someone was to try and escape an hour before that, at six, especially if they were super strong, they could sweep through the guards

– without hurting anybody seriously," he said with emphasis, "and there might be a few minutes when the cameras were off. If you went west, past the cafeteria and across the field toward the woods, there's a road behind the wall of the campus. A meta could clear it with a jump, easy."

"And what would I find there?" I was hollow, just waiting to see what he had in mind.

"Maybe nothing. Maybe a ride." He turned back to the door. "I wouldn't want to be accused of helping you."

"You're not," I said in a rasp.

He knocked on the door and left without further comment. After he was gone, I stared at the blank TV screen for a while. Decision made. You know what finally did it? What finally pushed it over the top? I saw at least one of the dead cops was a woman. She looked to be of an age where she might have a little girl. A little girl whose mom wouldn't come home tonight.

Sounds familiar.

I watched TV to kill the time without falling asleep. I found now that the decision was made, all the weariness of the last few days was creeping in, ready to overtake me. But I couldn't let it, not yet. They hadn't left me an alarm clock and I didn't trust myself not to sleep through this, or I would have tried to contact Wolfe in my dreams. I asked the guard at the door for some coffee. He sneered, made a sarcastic comment about how he wasn't my serving wench, and let me know he'd have someone else deal with it.

I couldn't wait to punch him in the face.

I'd never passed slower hours, not even in the box, without any visual or auditory stimuli but those I made myself. Every news report that rehashed the incident at the mall and all the new deaths seemed elongated, stretching into infinity. The metal hands of the clock that hung in my room moved as though they weighed tons rather than grams.

The last five minutes were the worst. I would follow the plan Kurt laid out. Even though I didn't trust him, I suspected he wouldn't have any problem taking me to die, especially if he could get away with it.

With two minutes left, I stared back at the news. The

timing was perfect: they were just beginning a montage of pictures of all the people who had died so far in this insanity. I watched their faces scroll by, some smiling and innocent – the children, mostly – some staid and serious, caught in candid shots. I would have wept, but my resolve was hardened. Soon enough, there wouldn't be any more.

I walked to the door at six, knocked on the steel and waited for it to slide open. When it did, the same guy that had told me that he wasn't my serving wench became my bitch instead, and I battered him against the opposite wall with a single punch. Not bad, considering he was at least a hundred pounds heavier than me.

Three more guards flooded the hallway. I pulled the gun from the first and heaved it at the farthest guy, and my enhanced dexterity scored a perfect hit; the butt of the shotgun clipped him in the jaw. I had seen people get knocked out before, but this time it was like slow motion; his eyes fluttered, he looked woozy for a second, then he dropped to his knees and flopped facedown.

I grabbed the closest guy to me as he went for his radio and yanked him forward, pulling him off balance with the ease of uprooting a small plant. I landed a hammerfist on the back of his head and he went down. I surged forward with a front kick, catching the last guy in the corridor in the stomach, knocking the wind out of him. I followed up with a punch that broke his jaw as well as knocked him out, giving the Directorate guards yet another reason to hate me. There were so many.

After the last one hit the floor, I looked down the steel-plated corridor. It stretched about a hundred feet in either direction, and there was no sound or movement. Most of the Directorate staff were out for the night, so this building was likely much quieter than, say, the dormitory building where all the metas and on-campus staff lived. Nonetheless, I crept quietly up the stairs to the first floor, where, without even leaving the stairwell, I found an exit door.

I studied it in a rush, making sure it wasn't an emergency exit that would set off a fire alarm. It didn't appear to be, so I pushed through the crossbar and opened it, sprinting out into the snow. I was back in my turtleneck, coat and gloves…the only thing I was missing was a ridiculous hat to keep my head warm. And I was headed home.

I ran across the snow, heading toward the woods. I passed the dormitory building, giving it a wide berth, snow up to my knees but still moving fast, when the alarm klaxons began howling. They might have found my handiwork in the basement. All those guards beaten senseless.

I didn't spare a thought for it, just ran faster. I was having to lift my legs high to clear the snow, but I was amazed at how fast I was moving. I went several hundred yards through two feet of snow in seconds. I reached the tree line and kept moving, trusting my reflexes to keep me from getting clotheslined by a low-hanging branch or plowing into a tree trunk.

Darkness appeared in front of me and I realized it was the wall. It stretched a good ten feet up and was made of solid block.

And I cleared it in a jump.

I landed on the other side with an inelegant roll, brushing off the snow as I got to my feet. I heard slow clapping coming from in front of me. Lit by the beams of headlights, Kurt Hannegan stood in front of his car. "Very nice. Now can we get out of here?"

I followed him, getting into the passenger side and shutting the door. He gunned the gas, wheels slipping on the wet pavement. "Where to?" he asked, hands gripping the wheel and his jaw clenched.

"Just drive me to my house," I told him, brushing the snow off myself. He shot me an angry look as he watched it land on the upholstery. "I have to let Wolfe know where to find me."

"Do it after I'm gone," he said with a scowl.

"Fine," I lied. "I'm going to sleep until we get there."

"Don't know why you're bothering," he shot back. "You'll be getting plenty of that soon."

I didn't respond to his dig, instead leaning back in the seat, resting my head against the side of the car, close to the window. The steady thrum of the tires against the road gave off perfect white noise, and the motion of the vehicle rocked me to sleep.

Darkness encompassed me, enshrouded me, took me away from the road and the headlights and that asshole Hannegan, and deposited me right where I wanted to be. Blackness surrounded me, swirled me into its vortex, and then, in the distance, I saw a spot. Burrowing through the dark, it got clearer and clearer, coalescing into a shape – like a man, but with black eyes, horrific teeth and a face that gave me nothing but fear. He drew closer and closer, a smile lighting his terrible features. A smile that broadened when I spoke.

"Wolfe…it's time to play."

23

I woke up, intentionally, a few minutes later to find myself rolling through the streets of my neighborhood. We'd left behind the wide open farmland, the stretches of suburbs and freeway, and entered the densely packed blocks of houses that had only a few feet between them. I lifted my head to find Hannegan looking around in all directions, as if he were expecting Wolfe to ambush.

"I don't think he's here yet," I said with a hint of amusement. Not sure where that came from. Gallows humor, I assume.

"I don't care; I'm not hanging around." He kept up his searching pattern. "You may be ready to die but I'm not."

"I'm not really ready to die," I said. "But neither are any of the people he's killing to get to me."

Hannegan grunted in acknowledgment, but did it so neutrally I wondered if he'd heard a word of what I said. He came to a stop at the end of a driveway and I looked up at the house. Unlike last time, I was sure it was mine. I opened the door and pondered making a sarcastic comment to him or lingering for a moment, but I realized I was more scared of what was coming than vindictive about what had happened in the past.

I wordlessly shut the door and I watched him swallow heavily, the sort of action that might make a gulping sound had I been in the car to hear it. He looked at me with hollow eyes and I could see his fear at the thought of facing Wolfe. He looked away and stomped the accelerator, slinging muddied slush on me as he sped away.

I sat there, freezing, in disbelief for a moment, sopping wet. "Screw it," I said and pulled my gloves off, throwing them into the gutter. I pulled my jacket off, also soaked, and tossed it on the ground. I took a couple steps toward my front door and faltered.

He probably wasn't in there yet. Probably. I found myself in no great hurry to find out. He was either here or on his way.

The chill wind combined with the lingering wetness of Kurt's spinout caused a frigid feeling that was eating into my bones. Still, I stopped at the edge of the driveway and scooped up a handful of snow. I felt the cold of it, the dull feeling of numbness that started radiating through my palm after I held it against my bare skin for a few moments. I couldn't have imagined two weeks ago that everything would end up like this.

I thought again about Zack and I wondered where he was, if he was still in South America. It didn't matter; I had no faith that M-Squad could take on Wolfe and win. I thought about his list of things, the things that I never got to do. That I would never get to do. Then I thought about the other list, the one I made after he left that night. Things he didn't mention, like having a first date…getting my first kiss…

I felt tears stinging at the corners of my eyes and I looked back to the house where I'd spent every hour and every day of my remembered life up until a week ago. Those four walls enclosed my life like a grave, and they would likely end up being my tomb, the place where my body would lie, maybe forever.

The hell of it was, with Mom missing, there really wasn't anybody else who'd care I was gone – care about me, the real me, not the supposedly super-powerful meta that everyone was chasing. Who's so powerful she can't even save herself.

I looked up past the trees that stretched into the sky. They'd been there for decades, growing in the ground here on this street. Clouds covered the sun, just as they had every day since I ran out the front door. I walked, slow, shuffling steps, each one an act of pure will, as I made my way to the door. I was going to die without ever even seeing the sun.

I remembered a few days before, when Wolfe first threatened to do what he'd done to this city. I recalled being so sure that there was not a soul that could stop him, but truthfully there was all along. The problem with being self-centered, as we humans are, is that sometimes we miss the obvious solutions when the effect on us is less than desirable. There was a person who could stop Wolfe. And it was me. I could stop him. And all I had to do was give him what he wanted most. And what I wanted least.

My hand felt the cold metal of the doorknob as I turned it, opening the porch door. I stepped inside and felt it slam shut behind me. I sat there in the semi-darkness, just breathing for a moment before I took my next step forward and entered the front door. I looked down, expecting to see the dead agent's body that had been left here last time, but it was gone. There wasn't a sound in the house, but outside I could hear a far-off police siren, probably answering the call of another person worried about Wolfe slaughtering them.

I looked around the living room as I shut the door behind me. It was still in scattered disarray from the battles it had seen in recent days. Wasn't your life supposed to flash before your eyes before you die? Not that I had a life; just a thin, cardboard cutout version of reality that involved me waking up every day, eating breakfast, reading books, working out and, if I was good, sitting on the couch that was upturned in front of me and watching an hour of TV before I went to bed at night.

It wasn't a life. My entire existence was circumscribed by the same walls I was looking at now, the walls of this house, and when I was bad, the walls of the box.

The box. That damned box.

I slipped down the stairs to the basement, leaving the wreckage of the living room behind me, replete with the smell of gore. The lights were still hanging overhead, the mats still bloody where Zack and I had left our contribution from the fight with Wolfe. I stepped over them and made my way to the corner to look at it.

It didn't matter if I grew ten feet taller, I would still look at it as a huge, metal, imposing figure. The side that swung open hung off its hinges, moved from where I left it. The last time…I tried to put the hinges back together, tried to set it right again, to make it look like it wasn't broken. It stood open, the darkness inside a silent reminder of days spent within.

I wish there was some brave, exciting reason why I tried to fix it, but the truth is that as irrational as it sounds, I feared Mom's reaction when she saw I'd broken out. It was the act of a scared little girl that vainly hoped her mother wouldn't realize that when she left the house, I was locked in a metal sarcophagus and when she got back, I was sleeping in my own bed and sitting on my own couch and going about my life unfettered by the metal prison she'd confined me to before she left.

Of course, she never came back, so it didn't matter. I wondered what Mom would say when she found out what happened to me. If she found out. I wondered if Wolfe had caught up with her, as well. Mom was a fighter; way better than me. If he did, I bet she hurt him before the end. The thought of the pen sticking out of his ear, blood trailing down his face, came back to me, along with the thought of tranquilizer darts and the knife I had buried in him last time I was here. Yeah. Mom would have given him hell.

"Little doll," I heard from behind me, turning to face the staircase. He strolled down, an idle man with all the time in the world. His nose was sniffing, as if he were savoring the meal he was about to eat. He paused at the last step. "So nice of you to call on Wolfe. I was beginning to question how many people I was going to have to kill before you'd pay attention…of course," he admitted with a broad grin, worthy of his name, "Wolfe can't take credit for all the kills the news has been giving to him…someone else has joined in on Wolfe's good times…"

"Who?" A brief spark of interest crossed my mind as my brain scrambled for ways to avoid the fate I knew was moments away.

A shrug from the beast. "Wolfe doesn't know. Wolfe doesn't care." A grin. "Wolfe cares about you, little doll.

Wolfe knows from the little samples how good you taste…now he wants the full course." He paused and wagged his finger at me. "Wolfe thinks you know that you can't beat him. But before we start, he wants to hear you promise you won't try."

An involuntary shudder passed through me and I gave my full effort to blotting out thoughts of what was about to happen. "I can't beat you," I admitted. "And if I kept running, I believe you will keep killing forever; everyone you could – men, women and children. It would never get better. It would be my fault. And that realization would sap every ounce of joy from my life – or what passes for my life – forever."

He took another step closer. "Wise, for one so young, to know the Wolfe so well. Wolfe is amazed that one so cut off all her life can feel connected to this world…but it matters not." He swept closer in one swift movement and I didn't resist as he closed his hand around my neck. "Wolfe is going to hurt you now…and this will go on for quite some time…until you can't resist even if you want to…and then, when you can't move, but you can still feel…then we'll start the real fun…"

He slammed me against the wall and it felt like the world ended. My ears rang as though someone had set off the planet's worst rock band in them, and it hurt like hell. My brain was swimming and for a moment the world spun upside down and then righted itself. Wolfe was still staring back at me with those black, lifeless eyes, like I was an insect he was studying. "I don't want you to move for your own good, little doll…dolls shouldn't move themselves when Wolfe plays with them…so this is for your own good…"

He reached back for a windup and threw me across the room and headfirst into the concrete. I don't know for sure that it fractured my skull, but the gawdawful cracking noise told me that either my bones or the wall had given. Blood covered my face, trickling over my eyes. I could only feel it, not see it, because my eyelids had snapped shut. He grabbed hold of me again and hauled me into the air. My hands twitched at my side.

"Wolfe wouldn't be doing this if you hadn't hurt him. He would have handed you over to his masters, like they wanted, all safe and sound, but you had to hurt the Wolfe…not once, not twice, but thrice…and now you're in his blood, and he needs you…and you need to learn not to trifle with big men…bad men…"

My eyes were lolling in my head as I tried to brace for the next impact, but I relaxed myself. Then he started to choke me, hard. I felt the stifling as I tried for a breath, then attempted to will myself not to breathe, hoping to get it over before he started having his fun with me, but I couldn't. My lungs strained and I began to panic.

I tried to gasp, but couldn't. No M-Squad was coming to save me. No cops. No…Mom. I was on my own.

Completely alone.

My eyes opened and my gaze lifted over his shoulder and I saw the box in the corner, door still open, almost leering, as though it were taunting me. Now the flashbacks came, at the end, as my pitiful life waited in the balance and I remembered moments I had tried to forget. All those years, Mom had held me in this house, like Wolfe was holding me now, keeping me captive, slowly squeezing the life out of me – and I let her, afraid of the box. Years of helpless imprisonment, putting aside everything I wanted out of my life.

It taunted me, in that corner. Years of being stuck in it, trapped, helpless.

Emotions poured over me like the icy water that had hit me earlier, a sudden, sharp shock. I remembered the last time I was stuck in that metal coffin, days without getting a breath of fresh air, and my fear built and built until I exploded, anger and hatred and sadness all rushing out. I pounded on the metal of the door, put everything into it and felt something I had never felt in all the times I had been in there.

It moved. The door moved, just a little. I hit it again and again and it budged a little more, and a crack of light from the outside peeked in. I hammered at the door, kicked, pushed at it, screaming, grunting, my weary and cramped muscles crying out to get free. The corner bent enough that I could stick my fingers through, and I pushed and the metal bent as I applied more and more pressure. With a final kick and punch I heard the top and bottom hinges strain and break and I ripped the door free, sucking in the breaths of life and falling to the basement floor, the cold concrete and breathable air letting me know that I was alive, and for once…I wasn't helpless.

I wasn't.

I stared back at Wolfe's soulless eyes and the same fury washed over me, the same desperate hunger for air and life. He held me at arm's length and my bare hands came up of their own accord and surged forward, wrapping themselves around his hairy neck. The black eyes looked at me in surprise and a smile found its way to his lips. His grip tightened on me as mine tightened on his neck. There was no way I would be able to kill him before he killed me, I knew that. And I didn't care. I would not die without him knowing that I wasn't a helpless, defenseless little doll just here for him to play with.

My fingers dug into his throat and he laughed. "You're going to have to squeeze much harder than that to make Wolfe feel it, my little doll. All you're doing is giving Wolfe a case of the tingles."

I gripped him tighter and he squeezed me so hard my head pushed back. I worried for a moment it was going to pop off, but I maintained my furious hold on him. I could feel a tingle of my own in my hands, likely from the fact that he was depriving my brain of oxygen. I dug my fingernails into his skin and I saw faint trickles of blood well up beneath them, even as I started to feel a sensation of lightheadedness percolate through my being.

"What…what are you…doing…?" Wolfe's words were choked, his eyes wide. I felt his grip slacken on my neck. I didn't dare loosen mine, and the lightheadedness I had experienced was growing into something more. The light in the room seemed to be brightening, amplifying.

"It…it BURNS!" He let out a howl of pain and batted at my hands. His claws dug into my wrists, scratching at them, drawing more blood that trickled down his fingers. I looked down to see it pooling in little drips on the concrete and then looked back to his face, awash in agony, and felt his weight start to drag me down. My hands were clutching his throat; my skin was hot and my head was throbbing, rushing with blood. I felt a heightened sense of…everything.

I suddenly realized the room reeked of blood and fear, and I drew in another sharp breath. Faint thumping noises upstairs were audible to me for the first time, and I could hear noises in the pipes and sirens blocks away, and all this over the whimpering and screaming of Wolfe. My skin was on fire with the heat of his throat in my hands, and I could feel the veins in Wolfe's neck pumping blood past my fingers.

"PLEASE!!" His voice shrieked, begging, pleading, filling the air in the basement. It was at that moment that I realized that if he could speak, I wasn't choking him – at least not effectively. "It hurts…SO…MUCH!" His words came out in a whimpering shriek. "Wolfe is sorry, little doll, please let him go, pleasepleaseplease…"

A few more wails of agony, one last whimper, and a death rattle filled the air. I held Wolfe by the neck and there was a bitter taste in my mouth as he went slack; his black eyes rolled back in his head, now truly lifeless. The lightheaded sensation filled me and I felt like I was floating, then flying, but not like I had when I went unconscious…instead it was like I was flying at a hundred miles an hour, even though I was still there in the basement, looking at Wolfe's dead eyes.

Though he weighed several hundred pounds, I held him up by the neck for several minutes, afraid to let go and empowered by the rush of whatever it was that was causing my head to spin. I finally let him slip from my grasp, and his body fell back, knocking over the box, which landed on the ground with a horrendous crash. Wolfe's body rolled off the side of it and slid to the floor, unmoving.

I took two steps back and slumped against the wall. My head felt like it was about to explode. My mind was so jumbled I couldn't control it; leaping in every direction, thoughts I could not have conceived of just a few minutes earlier were dashing through my head so quickly I couldn't even track them all.

I looked back at the two objects of my greatest fear and a heady feeling settled over me. I kicked Wolfe's shin with an outstretched leg. He didn't budge, didn't blink. He was dead.

And I was free.

24

I leaned against the wall, trying to catch my breath as thoughts whirled in my head. The creak of a floorboard focused me. I saw a foot appear at the top of the steps and tried to stand, then collapsed when I saw whose foot it was.

Reed tiptoed down the stairs and froze when he caught sight of Wolfe, then charged down the last few steps after he saw me, dropping to his knees at my side. "Sienna!"

"Yes?" I looked back at him, still wobbly.

"Thank God you're alive, you look…" He frowned in concern and his hand patted my forehead. "Uh…you…uh…"

"I think Wolfe did a number on me before I killed him," I replied through bloody lips.

He nodded agreement, looking somewhat gray in the face. He shifted from me and eased over to Wolfe on his knees and felt the monster's cheek. He looked back to me with an expression of fear and amazement. "He's dead."

"I just said that," I replied with an eye roll that left me feeling like my entire brain had done a backflip.

Reed shifted back to me. "I didn't believe you." His hands went to my neck and I felt the pressure of his touch for a few minutes; then he raised them in front of my eyes, covered in blood. "To answer your earlier question, yes, he did a number on you."

"Not the first time," I replied with a grunt. "But it's the last." I laughed, a light, airy laugh that turned into a hacking cough. Ouch.

He placed a hand on my forehead. "You're burning up." He tossed a look at Wolfe's body, then back to me. "How did you kill him?"

"I don't know…I just grabbed him around the throat and held on."

"So you strangled him?" His hand was resting on my forehead, as though he was trying to take my temperature.

"No…" I thought back to my hands around his throat, about him talking to me, pleading for his life. "He was still talking, so I couldn't have choked him to death."

Without warning, Reed yanked his hand away from me and toppled backward to the floor. He shook for a moment and stretched out as though he were convulsing. Crawling on my hands and knees, I moved toward him. "Are you all right?" I asked as he bucked once more and pulled himself to a sitting position. I reached out a hand and he batted it away, hard. I looked at him and his brown eyes came up at me laden with suspicion, a haggard look etched on his face, which was suddenly worn.

"Don't…touch me." His voice was violent, edgy.

I reached out again and he slid away in a hurry, hitting his back against the wall and sliding to his feet, looking down on me, his chest heaving as though he were fighting for a breath. "I said DON'T TOUCH ME!"

"What…is it?" I looked up at him from the floor, stunned at his sudden change in persona.

"Don't you get it?" He slid against the wall, moving toward the stairwell, still leaning against it for support. "You killed Wolfe…with your touch."

"What?" I asked, horrified. I looked at my hands and back to Reed, who had a look of revulsion on his face. "What…what am I?" A concern grew in me as I tried to wrap my still reeling mind around what had happened.

There was a sound upstairs, the noise of a door exploding open. Reed looked up and back to me, then took two steps toward a basement window and broke through it, springing with amazing agility through the hole and leaving a pile of broken, white-covered glass on the floor behind him.

The door to the basement flew open and heavy footfalls

came down the stairs. I struggled to my feet once more, looking at my hands, wondering if what Reed said was true and if I would have to use them again on whoever was coming after me.

I breathed a sigh of relief when Old Man Winter appeared at the top of the steps. He took a quick look at Wolfe, then called up the stairs, "Sienna is all right and…Wolfe is dead." He hurried down the last few steps to me, followed by a half dozen agents, all of whom goggled at the body of Wolfe, laying supine on the cold concrete floor next to the overturned box.

I braced myself against the wall as the agents formed a semi-circle around Wolfe and Old Man Winter stooped next to him. Ariadne came down last, followed by two more figures; Dr. Perugini and Dr. Sessions. Ariadne made her way over to me, following Dr. Perugini. Sessions made his way to Wolfe's corpse.

"No pulse, but no sign of trauma…" I heard Dr. Sessions rattle off as he leaned over Wolfe. "Are we sure he's dead?"

Sessions cast a look at Old Man Winter, who nodded. "He would not lie down like this. He is dead."

"I need you to sit down, sweetie." Dr. Perugini's thickly accented words washed over me and she and Ariadne eased closer, each going to one of my elbows.

"DON'T TOUCH ME!" I screamed at them, the thought of Reed's words still hanging in my mind. They both jumped back a step when I exploded, and I held my hands out to put them at arm's length.

"I don't get it; I see no cause of death." Dr. Sessions' words felt like an indictment of me.

"I killed him," I said into the silence that filled the room. "I killed him with my touch…"

Ariadne and Dr. Perugini exchanged a look. "If you say so," Dr. Perugini said with an air of patronization. She reached for me again, Ariadne a step behind her. "I need you to sit down and relax…"

Old Man Winter took two long strides from where he stood at the side of Wolfe's body and landed a long arm on the shoulders of Dr. Perugini and Ariadne. "Don't…" he mumbled in quiet warning, "…touch her."

They both looked at him in surprise, but Perugini's turned to annoyance. "She's injured. I need to get her back to the Directorate and treat her wounds."

Old Man Winter did not budge. "She'll be fine. Do not touch her without heavy gloves." His gaze fell over me again, and he turned back to where the agents stood around the body of Wolfe.

"Or what?" Perugini spat at him. "She's hurt, she's delusional, Erich! She's just been through a ridiculous level of trauma – you can't possibly think she killed this maniac by touching him." She looked after him, and he hesitated, and the chill of the cold air from the window filled the room, swirling around him as though it were embracing a very old friend. "Erich?" she asked again, note of disbelief filling her voice. "You don't actually believe her?"

He stared down at Wolfe for a long moment before he answered. "Certainly I believe her," he replied. His cold blue eyes swept back to Dr. Perugini, then to Ariadne, finally coming to rest on me. "It is as she said. She touched him, and he likely screamed and begged for his life, and she killed him with her hands. With her touch."

I felt a chill unrelated to the broken window as my eyes followed Old Man Winter's down to the corpse of Wolfe, the scariest maniac I'd ever heard of, dead, helpless, on the floor – the way I'd made him. I looked back up and the biting fear ate at me, doubts, horror, still swirling in my brain, which was rocketing at a mile a second. "What…am…I?" I croaked out at him.

"What am I?" I asked again, stronger this time. He did not answer me, instead turning away after gesturing at Wolfe's body as he swept up the stairs. Dr. Perugini reached for my elbow and I brushed her off, knocking her aside.

"WHAT AM I?" I howled at him as he retreated.

A voice, deathly familiar, prickled at the back of my mind, instilling a sense of calm that came from deep inside, an answer to a question that was asked and answered somewhere in the depths of me.

Soul eater, it said in a raspy, whispering voice.

Succubus.

25

"You're what would be known in mythology as a succubus," Dr. Sessions said in a voice pitched with excitement. We were back at the Directorate hours later. I had let Ariadne and Dr. Perugini coax me upstairs and into a waiting car after my question was answered from within. Although I was familiar with the myth of succubi, I knew that the answer hadn't come from me. And that left another question that I was sure I could answer, but didn't want to.

After a visit to the medical unit to make sure I was all right, Ariadne had asked me to see Dr. Sessions. I'd agreed. So there I sat, clad once more in a long sleeved turtleneck, jeans, and with a pair of heavy mittens they'd rummaged for me, on his examination table, him keeping an arm's length away while he talked.

"I thought that succubi...uh..." I blushed as I thought about having to ask the doctor the question that was on my mind. Ariadne and Dr. Perugini were both in the lab as well, hovering in the background. Perugini, in particular, looked as though she was ready to level Dr. Sessions, staring at him from across the room through half-slitted eyes. "...slept with men in order to steal their souls."

Dr. Sessions smiled, which at the present moment didn't creep me out as much as it might have a week ago. "No. Well," he rescinded, "you could, I suppose, but all that's necessary is the touch of your skin. You touch someone with your bare hands, or your face – anything involving flesh to

151

flesh contact, and they'll start to feel the effects of your power."

"Mom knew," I said in a low whisper. "That's why she had rule #4."

"Excuse me?" Sessions looked at me.

"My mom," I explained. "She had a rule that I wasn't allowed to wander around the house without being fully dressed, down to having on gloves at all times. I assumed that it was because we had to be ready to run at a moment's notice."

"Yes, your mother likely knew," he agreed, turning back to some printouts of the data he'd accumulated on me through our testing. "She was probably the source of your power; I suspect she was a succubus as well. It's very rare, of course; most of our data on succubi is apocryphal – in fact, there's only one in our records known to be alive." He chirruped with a twitter of excitement. "Well, three now, I suppose, counting you and your mother."

"How…do I kill someone by touching them?" I asked, still in disbelief.

"Looking for a scientific explanation?" He shrugged, still an air of whimsical amusement, as though he were so excited by the prospect of a new subject for study that he failed to realize that I might be feeling something other than what he was. "I can't explain it without studying the effect in more detail. Of course, we brought Wolfe's body back for study—" he pointed to a white sheet on a nearby table, covering a monstrous corpse—"which should be just a wealth of information. Since this is the first chance anyone's had to study a confirmed victim of a succubus, it's really a pioneering step…"

Victim. His words drifted past me after that, and as he kept talking, I thought about Wolfe as a victim. Wolfe had never been a victim of anything in his life until I came along. He made victims; he wasn't one. Until now.

Now he was my first.

"…so I'll be studying him. Of course there are tests I'll be wanting to run on you as time goes by, and hopefully we can get to the bottom of the root physiological causes of your power." Sessions clapped his hands together and looked at me with unsuppressed glee. "It's very exciting, isn't it?"

I cast a look back at Wolfe, still hidden under the sheet. "Thrilling."

It is thrilling, isn't it...

I ignored the voice in my head and turned back to Dr. Sessions. "A question about succubi...aren't they supposed to drain the souls of their victims?"

He entertained a high, giggly laugh. "Yes, according to anecdotes, incubi – the male counterpart of your type of meta – and succubi steal the souls of their victims, but of course they also are reported to do it through sexual contact, which is not what happened in this case." He pushed his glasses up on his nose, suddenly disheveled. "Right?"

A wave of revulsion passed over me. "I grabbed him around the throat, Doc."

"Oh, okay, that's what I thought." He recovered and shifted back to glee. "I think it doubtful you 'stole his soul'," Sessions said with a scornful laugh. "Bear in mind that also in the mythological descriptions is the idea that a succubus or incubus comes to their victim in their dreams, which is," he said with another giggle, "absolutely preposterous."

I stared back at him. "Right."

"I think you can see the myth and reality when it comes to meta-humans is somewhat divergent." He smiled. "Any other questions? Very good, then. Well, you get back to recovering under Dr. Perugini's able ministrations and I'll give you a call as soon as I have anything of interest to report."

"Doctor," I said as I stood. "This power..." He stared back at me, curious as to what I was going to ask. "Does this mean I'm never going to be able to touch anyone...ever?"

"Through heavy clothing you can. We'll need to do some study, but I suspect that there's a certain thickness of material that will prevent bleedthrough of your powers." He adjusted his glasses once more.

"I meant with my skin." My mouth was dry, but I didn't need a drink.

"Well...no, I...I think not," he stuttered. "We'll research the effect further, but it seems that if you killed Wolfe with your touch, then it will have the same effect on anyone else you happen to be in contact with." He seemed satisfied with his answer until he looked over my shoulder. I turned in time to see Dr. Perugini shaking her head in disgust and Sessions amended, "But...we need to do more research to be certain."

Dr. Perugini made a rattling sound of annoyance in her throat and reached up to place her hand on my back, avoiding touching the skin. Ariadne walked next to me and we descended into the underground tunnel back to the HQ building.

"So," Ariadne began, "now that Wolfe is out of the picture, have you given any thought to your next move?"

"Not really."

"You could stay here," Ariadne answered, pushing a lock of hair behind her ear.

"I don't have anywhere else to go," I replied, "so I suppose I will for now."

"I meant long-term," she corrected. "Our facilities and resources for meta-humans are unparalleled. We can help you learn how to control and harness your power."

Control and harness, two words that mean they'd like to make you their willing slave...

"Can we please focus on getting her to the point where she's no longer badly wounded before we start talking about anything else?" Dr. Perugini's irritation finally broke loose, causing Ariadne to do as the doctor ordered. Parting ways with us at the medical unit, Ariadne promised to stop by again later to check on me. Dr. Perugini walked me back to my bed, filling the air with florid Italian curses. I doubt she realized I knew them.

"Rest," Perugini commanded before she disappeared into her office. I lay back, resting my head on the pillow following the doctor's exhortation, and glanced around the medical unit. The curtains were down and the bay was empty.

They want to own you...they want to make you their property...run while you can...

"I can't yet," I said, voice no higher than a whisper. "I need answers."

They don't want to give you answers; they want you to work for them, to…kill for them.

I snorted, staring into the steel wall opposite my bed. "Let me ask you something…where's my mom?"

I don't know. And if I did, I wouldn't tell you.

"You're lying."

"Excuse me?"

I looked up, startled. Dr. Perugini had appeared from her office door and crossed the bay. "Who were you talking to?"

I tried to keep my expression blank. "Myself. Bad habit, I'm afraid. It's what happens," I said with a light chuckle, "when you have no one but Mom to talk to for years and years."

"Ah," she said. Her face bore discomfort and I could tell she felt sorry for me. "Here you go; something to dull the pain." She dropped two pills into my outstretched hand and reached to the side table where a pitcher of water sat, poured me a glass and handed it over. She watched as I dropped the pills in my mouth and drank half a glass. "Anything else I can do for you?"

"No," I said.

"You'll be healed by tomorrow. Nasty marks on your neck should all be gone by then. Skull fracture too; it's already almost knitted together."

"Thank you." I mouthed the words, not sure if I really meant them. I felt a sudden urge to hit her, to beat her bloody and then slam her head in the door until she stopped moving, and then…

"Are you sure you're all right?" Dr. Perugini looked at me, eyes searching mine.

I looked at the blank steel plating that covered the wall across from my bed, the shiny, reflective surface, then looked back at her with a practiced smile. "I'm fine. Just a little tired, that's all. And my head hurts. It's been a long day."

"Of course. I'll leave you alone. Just call out if you need anything." With a smile, she turned and went back into her office, closing the door behind her.

You wanted to do it, to beat her, to kill her…

155

"No, I didn't," I whispered, softer this time.

You did; I felt it; you're coming around to my way of thinking...

"No." I stared at the wall, and I could see just the faintest image of myself. "Tell me where my mother is."

Told you. Don't know...and I wouldn't tell you if I did.

Somewhere in her office, Dr. Perugini must have hit the light switch, because the medical unit was bathed in darkness, broken only by the faint light of instrument panels. I looked back at the steel, mirrored surface across from me and my face was gone, replaced by black eyes and teeth that looked unusually sharp; predatory, even. I smiled, and my voice came out harsher, lower and more rasping than usual.

"We'll see about that...Wolfe."

ACKNOWLEDGMENTS

I've heard it said that writing is hard. I disagree; writing novels is easy thanks to the people I have to help me.

Once more, my greatest thanks to my editorial team:

First of all Heather Rodefer, a real trooper, who pores over each page with ruthless precision, purple pen in hand. Her tireless efforts, real-time feedback, and fearlessness in telling me when something is simply not working help keep my work from becoming self-indulgent codswallop.

Second, I must thank Debra Wesley, who in addition to being the speediest to deliver her feedback, is also a constant source of wry humor, insight into the larger world of fantasy and sci-fi, and affirmation for whatever project I've just completed.

Third, Shannon Garza read through this particular volume multiple times, trying to figure out what grammatical sin I had committed that caused her Texan sense (it's like spider-sense, but for Texans) to tingle with displeasure. She ended up figuring out by pure instinct something that I thought I had fixed. Kudos to her for helping me smooth out that particular problem.

I shudder to think what any of these books would look like without the countless hours these three put in helping me fix the errors of perspective and thought, grammar and syntax. Keeping a story straight in my head is a lot of work and it'd be impossible if not for outside help like theirs.

Thanks again to Kari Layman for the affirming conversations that led me to go out on a limb and write this book. If she'd said it didn't sound that interesting, I probably would have worked on something else and Sienna Nealon might never have left her house.

Thanks also to Calvin Sams, who read through and gave some very helpful notes.

A special shout-out and thanks to Nicholas J. Ambrose, author extraordinaire.

The cover of this book was designed by Karri Klawiter of

artbykarri.com.

To the fans, the people who have been buying and reading my work and sharing your feedback, a hearty, hearty thank you. The best letters always seem to come on the days when I need them most.

And finally, thanks to my family – wife, kids and parents – for doing all that you do so that I can do what I do.

BOOK 2
UNTOUCHED

Prologue

Above the Podkannaya Tuguska River
Russian Empire
June 30, 1908

His skin was wreathed in flames, burning red and yellow, as he streaked across the early morning sky. Aleksandr Timofeyevich Gavrikov was not yet eighteen. *I can't believe I killed her*, he thought. *I have done murder.*

The air felt cold in spite of the fact that his skin was covered by a solid inch of fire. How *is that possible?* he wondered. The wind that whipped across his face did not affect the flames. *This is unlike anything I have ever seen...unlike anything Father has ever seen too, I think...*The smell of rank, stale water rose up from below him in the swamps. A river cut the land, the shine of the rising sun refracting off it. He was several hundred feet up, flying—*as though I were a bird*, he thought. *Without flapping my arms, I can fly! Just like Father.*

He felt a thrum in his heart at that thought. *He will hurt me for this; worse than he ever has before. Perhaps things would have been different if mother had lived,* he thought for the thousandth time, then dismissed it. *I am on fire and flying through the air and I have done murder. Had mother lived long enough to see this, the shock would have killed her.*

Seventeen years, he reflected. *Seventeen years of hell for me and Klementina. But no more.* The flames on his skin burned brighter as he thought about it, of all the abuses, the beatings, the nights he heard Klementina squealing and crying when their father went to her—

The flames that covered him changed, grew hotter. The cold air was warming around him, and he hovered a few feet above the water, staring at himself, his reflection, in the river below. *How many times, Klementina? How many times did he hurt you?* He and Klementina were forced to stay on the farm on all but the rarest of occasions. His sister was fair—*beautiful*, he thought. More beautiful than the peasant girls he had seen when they had gone into Kirensk. Her green eyes were hued with some blue, and her skin was tanned and freckled. Her blond hair hung about her shoulders as she carried buckets of water in from the well. She was far, far more beautiful than the girls he had seen in Kirensk.

He drifted close to the surface of the water, looking at himself. No skin was visible; he was a glowing fire, shaped like a man. *What...am I? Even Father does not burst into flames when he flies...*

"Aleksandr!" The word crackled through the air, and panic ran through him. He whipped his head around to see his father flying toward him from above, eyes narrowed, his teeth bared in rage.

I will get such a beating for this, Aleksandr thought. *I will be chained and locked in the shed for a week.*

He remembered the time when he'd had courage. A year earlier he had awoken to hear Klementina crying, his father slapping her in the only bedroom of their farmhouse. It happened so often, and every night it had, he turned over, shut his eyes tight, and covered his ears with his old, threadbare pillow. It almost shut out the cries of his sister and the primal, disgusting grunts of his father.

He had thought he couldn't bear it any longer. He had run into the room in the middle of the night and grasped his father by the shoulders, throwing him off Klementina. She huddled, clutching a sheet to her, moaning and sobbing, her eyes wide with fear. The first two punches had been so satisfying; he heard his father's nose break, watched the blood run down his lip. Then the drunken eyes had focused on him, and his father had brought a hand across his face in fury.

Aleksandr had gone flying across the room. After landing, he could dimly hear Klementina crying, saw her covering herself with the blanket as his father approached him. He could smell the awful night smells, the stink of sweat and fear. The blood was slick and running across his eye as his father leaned down to him. With another punch, everything went dark.

When he awoke, it was midday, hot, and he was chained to a stake in the middle of the shed. No water, no food, until after dark when Klementina came to him, bringing him some crumbs of supper and something to drink. Her eyes were black and swollen, and a trail of dried blood led from one of her nostrils to her upper lip.

He had not intervened since.

"Aleksandr!" The shout came again, and Aleksandr turned, blasting away from the river, up into the air above. The chill was back, the coolness of early morning, but this time it was fused with the tickle of the flames that wreathed him. His father was following, he knew. *He won't let me go. Not after what I've done.*

He climbed higher and higher in the sky, felt the chill increase. He looked down, and the Tunguska River was so far below that it was but a line. He felt the flames start to die, saw his skin peeking out from beneath the place where the fire had burned so hard only a minute earlier. *He'll catch me. He'll lock me away. I won't be able to stop him.*

The air was thin, and he couldn't breathe. He gasped for breath, but it didn't seem to help. He looked back; father was gaining on him, coming up behind him, his face fixed, eyes blazing in a way that told Aleksandr that this might be the last time...

He felt his father's hand close around his arm, felt it tighten, then felt the bone crack, and Aleksandr Timofeyevich Gavrikov tried to cry out with a breath he didn't have. His father had broken his arm, and the excruciating sensation felt as though someone had jammed a knife into his upper arm and twisted. He felt the pull of his father's strength, dragging him down, down, down. He fought, he struggled, but without breath he failed, sagging. He was pulled down, and after a moment he felt his breath return, felt the chill start to fade.

Felt the heat under his skin return.

"You have killed her!" His father's words were barely audible over the wind as they descended. "Your sister is dead because of you!"

"I did not mean to," Aleksandr's words came out ragged. "She touched me and..."

"You killed her," his father said again, and backhanded him across the face with his free hand. The smell of the swamp water below reminded him of the night smells, of the fear.

The heat under Aleksandr's skin grew, his breaths grew deeper and less forced. *He beats me during the day and tortures Klementina at night.* "You will never be able to hurt her again."

Another backhand was his reward. "I never hurt her!"

"You hurt her all the time." Aleksandr heard a menace in his own voice that had never been there before. It reminded him of the time he'd had courage. The heat underneath his skin was unbearable; it was burning, aching to get out. "I may have killed her this morning, but you have killed her every night since she was a girl."

"LIAR!" His father struck him again, and the heat became intense within him. His eyes were burning, his skin was burning, and suddenly it was on fire again, and his flesh was covered in flames. "What...?!"

His father yelped and his hand withdrew. Aleksandr felt himself fall for a second before he took over and felt the power of his own flight return. He hovered a few feet from his father, staring at the old man with unfettered contempt. "You have flown for as long as I can remember, Father." The menace was there. The courage was in his voice. His father was cradling his hand, a blackened, burned husk of what it had been: a strong, powerful limb that he used to beat his children. "It appears that I have taken more from you than I would have imagined."

"You are my son," came the ghostly reply.

"I am not. I am my mother's son." He felt the heat, still under his skin, even as the fire raged on top of it. "I am my sister's brother. I am Aleksandr; not Timofeyevich nor Gavrikov, because I want nothing of yours that I don't need." Without hesitation he flew at his father, slammed into him, and the searing under his skin unleashed as they fell toward the earth below. *Seventeen years of hell*, he thought, and it all came out at once—a torrent of rage, fire, flame, an explosion of his anger. He watched his father's skin blacken, his eyes disappear in the initial flash of heat, watched his flesh burn away, then the bone turn to ash and then dust.

The world went white all around, the trees below were like little pieces of tinder in the wind, picked up and flung through the air, the landscape flattening for miles in every direction. A screeching sound filled his ears, and cracks like thunder went off one after another.

When it was all over, Aleksandr Timofeyevich Gavrikov was no more.

And Aleksandr flew off, taking the only thing of his father's that he wanted.

The gift of flight.

1

Sienna Nealon
Present Day

I awoke in a cold sweat. The red light of the clock told me it was close to five A.M., and my eyes searched the room around me, trying to acclimate after another nightmare. I worked to get my breathing under control as I sat up, walls spinning around me. The only other light came from the windows and the far distant lamps that lit the Directorate campus.

The Directorate. That's where I was. A secret organization dedicated to policing humans with powers beyond the norm— metas, they were called. I still wasn't sure I believed that the Directorate did what they claimed to, but I had very little evidence as yet of what their true intentions might be. All I knew was that so far they'd helped me when no one else had.

I still didn't trust them.

My breathing returned to normal. I blinked my eyes a few times to adjust to the darkness and then I stood, letting my feet touch the soft, carpeted floor. The room smelled sterile, with just a hint of dust from what I assumed was the reconstruction it had undergone. I looked back through the glass, which was flawless, having been replaced only a couple days ago. Hard to believe it was such a short time.

Until a little over a week ago, I had been a prisoner in my

own home for over ten years. Mom kept me from leaving with a simple threat: if I got out of line, was disobedient in some way, offended her or didn't mind my manners, she locked me in a six-foot-tall metal sarcophagus. It certainly kept me from running. The drywall dust had a light and pleasant smell compared to the stench of being locked in that metal box for days at a time.

I had left my house in a rush, pursued by agents of the Directorate, who, at the time, I thought had ill intentions toward me. I'd met a guy named Reed who also helped me. Good looking, in a tall, dark and handsome kind of way, if you're into that. I kind of am. Maybe. He helped me get away from the Directorate for a while, but we got attacked by a beast.

The beast's name was Wolfe. He had lived for thousands of years, had killed countless people before we crossed paths, and after we tangled, he became obsessed with me. Everyone tells me I'm strong. Wolfe was stronger. So much stronger that it wasn't even a contest. He manhandled me, humiliated me, bent me, broke me, cut through a dozen or more armed Directorate guards, and left me in a bloody heap more than once.

I shook away the thought of Wolfe as I padded, barefoot, into the bathroom. I felt the cool night air against my skin. I was wearing only a bra and panties, less than I had ever worn to bed in my life, but there was a reason for it beyond simple tactile pleasure.

When I squared off against Wolfe for the last time, it was because he had held the entire city of Minneapolis hostage, leaving a trail of dead bodies until I came out of hiding and faced him. The Directorate higher-ups, Old Man Winter, his gal Friday Ariadne, and even one of the agents, Zack (he's a cutie, that one) begged me not to go up against Wolfe again. They urged me to wait until their highly trained team of metas, M-Squad, returned from a mission so they could handle it. But people were dying, and Wolfe seemed unstoppable. Since all he wanted was me, I went to give him what he wanted.

Meta powers are twofold. One, they have enhanced

strength, speed, dexterity—attributes far above a normal human's. I can lift heavy objects, run faster and farther, leap fences, and essentially do stuff that makes everyone but Superman look pathetic. I was reminded of this again as I went to take a drink of water after washing my hands and I accidentally burst the bottle, soaking the bathroom floor, the sink, and myself.

I shouldn't think about Wolfe while I'm taking a drink. Or handling anything delicate, come to think of it. But these days, it's hard not to think about him all the time.

The second set of powers a meta possesses is unique to each one, to his or her type of metahuman. Wolfe, for instance, had skin that was highly adaptable to damage. If he got shot, the next time it happened he was able to take a greater amount of that kind of damage. I saw a shotgun go off at point blank range and leave nothing but red marks on his skin.

It was in my final confrontation with Wolfe that I had discovered my other power. I am a succubus, possessed of the ability to drain a soul, or the essence of a person, with nothing but the touch of my skin. He had me in a chokehold, but I touched him, and he screamed, and I drained the life out of him.

Hence the bra and panties for sleepwear. If anyone came for me during the night, I wanted to be able to defend myself. I didn't think anyone would, but when you've been imprisoned in your own home for twelve years and then turned loose in a world where everyone wants a piece of you, it's easy to develop a sense of paranoia. Except it's not paranoia when they're actually after you.

I sighed, feeling the water dripping down my skin. I looked at myself in the mirror. I didn't know for certain, but I was pretty sure my meta powers also included enhanced hearing, smell, sight, taste, and feeling, because it felt like I could see every detail of the water drops that were tracing their way down my pale belly.

I wasn't very tall, about five foot four, and my brown hair was tangled from the way I slept on it. My eyes looked more blue than green, and I had acquired a couple of small freckles since the last time I had studied myself in the mirror. I had yet to see the sun, but I had spent enough time outside that they had formed, one on my cheek and one on the tip of my nose. I stripped, removing the wet clothing, and toweled off before I turned off the light.

As I turned to leave, something in the mirror caught my attention. A flash of black eyes, tangled, matted, dirty hair, far different than the slight mess that mine was, and a vision of wicked teeth, the type a predator would use to rip and shred its prey. The eyes watched me, and I could almost taste the desire for my blood—and something else, less savory.

So pretty, the voice came. *So pure and sweet and untouched.*

"Dammit, Wolfe," I said, my words coming out as close to a growl as I could imagine, "Can't you just go away?"

The unfortunate side effect of my power, one which I had told no one about yet, was that I now had Wolfe bouncing around in my head. He gave a running commentary on my life; his thoughts ranged from the mundane to the disgusting, and I got all of them—unfiltered, profane, and revolting. Living a life cooped up with my mother had kept me more or less innocent, and having this diseased freak sharing my skull was giving me nightmares, both figurative and literal, as I got to witness his crimes every night as I slept. And there were so many.

Can't go away, he whispered back. *You and Wolfe are bound together, little doll. Intertwined.*

I resisted the urge to vomit in my mouth and flipped the light switch, casting the bathroom in the bright aura of the overhead lamps. The reflection of Wolfe was gone from the mirror.

Such sweetness, he intoned, his words growing with verve in my head. *Wolfe would have touched you, Wolfe would have made you scream with pleasure—*

"You would have died," I said to my reflection, as though I could sense his presence behind my eyes. "Oh, wait," I said with mock joy, "You did. And it couldn't have happened to a more disgusting creature." I thought about it for a beat. "Actually, you dying did make me scream with pleasure—"

I felt a searing pain in my skull, one that dropped me to my knees. With my eyes almost squinted shut, I could only see blurry shapes in the mirror; one was flesh-toned, on its knees, the other was behind me, stalking back and forth—

I turned, but there was no one there. I fell back on my haunches, felt the cold linoleum of the bathroom floor against my backside, and lay down, closing my eyes and putting a hand over my throbbing head. "You're such a bastard," I said. "Why don't you tell me what you know about my mother?"

I stared at the ceiling, waiting to see if Wolfe would reply. He didn't.

Mom had gone missing about a week before the Directorate had ousted me from my house. Everyone here denied knowing anything about her disappearance. Wolfe knew something, I suspected, but in the last day or so of sharing skull space with me, he'd been cagey.

He was there, I could feel him, skulking in my brain. The headache was his doing. Whenever he had a burst of strong emotion, I felt its effects. Yesterday, when I was leaving the medical unit, a stay caused by my last fight with Wolfe, Ariadne had offered me different options of where I could stay on the Directorate campus.

"We have a variety of dorm rooms," she said, talking in a quiet voice, as though I were too brittle to be exposed to words spoken at normal volume. "Or, if you would feel safer, you could stay in the secure room in the Headquarters basement—"

"How about the dorm room I stayed in before?" I asked her, not sure where the question came from.

"The one where Wolfe...attacked you?" She took a step back, her eyes wide. "I assumed that there would be bad memories associated with...that place."

I had felt a little thrill run through me, a surge of pleasure at the memory of what he'd done to me there. It wasn't my feeling, which would have been closer to nausea, but it was strong enough to overwhelm my own emotions. "Yeah," I said. "I'll stay there."

Ariadne didn't have the most expressive face; it was reserved most of the time, and her red hair was always the only splash of color in her drab attire. Still, on this occasion, she had emotion—concern. For me.

"I'll be fine," I said. "He's dead. Nothing to fear from him now."

Oh, but there is. I ignored him.

Ariadne's fashion sense was prosaic; it was as if the dull and dreary winter weather was her inspiration. Wolfe threw out an uncharitable and crass thought about what he'd do to liven up her look and I ignored it even though it caused a vein in my eye to pulse. She didn't argue with me anymore after that, just let me go to my room—to rest, I told her. I didn't, though, not the rest of that day. Not until well after nightfall, and then I was plagued by the nightmares that had caused me to wake in a sweat.

The linoleum on the floor was causing my body to ache, and I felt a throbbing in my head. I sat up, felt the pain Wolfe had inflicted fade, and grabbed hold of the counter, pulling up to my feet. I stared once more into the mirror, looking at myself, my face, my eyes. There were bags underneath them; I looked tired.

I turned out the bathroom light and walked back out into the room, heading to the closet. The feeling that Wolfe had been watching me while I was nude left me unsettled; I dressed in silence, slipping on a long-sleeved sweatshirt and jeans.

The air was warm enough; I could feel an unseen heater fighting against the chill of the winter outside. The window was one-way, Ariadne had told me, a type of special glass that was tinted so that whatever happened inside could not be seen from outside, even if the lights were on. I had walked around the dormitory building and couldn't see anything but my own reflection, even at night, when I knew there were lights on inside.

I walked to the window with confidence that I was unseen. The ground was covered in snow, at least a foot deep if not more; the only disruption to its smooth, unblemished surface was the place a few hundred feet away where a path had been cut with a snow blower so people could walk and some footprints that were not fresh—mine. Far in the distance lurked a pine forest, the green needles blending with the black of night.

The sky seemed lighter than I remembered it being a few minutes ago. I stared out and saw a flat spot next to the headquarters building with heavy lights sticking up out of the snow around it, reminding me of a baseball game I'd seen on TV that was played at night.

I watched, looking through the dark, and saw figures standing on the concrete—the red hair of Ariadne was visible even at this distance. Old Man Winter was with her, towering above her small frame, and it looked like the wind was swirling snow around his legs.

Old Man Winter was the boss of the Directorate. Ridiculously tall, he looked like he was in his seventies, and his face looked as though it had been carved out of rock that had been exposed to the elements for too long. His eyes were the most piercing blue you could imagine, though even I couldn't see them at this distance. Standing next to him was a shorter man, a fatter one, and I knew it was Kurt Hannegan.

Kurt and I had a history of antipathy. He'd been the one that had helped me deliver myself to Wolfe, unbeknownst to Old Man Winter and Ariadne. Kurt and I had no love lost, not since our first encounter when he broke into my house and I pummeled him. If that wasn't enough, since I arrived at the Directorate I had caused the deaths of quite a few of his fellow human agents. None of them were intentional but I doubt it mattered to him; he didn't like me before that, and it wasn't the sort of thing that was going to put me on his good side.

The three of them stood to one side of the lighted area. The wind was blowing hard, and with the exception of Old Man Winter, they were wearing heavy coats. I pressed a hand against the glass and felt the chill seep through; the temperature outside had to be below zero. Two more figures joined them, one from the Headquarters building, the other cutting across the snow from in the distance. Based on the shuffle of the steps, I knew that one was Dr. Ron Sessions, the lab geek that the Directorate kept on hand. The other was shorter, her frame undeniably female, dark hair whipping in the wind. I suspected it was Dr. Perugini, the woman who ran the medical unit and had treated me several times since I arrived. When she turned, I caught a glimpse of her chiseled features.

Once Sessions joined them, the five of them stood to one side of the patch. I watched, waiting for something to happen. Ariadne appeared to be speaking to Sessions and Perugini while Old Man Winter watched, his mouth unmoving, and Kurt stood to the side, stamping his feet to ward off the cold. I could feel Wolfe stirring in my brain, wondering what they were up to. His thoughts matched mine, but I was trying to mask my thoughts from him. I had my doubts that it was working.

What are they waiting for, little doll?

"I don't know," I said. "Why am I bothering to answer your sick ass?"

Hard to resist the Wolfe, isn't it?

"Don't think that just because you're in my head that you have any idea what I think." There was a flicker of movement outside, and Wolfe didn't bother answering.

A helicopter descended. I recognized the type, my photographic memory reconciling what I was seeing with what I had seen in movies. It was a Black Hawk, and I could see the doors open as they descended. I saw a figure emerge, hanging out the door while waiting for the helicopter to touch down, a figure that was shorter than Old Man Winter by a lot. It was all I needed to see, and I had grabbed my coat and was slinging it on as I ran out the door.

Zack had returned.

2

I barely remembered to put my boots on before I was off and running. On the way out of the dormitory building I felt the cold air slap me in the face, but I didn't care.

Little doll seems very happy to see the flimsy agent. Wolfe wonders if she knows how useless the little man is to her, he breaks so easy, he would burn if she touched him...

"Shut up," I said as my feet found the path and I loped along, barely keeping myself from dropping to all fours the way Wolfe's instincts were compelling me to. "I'm not a dog," I snapped to the voice in my head. "I can't run on my hands and feet the way you can—could."

But it would be so good to see you on hands and knees again... A wave of revulsion washed over me and I tried to ignore it as I cut through the wintery air. *Why is this little man so important to make you run out in the middle of the night?*

"He's not..." I stopped talking when I realized I was giving the psycho in my head more fodder for taunting me. Besides, why was I running to see Zack? When last we had parted, it had been after he had extracted a promise from me to not go after Wolfe, a promise I had broken. Afterward, I had spent some time examining my thinking behind that promise and found it lacking; I believed I made it because Zack was hot. Tall, with tousled hair, brown eyes and in amazing shape. Downside: I suspected he was spying on me for Old Man Winter and Ariadne.

At that moment, I didn't care. Of all the people I had met

since leaving my house, Zack was the one I felt most connected to. After he left, things around the Directorate got much worse and—I hated to admit it—I missed having someone to talk to who was close to my own age. It's not like I had a ton of time to get used to it before he left, but still...I missed him. I felt a tingle of amusement that I knew came from Wolfe, and wished, not for the first time, that I could mentally slap the hell out of him.

I covered the ground between the dorm and the helipad quickly, arriving just after the helicopter set down. None of the observers noticed me as I slipped up behind them and I felt a thrill of predatory success as I stared at their backs and realized I could kill every last one of them.

I would have been disturbed by that, but Wolfe's thoughts were bleeding into mine with such regularity that unless he "spoke" in my head, I couldn't be sure whether it genuinely came from me.

I lurked behind them, and saw Ariadne say something to Dr. Perugini that caused Old Man Winter to look back at them both. "He was stable for transit," Ariadne said, then the rotors cut out her next words before I caught a few more, "...amazed they were able to catch him, really." Old Man Winter looked past Ariadne and noticed me. He stared, his eyes into mine, before nodding in acknowledgment. He spoke, something low, but loud enough that those around him heard it and looked, each of them finding me in turn.

I moved forward to join them, figuring that lurking in the shadows was a pointless game. I saw Zack, dressed in a paramilitary uniform, olive green overalls with a tactical vest, a submachine gun slung under his arm, and a headset covering his ears. He stepped down and tossed the headset back into the chopper. I could see him saying something to the figures inside.

He turned and strode across the pad to Old Man Winter. I half-expected him to salute, as though I were watching a war movie, but he leaned in and whispered something to his boss. While he did so, others were stepping out of the Black Hawk, four of them, in quick fashion. M-Squad, I figured.

A stir of interest from Wolfe kept me watching them rather

than Zack. The first one off the chopper was a man. He had a jaw that looked like it had been carved from an iron bar. It extended down, giving him the look of someone who perpetually stuck his chin out. His skin was dark, his hair black and short, military-style, stubble on the sides and just a patch of black on top. I couldn't tell what color eyes he had because of the dark, but they were moving fast and they were focused. They found me in the dark, surveyed me—not in the dirty way Wolfe had, but as a potential opponent.

The next off the Black Hawk was a woman. Her hair was short, blond, cropped in one of those boyish, pixie styles of someone who has no time and no interest in impressing anyone with it. Her facial structure was pronounced, Nordic, but her skin was tanned. She saw me, too, and watched me for long enough to do an assessment of her own. She was so severe, I wondered if she ever smiled.

The third off the chopper was a man with long, gray hair and a beard that matched it. The rotor blades stirred his silver locks, blowing them into his eyes, but it didn't seem to distract him. He gave me the same once-over as the others and halted by the door to the chopper.

The last guy off surprised me. I'm not going to mince words: he was fat. Not the size of a house or anything, but he was a big boy. The others were muscular, but his belly hung out under his fatigues. He was laughing about something as his feet hit the ground, but none of his teammates were laughing with him. His grin was not a happy one; for some reason I got a little dash of an unsettling feeling from looking at him.

He reached into the chopper and pulled something out, slinging it over his shoulder to carry. It was a tube, about six feet long, a couple feet wide and a foot deep. It reminded me of an oversized coffin at first glance.

Actually, it reminded me of the box my mother used to put me in, but smaller and more compact.

The big guy joined his comrades and the four of them walked across the helipad as the Black Hawk spun up the rotors and lifted back into the air. I turned my attention to Old Man Winter, who had finished his conversation with

Zack.

Zack moved to talk to Kurt. The two of them were partners the day they came to collect me from my house. I didn't know if they still worked together, because they'd had something of a falling out after Kurt tried to hit me at one point. I wasn't sure if Zack knew what had happened since then, but I doubt he'd be excited to know that his partner had driven me to an encounter with Wolfe.

I caught a subtle look as he was talking to Kurt. He held eye contact for just a second longer than he had to, and I saw a smile.

Ariadne broke away from the crowd and walked over to me. "You should be sleeping," she said, resting a careful, gloved hand on my shoulder.

"Am I not allowed to be here?" My words came out more bitter than I had intended. I thought that was because of Wolfe's influence, but given my past history with Ariadne, there was a strong possibility that it was all me.

"No," she said, remaining cool in spite of my acrid tone, "I just meant that I assumed you would be resting."

"I heal fast." I looked past her, trying to catch Zack's eye again. "I've rested enough, anyway." That was more defensive.

"I heard you broke into the cafeteria after it closed and took some food." She watched for my reaction.

I froze, trying to keep my eyes from widening. Had I done that? I managed to speak after a short pause that I hoped she attributed to my guilt at being found out. "It's better for all involved if I don't have to go to the cafeteria when I don't want to. Safer, really. It's like a public service." With the flight of the Black Hawk, things had gotten quieter on the helipad. "I'm surprised you don't have a helipad on the roof of Headquarters." I was desperate to change the subject by that point.

"We do." Ariadne crossed her arms and looked back at M-Squad. "But it'll be easier for Clary to carry his...cargo..." She nodded to the burden that the fat guy was carrying over his shoulder, "...to the science labs without having to navigate an elevator or stairwell."

"Big guy like that?" I inclined my head toward the coffin. "He looks like he can carry a lead casket for a ways." I stared at the object, but he had it inclined so that I couldn't see anything but the bottom and sides. I was beyond curious about what it contained; I wondered if it was the mysterious reason why M-Squad had been in South America for so long.

"I'm sure he can. But it's delicate, and it would be best if it were undamaged." She smiled, a tight, insincere one that told me worlds about how much of my question she was avoiding answering.

"Hey." Zack appeared in front of me, Kurt a few steps behind him.

"Hey," I said, feeling like the single greatest idiot in the world for repeating his greeting back to him. Genius level IQ, and I was still reduced to this by a boy. FML. (Yes, I know what it means.)

"I heard you broke your promise." He didn't come off as accusatory, which surprised me, and yet, didn't. If he was spying on me, getting into an argument seemed counterproductive. "But I also heard you killed Wolfe, so...good job." On the other hand, maybe he was just happy that Wolfe was dead. I knew I was.

If I was dead, I wouldn't be talking to you.

Shut up, I thought with all my might. I must have grimaced while thinking it, because Zack raised an eyebrow. "Yeah...I'm sorry. I just couldn't wait for you guys to get back." I looked away from him.

"Damn shame you killed Wolfe," the fat guy from M-Squad said, loud enough that it told me he'd been eavesdropping. I turned to find him leering at me; well, not so much me as my body; his eyes were looking below the equator and moving up slowly. "I was looking forward to tangling with him. But if he can get himself killed by a little girl, " he said with a laugh that sounded like a bark, " I guess he wasn't so tough, was he?"

"You're a moron, Clary," said the leader, the first guy off the helicopter from M-Squad. "You're just lucky most people judge by appearances, like you do, and write your fat ass off or you'd be dead ten times over."

"You think I'm fat?" One of Clary's eyes had squinted, drawing his puffy cheek up his face and causing it to wrinkle. "This is three hundred and twenty pounds of ripped steel." He waved a hand over his body. "And the ladies love it."

"The next lady to love your body will be the first, I'd wager." I said it before I knew I had, and heard the snickers from M-Squad, Dr. Perugini and Zack. Even Kurt seemed amused by my barb. The old guy in M-Squad let a low, rolling guffaw of purest amusement. "Unless you're resorting to picking up lovers from the graveyard," I said, pointing at the object on his shoulder, "in which case they're not loving you so much as—"

Clary turned a bright red and I watched him clutch the coffin a little tighter, and he let out a loud grunt. "I'm not gonna sit here and be insulted by some tweener punkass bitch."

"Yeah, you've got important things to do," the older guy spoke up. "You were talking about your damned motorcycle the whole time we were gone. You gonna go ride your 'phat hog'?"

Clary's embarrassment turned to glee. "Naw, your mom said she's busy tonight." He let out a high, long burst of laughter, one that was obviously fake, and turned to Dr. Sessions, slapping him on his skinny back and nearly waylaying the good doctor. "Come on, Doc, this son of a bitch is getting heavy."

I watched Doc Sessions nod and turn, leading the way toward the science building, Clary in tow and Perugini following behind them. When he turned to follow Sessions, the coffin dipped and I saw the top of it for the first time as he repositioned it to carry it like a backpack. It was flat, with a small window, just enough to show something glowing within, like fire in a bottle. He dipped it lower, and I saw something else—

Eyes. There were eyes staring at me from within. Plaintive, begging, filled with a fear that I knew all too well; the fear of a captive confined, one who might never take another free breath again.

3

"Who is that?" I asked Ariadne. I turned and caught a flash of her face pinched as though she had just pulled a splinter from her finger. I turned to Zack, and he looked away.

"Aleksandr Timofeyevich Gavrikov," the leader of M-Squad said to me. "One of the most dangerous metas you'll ever meet." He nodded at the capsule on Clary's back. "That's a containment cell Dr. Sessions designed to keep metas that have high energy projection abilities under control—without it Gavrikov could fry everyone."

"How'd you catch him, then?" I didn't throw any undue sarcasm into the words; I was curious.

"By not getting anywhere near him," the Nordic woman said, a slight smirk curling her flat lips.

"I think introductions are in order," Ariadne said. "Sienna Nealon, this is Roberto Bastian," she nodded to the leader, then to the woman, "Eve Kappler and Glen Parks," she indicated the older guy, who gave me a genuine smile, one that (surprisingly) didn't creep me out. "And of course the other gentleman," she strained at the word, "was Clyde Clary."

"Don't call him Clyde," Parks said, his gray beard reminding me of a thousand grandfathers I'd seen on TV. "It doesn't bring out the sparkling side of his personality."

"Sure it does," Eve said. "He sparkles like broken glass— then cuts you." Her smile became a smirk, a self-satisfied look that either Wolfe or I found insufferable and wanted to destroy along with the rest of her sculpted face. I think that was Wolfe. Mostly.

"Sir." Roberto turned to Old Man Winter. "Would you like us to make our report now or in the morning?"

Old Man Winter kept his silence. Everyone waited for his pronouncement, which came with all the gravity his position and deep voice afforded. "Come to my office at noon. We have other matters to discuss."

"Yes, sir." Roberto saluted, then nodded to Glen and Eve, and the three of them headed toward the dormitory building, Kurt in tow.

I looked back to Clary and Sessions, almost to the science building now. The capsule carrying Aleksandr Gavrikov looked heavy, and Clary was struggling to readjust it again. *Let him loose*, Wolfe said from somewhere in the depths of my brain.

Shut up, I told him, as if that would work.

If you let him loose, Wolfe will tell you what he knows about your mommy.

Son of a bitch. That immediately put me on guard; if Wolfe wanted someone out of confinement, there was no stronger indication that said person should remain under lock and key, preferably buried under several tons of soil, indefinitely.

You don't know anything, I thought back to him. *You're just lying to get your way.*

He was quiet for a split second, and a thought floated to the surface of my mind. *3586 Curie Way, Bloomington, Minnesota.*

I blinked, and Ariadne caught it. "Tired?"

"No." My mind was racing. "Just remembering something. Wolfe mentioned an address—3586 Curie Way in Bloomington. Is that close?" It wasn't a lie; I didn't say when he had mentioned it.

Zack, Ariadne and Old Man Winter were the only ones remaining on the helipad. Zack was the one who answered. "It's about forty minutes away. Ten minutes south of your house."

"Wolfe gave you this address?" Ariadne looked skeptical. Old Man Winter looked blank, as always.

"He did."

"Why would he give you an address?" Her eyes were narrowed, and you could see her crunching the odds in her head—wondering if it was some sort of trap. Leave it to Ariadne to ask the tough questions I wanted to avoid. I guess it could have been a trap, but if it was, it seemed counterproductive for Wolfe to kill me, since he lived in my head. I had this feeling that even after thousands of years of life, he was clinging to even this little half-life in my skull like lint clings to a sweater.

I chose my words carefully so as to avoid a flat-out lie. "I don't think he intended for me to survive our final encounter." True enough. "So anything he mentioned wouldn't have mattered, would it?"

I looked from her to Old Man Winter then Zack. All three of them were studying me with varying degrees of suspicion, which worried me. Even though what I was saying was technically true, I was leaving a lot out—lying by omission. Based on my experience with Mom, who could always tell when I was being false, I was a bad liar. Ariadne shot a look at Old Man Winter, who had a cocked eyebrow and very little else to tell me what was going through his mind. Zack was looking at the snow.

"Zack," Old Man Winter spoke. "You and Kurt will take Sienna to the address she provided." He turned, gracefully for a man with such a tall frame, and lumbered down the path to Headquarters.

The worry was evident on Ariadne's face. "Be careful," she said to Zack and me before following Old Man Winter.

Zack had his cell phone out and was already talking on it. I could tell it was Kurt by the way he was speaking. His cheeks were red and he shivered as he ended the conversation; I realized for the first time he wasn't wearing a coat. "You're cold," I said, feeling a blush for being so stupid as to state the obvious.

"Yeah, I should have grabbed a coat at the airport before we got on the chopper, but for some reason it slipped my mind. Was in a hurry to get back here, I guess." He cast a sidelong look at the retreating backs of Ariadne and Old

Man Winter. "I get the feeling that you're not telling us everything you know about that address."

"Oh, no," I said, "I've told you all I know about the address; it's as much of a mystery to me as it is to you."

"And Wolfe just...gave it to you?" His brow was furrowed and one eye seemed to be more closed than the other.

Now I had to be even more careful if I was going to avoid outright lying. "He hurt me pretty bad during the last fight, slammed me through a concrete wall." I tried to recall the final battle. "I don't know; maybe he was talking to someone else. I think I lost consciousness for a few minutes at that point." That was true.

"I see," he said. Doubt flowed through his words, and he wasn't looking at me. I felt a drop in my stomach. I hated lying to him, but I had to know what was at Wolfe's address. "Kurt's meeting us in the garage in five minutes."

I needed to know where Mom was, and I was sure that Wolfe knew something he wasn't telling me. I doubted she was there, but I also didn't think he'd give me the address if there wasn't some hint as to her whereabouts. Damn him; he was dead and he was still toying with me. I had to wonder if I'd ever be free of him.

I fell into step beside Zack, feeling the wind play through my hair, hoping it was blowing it in a sexy way. I self-consciously ran my fingers through it and found it to be tangled instead. I yanked my hand down as he turned to look at me, and I swore I could hear Wolfe's cackle ring through my head. In that moment I regretted he no longer had a physical body because I wanted more than anything to kick him in the balls.

"I have to ask," Zack started, and he looked at me, those brown eyes shining in the light of the helipad's spotlights, "Did you know you could beat Wolfe when you went after him?"

"What?" I was caught off guard by the question. I hoped it showed on my face. "No, I didn't think I had a chance against him. That afternoon I watched him wipe out a SWAT team and a half-dozen police officers without taking so much as a scratch. I didn't think anything could kill him."

I lowered my head, and felt a tingle of fear at the memory. "That's why I went. Only I could stop him."

"That's pretty damn brave," Zack said with a shake of his head. "I don't know too many people who'd throw themselves into the fire like that."

"It didn't feel brave." I felt a cold unrelated to the weather, something much deeper inside. "Someone who was brave would have confronted their problem long before I did, long before all those people died. What I did felt inevitable—and I just wanted it over."

"Most people," he said, "Wouldn't have forced a confrontation with that maniac after their first encounter with him. You did." He shook his head, I think in amazement. "How many eighteen-year-olds—"

"I'm still seventeen."

"How many seventeen-year-olds do you think would get choked out by some lunatic and then willingly go back for another round?" He laughed. "You're brave, Sienna. Maybe the bravest person I've ever met."

I felt a thrill at his words, then felt it go as I recalled the cold facts of the situation. "Yeah, but that second round cost you guys eight people. All so I could try and fight him."

"You didn't know that was going to happen."

"But I should have!" I felt hot, like something under my sweater was causing my skin to catch fire. "I was so focused on myself, trying to get what I wanted that I didn't worry about anyone else." I thought about that day, and suddenly it felt a little too close to what was happening now. Wolfe played his game and he did it his way; it was not unreasonable to think he might have allies left behind at the address he gave me, or a trap, or worse. I looked back at Zack, watched the mist from my breath blow in the air. "I need you to take me to the address and then wait in the car."

"Are you kidding?" His reaction was immediate dismissal. He didn't get angry, he scoffed. "I'm not letting you go in alone."

"I have to." I stopped walking, and he took another couple steps before he realized I wasn't alongside him and stopped too. "Wolfe doesn't play nice."

"I'm not helpless," Zack still stayed away from anger, but I could see the beginnings of annoyance in the way his eyes were wrinkling at the sides and how his mouth had moved from a smile to a flat line. "I can hold my own in a fight. Just because I'm not a meta—"

"It's not that you're not a meta." I aimed for gentle, soothing words. "If Wolfe set a claymore mine as a trap and it blows off my foot, it grows back." I gestured at him. "You'd never walk again."

I could see the wheels spinning as he struggled to put together an effective response. He started to say something, then stopped short, frustration pinching his handsome features. "I can't let you go in by yourself." His words came out mangled, as if he was at war internally. "But you have a point. Wolfe's not known for being subtle with his violence, so..." he took on the air of a man proposing a bitter compromise, "I'd be willing to let you lead the way while Kurt and I follow at a safe distance."

"A mile?"

"About ten feet. I doubt Wolfe bothered with explosives." He was firm; there was no more room to negotiate. I nodded and started to walk again. "And you don't know," he said, falling into step beside me.

"Don't know what?" I asked, confused.

"You don't know what would happen if you got an arm or a leg blown off. Yeah, it may grow back, or it may not."

"I heal pretty fast," I said. "I've regrown an awful lot of skin since I met you."

"Ouch."

"That's what I said." Deadpan. Perfect. He grinned at my wisecrack and I smiled back.

He walked a few more paces and I saw him gnaw on his lower lip. He turned his head to look at me. "You don't blame me for all the hell you've been through since..."

"Since you and Kurt rousted me out into the world?" I shrugged. "If it wasn't you, it was gonna be Reed or Wolfe. Reed might have been gentler," I needled him, giving him a wry smile, "but it all worked out, I suppose." Except I now had a psychotic mutant squatting in my brain.

"Yeah." He opened the door to the parking garage and held it for me. "I guess it did."

I heard Zack beside me, the squeak of the rubber soles of his boots on the tile floors, heard his breathing. I caught a whiff of his cologne and took a deep breath through my nose. I could feel the heat from the exchange positioned in the entrance nearby blowing on me.

Kurt Hannegan was waiting by the car, a thoroughly disgusted look marring his otherwise ugly face. I put my emotional turmoil to the side, because however bad I was feeling, I wanted to make sure that Hannegan felt worse. Again, if I could blame this on Wolfe, I would, but the truth is I loved pissing him off.

"Let's get this over with," he said with a grunt. He was wearing a tweed suit coat with brown patches on the elbow and a brown tie to contrast with his white shirt and dark pants. He had tried to comb the meager hair he had left on the sides of his head to the top in an attempt to...I dunno, revive the glory days, I guess, but it failed.

"You mean you haven't been looking forward to this?" I said, feigning hurt. "Kurt, didn't you miss me?"

"No."

"Sure you did," I said. "You missed me with your little popgun the first time we met. I think it's a metaphor for our entire relationship."

He looked at me, wary. "That I'll always be shooting at you?"

"And I'll always be dodging and kicking your ass."

We got in and he drove out of the garage without another word. It was a heated structure, with space enough for a couple hundred cars. The Directorate maintained a fleet of vehicles, along with the countless other things they kept—Black Hawk helicopters, weird and experimental weaponry, a host of agents, facilities all over the U.S. and the world. I had to wonder who funded it all, who ran the whole show, and what the real purpose was, if it was something different than what I'd been told.

Kurt kept the speedometer pushing eighty most of the way. We streaked through the farmland that surrounded the

Directorate, zipping along a state highway until we got on the freeway loop that circled Minneapolis and St. Paul. We headed east, as the sky showed the faintest hint of lightening in that direction.

After about twenty minutes we exited onto a street that held houses on one side and warehouses on the other. My pulse quickened as we neared our destination; I didn't think we'd find Mom, but I wondered what Wolfe was playing at. If he'd given me the address, there had to be a reason for it. It couldn't just be a dead end.

We turned onto a side street filled with small warehouses, all gray, all run down and drab, and Kurt stopped the car. We all stared at one in particular, with shiny brass numbers reading 3586 hanging on its dingy concrete block walls above a steel door.

I was out of the car a few seconds after it stopped, Zack and Kurt hurrying behind me. When I looked back, Kurt was looking around, nervous, and had his hand resting on his gut. I assumed it was because it was within easy reach of his gun, but maybe he just liked it there.

"We're gonna need a minute to pick the lock," Zack said when we reached the door. I shook my head, grabbed the handle and pulled. I heard a creaking before the mechanism broke free, the metal handle tearing from the door. I reached inside and pushed the guts of the lock out, then ripped the door open. I didn't wait for either of them to comment before I walked in, pausing inside to give my eyes a chance to adjust to the dimness.

It was all one big room with concrete floors and corrugated metal walls. There was a lump over in the far corner and I went toward it. The soles of my boots tapped against the bare concrete and each step sounded like doom as it echoed off the metal walls. As I got closer to the shape, my hand came up to cover my nose; a horrible smell filled the air and it got worse as I got closer and closer.

Zack and Kurt had flashlights on behind me, and I gestured for one of them to hand me theirs. Zack did. The beam played along the ground as I went toward the mass. It was big enough to be a person, it wasn't moving, and I hoped I wasn't about to find one of Wolfe's greatest hits.

"It smells like he killed something in here." Kurt gagged as he spoke, the choked glottal stop sound sending an echo of its own off the walls.

"Maybe he's keeping trophies," Zack said.

"You mean...body parts?" Hannegan didn't bother to hide his revulsion at the thought.

"I don't think Wolfe was a collector," I said. I knew it somehow, the same way I knew everything else, even though he wasn't talking to me right now. He was watching, waiting for me to find out what he'd left for me. I kicked the lump with my toe. It didn't move or squirm or anything. I knelt down, the flashlight shaking a little, and pushed at it. It was soft, cloth, and filthy.

I grasped it and it lifted with ease, a blanket all balled up. I shook it and it unfurled, and I sighed as I realized what it was.

"Bedding?" Kurt asked. "Is that...is that his bed?"

"Yeah. All balled up, like he was a hamster or something." I felt Wolfe bristle at my comparison, but I was annoyed. I shook it again out of a sense of irritation, and something came loose within the depths; I felt it moving inside. I shook it again and felt it tumble down, falling out of the sodden, filthy blanket.

I tossed the bedding aside and stooped to retrieve what dropped. It was a purse. Black, leather, no longer than my arm and with a broken strap. I opened it and shined the light inside. Frustrated, I turned it upside down and let the contents spill out to the floor. Lipstick, a cell phone, a few other odds and ends, and a wallet.

I picked up the wallet and noticed the name on the driver's license before I saw the face: Brittany Eccleston.

The picture was of my mom.

4

"How did you get this?" I mumbled the words, but I knew Kurt and Zack could hear them. I just hoped they assumed I misspoke or was talking rhetorically to Wolfe, who, as far as they knew, was not there.

Many, many stories I could tell you...but I have my price. The words were taunting, teasing. I killed him and he was still an absolute shit to me. At least he wasn't around to physically abuse me anymore.

"You think he got your mom?" Zack's voice was laden with concern, and it sounded genuine.

Kurt was more analytical. "No way to tell without more evidence." He pointed. "The strap's broken; he could have just ripped it off of her. The I.D. has her address on it, " he nodded to me. "This explains how he found her."

I wondered if I could chance another interrogatory toward Wolfe without attracting the curiosity of Zack and Kurt, but I decided against it. He'd wanted me to find this, to get curious, so I would do what he wanted. Maybe he knew more, maybe he didn't. All I was certain of was that he wanted Aleksandr Gavrikov out of that containment cell, and that scared me.

"Anything else in here?" It was Zack who asked the question, but Kurt who started shining his light around. The warehouse looked empty, abandoned.

"I don't see anything." I shone my flashlight to the corners, but all I saw were metal walls, through and through. I turned and started to say something but stopped and froze in fear as Kurt Hannegan got slapped down hard. The big man hit his knees and an arm wrapped around his neck. I watched his face turn red as he was dragged back to his feet, his portly body interposed between us and his assailant.

"Hi, Sienna," came a mild voice, a familiar one.

I shone the flashlight at the man who held Kurt. "Reed, what are you doing?"

I hadn't seen him since the day I killed Wolfe; he had fled from the basement before the Directorate arrived. He was muscular and it showed, even through his leather jacket. His dark skin stood out in contrast to Hannegan's face, which was turning red. His long brown hair was in a ponytail and he held a gun pointed at me then Zack, in turn.

"Well, well," Zack said, his own gun out and pointed at Reed. "If it isn't your old friend."

"Friend, enemy," I said, wary, "when they're pointing a gun at you, what's the difference?"

"A friend doesn't pull the trigger." Reed clubbed Kurt on the head, and I watched the big man's eyes roll up as he went unconscious. Zack tensed, as though he were about to shoot, but Reed held the gun up in surrender as he let Hannegan sink to the ground, letting him slide to the floor gently. "I have to talk to Sienna." He looked at me. "I don't want your boyfriend listening in either, but I'm willing to let him walk away instead of sending him off into the clouds."

"You can try—" Zack snapped.

"I can do it," Reed said. "You eager to cross me? I'm a meta, you're a Directorate agent. Do you want to find out what my power is just so you can try to keep her from having a conversation?"

Zack did not flinch nor lower his weapon. "You want to talk to her? Talk. She's right there."

"If I wanted the entire Directorate leadership to hear what I have to say to her, I'd visit your campus." Reed's lip curled at the end.

"You should come visit. I'd love to see you out there; it'd be fun to watch M-Squad beat you down and throw you in a holding cell for interrogation." Zack's eyes were narrowed, the gun still pointed at Reed. "I'm not letting her out of my sight."

"I'll go over to the corner with him, we'll talk," I said to Zack, who looked sidelong at me, mutinous. "It'll be fine. " I worried when he didn't blink, but he finally gave me a subtle nod of the head. He kept the gun pointed, following Reed, who joined me in a corner. "All right," I said when we were out of Zack's earshot, "what's so damned important that you had to crack Hannegan over the head?"

"That?" Reed chucked a thumb over his shoulder where Zack was nudging Kurt with his foot, trying to rouse him without taking the gun off Reed. "That was for him driving you back to your house when you went after Wolfe the last time." Reed's expression darkened. "It was only because you discovered your power that you even survived." He glanced back to Hannegan, who had yet to stir. "But you're still hanging around with him—with them."

"I haven't been presented with any other options," I said, bitterness inflecting my tone. "In case you forgot, right after I killed Wolfe, you freaked out on me and bailed."

"I didn't bail on you," he said. "I got the hell out of there before the Directorate decided to make me a test subject."

"You yelled at me."

"I'm sorry," he said with sincerity, " but I didn't want to get my soul drained. Besides," he looked wary, "I suspect your head is full enough now without me adding another voice to the chorus."

My eyes widened and I felt my jaw drop in shock. "You know?"

"If the Directorate had experience with incubi or succubi, they'd know too," Reed said. "They're trying to view metas through a scientific lens, and there's not one big enough yet to explain how metas work. Take this Gavrikov they just caught, for example," he said with a smile. "Explain to me scientifically how someone can fly without wings or sprout fire from their skin without burning it off?" He shrugged. "Maybe there's a scientific explanation, but it's so far outside our grasp right now that we might as well be talking about myth and magic, like the ancients used to describe us."

"How did you know about Gavrikov?" I kept my voice hushed.

"Everyone in the meta world knows about Gavrikov. He's been a legend and a whisper since he detonated in Russia a hundred plus years ago."

I squinted at him, trying to recall. "The Tunguska blast? I read that was a meteor."

His smile grew deeper. "There was no meteor; there was Gavrikov." He shrugged. "Or so the rumor goes."

"How goes the rumor about me?" I tightened my jaw.

He nodded, the smile sticking in place on his face, but no longer sincere. "It goes that your mother, Sierra Nealon, who everyone thought was dead, is a succubus, and has a daughter just like her. Whip smart, stronger than any other ten metas combined, and currently hiding behind the tender mercies of Old Man Winter in Minneapolis."

I absorbed his words. People whom I had never met were discussing me, as though I were some commodity waiting to be bartered. "How did you know I was here?"

"I've been watching the place for a few days, waiting for..." he hesitated, "...someone. Wolfe didn't bother to cover his tracks, so I expect the police will be here in the next day or so." He cast a look around. "Hope you found what you were looking for, because this is likely your last shot at this place."

I held up my mom's purse and I.D. "Know anything about my mom?"

Reed was cool when he answered. "A few things. Where she worked, known associates from before she disappeared, that sort of stuff." He looked back to Kurt, who was sitting up now. "Nothing I can share while you're still with them."

"You got a better deal for me?" I stared him down. "Because as I recall, when Wolfe was hot on my heels, you told me to stay put."

He shrugged. "Here in the U.S., I don't have a quarter of the force the Directorate could use to defend you. In fact, I'm with an organization that's big overseas, not so much here. The Directorate is king of meta activity on this continent, for now. But if you want to come with me..."

"Where?"

"Can't say until you decide to come along." He shrugged again. "Sorry for the secrecy, but we're not on the Directorate's radar and I'm of a mind to keep it that way."

I looked at him pityingly. "You just knocked out one of their agents; I think you're on their radar now."

"Heh, maybe me," he said, "but not we. They don't know who I work for. And I suspect it'll remain that way for some time."

I looked at him, a hard, long look. "Forget the background stuff. Do you know where my mom is?"

I saw pity flood his face, along with a sincere regret. "I don't. I'm sorry. If I knew anything that I thought would help, I'd tell you, but I don't. There are a lot of people looking for her, and not just from the Directorate. All the major players have people in town, but I think she's gone quiet. Maybe Wolfe got after her, maybe something else spooked her, but if she could disappear for all those years with you, she can hide even better without someone else to slow her down. Not to say you slowed her down."

"No, it's fine," I said. "I'm sure I did; it's probably why I was locked away all those years, to keep her profile low."

"Or to keep you out of harm's way." His voice got softer and his eyes lost their gleam. "These people that are after you now? At least you have the power to fight back. Imagine Wolfe coming after you when you were seven."

I shuddered, and deep inside felt Wolfe stir with interest at that idea. A few images floated to the surface of my mind, of places I'd never been, people I'd never met—young girls, all. I could taste bile rising in the back of my mouth and wished for nothing so much as the ability to drive his frightening psyche from my head. "That would have been bad. So what now for you?"

"I'll be around," he said. "I assume you're not taking me up on my offer?"

I lowered my voice even more. "Can you get this maniac out of my head?"

He looked over to where Zack and Kurt were waiting for me. "I don't think so. Once he's in, he's part of you from now on." He shrugged. "There aren't many experts on what you're going through, and I don't work with any. Counting you, there are three succubi on record. Only a couple of incubi."

I rubbed my head. "I'm losing my mind. I don't know how any of this works." I snorted in wry amusement. "I don't even know how my mom had me without killing my father, whoever he was." I thought about it for a moment. "Hell, maybe she did." I shook my head. "I know nothing about myself, where I came from, who my mother really is. You can tell me a little more, but I'd have to leave and go somewhere mysterious, somewhere outside the country?" He looked at me and nodded, and I knew he realized my decision was made. "Sorry," I said. "I think I'm gonna stick it out here a while longer."

"I figured. Like I said, I'll be around." He smiled, and with a gloved hand he brushed my cheek, sending a tingle through me. "You know how to get in touch with me." He turned and started away.

"Bad choice of words," I said to him with an impish smile. "I think the last thing you want is me touching you."

"There are worse ways to go." He laughed, shook his head, and disappeared out the door.

5

After I watched him leave, I returned to where Zack and Kurt waited for me. The older man held his head, and let out a near hissing sound when I approached. "Every time I go somewhere with you..." he said.

"You blame this on me? Last time we went somewhere together, I believe you made it out just fine." I smiled, and a look of panic crossed his features; the eyes widened, his mouth opened slightly and I would have bet his mouth was drier than the air outside. He looked at Zack, who was frowning. "I don't see anything else," I said, changing the subject to spare Kurt. "We can leave."

"Let me be the first to say, 'Thank God' at the thought of getting outta here," Kurt said with a grunt. He led the way, and I looked around, not quite forlorn but wondering if I was missing something, some subtle clue that might tell me more about where Mom was. I stared at the dark corners of the warehouse, as though I could sift the secrets out of the shadows if I only concentrated long enough.

"Come on," Zack said. I looked back to find him standing behind me, and his eyes were warm. He put a hand on my shoulder, and even through the heavy cloth I felt the gentle pressure. I didn't want to but I felt myself involuntarily close my eyes and wondered what it would feel like without his glove or my coat and shirt.

I forced a smile and buried that thought as Kurt yelled from the door. "Come on!" Without waiting for us, he pushed through to outside. Zack and I were only a few steps behind him as the door started to close, but before it did something silvery appeared with a flash and hit Kurt, sending the older man spiraling out of our field of vision.

I hesitated but was quicker to move than Zack. I burst out the door, felt my shoes hit the snow, the frigid air slamming me in the face followed by a metal-encased hand cracking me in the cheek. My feet left the ground and I landed in the snow. My jaw was on fire, and I felt the biting cold of the wet mush run down my collar. Before I had time to cry out, something punched me in the back of the head, and I felt a hand lift me to my feet.

I was dazed, but even so I recognized that what was in front of me seemed wrong. It was shaped like a man, but covered in metal. The figure was angular and the chest was boxy, like a robot I'd seen once in a movie. The head was roughly cylindrical with a rounded dome, giving me a flashback to the time Mom let me watch Iron Man on TV. I saw a metal fist raise and I squirmed to get out of the grasp of the metal man before the blow reached me.

I felt my coat rip along the collar as I pulled down and put my weight into it. Much as I might wish I was lighter when I looked in the mirror, I was thankful at that moment that I didn't look like a model as I slipped underneath the punch he had leveled at me. The metal man followed through and I heard a crunch. I rolled across the snow and to my feet, looking back to see he'd buried his hand in the concrete wall all the way to the elbow.

As he struggled to pull his hand back out, I realized he was grunting, which meant he wasn't a robot. I can't tell you how thankful I was in that moment; I was afraid that someone had perfected some sort of seeker droid and turned it loose on me. "All right, Full Metal Jackass," I said to him. "You want a fight, you sucker-punching Tony Stark wannabe?" I cracked my knuckles. "I'll give you a fight."

I darted low as he came at me again. I could tell from his breathing that the armor had some weight and heft to it. His fist whistled through the air in front of my face as he winged another punch at me. After it passed, I raised up and gave him a solid kick to the gut, just like I would have back when Mom and I broke boards in the basement. After all, I was a super-powerful meta, right? I should be able to break through steel; I had before, after all.

I heard a crack as I connected and realized that something had broken, all right—but I was pretty sure it was my foot. Full Metal Jackass went staggering back and fell over, which was the only saving grace in the whole thing, because I dropped to the ground, clutching at my foot, which felt like I had slammed it in a door well over a hundred times. I let out a stream of curses as I went down.

As I lay on the ground, clutching my appendage and plumbing the depths of my error in judgment, I tried to roll over. I had enough presence of mind to realize that the metallic monkey wasn't going to be down for as long as I was and that I needed to do something to avoid him and that screaming and rolling around wasn't going to do it. I got to one knee as I saw him rising to his feet, a hulking metal goliath. His eyes were two slits, and behind them I could see pupils staring back at me as I rested my weight on one leg. I raised my hand in a defensive posture that was purely for show; I doubted I'd be able to effectively evade him while hobbling.

"Hey Man of Steel!" Zack's shout caused him to turn. I saw Zack holding a very familiar weapon in both his hands. He'd been to the trunk of the car, clearly. "I bet you think you're invincible, beating up a girl like that. Boy, are you in for a shock."

I cringed, partly from his pun, partly from the ache in my foot as Zack discharged the weapon into the metal-suited man. A forked bolt of lightning arced from the barrel and made contact with the front plate of Full Metal Jackass's armor. The metal man shuddered only slightly, and then took a menacing step toward Zack, then another, before breaking into a run toward him, the electricity diffusing harmlessly off the metal as though it weren't conducting it.

I took two aggressive hops forward before the metallic tool could get any momentum and slammed into him with my shoulder, knocking him face-first into the snow. I saw a joint open between his helmet and his neck as he fell, a patch of exposed skin no wider than my fist that showed a strip of weathered flesh. I reared back, letting fly a punch aimed at the open spot. I connected and heard him shout in pain as his face slammed into his helmet, which impacted into the snow.

He started to stir and the gap in his armor closed as he lifted his head, making him effectively invulnerable again. "Let's get outta here," I said to Zack and limped my way to Kurt, slinging his bulky ass over my shoulder in a fireman's carry. I made my way to the car one hobbled step at a time. I threw Kurt in the back seat unceremoniously and heard him let out a moan as he landed on the padded cloth. I slipped into the passenger seat as Zack tossed the gun onto the floorboard at my feet.

In the rearview mirror I could see Full Metal Jackass rising to his feet as Zack floored the car. He didn't chase us, but his eye slits were watching as we slid out of the parking lot, following us until we rounded the corner and disappeared from his sight.

6

"Do you want to grab some breakfast with me?" Zack's words shocked me enough that I think my head spun. The ride back to the Directorate had been long and filled with Kurt's surliness. I didn't even bother to defend myself as he loosed a profanity-laden tirade about Reed colluding with me that lasted until we were well out into the farmland. I felt fortunate Zack was driving because with the fat man wailing and gnashing his teeth as he was, I had no faith he could have driven the car without putting us into a snowy ditch.

I blinked at Zack, amazed that he would offer after what had just happened, and I wondered if my head was twitching like Dr. Sessions did, brain trying to understand the question that was posed. "You want me to go like this?" I gestured to my coat, which was shredded from the collar to halfway down the back and hung open, the zipper ripped from the seam. My shirt and jeans were soaked and filthy, my hair was still wet from the snow in the parking lot and I could feel the grains of dirt in it. I couldn't see my cheek but the throbbing in it told me that I had a bruise of no small scale where I had been punched.

"You look fine and the cafeteria's bound to be open by now." He smiled at me and I felt my better judgment slipping away. "I'm starving. The last leg of the flight feels like the longest trip I've ever taken. Facing off with your friends in the warehouse didn't help matters at all." His voice hit a sour note and I couldn't tell if it was because of Reed or the armored ass.

"Friends? I don't know if you saw, but that armored tool damned near took my head off." I snorted, more from annoyance than anything, and it faded fast. "All right," I said, taken aback by his...I don't know, boyish charm. I felt my stomach roll over and knew that either I was hungry or Wolfe was reacting to my mooning over Zack. Forgotten was the fact that I avoided the cafeteria and the people who visited it, those people who hated me so. I watched Kurt limp off toward the medical unit for a once-over by Dr. Perugini.

The cafeteria was showing the first signs of life when we entered, with workers behind the glass counter adding food to the display and a few people already sitting at tables. The cafeteria was huge, a massive structure with glass windows for walls that stretched a hundred feet into the air on two sides, giving it an open feeling. I looked at the edges of the room and realized for the first time that the panes along the perimeter were doors that could be opened to what I presumed was a patio outside; with the snow covering the ground it was impossible to tell, but it seemed like there was an eating area out there.

The framework of the whole thing was metal struts that held the glass in place. I wondered idly if one could climb it, then wondered why I'd ever need to. I decided that I could, probably with ease, because the segments were no more than four- or five-foot square. On the opposite side of the room I shifted my attention to the cafeteria workers. When they saw me enter the line with Zack, several of them scowled. After we had collected our food, I let Zack lead me to a table by the windows, in the corner.

Others were here, a half dozen people scattered throughout the cafeteria. One caught my eye; a young man who I'd had words with in the past, here in this room. He'd been the only one in this place with enough guts to confront me after the first incident where I'd gotten agents killed. Everyone else had just gossiped behind my back. He had a rounded nose and his dark hair was curly and cut short. He hadn't caught sight of me yet, and was focused on the doll he was sitting across from.

When I thought of her as a doll, I shuddered. Damn Wolfe. She was tanned, with blond hair that fell below her shoulders, and green eyes that seemed very alight. Her smile was wide and genuine, and left me with the feeling that she had too many teeth, or they were too big for her mouth, or something. I wasn't jealous of her good looks, really. Well, not much anyway.

"Scott," Zack called out, stirring the young man out of his conversation. He turned and saw Zack and broke into a wide grin as he stood. Zack put his tray down and they did one of those manly greetings where they gripped hands and bumped shoulders.

The man he called Scott shook his head, his smile still wide. "When did you get back?" I wondered how well they knew each other.

"Just now." He nodded to me. "Have you met Sienna Nealon yet?"

Scott's features tensed and he looked me over. "Briefly."

I felt a flash of annoyance as I remembered what I probably looked like. "Have we met?" I kept a straight face. "I don't recall."

"My God," the girl next to Scott breathed. "What happened to you?"

"I got into a fight with a guy who thought he was the Black Knight," I quipped. "It turns out he didn't get so much as a flesh wound, but maybe next time things will be different."

"Sienna, this is Scott Byerly," Zack said. "He might be in training with the agents soon." Zack nodded back at me. "You better watch out, Sienna's pretty powerful. If she decided to go into training I think she'd give you a run for your money."

"Is that so?" Scott's reply was cool, far cooler than I would have given him credit for. He seemed like a hothead based on our first meeting. "I heard she might have some power, but there was a rumor she didn't have the..." He paused, as if searching for the right word, "...motivation to use it."

Courage, he means. Wolfe was so helpful. I was seeing red, and he was encouraging me to wrap this guy's head around the nearest table edge. I had to restrain myself to keep from showing Scotty Byerly exactly how motivated I was to use my power by throwing his limp and battered body through the nearest window. I wondered if I punted him how far he'd fly before landing headfirst in the snow like a lawn dart.

"Oh, she's motivated," Zack said before I could answer. "She killed that maniac Wolfe, you know."

"I heard about that!" Scott's companion bubbled with the enthusiasm he was lacking. "It's all everyone talks about since I got here, how this crazy meta killed dozens of agents and how she," she nodded at me, oh-so-helpfully, "went into a basement with him and was the only one to come out alive." Her eyes were as glowing as they had been when talking to him.

"This is Kat Forrest," Scott looked pained as he introduced her to us. "She just got here from our Arizona campus a few days ago."

Arizona Campus? I made a mental note to ask Zack about it later. Kat seemed to vibrate as she stuck out her hand for me to shake. I did, feeling the pressure of her grasp through the leather of my glove. "So glad to meet you," she squealed, and I could tell she meant it. "I don't know that I could have done what you did, facing off with that monster."

I pulled away as soon as I could, not wanting to find out if I could drain her soul through my gloves. "Thanks," I said, with as much sincerity as I possessed. "I'm surprised that everyone's talking about me in pleasant terms. It was my understanding that I wasn't very popular around here."

"Well, you're certainly popular to talk about," Kat said, almost gushing, "but I would have to say that the overall tone hasn't been terribly flattering." She looked a little chagrined, as though it was her sad duty to inform me that people hated me. "But it's difficult being the new kid in town, I know."

"Oh, you've had people say nasty things behind your back and send you a letter telling you that they hope you get raped to death, literally?" I kept my tone light and wore a smile, even as her face fell. Dark clouds gathered around Zack's eyes, and even Scott looked taken aback.

"Who did that?" Zack's voice was a low, strained murmur.

"I don't know. Does it matter?" I said.

"Yes. I want to know who it was," Zack said. I looked back at him, and his face was dark, as though he was in shadow.

"It wasn't the sort of work that the author would want to be associated with," I said.

"I wrote it," Scott said. "And it didn't say anything about anyone hoping you got raped to death. It said we all hated you for hiding while people were dying and we're rooting for him to turn you inside out."

I saw the punch coming, and I suspected that if Scott Byerly had any power as a meta, he did too. Zack took a long windup and swing that connected with Scott's jaw. The meta fell back, landing on his rump, his hand cupping his jaw lightly. "You done?" he asked, unconcerned.

"Maybe." Zack's hand quivered at his side.

"I didn't have to tell you." Scott sat on the floor, not bothering to get up.

"Which raises an interesting question," I said. "If you're so proud of what you did, why admit to it now when you left it unsigned before?"

"I'm not proud of it," he said with a shake of his head. "My aunt and uncle lived in Minnetonka. They got killed by that maniac while he was trying to root you out. And like I told you the last time we talked, I knew a lot of those agents that died for you."

"Which time?" I asked, voice laced with bitter irony.

He looked up at me, and I could see the loathing, the intensity with which he looked at me. "Both times."

"I was there." Zack's reply came out in staccato bursts, his whole face twitching with rage. "Sienna saved my life. I wouldn't have come out of that basement if she hadn't carried me out. I'd have been another body for Wolfe to torture."

It would have been so fun, Wolfe said in my head.

"Yeah, and?" Scott vaulted to his feet with the speed and agility of a meta. "There were a lot of other guys that didn't get carried out. Guys that we've known for a long time. Then she finally goes after him and miraculously kills him?" He smirked and I resisted the urge to give him a punch that I could guarantee he wouldn't see and would feel. "Why didn't she kill him sooner?" He threw his hands out. "Hell, HOW did she kill him? That's what I want to know—and nobody's saying a word about that."

"You want to see how I killed him?" There was enough menace in my voice that Byerly actually took a step back. "No? Then mind your own business." I wondered how much of his willingness to back down was based on the fact that I looked like I'd already been through at least one fight this morning.

I steered past him, guiding my tray toward the table in the corner that we'd been heading to before our detour. I sat down, my back to all of them, and started to attack my food with more violence than was necessary. It wasn't as if the eggs were going to stage an uprising and attack me, but I speared them on the end of my fork with enough vitriol to be certain.

Zack's tray hit the table in front of me a minute or so later. I'd heard him make a modicum of peace with Scott, enough that it sounded like they'd be on speaking terms but not enough that they'd be greeting each other like they did when we entered the cafeteria. He sat across from me and ripped into a strip of bacon with displaced anger. I didn't find it funny enough at the time to overcome my irritation with (still) being the most hated person on the campus.

"Amateur bullshit," Zack pronounced after throwing his bacon strip back on his plate.

"Excuse me?" I was halfway through a mouthful of eggs.

"When we take on the job of being an agent, it's understood that we're going up against metas. Most of them aren't that powerful. Some of them are." He stared at me, his eyes smoldering. "Policing metas is a dangerous business; especially since we have no powers and no way to know if we're up against an innocent person who's never done a violent thing in his life or the next psycho criminal who'll be glad to gut you and serve you for dinner." His eyes darted left and right. "It's a hazard of the business. Scott's got no right to take you to task for those guys dying."

"Maybe," I said, noncommittal. "You didn't have to deck him for it."

Zack licked his lips. "He didn't even feel it, did he?"

"Only a little," I said. "Why'd you do it?"

"Frustration." He let out a muted exhalation combined with an exasperated sigh. "I wanted to knock the crap out of Reed, too."

"Good job showing some restraint. If Reed really is a meta, he would have pummeled you, unlike your friend." My hand left my fork behind and I rubbed the bridge of my nose. "What happened in South America?"

"I went to find M-Squad." He put his hands on the table. "I found them."

"And a flaming metahuman in a casket." I stared him down and he tried to play it off but failed. "What happened? You got sent to retrieve them, but they were gone a long time; longer than Old Man Winter thought they'd be gone."

He concentrated, as though he were bringing up details of a story. "They were sent to our facility in the Andes Mountains."

"How many facilities does the Directorate have?" I crinkled my nose, trying to make it seem like an innocent question.

"Six in North America, two in South America, two in Europe, four in Asia, one in Australia, two in Africa." His eyes darted back and forth, looking up the whole time, as though he were trying to recall. "I think that's it. Anyway, they got sent down to the Andes facility—"

"For what?"

"Because the facility went dark. Completely offline, radio blackout, silence, dead air, all that. And we hadn't even had the facility that long—"

"What?" I frowned. "Was it new?"

"No, we took it over from someone else. Are you going to stop interrupting me so I can finish my story?"

"Sorry."

"So anyway, it went offline, and Old Man Winter had a suspicion he knew why, so he sent M-Squad down there with that coffin contraption after telling them about Gavrikov."

"I thought you said they went offline?"

"They did. Somehow he knew it was Gavrikov."

"How—"

"I don't know," Zack said, exasperated. "Because it's Old Man Winter, and he knows all kinds of things he shouldn't theoretically know. Do you want to hear the rest of the story?" I nodded, and he went on. "Gavrikov was there for some reason. He had come to the facility with something in mind. He killed the entire staff—about fifty people, in case you were wondering—and set up shop. Well, M-Squad started playing feint-and-parry, trying to get him boxed in so they could force a confrontation, but he wouldn't engage them directly."

He took a breath, and I jumped in. "Before, you said Gavrikov had energy projection capability..."

"Yeah, he flies and can throw fire. I heard from M-Squad he can even explode."

"Reed mentioned that Gavrikov was responsible for the Tunguska explosion in 1908."

I watched as Zack's jaw dropped open. "You told him about us capturing Gavrikov?"

I shook my head. "He already knew."

Zack's mouth became a hard line, his eyes looked down at the table, and I could tell he was suppressing a kind of deep internal fury. It was the wrong moment for it, but I actually thought it was damned cute. Outwardly, I gave no sign. I hope. "How did he know?" he asked, restraining whatever anger he was feeling.

"I didn't ask."

"If ever you get a chance again," Zack said, measuring his words, "do ask. This is something that only a dozen people in the world knew as of this morning."

"Sure. Though I think you're naïve if you believe he'd tell me. So did he explode for you guys? Wipe out a few square miles of real estate in the Andes?"

Zack was distracted, but he went on. "Not quite, but I guess Clary had him pinned in a building at one point and he blew up, left nothing but a crater. It took Clary a while to climb out of that one. Anyway, Gavrikov has a shield of fire around his skin, so tranq darts can't make it through—"

"So how did they get him?" I was getting impatient. I blame Wolfe. He didn't have much to do with this one, actually, but I blame him anyway.

"It was pretty ingenious, I thought," Zack said with a smile. "He wasn't willing to leave the facility. He'd just fly to a different building whenever they came for him, throw some fire if they got close, do anything to keep them at bay while he jetted off—"

"He doesn't sound so dangerous," I said. "Except for the fifty people he killed, I suppose." I felt sheepish. *He sounds like fun,* Wolfe thought. *You should let him out.* I ignored him.

"Anyway," Zack went on, "they managed to set a trap for him when I got there. They used me as bait."

"What?!"

"Well, I went in and tried to reason with him, pinning him in place while the hammer fell. See, I was a new face—he'd seen them for weeks on end while they went back and forth. They tried to talk to him at first, too, I guess. Didn't work out. Anyway, once he figured out I was human, he shot at me like a missile— I mean, he was gonna kill me, but Clary was positioned perfectly, took the hit for me, got a hold of Gavrikov and managed to knock him unconscious."

I was going over what he had told me, but it didn't quite make sense. "How did Clary put a hand on Gavrikov if he had his fire shield up?"

Zack's smile was smug. "Clary can change his skin. In this case, he shifted into some kind of metal. It was actually dumb luck; Clary moves a lot slower than Gavrikov, and if he had been even an inch to either side, he wouldn't have been able to grab him and club him out." He leaned back in his chair. "After that, we stuffed him in the containment unit and carted him back here."

"Bravo," I said in a hushed voice, thinking of the containment unit. It was tiny, a coffin by any other name, a horrible, claustrophobic nightmare. I tried to think of Gavrikov's victims rather than about the means of his confinement. I forced a weak smile. "I'm sure the world is better off with one less monster wandering around."

"I think so," Zack said, eating another piece of bacon. The

smell of my plate had stopped being appealing, so I watched him in silence as he ate, trying to think of something else to talk about. "You know," he said, "you still have quite a list to work through."

"List?" I stared at him, blankly.

"You know," he said. "Of things you haven't done—go to the movies, a mall, an amusement park..."

"Oh." I had forgotten that we had talked about that when last we saw each other. Nothing like having a mass murderer rattling around in your head to put some of the irrelevant things in perspective.

"You do still want to do those things, right?" He looked at me, all earnestness, and I couldn't flinch away from those eyes, those deep brown eyes, rimmed with concern. I got a sudden, uncomfortable feeling, like I was being put on the spot.

"Yeah," I said, and felt like my answer was burdened with a reluctance that seemed like metal scraping across stone. Slow and painful.

"How about this," he went on, "why don't we go out tonight—get dinner and see a movie. You can cross it off your list."

He smiled, and I felt my stomach twist. Did he just ask me out? Did I just get asked out for the first time? I blinked, almost in disbelief. Was it that he was spying for Ariadne and Old Man Winter that prompted this or had what he told Scott been true? Maybe he felt like he owed his life to me.

I mentally slapped myself. It wasn't like that, it couldn't be. After all, even if things went well and the date ended with a kiss, it wouldn't just be my first date—it'd be his last, and the next time I saw him would be at his funeral.

"Just friends," he added, as though that would make me feel better. It didn't. It made me feel a hell of a lot worse.

"Sure," I said with another weak smile. Wolfe was cackling again, that bastard. "Thanks for offering to...be my guide."

"It'll be fun." His phone rang and he answered, pulling it out of his pocket. "Yeah...I'm with her now, we're getting some breakfast. Sure, we'll see you in five." He finished his call and looked at me. "You're done, right?"

"What?" I didn't understand what he was asking until I looked down and saw my half-full plate. I hadn't taken a bite in several minutes. "Oh, yeah, I'm done."

"That was Ariadne. She wants us at Headquarters to talk about the warehouse."

"Okay." I stood, taking my tray with me to the nearest garbage can and dumping it in. I felt uneven; my head hurt a little, my heart hurt a lot, and I was once again suffering under the realization that my life had been so upended from what I was familiar with that I didn't know what I wanted.

I mean, even if he wanted me, I couldn't touch him, right?

7

Ariadne's office was right next to Old Man Winter's in the Headquarters building. His was cold and Spartan, and I expected the same from her based on her wardrobe. When Zack knocked on the door and she called for us to enter, I was surprised.

Her office had the same view of the grounds as Old Man Winter's, but that was where the similarities ended. Whereas he had a desk that looked like it was made of a massive piece of natural stone stacked on top of two others, hers was a warm cherrywood, with a workstation and hutch against the left wall and a more formal desk between her and the two visitor chairs. There were pictures scattered around the office of Ariadne with other people, ones that looked a little like her—a man and a woman who were older, another that looked like her sister, and a few of her with her sister and some kids.

"Dear God," she said as I came into the room. "Are you all right?"

"I'm as fine as I've been since I've gotten here."

She beckoned for us to have a seat. "Can I get you something to drink?"

"I'll take a whiskey on the rocks," I said without blinking.

She froze. "I have soft drinks..."

"Bummer," I said. "What'd you want to see us about?"

"About the encounters at the warehouse, and uh..." she blinked and shook her head. "Something else."

"Great," I said without enthusiasm. "Let's start with the 'something else' that you don't really want to talk about and work our way back to the warehouse."

"Fine." She tried to smile but it was so fake that it fell apart after about two seconds. "We have a forensics lab that can analyze the personal items from your mother that you found in the warehouse."

"I'm not hearing the 'something else.'" I leaned back in her chair with exaggerated casualness.

"Very well." She rested her hands on the desk between us, folding them, for some reason bringing to my mind the idea that she must have been a goody-goody in school. "I've been ordered not to have them analyzed unless you agree to see our on-site psychologist."

"Beg pardon?" My tone carried more frozen bite than the worst wind I'd experienced thus far.

"The Director would like you to see our counselor," she said. "Understanding you've been through something of a ringer lately—"

"He wants me to submit to headshrinking?" My eyes were so narrow that I was surprised I could see anything out of them. "If he thinks I'm gonna do that, I submit to you that his head has been in the icebox for too damned long."

One of Ariadne's eyelids fluttered at my remark as she suppressed whatever her first response would have been. "He thinks," she said, pacing herself, "and I agree with him, that you've been under a great deal of stress and strain—"

"Most of which seems to be the fault of your Directorate."

"—and we are concerned with your long term health, mental as well as physical," she finished without stopping to answer my accusation. "We are willing to help you in the search for your mother, but we feel that you've been through a high level of trauma in the last few weeks, more than is healthy for anyone," she held up a hand and I restrained my sarcastic response, "let alone someone as young as yourself. This is not a negotiation. If you want our help, see our counselor." Her hands went back to being folded on her desk as she awaited my response.

I caught movement from Zack out of the corner of my eye.

"It's not a bad idea." I turned to look at him, and I'm pretty sure my glare was more potent than any flame Aleksandr Gavrikov could have tossed out. "You've been through a lot—gaining powers, your mom disappearing, being locked in a metal box as punishment, being stalked by a psychopath, beaten, injured, watching a ton of people die and blaming yourself," he listed them as if he were ticking off points from a list. "It might not be a bad idea to talk to a professional about it."

"What will they tell me?" I felt the rage, but I leashed it. Wolfe was cackling, but I bade him shut up. "That it's normal to be stressed over being stalked by a psycho, imprisoned in your own house for over a decade, and finding out that you have superpowers?" I let the sarcasm fly. "I don't care what kind of shrink you've got, he's not qualified to deal with the crap I'd lay on him. I'd probably make him run screaming from the room, some of the stuff I could tell him."

Ariadne raised an eyebrow. "So you feel you should deal with these things on your own?"

I bit back an angry reply. Even with Wolfe circling in the back of my head, I knew there was truth to what she and Zack were saying. I had been through a lot, more than most people went through in their lives, I suspected. I'd been near death twice in the last week or so, had Mom vanish on me, and had a variety of other things, great and small, on my mind. I blinked. Actually, it *was* amazing I wasn't in pieces already, mentally. Maybe I was. I was hearing the voice of my greatest nemesis, after all, and he was dead.

"Fine," I conceded. "I will...talk to this...person." I said every word through gritted teeth. "When can you start looking over my mom's purse?"

"We've already started," Ariadne said. "Kurt had it delivered to the lab when he went to the medical unit. You'll get the results after the first session."

"Fine." I wasn't pouting, exactly. But close. "When can I meet with your psycho...analyzer?"

Ariadne's mouth was a thin line. "Right now. He's cleared his schedule to meet with you. He's in a different building."

She looked to Zack. "Show her the way?" He nodded.

"What did you want to talk about regarding the warehouse?" I was in a little bit of a huff, but I wanted to get this over with so I could get the next thing over with. Actually, I just wanted to get the whole day over with at this point.

"Your friend Reed. And the new threat." Ariadne had turned wary again, like she was tiptoeing around what she wanted to say so as not to set me off.

"I've only met Reed twice," I said. Kind of sad, but that made him my oldest friend. "And I have no idea who this new guy is. Just for the record, I'm calling him 'Full Metal Jackass' because he's a sucker-punching douchebag, and I hope you'll join me in that by putting it on his official file or threat designator or whatever you use to keep track of metas that cross you."

"Duly noted. We have concerns." She folded her hands again.

"So do I," I agreed. "Most of them involve your fashion sense, with a few left to spare for the armor-clad whackjob that bitch slapped me around a parking lot this morning."

She sighed, bowing her head in utter resignation. "We'd like to know who Reed works for."

"So would I. But I'd also like to know who Wolfe worked for, who this new metal man is, who funds the Directorate, exactly how many factions are out there involved in this dustup over metas, what all their goals are..." I shrugged. "I asked him some of these questions, and he didn't answer, so I'm not sure how I can help you."

Ariadne hesitated. "You could tag him for us."

"Tag him?" I felt a laugh rising from within and I let it slip. "Is that a crude aphorism for sex? Because I think that would kill him before he could answer any of your questions." I couldn't bring myself to look at Zack after I said it. I wouldn't have gone there, but as conservatively as Ariadne dressed, I had a feeling the reaction would be worth it.

It was. She reddened, her face turning roughly the same shade as her hair. "I mean with a tracer bug, if you should run into him again." She reached into her top desk drawer and her hand emerged with a small wooden case. She snapped it open, revealing a pen. "When you hold the clicker, it launches a tracking beacon that only we can follow." She slid it across the desk. "It has a range of about twenty feet when it fires, so make sure you're aiming the pen properly. It will cling to almost any surface, and it has ten tracers within it."

"Tricky," I said. "Reed would be pissed if he found out I was tracking him. I think he'd be less offended if I tagged him the other, more lethal way."

"I think he knows how to find those," Zack said from beside me. I didn't dare look at him yet. We'd faced death together, but I didn't want to see his reaction to my references to sex for some reason. Dammit. "Kurt used one of those to tag the bumper of his car outside your house the day we met, and it went offline after he left us behind at the supermarket."

I stared at the pen, picking it up and cradling it in my fingers. It was small, black, and slightly rounded. Looked fancy. "I always wondered how you guys had found us there." I held it up. "I'm not going to promise that I'll use this because I still don't work for you guys. But I'll consider it."

"Fair enough," she said. "What will it take to get you to trust us?"

"I notice you didn't answer any of the questions I asked a minute ago about who the players are in this meta conflict." I stared her down, making her uncomfortable.

"You want answers," she said with a nod. "I think we can accommodate that request. Let me talk with the Director. It will be a long conversation though, so let's plan for it to happen tomorrow morning. There might be other things we can discuss by then."

"Just to be clear," I told her. "This isn't an 'all or nothing' proposition. You don't get my trust all in one move, but this will help. Be honest with me and you build your credibility."

"That's a two-way street," she said with a flush.

"Which is why I'm going to see your master of mind

games." I stood and looked at Zack, now finally able to do so without profound embarrassment. "Care to show me the way to my mental doom?"

"You don't have to treat it like it's some awful, hellish scenario," Zack said once we were in the hallways outside Ariadne's office. "This is a good thing for you."

"Maybe. But it doesn't mean I want to do it." I was actually more scared that I'd inadvertently let something slip that I shouldn't, like the fact that the first man I'd ever killed was a houseguest in my mind, spinning wheels and talking to me. Even for a recent arrival from recluse-hood like myself, that didn't seem normal. But then, neither did killing people with a touch.

"Life's about more than just doing what you want to do," Zack said, terse.

"That's the story of mine."

"Right," he said. "Just try and let Dr. Zollers help you. He's good; I've seen him myself."

"What for?" Now I was very curious.

"Standard procedure for agents," he said, just airily enough that I didn't believe him. "We're in a high-stress occupation, so before they put us on field duty we get a full evaluation, and the doctor counsels us throughout our careers."

"What do you talk to him about?"

"Normal stuff. The pressures that come with being on call 24/7, ready to round up and suppress any meta that steps out of line."

"Suppress?" I giggled. "You mean kill?"

"Or capture," he said, bristling.

I felt my face fall. "Like Gavrikov." I thought of that coffin that they put him in, and I felt a familiar kind of sick.

The regret was there, on his face. "Yeah. Like him."

"Are there more?" I looked at him. "Have you guys captured a lot of metas?"

"Yeah. Our facility in Arizona has a prison where they're kept. It's far out in the desert, middle of nowhere."

"What do they do, these metas? You know, to deserve confinement like Gavrikov?"

"Gavrikov is unique," Zack said in protest. "Most of the

ones we have to confine—and it's very few, fortunately—are ones that are clear, obvious cases of metas using their powers to commit crimes. They're strong enough that law enforcement would have a hell of a time catching them."

"Like Wolfe?"

Zack cringed. "Not that bad. At least, none of the ones I've dealt with. Murderers, sure, some major thieves. But every one of them has committed enough crimes that you get the idea that they'll never be able to live in human society again without returning to the same behaviors."

"How many crimes is that?"

"Lots." He looked at me as we exited the Headquarters building, and he was all seriousness. "On average, twenty felony offenses, ranging from burglary to the big ones, the capital offenses, before we catch with them."

"Do they get a trial?" Again, I was curious.

"Not really," he said. "Usually we've caught them in the act, and our forensics are better than average. But it wouldn't matter; when we send them to Arizona, it's almost always for life."

"A life sentence," I mused. "So you guys are the judge, jury, and executioner."

"It's not like that." His voice lowered, and the defensiveness was on the rise within it. "These are criminals that the justice system couldn't contain if they wanted to."

"The government doesn't know about metas?" I shook my head. "They don't want to deal with them?"

"They know about them," Zack said. "I've heard they have a program in place for dealing with them if they catch them.

"And?"

"It's less charitable than ours. Our facility can allow even a truly dangerous meta some free rein, because our guards are metas and the staff are prepared. The government facility is a hole in the ground. They go in, they don't come out, and who knows if they're alive or dead." He looked at me. "You don't approve."

"I don't know," I said with a surprising lack of emotion one way or another. Bet I'd have felt different if I'd been in one of the Directorate's cells in Arizona. "I don't have a better solution, but I'm famed for my lack of trust."

"And?"

"Why would I trust you to faithfully execute a full criminal justice system, hidden where no one can observe or see it?" I shrugged. "I'm not going to get involved—for a myriad of reasons, including the fact that I'm one person, and I have no better solution—but it doesn't sound like a perfect use of power to me. It sounds worrisome, and seems like it has a high potential for abuse of prisoners and people. Kind of Draconian."

We lapsed into a vaguely comfortable silence, not saying anything as he led the way across the campus, which was just as well. If I hadn't been feeling so self-involved and worried about what was going on for myself, I might have thought more deeply about what Zack had been describing. It sounded ugly, but I had no time to worry about it.

He walked me to a building on a side of the campus I'd spent little time on. It was closest to the gymnasium but wasn't far from a host of buildings I'd never been in. Like the others, it wasn't marked well, I suspected on purpose. He held the door for me, which was a nice touch. I pretended to be too preoccupied to notice.

The hallways were long, brick, and like everywhere else in the Directorate they had a sterile scent to them. The building was older than HQ, the brick was faded, and it was quiet; only the hum of the overhead fluorescent lights could be heard. I wanted to believe I could hear the beating of my own heart, but I really couldn't. I was nervous, but not off the scale.

Zack stopped me at a solid wooden door. It had one of those silver name plates over it, and it read: Dr. Quinton Zollers, M.D. I grimaced inwardly. Not that I thought it would be easier, but having a psychologist without the M.D. appellation seemed less intimidating for some reason.

"You'll do fine," Zack said. In my nervous tension, I couldn't decide whether I wanted to kiss him or slap him, then remembered that they'd both have roughly the same effect. "Don't forget about our date tonight."

I froze. "Our what?"

"You know," he said, casual. "We're going to dinner, the movies, mall, all that?"

"Yes. Sorry."

"Not a problem," he said with a genuine smile. "You've got a lot on your mind. I'll come by your dorm at five to pick you up?"

"Sounds good," I said, relieved that he missed the source of my reluctance. After all, it was infinitely preferable that he thought I'd forgotten our rendezvous than that I was taken aback by him referring to it as a date. Because, of course, he meant nothing serious by it.

He was halfway down the hall and had not looked back when I reached for the door handle and swung it open. I found myself in a waiting room with chairs lined up against the walls and a fish tank in the corner. On the far wall was another door, solid, which I assumed led to the inner sanctum of Dr. Quinton Zollers, who would be helping me diagnose problems I didn't even recognize I had. I found myself surprised that Wolfe didn't have a funny comment for this situation, and then wondered if perhaps he was sleeping.

There wasn't another soul in the waiting room, so I made my way to the inner door and knocked, three sharp raps. A voice boomed out. "Sienna Nealon...come right in."

I took a deep breath, and swung the door open.

8

Dr. Zollers rose to meet me when I entered the room and to his credit didn't blink at the sight of my torn clothing. I had expected one of those long fainting couches, facing away from the practitioner. Instead, I was surprised to find a few comfortable chairs and an office that was set up more like a living room. A couch sat in front of me, a full sized one, and three chairs sat across from it, with a coffee table in the middle. Sitting in one of the chairs was a shorter man with dark skin that spoke of his African heritage, a goatee, and eyes that glittered as though he knew the punch line to a joke he hadn't shared yet.

"Howdy," he said, not extending a hand, keeping them both clasped on the armrests of his seat. The faint smile he wore went well with his eyes, and he inclined his head in greeting. "It's my very great pleasure to meet you, Sienna."

"The feeling is..." I hesitated, and knew I was letting loose a little too much sarcasm, "...mutual."

"I kinda doubt that." He sat back down and pointed at the couch. "Have a seat."

"Right here?" I pointed to the couch he indicated.

"Wherever," he said with a slight shrug. Then, as if sensing that my immediate thought was that the bed back in my room seemed like a good option, he added, "In the office."

I snapped my fingers theatrically. "Damn." I sat on the couch and stared at him. He stared back, still wearing that smile.

"So. What do you want to talk about?"

"Oh, I don't know. How about the season the Vikings are having?"

He raised an eyebrow. "You a sports fan?"

"Nah. I just thought it'd be more fun than what Ariadne wants us to talk about."

"What do you think Ariadne wants us to talk about?" He gave me a shrewd look.

"This is gonna be a brutally long session if all you do is ask me questions every time I say things." My eyes searched the walls for a clock.

"Why would you think that all I would do is ask questions?" His smile got broader. "Talk about anything you'd like, we'll go from there."

"Let's talk about the Directorate. How long have you been here?"

He thought about it for a beat. "About three years."

"How many doctors do they have on staff here? I mean, Perugini, Sessions, you...do they have a full-time herpetologist too?"

He nodded without any hint of levity. "For the reptile metas, sure." After a moment in which I was sure he was dead serious, he laughed. "Kidding. I don't know. I pay less attention to their staffing than I do to their staff."

"And your job is to help them..." I tried to find a phrase that would fit and be insulting, but I failed, "...psychologically decompress?"

"That's a part of what I do," he said, his voice smooth. "Agents get put in stressful situations, they may have to use violence in their work, and it's something that stays with them. Also, the metas we have here sometimes go through a rough transition. Though," he said with a sense of irony, "usually not quite as rough as what's happened to you."

"I was gonna ask how you manage to keep any of them here if what happened to me was normal."

"You probably know this, but what happened to you was not 'normal,'" he said. "I've counseled a lot of metas who have come here after realizing that they won't be able to fit in with their former lives the way they thought they could before. None of them have been attacked the way you were—hunted by a psychotic super-meta who wanted to capture you."

"Kill me," I said in a whisper. "He wanted to kill me. But not right away."

He gave me a tight smile. "I heard, but it'd be indelicate of me to bring it up first. Still, I guess that makes you unique."

"I'd settle for less unique. It's probably less painful."

"But you don't get to choose, do you?" He leaned forward in his chair. "You're a succubus, the first of your kind of meta that the Directorate has seen. Top of the power scale when it comes to your strength and speed, and you've been granted a different power than someone who could, say, affect the temperature in the room or breathe life into the dead or put someone to sleep with a song."

"Different." I squirmed on the couch, feeling a sudden desire to burrow into it, away from this conversation. "That's one way to put it."

"How would you put it?" The way he asked it was so smooth, so empathetic, that it touched a nerve in me and I didn't try to dodge, I just answered.

"I would say..." I took a deep breath. "That I've been disconnected from people my whole life. First, because I was locked in a house with my mother, and now because I can't touch anybody without killing them. That I'm doomed to go through life untouched, like a porcelain figurine set up on a high shelf, so fragile it might break if anyone were to take it out." I tasted bitterness in my mouth. "Except I'm not the one that's fragile. Everyone else is."

He stared at me and then nodded, real slow. "I can see how you'd feel that way." He paused, as though steeling himself. "Can I ask about your mother?"

"She's missing."

"That's not what I was gonna ask." He didn't look away, even though I did. "If this is too deep for the first time we've talked, go ahead and stop me, okay? But I've heard rumors, and I'm wondering if they're true. Did your mother beat you? Lock you in metal coffin?"

"Yes," I said in a muted whisper, "that is too deep."

"Okay." He nodded, picking up a notebook and a pen. "How about this? Let's go back to what you want to talk about."

"Um. All right." I thought about it. "Do you have to report everything I say to Ariadne and Old Man Winter?"

He smiled, but it was overly cool. "Professionally, that would be unethical. You and I are stepping into the territory of doctor and patient, which means that there's confidentiality that extends to whatever we discuss in the course of that relationship. So, no—I'm not reporting to the higher-ups on what we talk about here, unless what we talk about here crosses the line—"

"Into something dangerous?" I asked, an odd sense of numbness falling upon me. "Into something threatening?"

"Exactly. Ariadne and Mr. Winter want to make sure that you're mentally healthy." His eyes were focused on me, but not in the uncomfortable way that Old Man Winter did. They were warm, and knowing, and that was why I couldn't meet them. "I don't think I'm revealing any big secrets when I say they have high hopes for you. The Directorate may be one of the only places you can safely exercise your powers in the world, that could give you a path, and some meaning if you wanted it."

"They want me to join M-Squad." I said it while looking at the laces of my shoes, studying a little piece of snow that had caught on the edge of the rubber sole and hadn't quite melted yet.

"They see a path there for you." He looked down at the notebook. "They see a natural fit with what your mother used to do in the old days for the Agency. From what I've heard, you have a certain fearless quality and tenacity that would serve you well in a variety of walks of life."

My mouth felt dry. "What if I don't know what walk of life I want to tread?"

He paused before answering. "Then I'd say you're probably an eighteen-year-old."

"I'm seventeen."

He laughed, a low, quiet one that actually brought a smile to my face. "From what I've heard, you have a lot of

222

confidence—a lot of brass, I'd say—in standing up to adults who seem like authority figures. Not mouthy, pointless defiance. Rebellion is a natural teenage quality, but most teens are not gonna confront a guy like Erich Winter about much of anything."

He put down his pen and notebook on the table at his side and looked back at me. "You've got confidence in some areas that most others your age don't. But here's the thing about self-confidence: a lot of it comes from knowing who you are, and knowing that whatever problem that comes your way, you can solve it." I looked up and met his gaze. "So do you know who you are?"

I cleared my throat before answering, and it still came out crackly. "Not really."

He put his hands up. "There's your answer. If you don't know who you are, it's kind of tough to know what you want, at least on more than a basic 'eat-sleep-play' level."

"But wouldn't you think..." I swallowed hard before continuing, "after all I've been through, especially with the changes and revelations lately that I might have a hard time with that? That I might struggle with who I am and what I want?"

He laughed. "God, I hope so. Otherwise I'd be worried. Metas and humans aren't that different in a lot of the things they go through, but metas deal with their process of growing up differently when their powers start to manifest. Every human struggles to find their place in the world. Sometimes you feel like you're in control and in charge of your life and everything is grand. Other times you feel powerless and insignificant. If you didn't experience these same feelings of grandeur and wonder and worry...you wouldn't be human." His skin crinkled around his eyes with his smile. "Whatever else you may be, meta and all that, you are human. And normal, for what you've been through."

I felt a knot in my throat and a burning in my eyes. "I don't feel normal."

"Yeah," Zollers said with a drawl. "That's normal too." He leaned forward, features animated. "You've been through hell and a little more, but no teenager knows what 'normal' is. So," he finished with a smile, "in that regard you're as 'normal' as anyone else your age. Hell, most adults feel that way too, just not as consistently. Now...do you have anything else you want to talk about?"

I opened up, a little at a time. I didn't tell him everything (especially about Wolfe) but I did tell him a lot. An hour flew by as he asked me questions about life in our house, about being punished the way I was by Mom, about how I still missed her, even in spite of all that. About how I wanted some part of a normal life, or at least what I envisioned as a normal life in my TV-influenced brain.

I got close to letting it all go, but I just couldn't. I let him know more than almost anyone, which wasn't saying much, but there was something else, something below the surface that I couldn't define, and I wanted to keep it that way. For now, at least.

When I left, it was with another appointment scheduled for a couple of days later. I walked out of the doctor's office feeling much different than when I had gone in, lighter, somehow. As much as Zack wanted to talk to me, I couldn't have felt comfortable telling him even half the stuff I had talked to Dr. Zollers about. And I still hadn't told him the worst of it.

The sky was slightly brighter when I walked back outside, though there was still no break in the clouds. In spite of it, I could see the lightness in the sky where the sun must be hiding, and felt the slight creep of a smile at the corner of my lips as I trod across the salted sidewalks, back to the dormitory I was calling home.

9

"You should try the bacon-wrapped dates." Zack wore a smile as he extended the plate toward me. I looked at it with hesitation born of my confusion at the word date (again) but I grabbed one of the little delicacies from the plate and tentatively put it in my mouth. I was rewarded with a lovely tang followed by a sweetness. I felt like it was a little symphony being played on my tongue, and I couldn't have been happier about it, although I did have a brief vision of Zack wrapped in bacon that I shook out of my head to the sound of Wolfe's laughter.

We were in a restaurant at the mall; an Italian place with an Italian-sounding name, lots of warm wood finishes, smooth tableclothes, and the smell of the freshly baked bread lingered in the air, enticing me. I picked up a slice from the table and dipped it into the plate of olive oil and parmesan cheese our waitress had made before I took a bite. Heavenly.

"I take it this isn't how you ate at home?" Zack's smile had morphed into a full-blown grin. Outside, the last light of day was shining in through the external windows of the restaurant. It was built into the side of the mall, which I hadn't walked through yet. I felt a buzz of excitement to be able to explore when I finished eating. It was one of the best dinners I'd ever had and we weren't yet past the appetizers and bread. Hell, I'd never even had a meal with an appetizer course before. Fancy.

"Lots of ramen noodles, some TV dinners, occasionally

hamburgers made in a skillet," I said. "I think Mom attempted turkey once, with tragic consequences for the bird and us."

He made a face. "Sounds tiring, eating the same thing over and over." He grabbed a bacon-wrapped date by the skewer and popped it into his mouth as I devoured another. "Pace yourself. You'll want to leave room for dessert."

"I don't know where I'll find room for that."

But I did. After my steak, I had some of the chocolate cake. It was richer than any Mom had ever brought home (on the rare occasions she brought one home). When I was done, I felt fuller than maybe I ever had. "I think you're glowing a little bit," Zack said.

I smiled back at him, a long, lazy one. "I'm surprised I don't feel sick after all that food." I paused for a beat. "And I'm not surprised I feel better."

"Yeah, Doc Zollers does wonders for people." He looked around. "Want to go for a walk? You probably have a meta-strength metabolism to keep you thin but I promise you, my physique doesn't come without a ridiculous amount of work."

I tried not to stare at his body because I already knew it was good. Instead I focused on his eyes. "A walk sounds like a good idea."

He paid for the meal and we left, walking outside until we reached the "official" entrance to the mall. A massive bookstore was to my left, and shops were clustered on my right down either side of a long hallway. We walked along, oddly silent, though I kept looking at him out of the corner of my eye. Every once in a while, I'd catch him looking back, and like a chicken, would pretend I was looking past him at something else.

It wasn't hard to pretend that, actually. The stores were a barrage of colors, lights, and products that I'd seen advertised on TV but had never laid eyes on in real life. I stopped at the first of the clothing boutiques; there was a plastic figure, life sized, with no features, wearing clothing in the window. I frowned at it. The dress it was wearing was black and sheer with a low cut neckline and a high hemline.

"Nice dress." Zack's voice had a far-off quality to it.

"I agree. But what's that it's on?" I studied the plastic creation, as though I could discern what it was just by staring.

"Haven't you ever seen a mannequin before?"

"No. What is it?"

"You know," he said. "Fake people."

"Like Southern Californians?"

He laughed and I gave up. I'd heard of mannequins before, but I couldn't recall ever seeing one on TV. We walked past a store filled with mobile phones and I had to curb an impulse to run inside and snatch one up to fiddle with it. Sure, I'd seen people in the Directorate use them, but to me they were still something out of fantasy. We hadn't even had a regular phone at home.

We rode an escalator up to the second floor where the movie theater was. The box office had a short line in front of it, and movie posters were plastered into frames on the walls on either side of us. Behind us was an opening that looked down on the first level of the mall and across the wide space to the walkway opposite. Intriguing smells wafted over to me: popcorn from the movie theaters, and from the food court behind us the scent of burgers, Chinese food, and maybe hot dogs; I wasn't sure.

We'd decided in advance what to see, and I heard Zack buy two tickets as I continued to look around, mesmerized by the sights, sounds, and smells that were all around me.

I was staring at an ice cream stand when a flash of dark hair across the gap caught my attention. A woman had been standing at the railing, and I hadn't noticed her until she moved. Her hair was long, like mine, dark and stretching down around her shoulder blades, and for some reason it looked wild and unkempt to me. She was close to middle age, wore a red dress, shorter than the black one I'd seen before and cut lower at the neck. She turned and I saw her profile. My heart jackhammered at the sight of her, the realization.

It was Mom.

10

I was moving the moment it hit me, my feet pounding along the floor. I jumped to the railing and leapt across the wide gulf that separated one side of the second floor from the other. I landed, feeling the pressure of the impact run through my knees and ankles, but I felt no pain in spite of having cracked my foot earlier in the day. The woman in red turned, only a few feet in front of me, and her eyebrow raised when she saw me breathing heavily from the exertion of my running leap.

It wasn't Mom.

"I'm sorry," I said. "I didn't mean to scare you." My mind was racing. From a distance, she had seemed like a dead ringer. Up close, it was obvious that it wasn't Mom. "I thought you were...someone else." Mom never wore makeup; this woman's eyes and cheeks were covered in it, giving me the impression that she was fighting the clock with everything she had, even though she was still pretty. Also, I was a little surprised by her lack of a coat given the weather—even more so by the dress.

Her eyes were cool, and she looked around, as though she were trying to decide where I had come from. They froze on my cheek as Zack ran up behind me. She stared at him, then back at me, with eyes that were filled with a sort of concern. "Did he do that?" She pointed at my cheek and I remembered that I had a bruise from my fight earlier.

"What? No," I said with a little laugh. "He didn't hurt me.

He couldn't."

"Oh," she said. "Sorry I'm not who you thought I was." She turned to walk away. I watched her go, noticed the sway of her hips, and wondered what kind of a man would be attracted to a woman so obviously starved for attention.

There was a hum from the crowd gathered around me; people were talking, those that had seen my jump, low, muttered voices of incredulity. I think I heard someone mutter, "PCP."

"Way to stay nonchalant." Zack eased up beside me. He watched her go, his eyes never moving off her backside and answering my internal question about what kind of man would be attracted to her. The looks of others as she moved through the crowd provided more clarity; apparently, any man with a heartbeat. I looked down at my simple turtleneck and jeans with my new heavy coat. Practical, I supposed, especially for the girl who kills with a touch—but not likely to generate the kind of attention she was getting. "What is she wearing?" I said it mostly to myself.

Zack answered anyway, watching her as she walked away. "Damned near nothing."

"In this weather? It's winter. Isn't she cold?"

She turned and Zack's eyes alighted on her chest. "Looks like it from here."

I looked back at him, and I tried not to make it a glare, but I failed. "What?" He looked at me with slight alarm, as though he had no idea why I was irritated with him. I looked to the store that the woman had exited, and sure enough, on one of the mannequins in the window was the exact same dress I had just seen on her.

I drew closer to it, but this time not to look at the mannequin that wore it. I felt my gloved hand touch the glass, as though I could connect with the dress behind it, feel the silk between my fingers. It was a symbol of all I could never be. All I could never have. "Nothing," I said after another moment. "Can we go to the movie now?"

"Sure." He stepped out of the way and held out an arm as if indicating I should go first.

Most of the movie I spent buried in my own head,

frustrated. I mean, hadn't it been obvious that I wasn't destined to be able to touch anyone, anytime? I cursed myself for my foolishness; Zack didn't want to die, and a relationship with me was just that, a death sentence. At least, if it was to involve anything other than conversations. And if there was absolutely no physical component to a relationship, was it anything other than a friendship?

A guy like Zack had friends. I was fairly certain he could have his pick of any number of women, too. Why wouldn't he look past me at some devil woman in a red dress? Even if she was twenty years older and taller and more shapely and knew how to apply cosmetics and bleh. Was it possible to hate someone you didn't know and hadn't exchanged more than a few words with? I even envisioned walking up behind her, taking off a glove and giving her a little touch to the arm. Not enough to kill her, just enough to zap some of the prettiness away.

Then I cursed myself for being petty and tried to watch the movie. It wasn't easy; it had no plot and a lot of explosions. I felt my mind wandering for minutes at a time and when it came back, I found I hadn't missed much.

Afterward Zack offered to walk around the mall for a little while longer but I declined. I suspect he saw through my terse answer, but he didn't say anything as we walked to the car.

It was a quiet ride back to the Directorate. Even though I could have sworn it was only about twenty minutes, it felt like an hour. We pulled into the parking garage and he stopped the car. I started to turn to him to say good night, but he preempted me.

"Did I...say something or do something that pissed you off?" He was staring at me, earnest, for all his faults.

"No. I'm sorry," I said. "I thought that woman in red—I thought she was my mom, from a distance. She looked like..." My words trailed off.

"Ah," Zack said with a nod. "I wondered what would possess you to jump across the mall like that, in public and in full view of a hundred people. It all makes sense now."

"Why didn't you ask me before?" I stared straight ahead,

looking hard at the concrete wall that was just in front of the hood of the parked car.

"In my experience, if a woman seems upset, it's better to wait a little while before you probe to get to the bottom of it," he said. A sage, he was. "You know," he said with confidence, "in case it was something I did, I didn't want to make it worse by seeming like I didn't have a clue."

I heard Wolfe's laughter ringing in my ears and I saw red. "Of course it wasn't you," I said, calm. How did I manage that calm? No idea. "Well," I said with an urgency I couldn't define, but that welled up along with a hundred other emotions I didn't want to give voice to, "good night." I grabbed the handle to the car door and forced it open, rushing to get out before he could say anything else. My hand gripped it tighter than I intended, and I heard a squeaking noise as I stood up, and I looked down to find the door hanging free of the car, loose in my hand.

I stared at it with incredulity for a moment before a torrent of bitter anger burst loose somewhere within and I screamed a curse. I hurled the car door as I stomped away from the vehicle toward the nearest exit. I heard it crash, the window breaking when it hit the wall, and I heard it bounce into something else. The earsplitting sound of a car alarm going off echoed through the whole place as I pushed my way out of the garage's exit door and blissfully found myself out of the garage and on the snowy grounds of the Directorate.

11

You should let your anger out to play more often, Wolfe said a little while later, as I was about to get into bed. *It's quite becoming, little doll.*

"You're a hobo who's living rent-free in my brain," I said out loud as I turned down the covers. Someone had snuck in and made the bed and cleaned the room while I was out. At another time, I might have been impressed with the turndown service. As it was, it was added to the pile of things annoying me, the lack of privacy I felt in this place.

No need to get so hostile. Wolfe's tone (in my head, the bastard still has a tone) was leering, taunting. *Wolfe was paying you a compliment.*

"I need your compliments like I need another mysterious enemy trying to kick my ass," I said, flopping down. "Since I already acquired another of those today, I'll pass on your 'kind' words."

Poor little doll, whose life is aught but mysteries and lies, he said, almost soothing. *So troubled, so sad, so...delicious. And how you feel about the agent is even more tasty.*

"Go screw yourself." I buried my head in the pillow.

There, there. What if Wolfe could make some of the mystery go away?

"Like you did with my mother? Thanks, but that turned out to be more mystery."

Such a shame, Wolfe was going to tell you all about the man in the metal suit...

I raised my head up. "You don't know anything about

him."

Wolfe snickered at my uncertainty. *David Henderschott, age 58. He doesn't look it, of course. He ages well, like powerful metas tend to. He was pretty too, before someone...*He paused in his narrative and I could almost hear a squeal of excitement in my head...*cut him up. Now he's not so pretty anymore. Very strong, though.*

"Why is he wearing armor?" I clutched my pillow in my hand. "To hide what you did to him?"

Wolfe laughed, a shallow, short bark. *His skin can stick to whatever it touches. He used to use it to rip the flesh off his foes, but Wolfe taught him the error of his ways, oh yes he did. Now Wolfe would guess he's scared to come out and play.*

"Who does he work for?"

Tsk, tsk, little doll. What will you do for the Wolfe?

I smiled, but it wasn't one of deep satisfaction. "I'm not doing a damned thing for you." I flipped the switch by the bed that triggered the lights. "Night night."

Oh, little doll...you'll be sorry. Without another word, it was like he picked up and went to another corner of my mind and lay down. I had a vision of him, like the proverbial dog licking himself, and I got disgusted and tried to put it out of my mind.

Sleep was horrible, filled with a hazy nightmare. I walked over snowy fields into a building with brick sides and down long, yellowed corridors. I saw fire, blazing, hot, heard words spoken that I couldn't understand, and then felt the wind at my face as I ran.

I awoke as an explosion flipped me into a snow bank.

I blinked in shock as I felt the damp cold slide down the back of my shirt for not even the first time today. I got my bearings and vaulted to my feet. There was noise behind me and I turned. I was standing in the middle of the campus, somewhere between the Headquarters and where the science building, where Dr. Sessions had kept his lab, had been only moments before.

There was still some of it left, but what there was happened to be covered in flames, the fire stretching up to the heavens. I ran toward the building and felt the heat wash over me the closer I got. The brick building had once been three stories; now only a few spots remained where more than a few feet of brick stood at a stretch. I wondered if anyone could have survived just as I saw a shadow moving around behind one of the walls.

I heard screaming, shrieks everywhere around me. The heat from the burning building was intense, the smell of smoke pungent and overpowering. I looked and saw others had come, flooding across the campus toward the site of the calamity. One of the screaming voices caught my attention; it came from within the burning building.

I moved toward the wreckage and jumped over the nearest wall. I felt my flesh start to char, smelled the flames and the tang of what I suspected was the first degree burns that were already causing my skin to redden. I saw a lone figure on the ground, scorched from head to foot and I reached out, grabbing hold of him and lifting him into my arms. I vaulted back over the wall and tried to carry him away from the building. A pitched squeal stopped me long enough to look down.

It was Dr. Sessions. I was carrying him like a baby in my arms, and I hurried away, not wanting to look at him, just trying to get away from the fire. The smell of burning meat was everywhere, in my nose, in my eyes, in my throat and it was threatening to make me gag, cry or throw up. Maybe some combination of the three. The heat was steadily getting weaker until I ran into something and fire burst around me.

I fell on my backside, Sessions still in my arms. I looked up and saw the same eyes I'd seen only a day before, behind the glass of a containment cell as Clary carried it away from me.

Gavrikov.

I drew a sharp breath as I looked at him. He was wreathed in flame from head to toe, not an inch of flesh visible. The fire stood out, reaching a few inches from his arms, his head, from everywhere. His eyes were something else entirely, just a shadow and a shape, with no hint of a pupil or an iris, as though they were nothing but spheres surrounded by a living, breathing fire.

He drew up in front of me and I remembered what Zack

had said about him, about his power to control flame; he could start an inferno right here with me at the heart and there wasn't a thing I could do about it other than chuck a charred lab rat at him and run. And that was iffy.

He stared down at me with those burning, empty eyes and raised his hand. I scooted Dr. Sessions off me, laid him on the snow with only a murmur of pain from him and stood, wary and ready to dodge, for whatever that might have been worth. I stared at him, he stared back at me.

"Thank you," he said, his voice no more than a whisper. "Thank you." I looked at him, confused but still tense. I braced for whatever he might do. He seemed as though he might take another step, lifting a leg off the ground, but instead his other leg joined him and he hovered a few feet above me. "Your kindness will not go unrepaid."

I felt a clutch of unnerving suspicion inside, but before I could question him, he shot into the sky in a blur, and he was gone.

Dr. Perugini was beside me in the next moment, bending low over the body of Dr. Sessions, barking commands to others around her. I turned to look at him and realized that his flesh was charred, hideous. His lab coat was burned perversely, his glasses fused into his flesh. His clothing was blackened, what was left of it. I couldn't see a single place where he wasn't burned, and I wondered how he could still be alive.

"Sienna," Ariadne cut through the chaos and I realized with a shock that she was wearing a robe, a red one, silken and utterly out of character for what I would have suspected of her. "What did you see? What did he say to you?"

I couldn't take my eyes off Dr. Sessions. "I don't know," I lied, far too nimbly. "Is...is he going to be okay?"

"Does he LOOK like he's going to be okay?" Dr. Perugini nearly screamed the reply, her distress increasing the potency of her accent. "I need..." Her head spun around until it alighted on Kat Forrest, who was standing in a nearby knot of metas in nothing but a tank top and briefs. "You."

The delicate, gushing girl who I had met earlier in the cafeteria stepped forward, tentative. She shook from the cold, and her breath came out in great clouds as she walked in halting steps toward where Dr. Perugini waited for her. "He doesn't have all night!" Perugini snapped and Kat quickened her pace, dropping to her knees in the snow. She reached out, her hands curled up tight to ward against the cold. She unfurled them, bringing them to Sessions' face. I may have imagined it, but it seemed like the snow was melting around her legs.

Her hands were on his face, the soft light of the overhead lamps illuminating the nighttime scene. He moaned when she first brushed his cheek, then again when her fingers anchored around his cheeks. The charred and blackened flesh seemed to grow redder around where her hands rested and Sessions grunted in pain. Then he started to scream.

I made a move forward, shrugging off Ariadne as she grasped at me. I felt a hand land on my shoulder and I started to turn and attack, but as I moved to do so, the hands released me and I was left staring at Scott Byerly, his hands raised as he took a step back. "Watch," he said.

I did. Sessions was still crying out—in pain, I thought—until I looked back and saw that around her hands, fresh skin was springing up on his face, replacing the cracked and blackened with new, pink flesh. It spread out in an effect that rippled over his visible skin. New hairs sprang from his once bald head and his shrieks became a low moan then ceased. His head dropped to the ground and he let out a long, deep exhalation.

"Pulse returning to normal," Dr. Perugini said, her stethoscope on his chest. "He's in stable condition." She snapped her fingers and someone slid a stretcher and a backboard into the snow next to Sessions and they started to load him onto it.

"How did she do that?" I asked, low, but loud enough to be heard.

Scott Byerly was the one who answered. "She's a Persephone-type. She can give life with a touch."

"Give life?" I stared at the girl, still on her knees in the snow, which had indeed melted around her legs, brown grass visible against the tan skin of her thighs. I looked closer;

blades of grass were turning green and waving against her sun-kissed skin, and it wasn't my imagination. It was almost as if they were trying to touch her. "Persephone was the Greek goddess of seasons. She couldn't give life to people, just to plants."

He shrugged. "I said Persephone-type, not Persephone herself. It's based on myth and legend, after all." He stared me down, and I saw a hint of a smile poke at the corners of his lips. "What are you?"

I looked away, back to Kat, who was sitting on the ground, resting, her eyes closed, gold hair flowing around her face, which was red from exertion. She looked at peace, and she sank back, laying flat on the ground, embraced by the patch of green in the midst of all the snow. Her breath was still coming in and out with regular certainty, the steaming heat of it boldly visible against the bright lights surrounding us. I saw the calm around her, watched the grass play at her fingers, touching it, tickling it, and I felt a surge of envy.

They were carrying Dr. Sessions away now, away from her, the girl who had given him life, returned it to him with her very hands. I looked back at Scott Byerly, and his eyebrow was raised in expectation. "Me?" I asked, and I felt hollow inside, empty of everything, even Wolfe. "I'm her opposite—everything that she isn't." My jaw hardened. "I'm death."

12

I didn't sleep for the rest of the night. I'd left Scott Byerly and his stupid question behind with my cryptic answer, not even bothering to gauge his reaction. Well, maybe just a little. His face scrunched up as I was turning from him. I can't say that was satisfying, but it was better than stopping to explain the literal truth I had told him.

I am death. My touch brings it. Where Kat Forrest was a tanned, lovely, blond-haired princess of life, I was a dark-haired, pale-skinned angel of death. Her green eyes represented life; my bluer ones represented winter and the end of that life.

Worse than the nasty comparisons that witnessing Kat's power had spawned in me were the questions. What was I doing outside when the building had exploded? Why couldn't I remember it? Why was the flaming lunatic so thankful to me?

When I returned to my dorm room, I had to take another shower. The fall and the fire had done a number on me. No one had asked, probably because they hadn't seen, but my leather gloves had burned to my skin on the back of my hands. I ripped them off, the leather shredding and pulling the flesh in patches. I let them bleed out in the shower, the diluted red standing out against the cream-colored tiles that surrounded the drain. I watched the little stream of maroon as it came in streaks, circling the inevitable.

My hands still itched by the time I was done, along with a

few places on my chest and legs where the same thing had happened. Good thing the Directorate seemed to have their finances in order, I reflected as I tossed my previously new outfit in the garbage. I was going to cost them a lot of money if I kept ruining clothes at the pace I was going.

The bruise on my cheek from earlier was gone, I saw as I looked in the mirror. One plus was that since I had awoken in the field, Wolfe hadn't made a peep. I wondered if he was sleeping. Or maybe the explosion scared him into a kennel in my mind.

I returned to my room and stared out the window for the rest of the night. I had a very, very nasty suspicion about how things had unfolded the night before, based partially on my dreams and partially on the fact that Wolfe had very much wanted to get Gavrikov out of his cage. He should have been overjoyed, swinging from the metaphorical rafters in my head at the fact that it happened, but he was dead quiet instead.

Not good.

The sun rose without me seeing it, once more hidden behind the clouds. I was disgusted enough that if I could have somehow wished myself to Tahiti and left this awful city behind, I would have. Actually, that might not have entirely been because of the sun.

A note was slid under my door shortly after sunrise, suggesting I attend a meeting with Ariadne and Old Man Winter in his office at 9 A.M. I shrugged when I saw it, trying to play cool in case there were cameras watching, but inwardly I trembled. Did he know? Could he know? What had I done?

I skipped breakfast. My stomach was tied in knots anyway; why bother to give it something else to bitch about? I walked to the HQ building when it got close to time. The air was crisp—actually, I'm romanticizing, it was still brutally cold, just like every day since I left my house. Tahiti was sounding better and better. There was still a smell of burning in the air and when I passed in sight of the science building, my suspicions were confirmed—it was still smoking. The smell it gave off was acrid and awful and stuck in my nose, tormenting me even once I was inside Headquarters.

I knocked somewhat tepidly on Old Man Winter's door. I was early, and a sizable part of me (all of me, if we're being honest) hoped he wasn't around. It opened to reveal Ariadne, her usual smile forced across her face. "You'll have to forgive us," she said as she ushered me to a seat, "It's been a busy night and we haven't had much time to prepare for this meeting."

"'Busy'?" I looked out the window behind Old Man Winter, who was sitting placidly behind his desk as always. His eyes had yet to remove themselves from me since I walked in, but I was used to it. It wasn't like he was undressing me mentally—at least I didn't think he was—it was more like he was always assessing, testing me, my willpower. I could swear he read the lies in how I moved, my reluctance to even be here. I worried that if he stared long enough, he'd be able to root out that I was carrying my own worst enemy inside my head, and that wasn't figurative speaking. "I'd hate to see what you'd be talking about if you started pulling out the really descriptive adjectives—you know, like calamitous, explosive, apocalyptic—"

"Yes, well." She cut me off, her politeness for once infused with iron. "It's not as though this is the usual for us."

"Sure, sure," I said in what sounded to me a very Midwestern way. "Last week, near-invincible psychos, this week, men who explode into flames and girls who touch the dead and bring them back to life."

"Even for us," she said, "that's not normal."

"When you're dealing with people who have powers like ours, what is?" I said it airily, but the word stuck in my head. Normal. What was normal? Everything I wasn't, at this point. "Is this about the history lesson I asked for?"

"Yes." Ariadne seated herself next to me. "It's also a briefing on the state of meta affairs in the modern age."

"Ooh, a briefing," I said. "I feel like I should be wearing a colorless pantsuit." I blinked at Ariadne, dressed once more in monochromatic businesswear. "Like that." I blanched inside and Wolfe howled with laughter, the first sound he'd made since last night. The sad part was I couldn't blame that one on him; there was something built into my relationship with Ariadne that made me want to insult her more than anything.

Her face was drawn, her eyes lowered. I wondered, far in the back of my mind where I hoped Wolfe couldn't see it, if my constant slings and arrows at her were actually hurting her feelings. *If so, she should get thicker skin*, Wolfe said, shattering my illusory idea of having private thoughts. I rolled my eyes, possibly insulting Ariadne further. Unfortunately, I couldn't tell her that I wasn't rolling them at her, but at the asshole brainclinger.

Old Man Winter stood, drawing my attention from Ariadne. He pulled himself up to his full height, towering over the two of us, and walked to the window, looking out on the campus. He seemed to focus on the remains of the science building in the distance. I waited for him to say something, and after a minute of silence I spoke. "How can you manage to keep this place secret after an explosion like that?" I looked from him to Ariadne. "It's not like that was quiet; it had to be audible for miles around."

"There is nobody around for miles," Ariadne said. "But you're right, it was heard in the next town over. Fortunately, the local law enforcement are in our back pocket, which means it won't be investigated, and it seems the media is still too focused on Wolfe's reign of terror to give this any thought."

"Got your own little cover up going on," I said with grudging admiration. "I suppose you guys have it all figured out, keeping things secret and hidden from the normal world."

"It has not always been so," Old Man Winter spoke finally, his low timbre crackling with a surprising amount of energy. "But the modern history of metahumans has been one of hiding our existence from the rest of the world, of letting ourselves fade into myth and legend and cloaking our activities so that humanity does not become suspicious of those of us who have abilities beyond theirs."

"You were around when metas walked tall and proud," I said. I couldn't see his reaction, not even in his reflection, but I suspected it was insubstantial. "Why the change?"

"Why, indeed?" His hand reached out and touched the window. "Metahumans did not just walk among humans in the days you speak of, they ruled mankind. We were gods among men. A thousand humans with spears and swords could not defeat a single strong metahuman. Entire armies tried and were wiped out in battles so bloody that they became the stuff of legend—and we became the bane of human existence and the single greatest obstacle to the freedom of men.

"Imagine a meta possessed of the will to become a conqueror, someone with the strength of a man like Wolfe, but more cunning and less psychotic." I heard a grumble in my head from Wolfe at Old Man Winter's assessment of him. "That was the story of a hundred dictators who threw their will onto the huddled masses of humankind, over and over again through the millennia, from the Greek gods of old to later, more subtle attempts of men like Rasputin to assert their influence over world powers."

"Why were the later ones less obvious?" I asked him out of genuine curiosity.

"Your experience in fighting metahumans is colored by your encounter with Wolfe." He was calm, dead calm. "Most metas are not immune to bullets. Technology has been the greatest equalizer for mankind. Whereas a superpowered metahuman might defeat an entire army in the old days, now he must contend with rifles and machine guns, bombs and explosives. Against the might of a modern army, with training, discipline, and handheld weapons with more ability to kill than entire armies of the ancient world, all but the most powerful among us would fall. Take yourself for example." He turned to me, those ice blue eyes seeming to glow against the backdrop of the gloomy sky.

"In the days of old, one with your power and strength, the ability to kill with a touch, to move faster than any human foe, with power enough to kill in a single blow and drain them with agonizing pain should they touch you—you would have been a goddess. Because of your speed, your dexterity, your strength, with a sword in your hand, you could have killed a thousand men and watched the rest flee in fear. Even the arrows of archers would have to have been lucky indeed to bring you down.

"But now, a man with a single gun could end your life with a well-placed shot." His finger traced a line ending at his forehead. "Certainly, you are more resilient than a human, and a wound to anything but your head would not kill you, but if one knows what they are facing...well," his voice trailed off for a moment, "it's not as though bullets and bombs are a commodity that mankind is soon to run out of."

"So metas have spent a good portion of history trying to conquer people." I shrugged. "Not a huge surprise. I've studied history. Why should we be any different than the rest of mankind?"

"Because we can be better," he said with a low intonation. "The story of mankind is one fraught with struggle, true enough. But it is also the tale of a people reaching for more, desiring more than to be static, immovable, and mired in the mistakes of the past. If we are to be nothing more than a warlike people, forever locked in a struggle for dominance, then the metahumans are of no more purpose than any other weapon or person of power in the modern age.

"The need for secrecy has become a paramount concern, especially as governments possess more and more means to control metahumans." His eyes were dull, almost sad. "We dare not challenge them openly, and thus far America has been content to let us rest in the shadows so long as we are not an open threat. I have worked with those in charge of the country's response to metahuman incidents. They have little to no desire to round up a small minority of people for internment or worse so long as we keep a low profile. Other governments..." His words drifted off, along with his gaze, "...are not so reticent."

Ariadne leaned forward. "Approximately three hundred and fifty metahumans were killed at a Chinese government facility less than a week ago."

"That's..." I let my mind run with the numbers I knew and came back with an answer. "That's over ten percent of the metahuman population, based on the number you gave me.'""

"It is." She sat back and drew a deep breath. "We don't know what happened; reports are somewhat sketchy. The facility was supposed to be a training center for the People's Liberation Army's metahuman development program. Either they destroyed it after deciding that it wasn't worth the risk or someone else did it for them. Either way, the meta population took a steep dive last week."

"Ten percent?" My words were almost a croak, no more than a whisper. "I believe the literal term for that is 'decimated'." I had never met even one of the people killed, but somehow I felt a connection to them because somehow we were the same.

"True enough." Ariadne's hands landed in her lap. "These are the sort of things that happen every once in a while. We live in a world where metahumans keep their powers secret—unless they're—"

"Troublemakers? Ne'er-do-wells?" My hands found the padded armrests of my chair, felt the cool metal where the leather padding ended and squeezed it, more out of a desire to feel some pressure than anything else. "Like Wolfe." I felt him stir in umbrage within me and ignored him.

"Similar." It was Ariadne who answered, again. "Usually a meta doesn't openly declare, committing crimes, harming people, unless they've decided to start shirking societal conventions and live by their own rules. At that point they've become a threat, both to human society and the collective metahuman secret." She shrugged. "After all, it's not as though we have something that can make a person forget when they see something crazy—"

"Like some beast rips through a dozen cops in a mall parking lot?" I saw a brief reflection of Wolfe's grin, like a Cheshire cat, in the window as I turned from Ariadne to Old Man Winter.

"That's not one we can explain our way out of," she said. "We had to leave it to the media and the government to spin it." She smiled. "Did you hear what they finally landed on?" I shook my head. "A biker on PCP and cocaine that was wearing multiple Kevlar vests under his clothes."

"I suppose he was rather scruffy looking." I ignored the shout of outrage that echoed through my head alone.

"But it's at those points that someone has to get involved, for the good of society. Once someone crosses that line, if there's no one there to stop them, they spin out of control, as though the taste of power over people and freedom from consequence is a narcotic that takes them over."

"That's where the Directorate comes in," I finished for her. "But what about the other groups? They don't do the same?"

Ariadne looked uncomfortable very suddenly. "Keep in mind our primary mission is policing the metahuman population, not spying on other groups that have metahuman interests—"

"Which is a fancy way of saying what?" I looked at her evenly. "That you don't pay attention to them? Don't know who they are?"

"We don't," she said. "We're aware that there are other factions out there, but none of them have strong roots in the U.S. yet, and we've been more focused on small scale threats and awakenings than some dread conspiracy—"

"You don't have a clue about any of them, do you?" I shook my head in near disbelief.

"Not so," Old Man Winter said from the window. "The boy you have had dealings with—his name is Reed Treston, and he works with an outfit based in Rome. They appear to be a group concerned about government interventions against metahumans but most of their operations are in Europe."

"What about Wolfe?" I sat up in interest, and I could feel him rattling around inside, almost as though he were holding his breath to find out what they knew about his employer.

"We know less," Ariadne shared a look with Old Man Winter. "Almost nothing, actually. They're a group possessed of incredibly strong metas, like Wolfe."

"And this new guy," I told her. She looked at me quizzically. "You know, the guy with the metallic complexion? He's with Wolfe's outfit."

She looked to Old Man Winter, then back to me with a furrowed brow. "How do you know that?"

"Well if he's not with the same group Reed is, then it stands to reason he's with Wolfe's group, unless there's another power out there that wants a piece of me?"

"There are several others," Old Man Winter said in his low rumble. "None of which we know much about."

"How is it you guys can be so well informed that you found me but you have no idea who your enemies are?" I sighed more out of disbelief than despair. "You don't want to know anything about your competition?"

"There's been a proliferation of metahuman groups in the last few years," Ariadne said, twisting a lock of her hair around her finger. "It's something we've recently begun to pivot to address, but it takes time to put an intelligence network in place and develop useable intel. We are working on it. But that's not why we asked you here." She took a deep breath. "Did this answer your questions about the larger history of metahumans and the role they play in society?"

I hesitated. "Yes," I said after a moment. "It's far from complete, but I get the gist. I'm still wondering about a few things—like the Agency, what my mom did for them and how they were destroyed," I said when she looked at me with a curious expression, "but that's not something I expect to know the answer to right now, today."

"It's something we could cover soon, perhaps in our next conversation." Ariadne's hands left her lap and went to a folder on the desk, sliding it across in front of me. "But all that is ancillary, unrelated to the real mission—which is why we wanted to talk to you."

"I see." I felt a nervous tension run through me. Did they suspect my involvement in the destruction of the science building? I felt an involuntary shudder inside and couldn't dispense with the idea that somewhere inside me. Wolfe was suddenly very cagey.

She opened the folder and pulled out four photographs, arranging them neatly in front of me. One was a picture of a family of four, another of a police officer, the next of a young woman not much older than me, and the last of a mother and young daughter. "This is why we're here. Last year a metahuman named Darrell Seidell went on a crime spree. He was nineteen and already had three felonies to his name before his power manifested."

She pointed to the family of four, all blond, with two girls. "He staged a daylight break-in at this couple's home—Rick and Susan Ormann of Champaign, Illinois. Rick was a lawyer, Susan worked for a local bank. They had a nice house, so nice, in fact, that Darrell chose it out of dozens of others to break into. He went there to steal from them— maybe a TV, some jewelry—and he ended up killing both of them, then their kids." She moved her finger to the picture of the police officer. But not before Melanie, the Ormann's eight year old daughter, called 911 and this man, Officer Lance Nealey, responded."

She picked up the picture of the cop, and I couldn't look away. He was young too, probably in his twenties, around Zack's age. He had cocoa skin, big brown eyes, a warm smile, and his head was shaved. He was the perfect picture of a cop, the kind of image that was everything my skewed perspective thought a cop should be. He just...looked like a nice guy, there to help. "Seidell killed him and stole his cruiser, escaping the scene. That night he stopped at a convenience store outside Ottumwa, Iowa and ran across this girl, the clerk, Jeannie Sabourin." She handed me the picture of the young woman and I took it, even though I really didn't want to and forced myself to look into the girl's face.

"She was a high school senior who worked at the store at night to help make ends meet for her family." Ariadne shook her head, a kind of muted rage present on her face that made her pause. When she went on, her voice cracked. "She had been through one robbery already and knew to give him whatever he wanted. She went with him into the back where he assaulted her and once he was done, he killed her."

Ariadne paused, and I watched her face twitch as she struggled to maintain her composure. When she began again, her words came out strained. "Afterward he went behind the convenience store to the low-rent housing complex where he found Karina Hartsfield smoking a cigarette outside her

247

patio door." She moved to the last photograph. "He killed her and stole her car, leaving behind her four-year-old daughter alone in the apartment." She pointed to the child in the photograph with Karina Hartsfield. "Odds are good that if he'd known she was there, he would have killed her too."

"Seven people dead." She reached back into the sheaf of photos and pulled out a half-dozen more, scattering them in front of me and causing me to hold my hand in front of my mouth as I heard a small gasp escape. They were photos of bodies, burned around the torso, the hands, the legs, burned so their insides showed and I nearly gagged from seeing them. "See, Darrell Seidell is what we'd call a fire jotnar—a fire giant, from the same Norse myths as," she looked to Old Man Winter, "well, you know. Not nearly as potent as our friend Mr. Gavrikov, but up close, he's the breath of hell brought to earth. Without anyone to stop him, he was free to keep driving west, leaving burned corpses and sundered families in his wake."

She pulled newspaper clippings out of the stack. "Want to read his press reports?" They were emblazoned with headlines, "Killer Burns Family to Death One by One, then Kills Police Officer" and "Arson Killer Claims Two in Iowa."

"What..." I felt myself speak in a hoarse whisper. "What happened to him?"

"That part isn't in the clippings." She reached into the file and pulled out another page, handing it to me.

It was a report, signed by Roberto Bastian, the head of M-Squad. I skimmed it then looked up to Ariadne. "Your people caught up with him halfway to Des Moines."

"They wrecked his car, beat him to a bloody pulp," she said with a haunted look, "and dragged him back here where we slapped him in restraints and sent him to Arizona to spend the rest of his life in a deep, dark hole in the middle of the desert." Her eyes found mine, and I looked away first. "This is why we're here. To protect people from this sort of monster." She picked up another file from a stack to her left, slapping it onto the table in front of me, followed by another, and another. They weren't loud, but the sound of the paper hitting the rock of the desk made me flinch each time. Finally she grabbed the rest of the pile and let them fall in front of me with a thud.

I stared at it, then pulled a file from the middle of the stack, opened it, and thumbed through. It was a series of reports from an incident in Birmingham, Alabama, that was handled by their Atlanta campus. A murder committed by a kid who was no older than me. Then another, and another. They caught him on his sixth victim. They were all committed in the course of robberies; three in the same incident. Every last one of them had been beaten to death.

The next file was from Chicago and detailed a rapist working the South Side that was putting every victim in the hospital and a few in the morgue by what the victims described as "one horrific punch." And only one. Impossibly strong, the report concluded. The rest of the file laid out the evidence against the creep: the witness statements, the agent investigation. The final report was signed by Zack Davis.

I flipped through about fifty of them, not reading every detail but taking them all in. Every crime was like something you'd see in a movie or maybe a police blotter. Some of them were a decade old or more; some were very, very recent. They were from all over the country, and each one had a trail of evidence cataloged, indicating why the agent or meta investigating believed the person they caught was the guilty party. And almost all of them were slam-dunk obvious.

I closed the last file, a robbery/murder, and put it on the stack with the rest. I swallowed hard, wishing somehow I could scrub all that I had just read out of my brain, along with all the things Wolfe did to me and the things he'd shown me in flashes through his memories earlier. I felt a desire to run far, far away to a place where people didn't do things to other people like I saw in those files and in Wolfe's memories...and in my own. Too bad there wasn't a place far enough I could run to find that. "Why did you show me this?"

"Because this is the 'solved' stack." She reached behind Old Man Winter's desk and pulled out another stack, almost as big as the first and lay it in front of me. The solved stack's folders where manila; these were red. "These are unsolved, crimes where meta involvement was suspected but the perpetrator couldn't be located because they didn't make a big enough noise and we only have so many agents and resources." She raised an eyebrow at me and opened the first folder. "Take this one, for instance...thirty-eight-year-old man dies in an attempted robbery. A witness said that the perpetrator seemed to have extra arms growing out of his sides that restrained the victim while the robber beat him to death."

"That's...horrible." I was suddenly hyperaware of Old Man Winter looking at me. I felt like he was sifting me, trying to filter through to my core, and I suddenly didn't care for what he might find there. The anger made me bite back at Ariadne, hard. "I'm sorry he died, but I don't see how anything I do is going to matter. I have my own problems, and I'm only—"

"A little girl?" There was no accusation in her words, but they slapped me just the same. "A teenager with more strength than twenty men and a power that could keep any physical assailant at bay."

"This isn't my problem." I wanted to be firm. I needed to find Mom.

"So it doesn't matter if it doesn't involve you?" That time there was accusation, and it stung. I wondered if my verbal lashings hit her half so hard as hers hit me.

I reddened. "I'm a teenager; I'm pretty sure it's a biological imperative to think that way."

"I guess you're pretty normal, then," Ariadne said, staring me down.

"But you can be better." Old Man Winter said it from behind his desk, leaning forward on his knuckles to look close at me. I didn't cower from his stare, but I felt a bit of withering. Wolfe was nowhere to be heard, not that I felt like I could count on him for moral support. "You are not some schoolgirl whose blissful ignorance of the harsh realities of the world cloud her eyes with starry dreams of happy endings. Are you?"

"I'd like a happy ending," I said. "But I don't ignore the

fact that the world can be cold and brutal and that there are people out there who exist solely to hurt others."

"Then you know that someone has to protect ordinary people." Ariadne leaned forward again and her red hair flared against the dull background of Old Man Winter's office. "They can't protect themselves against what waits for them out there. They have no defense because they don't know what they have to defend against. Metahumans move too fast, hit too hard, for an unprepared person to fend them off. Only someone who's well prepared—and armed, actually—stands a chance against them, and then only if they don't get taken by surprise."

"Same old story," I said, swallowing hard again. "Why are you telling me this? What do you want me to do?"

"Even when you find your mother," Old Man Winter spoke, his quiet voice devastating for some reason, "at some point you will have to decide what to do with your own life, how you wish to spend it. You are nearly a woman grown, and you need to find—"

"A job?" I licked my lips.

"A path. A career. Maybe even...a purpose," Ariadne said. "Something you can do that you can believe in, that will challenge you, that won't leave you hating your life and questioning why you're even doing what you're doing." She laughed, a low, quiet laugh that had no real mirth behind it. "Unless you'd like to get to age forty and wake up to wonder where your life went."

"Forty is a long ways off for me." I looked at my boots. Most eighteen-year-old girls wear shoes; I'm in boots. Most girls my age wear dresses sometimes, go to school, look forward to prom and graduation. I'm stuck in outfits that cover me head to toe, I've been home every day, week, and year for over a decade, and all I have to look forward to is finding my missing mother so...what? I can go back to living like that?

"It'll be here before you know it." Ariadne snapped her fingers in front of her face. "It goes fast. And the question you'll be left with is if you just got by or if you actually made a difference." She slid the stack of files away from me. "We don't expect you to make a decision right now." She pulled out a lone piece of paper and placed it in front of me. "Working for us as a meta will have its rewards—more money per year than most eighteen-year-olds make, along with other benefits—"

"I'm not super concerned with a 401(k) right now." I glanced at the sheet. Money meant almost nothing to me, largely because I'd never had any opportunity to use it. I truly didn't know the value of a dollar, nor what it bought. "What do you want me to do? What would happen if I said yes?"

"You would enter training with M-Squad and agent trainers, learn how agents operate, field procedure, all that. After some basics, you'd be assigned a more experienced partner and learn how to be a 'retriever'—someone who tracks down rogue or awakening metas and brings them back to the Directorate either through peaceful means, or, if necessary—"

"Cracking skulls?" I glanced at the compensation sheet and wondered if $100,000 per year was a lot or a little for a girl just starting out.

"You never seemed like you had a problem with physical violence before." Ariadne was unrelenting. "Like, say, when you battered Zack and Kurt, or when you went looking for a fight with Wolfe—"

"I don't." I looked up from the sheet to her. "I don't have a problem breaking the teeth out of anyone who does the things that you've showed me in the files." I felt my jaw clench as a little surge of pleasure from Wolfe ran through me at the thought of inflicting pain on others. "But I don't know that I want to be a retriever for a living, always chasing down some fugitive meta who might kill me if I screw up. And I don't know that I could…" I struggled with the words. "I mean, killing Wolfe was an accident. I don't know if I could…do that…to someone else. "

"It rarely comes to that, " she said. "And retriever's not necessarily the end of the line. You could move up, join M-Squad, move to another branch, work into one of our training positions to teach and guide the metas here at the Minneapolis branch—"

"Because that's the place for me, guiding the next generation."

"—or you could move into administration." She shrugged. "There are a lot of places you could go. We're a big operation. You could see the world, help us expand overseas if you wanted. You'd have the satisfaction of knowing you're doing some good."

"I hear you say it," I picked up the compensation sheet between my thumb and forefinger, "but how do I really know it's true?"

"Trust is a two-way street," she said, standing. "It won't happen overnight, but if you're out chasing these people down and you see what they do, you'll eventually come to realize that we're the good guys. We don't expect a decision right now."

"You have a great deal to think about," Old Man Winter said. "You stand at the edge of the rest of your life. The decisions you make now affect everything from here on. Gone are the times when simple and inconsequential matters governed your life. It is now the time for you to choose who you want to be, what you want to stand for, and what you want your life to reflect." He walked around the desk, buttoning his suit coat as he walked to the door and opened it for me. "So few people get to truly steer their course the way you have the chance to now. And the question before you is—will you strive to be normal and live an ordinary life? Or will you do what no one else can do—and be more?"

13

I carried the compensation sheet with me, crumpled in my fist, when I left the meeting. I had read through it, though I confess I was in a haze as I left them. One item stuck out, though—a $10,000 bonus to be paid when I signed on for the training program. I still didn't have a great concept of how much that would buy me, nor what I would do with it. The sheet indicated I could continue to stay on the campus free of charge with all meals provided.

The meeting had taken longer than I expected and I'd skipped breakfast. I had a lot on my mind—after all, the question of how Gavrikov got out of his box was a pretty good one, and I hoped my theory was wrong. We hadn't discussed Full Metal Jackass in much detail; not that there was much to discuss. Why did I doubt he was the sort to just give up and go home after one encounter that went awry?

Probably because he dressed himself like a submarine and paraded himself into town in hopes of capturing me. You don't dress like that unless you're a hopelessly delusional loser who will continue to swing for the fences long past the time you should have returned to the dugout.

I entered the cafeteria at half past eleven. It was crowded already. I made my way through the line, again ignoring the animosity of the workers as I gathered my food. I was picking my way over to the far wall, prepared to eat by myself (again) when I caught sight of Zack, sitting with his back to me. I took one step toward him and halted. He was at a table for four and it was filled. Kurt Hannegan sat next to him and Scott Byerly and Kat Forrest sat opposite.

I began to slink back toward the window when Kat waved at me, her big eyes and a wide smile visible even from across the cafeteria. An inward feeling of desperation enveloped me as she tried to wave me over. I sighed and closed my eyes, and when I opened them, Zack was also gesturing for me to join them. He got up and pulled another chair over. With greatest reluctance, I made my way across the room and endured the enthusiastic greetings of Kat and Zack and the muted one from Scott. Hannegan ignored me, I ignored him, and we were both the happier for it.

"Scott has something he wants to tell you," Zack said as I sat down. I could feel my motions reduced to a severe stiffness, as though all my joints were locked together and it was only through acts of absolute will I could bend them to seat myself. I looked at Scott, who was at my left, and had his head bowed.

"I wanted to apologize," the young man said, his face angled toward the table. Kat and Zack watched him while Hannegan continued to shovel a burrito into his face. "I didn't really know you when I wrote that note and it was wrong and inappropriate." He managed to look up and I got the impression that he was rather like a child caught doing something he shouldn't. "I'm sorry."

"All right," Zack said. "Now we can put all that unpleasantness behind us." He looked at me, the satisfaction disappearing from his face. "Right?"

I thought about arguing, but what was the point? Byerly couldn't have hated me any more than I had hated myself when he'd written it. "Sure," I said. "Bygones and forgetting and all that." I picked up the burrito from my plate. The smell of beans, rice and chicken wafted up to me, tempered with the tang of the salsa and guacamole.

"What did you talk with Old Man Winter and Ariadne about?" Zack asked just as I was taking my first bite.

I finished chewing before I answered. "How did you know about that?"

"I went to see Ariadne this morning and the secretary told

me she was in a meeting with the two of you and couldn't be disturbed." He took a sip of the water sitting in front of him.

"History of metas, remember?" The burrito was slippery in my gloves and Byerly was giving me a funny look as the salsa dribbled down the leather and onto my sleeve. I dropped the burrito and wiped at it with a napkin.

"Uh huh." He chewed as he answered, kind of skeptical. Hannegan still hadn't looked at me and Kat hadn't taken her eyes off me yet. I wanted to knock her chair over with her still in it. Or maybe Wolfe did. No, it was probably me. "You guys talk about anything else?"

I remembered the compensation sheet, tucked away in my coat pocket. "Yeah," I said. "A couple things."

"They offered you a job, didn't they?" This came from Hannegan, who had stopped eating and was frozen with a taco halfway to his mouth.

"Yeah." I felt myself flush. "So?"

"Doing what?" Scott Byerly did a flush of his own, his ruddy complexion suddenly redder.

"As an agent?" Zack was looking at me in wonderment. "A retriever?" He looked down at my side and my eyes followed him a moment later. His hand was already in motion and he snatched the compensation sheet from where it was dangling out of my pocket. I didn't try to stop him, and he stared at it, eyes narrowed as he focused, Hannegan leaning over his shoulder. "Wait, this isn't an organizational chart...this is...this is...whoa." Zack's jaw dropped and he looked at Hannegan in near-astonishment. "I don't get paid that much. Do you?"

"Hell, no," Kurt said, scowling. "And I'm near the top of the pay scale!"

"But at the bottom of their estimation, apparently," I said and ripped the paper out of Zack's hands.

There was an eerie quiet around the table that lasted almost five seconds before Scott Byerly spoke. "Can I see that?"

I let out a small noise of exasperation and thrust it at him. "Sure. Why not?"

Kat Forrest looked over his shoulder as he looked down the page. "Wow," she said. "They must think you're really powerful to offer you so much."

"I'd offer you more to leave," Hannegan said under his breath.

"This is..." Byerly blinked a few times in rapid succession and then handed the page back to me. "A very nice offer. I wish I'd gotten one." I saw his jaw tighten as he said it.

"The day will come, my friend," Zack said. "Probably soon, in fact—" A low buzzing filled the air and he reached down, pulling out his cell phone and studying the screen. He looked to Kurt. "Ariadne wants to see us."

Kurt paused in eating, his mouth full. "Now?" Flecks of half-chewed food rained onto the table and I looked away.

"When was the last time she made an appointment to see the low-paid help?" Zack stood and pulled his coat off the back of his chair. "Yes, now." He looked back at the three of us still seated. "You guys take it easy." Hannegan followed him out, a taco clenched in his chubby fists.

"Congratulations on your offer," Kat said, her eyes shining. "That's really amazing. Not too many metas get asked to go through the training program. You should be proud."

"Why?" I took a bite of my burrito and then wiped my glove on a napkin. "I didn't do anything except be born a meta."

"Well, you killed that psychopath." Her smile glittered like a spotlight shining directly in my eyes, annoying me.

"Yeah, you did," Byerly said, then leaned closer. "How did you do that, by the way?"

I felt still, as though a great slab of ice had frozen everything inside me. "I told you—I'm death."

"What does that mean?" He leaned even closer, almost whispering. "You're an efficient killer? You're super strong?"

I felt an ugly thread tug at me inside, felt Wolfe doing something, though I couldn't tell what. I ignored him. "It's none of your business."

"Are you a human time bomb? Like the guy that blew up the science labs?" Byerly kept pressing, and I could feel the warmth of his breath on my cheek, he was so close—too close. "Can you throw energy or maybe—"

"What I can do—" I started to scoot my chair away from

him but he landed his hand on my arm, stopping me. "If you really want to see, just keep your hand where it is. If you don't, move it."

"Maybe I want to know." His eyes were focused, boring in on me and I saw something else in them, an intensity.

"Scott, let her go—" Kat's plea went ignored.

My glove was already off. Wolfe had moved my hand without me even knowing it and it was on Scott's cheek. He started to recoil, but I anchored my thumb and forefinger, gripping him on the neck. Not hard enough to choke him, but enough to let him know I had a good hold on him. His eyes widened in surprise, then narrowed in anger, and he brought a hand around, maybe instinctively, to hit me. I knocked it aside and jerked him to his feet.

I saw the anger vanish, replaced with creases in his forehead from the first stirrings of pain. "Ouch," he breathed, consternation knitting his brows together. "Ow...oh..." He sucked in a sharp breath and grunted. After another second he let out a squeal that drew even more attention from those around us and then he let out an earsplitting, agonized scream that started a scramble for the cafeteria door, people falling over each other to get the hell out of there.

"Put him down!" Kat was on her feet, shouting at me. I strained, trying to regain control of my hand, but Wolfe was in charge, holding the rest of me still. I lifted Scott Byerly off his feet and he shuddered in the air, convulsing, his eyes rolling back in his head. I looked on, horrified, unable to stop it.

I felt a blow land on the back of my head and I flew forward, releasing my grasp on Byerly. I plowed through three tables, heard some things break that sounded like it could have been me or the furniture, I wasn't sure which. I came to rest twenty feet away from where I had started, a medley of other peoples' lunches smeared on my clothes. Kat was already at Scott's side and Clyde Clary stood not far away, his lips twisted in an amused smile. "Clyde," I said, using my sleeve to mop some blood from the back of my head where he'd hit me.

"Girl, ain't no one calls me Clyde," his pudgy face went angry quickly.

"I think I just did." I stood up. "But if you'd prefer, I could just call you fatass prick—"

He charged at me, broad shoulders flashing underneath his shirt, the skin around his neck rippling, turning into something different. It looked like metal in the brief glimpse I got before he put his shoulder down and stormed at me. He moved fast, especially for such a big guy.

I grabbed the nearest table, heavy and metal, and heaved it at him. It spun, hit him in the face and ricocheted off at high velocity, flying through one of the upper windows of the cafeteria. He moved off his course not even a millimeter, his head now the same dull metal that I had seen beneath his shirt. I dodged out of the way just in time as he shredded the tables behind me, shards of them flying through the air.

"You're dangerous. I like it." He smiled and grabbed a table of his own as I rolled to my feet and he chucked it at me. It skipped off the floor, a hubcap of spinning death that grazed my shoulder as I dropped below it and heard the shattering of glass behind me. He threw another, then another, and I dodged them, executing some gymnastic evasions I wouldn't have been capable of even a month ago—before my powers manifested. I looked around for a weapon—any kind of weapon—that might be effective against a hulking slab of metal.

He stomped toward me, malice in his eyes. I met his attack, ducking his punch and grabbing his arm with my ungloved hand as he started to pull it back. I gripped onto the slick metal and held tight, waiting for a reaction; it was cool in my grasp. The big jackass looked at me, then down to my hand, then back at me and split into a broad grin. "Your succubus trick only works on flesh." He pulled his arm back, yanking me off balance and lifting me from the ground. I managed to hold onto him, but only just.

A second later I realized what he was doing. As soon as he pulled me toward him, he set me up for a punch with his other hand. His fist made contact with my midsection and I felt all the air leave my lungs in a rush, worse than any physical pain I'd felt since Wolfe had near-gutted me. I flew through the air, landing with a crash on a metal chair that promptly upended. I heard more things break when I landed and this time I knew it was me, not the furniture.

I sat up, clutching at my ribs. There was blood in my mouth, the metallic taste unpleasant enough that I spit it out. Clary stalked toward me from across the room; his punch had thrown me almost a hundred feet, from the middle of the cafeteria to near the kitchen.

"Any suggestions to keep us from getting pummeled?" I muttered the words under my breath, but Wolfe was silent. If ever there had been a time when I could have used the help of the world's most brutal infighter, this would have been it. I looked around and my eyes widened as I remembered something, a possibility. I made for the kitchen, hobbling as fast as my wounded frame could carry me, Clary not far behind.

I jumped over the cafeteria line and the serving stations with one good leap. As I reached the kitchen doors I heard Clary crash through them behind me. "You can run girl, but you can't hide!"

"You can spout cliches," I said, "but you can't find a woman who'll enjoy your company."

I plunged into the kitchen and heard the screams of the serving ladies, who had all run inside to hide after the altercation started in the dining area. There were a half dozen of them, all wide-eyed. "Get out!" I said as I pushed past them. I stopped next to the freezer and swung the heavy door open, then checked my placement. He would have to charge through a preparation station in order to get to me, with an obstructed view, and if he wasn't paying much attention (which I assumed was his usual state) he'd go charging into the freezer where with any luck I could shut the door behind him.

Clary stopped at the entrance to the kitchen. "Come on, now, girl."

"I'm not going anywhere with you," I said, holding my arm. It was actually the least of my pains, but the others weren't easily reached and pulling it closer seemed to ease the torment in my chest.

"Have it your way, then." He lowered his head. "I'll let Old Man Winter decide what he wants done with you once you're good and out." He barreled toward me, not bothering to use the aisles, charging right through the prep station, tearing the vent hoods out of the stove, destroying a cook top and counters, metal flying in every direction.

I watched him for as long as I could, but once the debris started flying my way I dodged sideways, behind the heavy door of the freezer. I hit the ground and my chest and side screamed at me. I watched him run past me into the freezer, hit the wall and bounce off, then heard the crashing of a side of beef and cartons of God knows what hitting the floor. I kicked the freezer door and it swung closed. I wrenched myself up and yanked the pin off a shelf nearby and plunged it into the lock.

I took two steps back and fell down, breathing a sigh of relief. Everything still hurt, but at least that idiot was contained where he couldn't do any harm—

That thought lasted less than the second it took for the door to the freezer to come exploding off its hinges. It flew through the air above me, skipping across my left shoulder and leaving a gash over an inch deep. I was pretty sure it broke my collarbone, but it was hard to tell among all the other agonies.

"Nice try." Clary sauntered over to me as I squirmed on the floor. I heard a hissing that I thought was in my head until I realized that the idiot had severed the gas line to the stove when he charged through. "Ain't nothin' can hold me."

"I think you've confused 'can' with 'want'," I said through gritted teeth. "For example, a woman 'can' hold you, but none of them 'want' to—"

He grabbed me in a clawlike hold around the neck and picked me up in a manner that reminded me of the way Wolfe had manhandled me, beaten me, abused me. Clary's piggy eyes leered at me from behind his smug smile and I hated him, wanted to crush him, but now I couldn't breathe.

The eyes.

I stared down at him. Sure enough, Wolfe's voice was right—his skin was metal but his eyes were the same white as always, the blood vessels visible on the sides.

My fingers lanced out and I stabbed him with my thumb right in the socket. I did not hesitate nor pull my strike and he screamed in uncontrolled misery. I fell to the ground, unable to catch myself. A lancing pain ran up my entire upper body after the impact, and I floundered on the floor, holding onto my sides.

"YOU BITCH!" Clary stomped and I bounced a few inches into the air before landing again. It hurt more. "YOU TOOK OUT MY EYE!"

"Honestly, it wasn't one of your best attributes," I muttered. "Not that you have any good ones." I managed to get to my hands and knees and looked for something to use as a weapon since it had become obvious that he was unlikely to present me with an opportunity to stab out his other eye. There was a ringing in my ears that went along with the hissing. I saw a fire extinguisher and it dawned on me that it was probably a better choice than anything else. I grabbed it and crawled along on my hands and knees, trying to avoid his blind rage behind me.

I had reached the door when he finally realized I wasn't near him anymore. "Hey! Where do you think you're going?"

I used a countertop to pull myself up and turn back to him. "Me? I think I'll go for a quiet drink somewhere. Care to join me?"

He had started towards me but stopped, his head snapping back, his jaw opening slightly. "Really?"

I grimaced. "No. Not really. I'm going to get medical treatment. You? You can burn in hell. Literally."

He stomped his foot again and his jaw made a scraping noise as he ground his teeth together. "Damn you, girl! What am I supposed to do with one eye?"

"You could be huge in the kingdom of the blind." I reached back and flung the fire extinguisher with all my much-vaunted metahuman strength.

And it missed him.

He smiled as it sailed by. "You missed—"

It hit the side of the metal countertop, hard, and sparked. I had the intense satisfaction of seeing him look back, confused, before the fireball blew me out of the room.

14

"You!" I awoke to the sound of Dr. Perugini's less-than-dulcet tones. I stared up at her when my eyes opened. Her dark complexion was flushed, her eyes on fire as she glared down at me in the hospital bed. I took in the medical bay around me and saw Clary in the bed next to me, a bandage over his eye. Scott Byerly was across the way, Kat at his side, casting the occasional furtive glance at me.

The doctor poked her thin index finger in my face. "You keep causing me so many problems!" She let out a string of curses in her native Italian. "I used to have a nice, peaceful life! Since you get here I have nothing but bodies all the time! Before, I work on my novel and clean my instruments. Since you show up, all I do is fix hurt people!"

I coughed and tried to sit up. "Your job description includes that, I believe." Her eyes blazed and she pulled her finger out of my face and grabbed a tongue depressor out of her jacket pocket. Without a word she poked me in the side. "OW!" She did it again. "OW OW! What the hell?! Were you absent the day you were supposed to take the Hippocratic Oath?" My fingers found my wounded side where she had poked me. "Pretty sure it includes something about not doing harm."

"Not doing harm?" She thrust the tongue depressor in my face and wagged it at me. "You are a fine one to talk! All you do is harm—to yourself and others! All I do is clean up your messes! You are a menace!" The way she said it made me chuckle, which did not improve her mood. She whirled and marched away from me, back to her office. She slammed the door and dropped the blinds, giving me one last glower before her face disappeared.

"You awake, girl?" Clary's stupid drawl drew my attention to him. He was laying on his back one bed over, a bandage over his eye.

"No, I'm talking in my sleep." I tilted my head to look at him. "What do you want?"

"That was a cheap shot, blowing me out the back of the building. Hurt a lot too, when I woke up." He blinked with his one good eye.

"Oh, yeah?" I adopted a disinterested tone. "I'm so *not* sorry." It took a minute for him to register what I'd said.

"Yeah, well, I'm not sorry I busted your guts." He guffawed. "That was the best tussle I've had in a long time. Cojones. Girl, you got 'em."

"Actually, I don't." I turned away from him and stared straight up. "But it doesn't surprise me that you wouldn't know that about women."

He looked at me, blank. "That was a good fight, you hear me? That was good." He put his hands behind his head and leaned back and smiled like he'd just won a prize.

I was about to tell him just how dumb I thought he was when the door clicked open. "I can assure both of you that what you did in the cafeteria was *not* good." Ariadne stood silhouetted in the entry to the medical bay, a paper in her hand and a fury in her eyes that was only a couple degrees shy of what I'd seen from Dr. Perugini. "Thirteen people with minor injuries, Byerly—" she seemed to be flustered, searching for a word, "—soul drained or death touched or whatever, Clary lost an eye, Sienna with a host of broken bones and severe blood loss, and OH, let's not forget! Over a million dollars in damage to the cafeteria!"

She made it across the medical bay and slapped the folder in her hand down on Clary's tray. "She's not even eighteen, Clary! Did it not even occur to you that she might have made a rash decision—a mistake—in attacking Byerly?"

"Well, no," the big man said. "She was draining him pretty hard. I just wanted to put her down, you know—"

"Rhetorical question, Clary!" She thumped her hand on the tray, stunning him into silence. "Try to pretend you've never assaulted anyone before! It's not your job to break up a cafeteria altercation by bludgeoning the offender to death; it's your job to pursue the dangerous metahumans we send you after." She pulled back after delivering the last directly to his face, causing him to flinch. "Get it straight. You're not a four-year-old. Keep your damned hands to yourself and stop looking for a fight everywhere you go."

"But—"

"If the next words out of your mouth are anything besides 'Yes ma'am, I'll never do anything like it again' then I will personally have Bastian come down here and deal with you." She faded. "He wanted to, desperately." Clary shrank away, almost seeming to recede into the bed.

I snorted and instantly regretted it. Ariadne turned her withering stare on me. "Don't get me started on you."

I coughed and tried to look contrite. "I'm sorry. I...overreacted when Scott put his hand on me."

She continued to stare for a second longer then shook her head in disbelief. "Overreacted? You nearly killed him. How is that an overreaction?"

I thought about it for a moment and shrugged. "Because it sounds better than the way you put it. He wanted to see what I could do in the worst way. So I showed him. In the worst—"

She let out a noise of disgust. "Is that how you're going to operate if we train you to be an agent?"

Clary looked up in surprise. "You're gonna make her an agent?"

"Shut up," Ariadne spat at him and whipped her head back around to me. "You wrecked the cafeteria and blew up the kitchen. You could have killed somebody."

"Um," I shook my head, "I believe that the persons most likely to have gotten killed today were myself and Byerly, in that order."

"What about me?" Clary's face was puckered, as though he were insulted by what I said.

"You don't count." I looked to Ariadne, who was steaming. "He was trying to kill me! I just repaid the favor." I looked down. "If it's going to be a...um...an insurmountable obstacle—"

"It's not an insurmountable anything." Ariadne's withering stare turned to a simmer. "But if this is what we can expect from you as an employee—"

"I didn't mean to." I said it low, almost under my breath. "It just got out of hand, I'm sorry." An ugly thought occurred to me. "Oh, God. If I take the job, does that mean you'll be my boss?"

She folded her arms in front of her. "Yes. Why?"

"I think that might be a dealbreaker." I tried to sit up. "There's no way I'm going to be able to not make insubordinate wisecracks about you."

"Tell me about it," Clary said, nodding his head.

"I said wisecracks, not dumbasscracks."

"I think we can typically overlook incidents of..." she paused, "...over-exuberant verbal witticisms. However, failure to follow orders is looked down on, as is destroying campus property." She frowned. "Or in your cases, the whole damned campus."

I stiffened and wondered if she was accusing me of blowing up the science building. It didn't seem fair, since I was being held responsible now for two incidents which were started by the houseguest in my skull, that mongrel that still needed to be housebroken and taught not to play with other people's bodies.

"Be that as it may," she looked daggers at Clary and then turned back to me, "we can overlook this, but any further incidents would provoke our full displeasure."

Clary looked at me. "They're gonna let you skate!"

I looked over at him. "Yeah. Awesome." I turned back to Ariadne. "Anything on my mother's stuff yet?"

"What?" She took a step back. "Oh. That. Our forensics lab was in the science building."

I took a deep breath and let it out slowly. "So it's gone."

"Yes." She wavered, looking as though she wanted to offer me some sympathy, but thought the better of it. "I'm sorry."

"Bummer." Clary was nodding his head, then he brightened. "When do you start training? Cuz that'll be fun."

267

15

I walked out of the medical unit under my own power shortly before nightfall. My broken bones were knitted, though my skin still had scabs in numerous places that would take until the next day to heal.

"Get out and don't come back!" Dr. Perugini shouted as the door swung closed behind me. Clary walked out along with me and I kept an eye on him, though he was whistling a pretty happy tune the whole way out. Turned out that Kat Forrest had given him his eye back with her healing power after I blew up the kitchen. It took a little while before Perugini was sure it was fine, but when she ripped the bandage off I almost fell off the bed in shock. No wonder he wasn't holding a grudge.

Byerly had left a few hours earlier. It was awkward after he woke up. Clary leavened the moment with a few choice jokes that were fairly graphic and involved my powers and how they'd affect someone in an intimate setting. Needless to say, Byerly didn't laugh and neither did I, and when Perugini pronounced that he was in fine form after Forrest's ministrations, no one was more relieved to see him gather his clothes and dart out than me.

"You wanna get something to eat?" Clary asked me as we cleared the Headquarters building. "I'm starving. I didn't get my lunch before we got into it, y'know." His earnestness would have been endearing if he hadn't been trying to beat the daylights out of me only a few hours earlier.

"I'll pass." I left him behind, walking back toward the dorm. I was hungry too, but I doubted I'd be welcomed in the cafeteria for a while—assuming it was even operable at this point. I had a feeling that the below-zero temperatures I'd encounter would make any sort of meal eaten there a chilling experience. And that was just from the pissed-off people. We'd broken a lot of windows, which meant it'd also be literally cold in there.

I went back to my room, closed the door, and dug into the stash of food I'd gotten from my apparent burglary of the cafeteria a few days earlier. There was no doubt in my mind that Wolfe had done it, taking my body for a joyride while I slept. Now that he'd taken control during my waking hours, that was even more worrisome. I could tell Ariadne and Old Man Winter, I suppose, but only at the risk of being locked away and never allowed out again. I didn't enjoy the thought of a cell of my own in Arizona, so I'd decided to play the whole incident off as me being reckless. I assumed it worked. It was hard to say.

"How do I get you out of my head?" I asked the question aloud, but no answer was forthcoming from inside or out. I chewed on a piece of beef jerky and sat down on my bed. No one but another succubus could answer my question, and the only one I knew of was Mom.

It occurred to me that I had a few powers to go along with the fatal touch of my skin, one of which was something Wolfe had called "Dreamwalking"—the ability to touch the minds of others while sleeping. I'd had conversations with Reed and Wolfe by doing that, and all it took was a willingness to fall asleep while concentrating on the person I wanted to talk to.

I was a little afraid to sleep after the control Wolfe had exerted on me, but I was more afraid of having to admit to Old Man Winter and Ariadne that I had him in me and that he was taking control. I finished my beef jerky, chewing slower and taking more time than was necessary even for that tough stuff.

When I was done, I lay my head down on the pillow and clicked off the lights. I thought of Mom, of the house, of the old days when we were a family. I could feel the tug of fatigue on my eyelids, but I lay with them wide open in the dark, worrying over what might happen when I closed them. Wolfe was a monster, a beast that I had once hoped I could put down like a rabid animal. Instead he was cohabitating with me in my own body.

It was bad enough when I only heard his voice. Now he'd set free a crazed man who could explode with the force of a bomb and turned even more of the Directorate against me. If I took the job they offered me, there would be no doubt it was going to be a hostile working environment. Most of the metas I encountered in the halls had done a swift direction change when they saw me coming as I walked back to my room.

I lay there in silence, the only noise coming from the warm air rushing through the vents above me. I could hear a tap-tap-tap of metal in the ventilation system somewhere as the ductwork vibrated from the furnace-heated wind that pushed through it. I could smell that clean, sterile scent that lacked the authentic aroma of a house. The whole room felt less lived-in and more generic, as though it was a room made for anyone. My room at home was mine, made for me. I looked at the blank walls, lit by the glow of lights outside, and thought that maybe I should get a painting or something.

The sheets were cool against my skin. It was comfortable, neither warm nor hot. The spice of the beef jerky lingered on my tongue and I thought about getting up to brush my teeth, but now I was drifting and it was too late. I tried to bring my thoughts back to Mom but things were hazy.

I woke to an insistent knocking on the door. The drowsiness was overwhelming, a fog hanging around my head. I tried to ignore the sound, but the thumping grew louder and the interval between it shorter and shorter until I finally shook off my covers, pulled on a pair of long gym pants and a t-shirt and threw it open. "What?" I wasn't kind about asking.

Zack was waiting outside, Kurt behind him, leaning against the wall. "Get dressed. We're going."

"Going where?" I was so bleary eyed at that point that my

thoughts were coming in fits and starts. For a fraction of a second I wondered if they were there to try and dispose of me.

"We got a vague report of a meta causing some trouble at Eden Prairie Center—the mall we were at the other night, you remember? Ariadne wants you to come along."

"What?" I blinked twice and rubbed my eyes, still trying to shake off the sleepiness. "I don't work for you guys." I shook my head and added, "Yet."

"She still wants you to come along. She said to call it a ride along, and if you didn't like that, to call it penance for the cafeteria because M-Squad is busy chasing down a lead on Gavrikov a hundred miles south of here." He chucked his thumb back at Hannegan, who waited, staring out the window in the hallway. "We'll wait for you out here. Think you can be ready in five minutes?"

I looked at him with great pity. "You don't know many girls, do you?"

He cracked a smile. "Ten minutes?"

I shut the door on him. Thirty minutes later and after some insistent knocking at one point, I joined them in the hall, wearing what was probably my eight hundredth black turtleneck and jeans since coming to this place. I'd pulled my hair back in a ponytail and someone had left another coat for me in the closet, the same kind of black, heavy wool that I'd been wearing all along. I was growing a little tired of the flimsy boots they'd been giving me and made a mental note to ask Ariadne for some with a steel toe if I was going to keep fighting people bigger than I was.

"I don't get it," Hannegan said as we walked toward the garage. "What took you so long? It's not like you're wearing any makeup."

I blushed. "Shut up." I had actually been trying to get my hair to lay flat, but after sleeping it was a mess, which is why it ended up in a ponytail. Again. "What are we going to investigate?"

Zack frowned as he opened the door to the garage and held it for me. Hannegan darted his bulk through first, drawing a look of acrimony from me. "There was some sort of altercation earlier today, some local youths tried to get tough with a guy and he smeared them all over the pavement." Zack looked over at me as he let the door swing shut behind us. "Literally. Two of the youths died, and the others said the guy moved so fast that it was like he was blurry."

"Why are we doing this now? Isn't it Saturday night?" I opened my own door to the car and got in the backseat as usual. "I thought people only worked 9 to 5 on Monday through Friday?"

"Most people do," Zack said. "But you don't wanna be normal, do you?" He winked at me and put the car in reverse, backing out of the parking spot.

I ignored the leering grin from Hannegan. "Perish the thought."

When we got to the mall we circled, passing a department store with a roll of police tape staked out in a circle on the sidewalk. "That must be where it happened," Kurt said.

"You catch on quick," I said. "Was it the 'POLICE LINE DO NOT CROSS' written in big letters that tipped you off or the fact that there's a smear of blood on the sidewalk that looks like someone slaughtered...well...you?" He shot me an acid look that brought a big grin to my face. "What's the matter? Am I annoying you?"

"Annoying is the Facebook statuses my twelve-year old niece posts. You are a hazard," he said, shaking his head. "'Like for a rate'—what does that even mean?"

I frowned. "A rate? Like an hourly rate? Like a hooker?"

"It's for photos," Zack said. "They 'Like' your status and you tell them how you think their profile picture looks."

Kurt nodded his head as though a mystery of the universe had been revealed. I looked at the two of them and asked the dumb question. "What's Facebook?"

"You don't need it," Hannegan said. "You have no friends."

His barb hit home and I tried to ignore it, not bothering to come up with a reply. It's not like he was wrong.

We parked and walked to an entrance after passing the police line for a quick look. "Without a chance to look over the forensics, checking out the scene won't do us much good," Zack said as we entered.

The mall was much more crowded than it had been the last time we were there. It felt like there were people packed from wall to wall in the place, a throng that was moving, bustling. There was a hum as we passed the food court and the smell of all sorts of goodness reached my nose. I stopped and sniffed, feeling a little bit of salivation in my mouth.

"Come on, shut-in," Hannegan said, passing me. "We've got work to do."

"I'm hungry," I said. "I don't know if you heard about it, but someone got into this big fight that destroyed the cafeteria and so I haven't had anything to eat since lunch."

Zack shook his head, stifling a laugh. "Let's sweep the place once and we'll grab you a burger as we come back through."

"But I want a burger now." I looked plaintively at the restaurants and took another deep breath through my nose. "What are the odds some meta killed two people earlier and decided to hang around the scene of the crime?" My gaze drifted to a couple cops, standing off to the side, watching the crowd pass by.

There was the sound of breaking glass behind us and I turned as people started screaming and someone went flying through the air toward us, tossed like a child would throw a toy. "Good odds, apparently," Zack said, reaching into his coat and drawing his gun. "I'd take 'em."

The crowd started pouring past us, women and men alike shouting and crying out. I jumped onto a nearby planter to get a better vantage point. I made it up in time to see two policemen go down hard under the assault of a familiar figure—a guy with metal plates on his body. "Damn," I breathed. I used the planter to vault over the retreating crowd, leaving Zack and Kurt far behind.

Full Metal Jackass held one of the police officers by the arm. The guy was screaming and crying, probably because he was on his knees and his arm was twisted in a way that would not be comfortable at all. After a moment, Henderschott yanked him up in the air and brought him down with sudden, violent force. I heard the snapping of bones and sinews and the officer went still. I stared at Henderschott, he stared back at me, those eyes glaring at me from tiny slits in the metal helmet. "I feel like we haven't been formally introduced," I said. "I'm Sienna, but you probably know that. And you're David, right? David Henderschott?"

He froze, then nodded once, slowly. He had yet to make an offensive move toward me. "So, David—hope you don't mind if I go on a first name basis with you, since you're trying to kick my ass—you're all alone in the big city, you're supposed to hunt down a girl, and so you decide to murder a couple of locals to draw out the group she's hiding with, get a bead on them and follow them back to where they work, am I right?" He nodded. "But something happens you couldn't possibly suspect—they actually bring the girl with them! What fortuitous luck! You must be having the best day." I stared him down. "What a contrast with your life thus far." He was frozen in place. "What's the matter, David? Wolfe got your tongue?" I smiled at him wickedly.

That lasted about two seconds before he grabbed at his belt and threw something at me. It was small and circular, and I flipped back as it sailed only an inch over my nose. I hit my back and sprung to my feet like Mom taught me, already in a fighting stance. I heard a strangled cry from behind and chanced a look.

Kurt and Zack had made it through the crowd and were standing behind me. While I had dodged what he threw, Hannegan hadn't. It was a collar of some sort and it had caught him perfectly, locking around his neck. He was shaking like a cartoon character caught in an electrical current, screaming, and I could have sworn I smelled urine and worse. Zack took a step toward him, but stopped, afraid to touch him as the big man fell to his knees.

I turned back and dodged another thrown collar. I watched it sail by and as I got back up, Henderschott charged at me. I jumped on top of the planter closest to me, vaulting up and running down the side of it toward him. I came off in a running jump side kick, the kind I used to break boards with Mom. I hoped the heavy sole of my boot would protect me from hurting myself on his helmet.

It mostly did. I hit him where his face would be and I felt the shock of the impact up my leg. It hurt, but not too badly. My knee was locked into place and it held. He had been barreling toward me full steam when we hit and the strength of my kick lifted him off his feet, delivering him on his back as I landed just past him. My leg buckled when I hit the ground, but I managed to stagger and recover, keeping my footing as I swung around to deal with him.

He was flat on his back, legs and arms in the air as he tried to rock to his side. "So, who are you really, David?" I said as I took a couple steps toward him. I reached down before he could roll over and grabbed him by the bottom edge of his helmet. I hoped two things—one, that Wolfe hadn't lied to me, that his skin wasn't going to unstick to his helmet while I was doing this; and two, that I was strong enough to pull off what I thought I could. "Just some asshole working for the same people as Wolfe, hunting down innocent metas who don't stand a chance against your superior experience?" I heaved him up and swung him by the head like a hammer at a track and field tournament (thank you, Olympics).

He flew twenty feet through the air and made solid contact with the wall, crashing through the plaster and leaving a massive hole. I knew I had to press the attack now, while he was dazed, or risk getting stomped when he got his bearings again. I didn't know if he was stronger than I was, but he certainly didn't take damage like I did, not with his armor on. I stepped through the hole and saw him on the ground against a concrete wall. We were in a passageway only a few feet wide, with lights overhead.

"Or are you just some sick douchebag who got a hard-on reading Iron Man comics as a kid?" I grabbed him by the leg, dodged the kick he aimed at me, heaved him into the air a few feet and brought him down on his forehead. "Were you the kind of guy who got way too excited at the thought of being Tony Stark? You know he's not a real person, right?" I repeated the process twice more, producing a satisfying clang of his face meeting the concrete before he managed to twist and kick, sending me flying back.

I blasted through the drywall and hit the floor out in the mall. With a cringe, I rolled to my feet.

"You okay?" Zack appeared at my side.

"I'll be fine once I mash this comic book geek into paste in his own suit." I rubbed my chest where the kick had landed. "How's fatboy slim?"

"He'll live," Zack replied as I walked to a nearby wall and opened a box containing a fire extinguisher and pulled it out. "What are you doing?"

"I'm on a roll with these things. Shhh." I held a finger up to my mouth and positioned myself next to the hole in the wall after I pulled the pin out of the spray mechanism. I waited and sure enough, Henderschott didn't disappoint, sticking his head out of the opening. I jumped out and yelled "BOO!" mostly for effect, and depressed the trigger. Foam shot out, covering his face, the slit for his mouth and the eye holes—which was the point. He staggered back, clawing at his face. I ducked through the hole and went beneath his flailing arm to get behind him. Once I was, I put my back against the wall and jumped as he edged backward toward me, using the strength in both my legs to give him a hearty shove.

He went sprawling back through the wall and landed facedown with a clang, his metal chestpiece landing on the tile floor. He ripped at his mask and I smiled; he couldn't see a thing because I had covered his eyes with foam. "Looks like you need some glass coverings on your helmet with some little windshield wipers." I grabbed him by the helmet again and lifted him over my head, slamming him to the ground. Fragments of tile shattered and flew everywhere; I saw Zack dodging away from us. I lifted him again and started to bring him down but I felt him slip out of his helmet on the downward arc.

Henderschott bounced and landed on his hands and knees, his head exposed. His hand came up to his face and wiped the powdery film of the fire extinguisher away from his eyes as he rose to his feet and his hands dropped to his side. His face was scarred, hideous, with scars from his forehead to his chin. One of his cheeks was sunken in, like the flesh had been stolen from it. His teeth were jagged, what of them were left, and his jaw hung at a funny angle.

I cocked my head and looked at him, pretending to appraise. "You know, I liked you better with the helmet. Here." Without telegraphing I threw it at him, as hard as I could. He didn't dodge in time, didn't even get a hand up. The helmet hit him in the nose and a geyser of blood erupted as his head snapped back. He staggered, moaned and his hand came up to his face. After a second of trying to clench his nose with his metal encased fingers I saw him drop one of his gauntlets to the ground. He held his hand over his nose, but it didn't do much good. He was bleeding badly; it was slick down the front of his armor.

He looked to be unsteady on his feet and I pulled my gloves off one by one, tucking them into my pocket. He looked at me, his eyes watering. In the distance I could hear police sirens. Henderschott heard them too, his eyes flicked around and he turned and ran into the department store to the side of us. I took off after him in spite of a shout from Zack. "Get Kurt out of here!" I yelled back to him. "Pick me up outside!"

I saw Henderschott running through racks of clothing, flinging them aside, metal and fabric all around me. There were shouts and screams as people tried to get out of his way. He was slower than I was but he made good use of the obstacles in the store to slow me down. He heaved a circular rack that was five feet in diameter at me and I was forced to dodge to the side, pulling a stroller with a kid in it along with me.

I landed on all fours, staring at the face of a very scared baby before jumping back to my feet and returning to the chase. I heard a scream of gratitude from the kid's mom and the beginning of a serious cry from the kid as Henderschott blasted through the glass exit doors feet first. I wondered why he had jumped through them that way until it occurred to me that with his head unprotected he'd get sliced like lettuce if he had plowed through the glass in a shoulder charge.

The window shattered as he broke through it. He landed

on his back just outside the door and grabbed a trash can from the sidewalk. I had just rounded the corner and was about to follow him through when he whipped the trash can at me. It was big, looked to be encased in concrete, and it blasted through the windows that hadn't already been broken between us. I was forced to throw myself out of the way to avoid a shower of broken glass that cut through the air where I had been standing only a moment before, shredding the clothing on the rack behind me.

I picked myself up from the floor and looked up to find Henderschott gone. I ran outside through the glass he had broken, my hands ready to seize him by the face and drown him in unconsciousness, but as the biting chill of the outside air prickled my hands and face, I looked to either side. He was gone. Just in case, I looked up the side of the building. No sign of him.

What there was a very clear sign of, however, was police presence. Red and blue lights were flashing at the entrances and more were lighting up the night at all corners of the parking lot. A car screeched to a halt in front of me, Zack at the wheel and Kurt sprawled out in the back. Zack made a frantic gesture for me to get in, which I did, and the tires squealed as we made our getaway.

16

"What happened to the armored guy?" Zack's hands were clenched tight on the wheel as he steered us through the parking lot and to an exit that didn't have red and blue lights swarming along the road it led to.

"I don't know." I pulled my gloves out of my pocket and slipped them back on. "He threw a trash can at me and when I got back up, he was gone. I guess he hid in the parking lot."

"Doesn't matter now," Zack said, sending me a tense smile. "With that many police officers on the ground, we would have had a hell of a time apprehending him."

"Not as tough as you think," I said. "All I needed was another minute without the cops and I think I could have put him down."

He looked from the road to my hands, now back in their black leather sheaths. "You really would have done it?"

"I would have knocked him out." I looked at Zack's earnest eyes. "I think I can do that without killing someone. I mean, I don't really want to...you know."

"Yeah." He turned back to the road. "I know."

I looked to Kurt in the back seat. He still wore the collar but seemed to be unconscious and presumably no longer electrified. Zack pulled out his cell phone and made a call to Ariadne, filling her in on the encounter at the mall.

When we returned to the campus, we did not head to the garage but instead to the small underground parking area under Headquarters. When we pulled up in front of the

279

door, Dr. Perugini was waiting along with Ariadne and Kat Forrest. When she saw me, the doctor began wagging her finger before the vehicle had even stopped. "You! I knew it was you!"

"I didn't do it," I said, shutting the door behind me and opening the one to the backseat.

Perugini's eyes narrowed. "Why is it that I do not believe you?"

"Isabella," Ariadne said with excess gentleness. "Perhaps you could make sure Hannegan is all right?"

"I will treat him," she snapped. "What is this?" She leaned down and pointed at the collar around his neck.

"Some sort of electricity-based capture collar," Zack said. "It was meant for her," he inclined his head toward me, "so it's probably pretty damned strong."

She poked at it, and Hannegan jerked and screamed, electricity running through his body. I jumped back from the door, leaving him plenty of space to writhe about. He fell out of the backseat, landing on his shoulder and coming to rest in a heap on the curb. Everyone else kept their distance except Dr. Perugini, who stood only a few inches away. "I need to get this off of him." She whirled to Ariadne. "I need the lab rat."

Ariadne looked taken aback. "Dr. Sessions? Perhaps you remember he was flambéed last night? He's on leave."

"Unless you want Hannegan to leave the planet, get me the lab rat so he can get this *maledetto* collar off of him!" She spun back to me. "You! Make yourself useful and pick him up!"

I did. Zack stared at me as I set Kurt down on the gurney and Dr. Perugini strapped him in across the midsection and legs. She jerked her head toward Kat, who had been watching the whole exchange so far without saying a word, looking like someone in far, far over her head. "Can you tell me how hurt he is?"

Kat blinked a few times then stepped forward, laying her hands on his face. She didn't look quite as tanned as she usually did; in fact, her face had a kind of pallor about it and she looked almost gray. I started to ask if she was okay but I remembered that when last I had seen her she was trying to undo my handiwork on Scott, so I shut up. Her hands hovered over his face. When she withdrew them she appeared to be unsteady on her feet. "He's hurt, but not too bad," she said. "Some nerve damage, I think. Maybe some tissue damage to the heart, I can't tell." She looked up at us, weary sadness filling her face. "I'm sorry. I can't do anything to help him, I'm too exhausted."

"That's all right, sweetie," Perugini said, soothing. "That tells me most of what I need to know." She looked back to Ariadne. "Sessions. I need him now."

Ariadne nodded and pulled out her phone. "I'll have him meet you at the medical unit." We watched as Perugini pushed Kurt inside on the gurney, Kat trailing behind her. Ariadne was on the phone for less than thirty seconds and when she got off, she gave Zack and I a wan smile. "So, it was a trap?"

"I think so." I answered before Zack did, causing him to blink in surprise. "This guy wanted to stir up enough meta trouble to get the Directorate involved and tail your agents back here so he could find me."

"How did you know who he was?" Zack stared me down, drawing Ariadne's attention to me as well.

I almost panicked, then realized that there was an easy answer. "Reed told me this guy was looking for me but he didn't know when he was gonna show up."

Ariadne let out a sigh of exasperation. "You could have mentioned this before."

I smiled weakly. "Trust."

Ariadne crossed her arms in front of her. "Fine. Give me his name and I'll see if we have anything on him." She looked me over. "How are you feeling?"

I thought about it before I answered. "I'm fine. It felt...really good to win a fight for once." I frowned. "Without getting pummeled to a near-death state."

"Try and make a habit of that, will you?" She looked back to the door where Dr. Perugini had gone only moments before. "I don't think *il dottore* is very pleased with you at present."

"I'll add her to a list that's growing by the day," I said. "I don't know what it is that makes people so angry with me."

"Perhaps you insulted her," Ariadne said with only a touch of irony. I let it pass. I actually did feel good. She turned to Zack. "I'll expect your report tomorrow morning." With a nod at me she went back into Headquarters, leaving the two of us alone.

"Anything else you want to tell me about the man in the iron lung?" Zack looked at me with hard eyes as soon as she was gone.

"Umm." I pretended to think about it. "His name is David Henderschott, he's a Pisces, he likes long walks on the beach at night, and his favorite drink is a fuzzy navel. He's also a fan of Streisand movies, and he listens to Nickelback when he's alone and in the shower." I snickered. "I might have made a few of those up."

Zack did not appear to be amused. "I'm not surprised."

"Well, seriously, I mean I don't know anything else about him except that his skin is what binds those metal plates to him." I shrugged, my arms expansive. "I only have the basics."

"And you didn't mention this before, when we first encountered him?" Dark suspicion glassed over his eyes.

"Like I told Ariadne, we're not to the full-trust stage yet." I stared him down. "Give it a little more time, maybe."

"Time," he said with a shake of the head. "I don't know what it's going to take, but I doubt it's just time. I'm gonna go check on Kurt."

He left, and I felt a stab of guilt for lying to him. I exited the garage through a side door, stepping out into the winter night. It was starting to snow, the flakes landing delicately on my shoulders. Had I been less preoccupied, I might have tried to catch one on my tongue. Yeah, I'd just dealt a hell of a beat-down to Henderschott, but he wasn't dead, and for some reason, I suspected he'd be back. Wolfe was still somehow able to take control of my body at unfortunate moments (not that there would ever really be a fortunate moment for him to assume control) and because of him, I suspected I'd let loose an extremely dangerous meta to wreak untold havoc upon the world.

Did that mean anyone Gavrikov killed was another death on my conscience? I already had 254 that I blamed myself for. I'd kept a very careful accounting, sadly enough, and that was the tally. Sure, I hadn't physically killed any of them myself (except Wolfe) but I regretted them all (except Wolfe).

I entered my room, shutting the door behind me. I had been tired hours ago; now I was exhausted. I threw down my coat, noting white powder spots from the drywall all over the exterior and a nice rip along the back, presumably from the fight with Henderschott, and I wondered if I should be worried. Did most seventeen-year-old girls get into as many fights as I did? I doubted this was normal for anyone but the worst delinquents.

A knock at the door jerked me out of my thoughts. I looked at myself in the bathroom mirror. Drywall dust was speckled through my hair and I had three visible rips in my shirt. I sighed and went to the door.

When I opened it, I was faced with a man I'd never seen before. He had a deeply pale face, his hair was brown and short, and his eyes were bright blue, in a shade that glittered even in the dim light.

"Yes?" I looked at him as I spoke. He was older, probably in his thirties or later. "Can I help you?"

"May I come in?" He spoke with a heavy accent that sounded Russian or Slavic.

"Umm...do I know you?" I looked at him, trying to determine if I'd seen him before. He wasn't Henderschott, I knew that much. His face was normal, handsome even, though pale.

"Can I please come in?" He looked back down the hall, furtive, and lowered his voice to a whisper. "I saw you outside and followed you back here so we could talk."

"Saw me outside?" I drew the door a little closer to shut. "There wasn't anyone outside just now. The campus was deserted." I straightened, trying to project the image that I was strong by drawing myself up to my full height. I doubt it worked. At 5 foot 4 inches, I was shorter than almost everyone. Including him. "By the way, telling a girl you followed her back to her room? Not exactly a turn on. Kinda makes you sound like a stalker."

He brought his hand up to his eyes as though he were frustrated, massaging his temples. He looked out at me from behind his fingers. "I need to talk with you." He pulled his hand away from his face and held it up. I stared at it, wondering what he was going to do next when the tip of his finger burst into flames. I yelped in surprise and the flame spread across his entire hand, stopping at the wrist. With an abrupt flick of his fingers, the fire died and his flesh returned.

"Aleksandr Gavrikov," I whispered.

He stared down at me with those intense, blue eyes, and I swore I could see a hint of fire deep within them. "Yes. Now can I come in?"

17

I took a few steps back trying to get away from him, but Gavrikov took it as a sign to enter. He closed the door after checking the hallway again. He pressed his back to the door after shutting it. He was haggard, his face pale, the coloring washed out. Big beads of sweat ran down his forehead and he was breathing heavily.

I didn't want to ask, but I did it anyway. "Are you all right?" The backs of my thighs felt the soft impact of the edge of the bed; I could not retreat any farther without making it obvious.

"What?" His accent was more pronounced and he blinked a few times, as though his eyes were hurting him. "Oh. I have not been..." He stared down at his hands, as if seeing them for the first time. "It has been very long since I last quenched the fire." He took another deep breath. "I don't think I've done it since..." He looked up, concentrating as if trying to recall. "Not for over a hundred years."

"Uh...how do you eat?" My brain screamed at me for my stupidity, asking him dumb questions when I should be jumping out the window, running far, far away from the man who blew up an entire building last night.

"I don't," he said with a grim smile. "When I am afire, I don't need to eat, I subsist on air—it keeps the flames burning."

"Oh." I pondered that. "You don't like being human?"

He looked down at his hands again. "Flesh is easily hurt.

285

Not so with flame; it can be elusive, unquenchable—and it feels no pain."

"Ah," I said, still feeling dumb. "So...what do you want to talk about?"

"Have a seat," he offered. I don't know why, but I sat down on the bed. If he burst into flames, it wasn't likely to matter whether I was standing or not. He walked past me to the window and looked out. "I have to thank you again for freeing me." He looked out through the glass, then to either side as if he were trying to find curtains.

I shook my head when he turned back to me. "The glass is mirrored. No one outside can see us."

His hand touched the window and he looked at it, curious. "So many differences since I was a child. We did not even have windows in the house I grew up in."

"Yeah, me neither, for all intents and purposes," I said, drawing a surprised look from him. "I had a somewhat unconventional childhood."

"Unconventional." He nodded and half-smiled. "I like that. I had an unconventional childhood as well."

"So." I felt a little awkward, and I still wondered why he was here. "Mr. Gavrikov—

"Please," he said with a wince. "Call me Aleksandr."

"Well, I was trying to be a little more formal—"

"I hate that name. " His mouth was a thin line. "I am only Aleksandr."

"Okay." The awkwardness did not abate. "Why are you here?"

He kept his distance, walking over to the desk and the computer that I had yet to use. He pulled out the chair and tentatively sat down in it. He was still sweating profusely and I wondered if he was suffering some sort of withdrawal from not using his power or if he was simply nervous. "Your Directorate—"

"Let me stop you right there," I said, drawing a look of curiosity from him. "They're not mine. I've only been here a couple weeks, and mostly because I have nowhere else to go since that psychotic Wolfe," I felt him stir inside but he kept blissfully silent, "was chasing me down."

"Wolfe?" He squinted at me. "You drew the ire of the beast and yet live?"

"Drew his ire?" I snorted. "I drew more than that."

"No matter," he said with a wave of his hand. "I have heard the legend of this beast. Help me and I will kill him for you."

"Too late. I already killed him."

I watched Aleksandr's face drop, a hint of disbelief permeating his clenched expression. "You killed him?" He pointed his finger at me. "You? You did this...by yourself?"

"I—" I tried to find an easy way to explain but failed. "Yes, I did."

"Very impressive." He nodded. "It explains why you were able to help me escape the lab. But I still need your help to free another."

"Um...free them from what?" I tried not to overly worry about it, but I suspected that my potential new bosses here at the Directorate would be less than pleased that I had helped Gavrikov escape. I suspected they'd be even more peeved if I helped him break someone else out. As if having Wolfe running through my head wasn't a bad enough mark on an employment application.

"The Directorate has imprisoned someone at their Arizona facility." He took a deep breath. "Someone I must help."

"Umm, I don't think I'd be able to help you with that," I said. "First of all, I don't know where that is; second, I have zero pull with this organization." I laughed under my breath, but it died after a second when I caught sight of his face. "Truth is, I've done a few things here that would be likely to land me in their jail before too much longer."

"I need help," he said again, this time almost pleading. "I don't care if it costs my life, I must get this person out of their hands."

"I can sorta understand that. Who is it?"

"My sister, Klementina." He took a deep breath. "Only...it is not her."

I let the air hang with silence while I tried to digest that. "I'm sorry...what? It's your sister...but it's not?"

He stood suddenly and his breathing was heavier. His eyes

moved left and right, and he twitched. "My sister died in 1908."

I started to wonder if I was dreaming, because of the surreal nature of the conversation. Then I remembered that I could talk to people in my dreams, and wondered if me being dead was a simpler explanation. My head hurt, mostly from being confused. "So they imprisoned her corpse?"

"No." He stood and started to pace, his agitation becoming greater as he went. I could have sworn I saw thin drifts of smoke waft from him. "She died...but somehow they brought her back. Except it is not her, because she does not remember anything."

"Like a clone?" I know my eyes were wide, and I was trying not to do anything to set him off, but by this point I was fairly sure he was crazier than I was. And with a psycho nutter in my head, I was probably pretty crazy by any objective measure.

He snapped his finger at me. "Yes! A clone. I worked for...an organization. After a time, I heard rumors that they were working on something. Something for me, as a gift—they wanted my loyalty, to buy it forever. But the facility at which they were working on this gift was lost to an attack by your Directorate. So I went there. I found the scientists that have taken over, but they have no answers for me. All the research was moved when the Directorate took over the facility, and now all that is left are files, some videos. I see her in the records, her face, Klementina's. Somehow they brought her back, but the Directorate took her away with the other research subjects and sent her to Arizona."

I had a sudden, annoying suspicion that sent my skin to tingling. "Describe her for me."

"She was tall, with long blond hair, and green eyes. When I saw her last, her skin was tanned from working our farm. In the pictures I saw, she is still so." He halted in his description and anguish flowed across his features. "Please. You must help me. I have to tell her—" He choked on the words. "I have to make it right."

"Hrm." I thought of Kat Forrest, our new arrival from Arizona, and wondered about the likelihood that Old Man

Winter would have had her brought up here, thinking that he was about to capture Gavrikov. "Did she have any powers? You know, like you?"

"No," he said with a shake of his head. "She was kind, and gentle. When father would—" He looked away. "She would come to me, try to soothe my injuries."

"Uh huh. So would you say she had a," I swallowed, "healing touch?"

"I suppose you could say that." He paced back to the window. "I owe her...an apology. I failed the Klementina that was my sister." He whirled to face me and all I could see was the resolve on his face. "I owe her—this shade of her, at least—freedom. I must get her free."

"I can appreciate that you have," I scoured my mind, "unfinished business or a debt or whatever. But, um...when I said healing touch, I meant literally." He looked at me in confusion. "Can her hands heal wounds, grow flowers, stuff like that?"

His brow was furrowed. "I—"

For the second time since I'd been here, the giant window that ran across the entire wall behind my bed exploded inward. I dropped, using the bed for cover as glass flew over my head and I felt a blast of heat from where Aleksandr had been standing. I poked my head back up and found Clary, skin turned into some dark rock, stepping through the window. Behind him I saw the outlines of Parks, Bastian and Kappler, lurking about a hundred feet away. Gavrikov was already covered in flame again, hovering about a foot off the ground. The influx of outside air had turned the room a frigid cold in seconds.

"We went all the way down to Fairmont tracking you," Clary said as he dropped onto the floor, shaking the room. "Found your handiwork. Blowing up a propane truck, Gavrikov? Not cool." Clary hesitated and his voice turned gleeful. "Actually, I bet it was cool to watch when it happened, but now it's just a big damned smoking crater and a hell of a lot of lanes of I-90 that ain't gonna be open again for a longass while. And that poor trucker's family—"

Aleksandr didn't let him finish his sentence. He heaved two

enormous fireballs at Clary, one of which burned the big man's clothing off, exposing a chest of blackened stone. "I liked that shirt," he said, staring down. "You better not—" Gavrikov fired two more blasts at him, each worse than the last. I felt the air turn superheated around me and closed my eyes to protect them from the intensity of it. Every single bit of the flame that Aleksandr had thrown at him had bounced off, hitting the walls of my dormitory room. The drywall had begun to blaze in four places and the carpet was beginning to catch fire.

"You're gonna burn the girl's stuff up, Gavrikov!" Clary shouted at him.

I was coughing, but I managed to get out, "I don't own much of anything."

"Well you're gonna burn the girl up, and she's already hot enough without your help!"

I was crawling toward the exit to keep that from happening, although I did blanch at Clary's comment. I heard a fire alarm klaxon start wailing and then the sprinklers activated, and suddenly I was no longer hot but now cold again as the chill water soaked me through my already damaged clothing. I stopped at the door and used the wall as an aide to pull myself up. There was smoke billowed at the ceiling, but Gavrikov and Clary were already outside. Kappler, Bastian and Parks were circling them, but keeping their distance.

I watched them out the window. Gavrikov was throwing fire at Clary ineffectually. Clary advanced on Aleksandr but every time he would get close, Gavrikov would fly away and hurl another burst at him, with an occasional shot toward the other three to keep them at bay.

"Aleksandr," I called, staggering to the window. By now, the sprinkler system had almost extinguished the flames in my room and the carpet was sodden, squishing underfoot with every step. "He's invulnerable to your attacks! Get out of here before they capture you!"

With that, Parks, Kappler and Bastian, all three of their heads swiveled toward me, as if seeing a new threat for the first time. "I'm not getting involved in this," I told them, hands raised, as I stepped over the window ledge and into the snow. "Just hate to see him get overmatched and pummeled."

As I stepped out, I saw a ring of black-clad agents in the distance, along with Old Man Winter and Ariadne. They were far enough away that I could only distinguish them by Ariadne's red hair and Old Man Winter's staggering height. It occurred to me that they either saw Gavrikov enter my room through a security camera and figured out who he was or else they were listening and/or watching my room.

Gavrikov floated away, drawing Clary charging after him. He reached a distance away from me and then with a flash of heat and light he shot back toward me, stopping a foot or so away. "Will you help me?" His voice was different now, laced with a kind of crackling heat, something that sounded far different from human.

"I..." I stopped and looked around, the agents closing in, ringing us. Gavrikov turned and saw them and he burned brighter, as though ready to explode. "No! Wait!" He turned back to me, his head whipping around, the fire burning brighter. I held out my hand. "I'll help you, but you can't hurt them! Please! Just go for now, come find me when things have calmed down, I'll..." I looked at the agents charging closer, Old Man Winter with them.

The air grew colder; I could feel it because I was soaked from the sprinklers and I felt ice start to form on the outside layer of my clothing. "Go!" I said. "Get out of here!"

He looked around once more and the heat blazed hotter around him. A short blast of fire filled the air in front of me, knocking me backward over the window frame. I landed on my back with a wet splash in my room, a stinging pain in the hand I had held out which quickly moved down my wrist and stayed there. My head ached from the landing. I saw a streak of fire trace across the sky like an angry star, flaring in the night until it disappeared.

Faces appeared above me, and I didn't feel like I could fight my way through all of them or adequately run, so I just lay there. Clary was the first to climb into my room, followed by the rest of M-Squad, then a few agents, all wearing their tactical gear and black masks. One of them pulled his off; it was Zack. He shook his head at me in deep disappointment.

"Yeah, I know. Save it," I said, feeling surprisingly weak. His disappointment changed in an instant, into something more approaching horror. His mouth was open, his normally handsome face twisted in disgust. "What?"

"Sienna," he gasped as Old Man Winter appeared in view above me with the others. "Your hand."

I looked down at my hand, the one I had extended toward Gavrikov, but it had nearly vanished, all the way to the wrist. There was no flesh, no muscle, no connective tissue left— only bone, scorched, blackened and bare.

18

They took me to the medical unit, where no one spoke to me, not even Dr. Perugini. The rest of them were just quiet, but Perugini was irritable and glared at me constantly, in addition to giving me the silent treatment. She injected something into my other arm and I didn't stop her, mostly because M-Squad was standing around watching me. Before my eyelids fluttered and I drifted off, I reflected that I wouldn't be surprised if I woke up in a confinement cell. Whenever they allowed me to wake up.

I came to still in a bed in the medical unit. The room was dark, and there was not a sign of anyone else, even in the dim light. A machine to my right was beeping every few seconds. My hand hurt, which was funny because it wasn't there the last time I checked. My mouth was dry and my arms were restrained, a large steel bar locked into place across my upper body and another at my waist. My hands were pinned beneath them so that I couldn't even get enough leverage to move them a half inch. My right hand, the one that was missing, was encased in a box of some kind, but it was difficult to see with the bar across my abdomen.

Also, I had an itch on my nose and had to pee worse than I've ever had to before.

I didn't want to say anything, but those two urgent needs brought words to my lips faster than anything else could have. "Hello?" I was hesitant, almost as if I was afraid of who would answer.

The door to Dr. Perugini's office opened and she stepped out, her hair pulled back. I heard the click of her high heeled shoes on the floor and when she got close enough, saw the weariness in her eyes as she stifled a yawn. "I've grown so tired of you I can't help but fall asleep in your presence."

"I've grown tired of being here, Doc." I chafed under the bands keeping me in the bed. "When can I leave?" I felt tension as I waited for her answer.

I was surprised when it was hysterical laughter. She bent double, hand over her face, clutching at her sides. After a few minutes, she stopped, letting out one last chuckle (that I suspected was fake) and turned serious, looking daggers at me. "Oh, I'm sorry," she said, her voice rising, "it takes a while to REGROW AN ENTIRE HAND!" She shook her head self-righteously and took a needle out of her pocket.

"Hold up," came a voice from the door. I looked past her as she turned and saw Dr. Zollers standing there, hands folded over his sweater vest. "Don't administer that just yet." He walked over to the bed and looked me over. "Living a little rough, Sienna?"

"What can I say? I live a hard-knock life." There was a steady, thrumming pain coming from my missing hand. I had a suspicion that I was getting some new nerve growth.

Zollers chuckled. "I wasn't even talking about that. I was talking about the personality conflict you've got going on inside. You know, you versus the beast within?" He leaned closer. "It'd be a hard thing, living your life when you've got Wolfe in your head."

I blinked at him in disbelief, and I felt all the blood drain from my face. "How did you know?"

"Old Man Winter told me," he said, straightening back up. Perugini watched him with a glare and he smiled at her. "He's suspected for a while now. But thanks for confirming it."

"I didn't want to tell anyone," I said. I felt the slow gut-wrench of fear settle over me. If they weren't going to lock me away before for aiding Gavrikov, this would surely do it. "I figured you'd all think I was crazy—or worse. And when he started taking over my body—"

"You should have said something." He pulled out a needle of his own and pulled the cap off it with his teeth. "We might be able to control him with medication. Or some dog treats." He smiled.

"So that's what makes a good headshrinker," Dr. Perugini said with a roll of her eyes, "an overdeveloped sense of irony and a willingness to engage in psychopharmacology."

"That and a bitchin' sweater vest collection." He tugged on the front of his outfit. "You like?"

Dr. Perugini snorted in disgust. "She's in a lot of pain. She needs something to help with that."

He raised an eyebrow at her then looked down at me in the bed. "Pain she can deal with, I think. Crazy is a whole different problem, and typically more serious. Make no mistake, having Wolfe as a mental hitchiker means you are opened up to all sorts of crazy."

I gulped. "Will this make him go away?"

"I doubt it," Zollers said. "This is just gonna take the edge off a little. It's called Chloridamide. It's a low-grade antipsychotic; it hasn't quite passed the FDA yet, but I think it'll be just the thing to keep you calm for a bit while we work out what to do."

I smiled weakly. "Any side effects?"

He shrugged. "Nausea, vomiting, burning while urinating, blood loss, diarrhea, liver failure, renal failure, heart failure, cancer, tumors, paralysis-"

"Nice." I faked a smile. "You're joking, right?"

He laughed. "Wouldn't matter if I was serious. You're a meta, you shrug off all that stuff." He took a sterile swab from Dr. Perugini and rubbed it along my arm where my sleeve was rolled up. "Except the burning while urinating. That would probably still sting."

"There's a cautionary tale in there somewhere," I said, sarcasm tingeing my words. "How did Old Man Winter know I was carrying around Wolfe with me?"

Zollers smiled again as he injected the needle in my arm. "You're not the first succubus to cross his path. I think he's playing things a little close to the vest, though. Big surprise, coming from him, right?" The last words were delivered with unrepentant sarcasm. "But as he is the boss, that's his prerogative, I suppose."

"Yeah," I said, my head starting to grow hazy. "I get the feeling it's not the first time."

"You're probably going to sleep for a while," Dr. Zollers said. "This is something new for your system, and one of the genuine side effects is drowsiness, which is working along with the fact that you're tired because your body is healing. You'll build up some resistance after the next few doses and pretty soon it won't affect you at all, okay?" He took care rolling my sleeve back down, making certain he didn't touch my skin, even with the latex gloves he was wearing. "When you get out of here, you'll go talk to Ariadne and Winter first, but they'll tell you I'm next on your list after them. Doesn't matter if it's day or night, you come see me."

I stared up at him. His chocolate skin was blurring, running into the white ceilings in the most bizarre mixture. "Why?"

My eyes were already closed when he answered. "Because together, we're going to find a way to put Wolfe in a cage."

19

I awoke again to the beeping of the machines, this time with Dr. Perugini standing over me. "Oh, good, you're awake," she said without enthusiasm.

"I had to pee before I fell asleep," I said. "Did I..."

"You got a catheter after Zollers injected you." She delivered the news with a little snippiness. The restraints were gone, though my hand was elevated. The flesh on it looked to be an angry red, with blisters standing out like little white bubbles against a torch red background. Also, now it itched.

I rubbed my eyes with my good hand. "I'm hungry." My stomach growled as if to emphasize the truth of my statement.

"I'll send for the cafeteria to bring you something in a few minutes."

"Poison?" I asked with a smile.

She ignored my wisecrack and used her stethoscope to take my pulse, avoiding touching my skin even with her gloves. "You are nearly back to normal, which is good because I want you out of here as soon as possible."

"Oh, I don't know about that, Doc." I said trying to be coy, but I think it came off sneering. "After all, I can't do any more damage when I'm here. Once I'm out in the world, it'll be no time at all before you've got the medical unit full again."

She let out a hiss that startled me, it was so violent. "You," she said, spitting it at me with the same vehemence as the Italian curses she so frequently used.

"Me what?" I shot back. "I didn't ask for any of this—not my powers, not my mom to disappear, not Wolfe to come after me, nor this Armored Assclown. I wasn't looking for Scott Byerly to grab at me when Wolfe was so close to the surface of my mind, and I damned sure wasn't spoiling for a fight with Clary! I didn't ask Gavrikov to vaporize my hand, I never wanted a single person to die—but they all happened, and I can't do anything about them now."

"*Porca miseria!*" She withdrew her hands and took a step back, and for a moment I thought she was going to spit on me. "Oh, yes, you have had such a miserable time. So many bad things have happened to you, poor you, nobody else has it as bad as Sienna." Her voice came slow, mocking me.

It smarted. Enough to bring that curious burning to my eyes, the one I wished I could disavow. I hate crying, and I wasn't going to do it in front of an enemy. Not that I had many friends at this point. Or ever. "Yes, I have had a miserable time. And you don't hear me griping about it."

"No, not griping," she said, almost as if she were agreeing. "Moping. Sulking. Stewing, I think they call it also? You are a girl, about to be a woman, yet you act like a child."

"Act like a child?" I almost choked on it. "I've had all these things—"

"Happen to you, yes, such miseries, I already acknowledged." She folded her arms. "So sad, no one in the history of the world has ever been through any worse."

"Been through?" I almost choked on my own words. "How about 'still going through'. They're still after me, the people who sent Wolfe—I still have him hanging around in my brain—"

"You are not the first to go through that, either." She shrugged, as though it was a matter of little consequence. "You're hardly the first succubus. They made it through somehow, so will you muddle through—if you ever decide to stop moping."

"You know, I think after all I've been through, I'm entitled to a little— "

"No, you're not." She cut me off. "You're not entitled to a damned thing. This is where Ariadne and Old Man Winter make their mistake with you. Yes, you have had a hard life up to when you left your house, being locked in, boxed up, crated, whatever you want to call it. You leave your house, all hell breaks loose and worse. All this is true. You have had very bad things happen to you, no denying. But you take responsibility for the things you shouldn't and take no responsibility for the things you should." She threw her arms up in the air. "You will be a bitter, pathetic shell of a person if you continue down this path."

"Well, awesome." My words were acid. "Because I've always aspired to be like you."

A self-satisfied smile made its way across her face. "I hurt your little fragile ego, so you lash out. Very mature."

"Yeah." I tasted bile in the back of my mouth. "Well, I'd call you old school but you're really just old. Die already."

Her hand came down and slammed the bed and I jerked back, reacting to the idea that she might actually hit me. "At some point you have to accept some responsibility for your actions. Not Wolfe's. He killed all those people, not you. If you blame yourself for those, you are stupid. But now you want to blame Wolfe for some things you control. It's not always him that lands you in trouble. Bad things happen to all of us. You cannot control bad things that happen to you any more than you can control the weather. It's less about the things that happen and more about how you react to them."

She turned away and stalked back to her office. "Or you can sit here in your little pity party and let whatever life you could have pass you by—be a vegetable of sorriness, feeling bad for yourself, curl up in a little ball and waste away, waiting for momma to come find you and hoping those people you didn't even see die will somehow vanish from your conscience."

"Why do you care?" I snapped it at her, trying to find some way past her infuriating facade. "I'm just another patient, another pound of flesh for you to minister to. Why does it matter?"

She stopped at the door to her office, put her hand on the frame and rested on it for a split second before turning back to me. There was emotion peeking through from behind a wall, some reservoir of feeling that I couldn't see the depth of. "Me? I don't care what you do, whether it's waste away in a little ball of sadness or become a useful, productive, happy member of society. Neither one matters to me." She pointed at me. "But if you're going to do the former, at least leave so I don't have to watch you throw your life away?" She smiled all too sweetly. "Okay? You can go now." She turned and I heard her office door shut softly and her blinds closed a minute later.

20

I pulled the IV out my arm and slapped some gauze on it, along with some medical tape. I didn't see Dr. Perugini, but the blinds in her office moved a few times. She was watching, I knew it. I stormed out in my outfit, burnt and haggard once more. I didn't even want to know how much of a mess my hair was, but I saw it anyway in my reflection on the metal wall.

I rode the elevator to the top floor and found the offices abandoned. I could see out the windows that darkness had fallen. A clock nearby told me it was the middle of the night. Old Man Winter and Ariadne were not in their offices, which both were locked.

I walked out the door to the Headquarters building and found myself in the middle of a light snowstorm. Again. I kicked a trash can savagely, sending it hurtling across a snowfield. I started back toward the dormitory building at a brisk walk, as though I could exorcise the demons of Perugini's words by walking them off.

I was already in the building and almost to my door when I remembered that Gavrikov had burned my room. I stopped outside the door, which had caution tape across it and gave it a gentle push. It swung open and I found the space covered from the outside by several tarps. The broken glass was gone from the floor, as were the carpets, leaving bare concrete.

The room was frigid and the furniture was all gone—desk, bed, everything. The walls had already been replaced, the scorch marks gone, vanished with the addition of fresh drywall. It hadn't been painted yet, giving the place the smell of a construction site.

I walked into the closet and found the clothes were missing. I smiled as I wondered if the Directorate had finally run out of jeans and turtlenecks in my size. My smile vanished when I realized that would bode ill for me; my current outfit was scorched, stunk of acrid smoke and was missing a sleeve.

I heard the scrape of a footstep on the concrete and all my amusement vanished as I sprung to attention. I stood in the darkness of the closet and heard someone walk to the door, opening it wide to let light from the hallways outside my room filter in. "You were supposed to come see me." Dr. Zollers stood in the doorway, leaning against the frame in the way of a man who'd been awakened from a deep slumber and might return to it while standing there.

"Dr. Perugini called you?" I took a step toward him and he nodded. "I thought maybe it could wait until tomorrow."

"Well, that was dumb," he said and turned, then gestured for me to follow him. "Let's go."

I went with him, out of the dormitory building, back to his office. He didn't talk the whole way there and I started to wonder why, but when we got to his office, he poured a cup of coffee and gestured for me to sit. He yawned, took a big swig of his mug and cracked a smile. "Much better." He pointed to his cup. "Want some?"

"No, I had a bad experience with coffee." He looked at me quizzically. "I tried to drink it with meatloaf. It was my first time with both of those things, so..." I shrugged.

"All right, so let's talk." He put his mug down and picked up his notebook, all business. "You've got a maniac in your head."

"Plus Wolfe," I said with a smile.

"Clever. How's it feel?"

"Being clever? Damned good. It's my only vice." I grinned, then turned more serious when he didn't smile back. "He mostly just talked, until recently. Smarted off and whatnot. Told me a couple things—like where his lair was, who the man behind the armor was."

"When did you figure out that he could hijack your body?" He was already writing feverishly, but paused to look up when he asked the question.

I looked away, uncomfortable. "Um...probably when the Science Building exploded and I woke up in the snow with no idea how I got there." I hesitated. "But I had a suspicion before that. Ariadne said they had footage of me breaking into the cafeteria and I didn't remember doing it."

"Sleepwalking is not usually a good sign, even if it's just to get something to eat." He put down the pen and looked up to me. "We have no scientific idea how you drain a soul. Sessions is mystified." Zollers stopped to smile. "He's always a little confused, but this one started him on all the possibilities of other mythological powers that might hold some truth. For example, the ability of a succubus to influence dreams?" He waited, eyebrow raised, as though he were expecting an answer.

"Yeah." I nodded. "I can contact people in my dreams. It's a kind of weird, two-way communication dream. Like a video conference, but entirely in my head." I frowned. "Like a hallucinatory video conference."

"Anything else you haven't been telling us?" he asked with a cocked eyebrow and a half smile. It could have come off as an accusation, if anyone else had done it. Zollers pulled it off like a pro. I think I smiled when I shook my head. "All right. So...how are we going to get the Wolfe under control?"

I shrugged expansively. "I dunno. You're the doc."

"Yeah, and you're the patient and the one that has to live with him in your head." He leaned forward in his seat. "Which means you stand to lose a lot more than I do if we can't. The good news is, Old Man Winter assures me that succubi have been living with this particular quirk for thousands of years, so I assume it's manageable somehow." His face squeezed into a look of concentration. "Obviously it'd be easier if we had some firsthand experience from someone who'd been through it, but..."

"Since I'm the only succubus currently available to talk to..." I shrugged. "On my own again. Big shock."

"Is that a note of self-pity I hear? Cuz' that's not an attractive quality."

I rolled my eyes. "Because being attractive is my biggest concern." I tugged on the shredded turtleneck and stared down at it. "Actually, even if it was, it'd be near impossible given the crap I've gone through lately."

"There it is again!" He pointed the end of the pen at me. "That little quavering of self-pity in your voice."

"Oh, who cares?" I threw my hands up in the air. "So I feel a little sorry for myself sometimes. So what?"

"Because it doesn't do a damned thing to make you feel better." His dark eyes were locked on mine. "Yeah, you had some stuff go wrong in your life. Real wrong, in fact. I feel bad for you. But wallowing in it won't make you feel better."

"This conversation is getting repetitive." I drummed my hand on the arm of the chair to emphasize my point. "Perugini gave me the same line. Couldn't quite figure out her angle, though. She doesn't like me, after all."

"She doesn't hate you. That's important to realize."

"Why is that important?" I was close to beyond caring. "Whether she loves me, hates me, or wants to kill me, the message is the same. You guys think I'm being self-indulgent, I think I'm justified—at least a little bit. It's not like I'm whining to anybody but you about how much my life sucks."

"Got a question for you." He looked me in the eyes. "If you're thinking about yourself and how bad things are for you, how much time and thought are you devoting to other people?"

I glared at him but didn't argue his point. "Go on."

He shrugged. "Seems to me if you're that worried about being alone—enough that you've mentioned it both times we've talked, you'd look at what you could be doing that's causing that situation. Self-involved people don't tend to make the best friends because they're too busy thinking of their problems. Ones that are bitter and hurting tend to be the ones that push others away, sometimes with their actions, sometimes with their barbed tongues.

"So congrats." He clapped twice for me. "You had a bad

past. You've got stuff going on right now that I wouldn't want to have happen to me. But everything you're doing that's alienating people around you is because you're so busy worrying about who to trust that you're missing how trust gets built. You're missing how to connect with people on a basic level and get to know them—and you're giving up the possibility of a future because you're stuck in your past. Your mom, the abuse—yeah, she abused you, get it straight in your head."

"How can I have a future? How can I connect with anyone?" My words came out in a rage, but I felt the burning of curiosity at what he might say. "I can't touch anyone— ever! Without causing them pain or death. And there are a ton of people no longer walking this earth because of me, because of what I didn't do, because I hid while Wolfe was on the rampage, trying to draw me out."

"Yeah, that happened," he said. "But you went into the basement to face him knowing you were going to die, didn't you?" I nodded. "That was your penance, kid." I didn't take umbrage at him calling me kid, surprisingly. "Yeah, a lot of people died at the hands of that maniac, but you didn't wrap your fingers around any of their throats, didn't kill a single soul up to that point and hey—news flash, you haven't killed anyone since! You are not a killer, Sienna. You went in there to die, knowing he was going to eat you alive and do God-knows-what to you. You knew and you went anyway. You faced the fire and you walked out the other side. Yeah, it's not all spun out yet, and there's the little complication of him mind-jacking you, but past examples say that that can be settled. So my question is—are you gonna blame yourself forever for stuff you didn't even do?"

"I..." My voice was ash. "I don't know. They're all dead, and I'm alive."

"Mm-hm. Got a way to fix that?" I shook my head. "Did you do it? Really do it? Go out there and kill a swath of people?" I shook my head again, this time tears welling up. "Forgive yourself. Explain it however will get you through the day—that you couldn't have stopped Wolfe then anyway, that it wouldn't have made a difference, he would have killed just as many people over the next hundred and thousand years he lived—whatever it takes to reconcile in your head that it was not your fault. Anyone who calls you weak for not wanting to die is an idiot. If that includes you, then stop being an idiot."

"I could have gone sooner." My voice was even hollower now. "I don't have a future." I looked up at him and the lump in my throat was big, enough that it was choking me, enough that a little sob escaped and I wanted to hit myself in the chest for letting it out. "I lost my future in the moment I killed Wolfe—when I found out what I was. Even if I got past all the rest, I still have no future, not a normal one anyway. I can't touch anyone. Ever."

"Can't touch anyone? Your mother was a succubus, yes?" He waited for me to nod. "You're familiar with human biology, how we breed? Explain your existence, please."

"I don't know. She could have," I faltered, "artificially, you know. I never asked her the finer details because I didn't know what she was at the time. There are ways it could have happened without touch, real touch—but none of that changes anything. I can't lead a normal life. I can't have a normal relationship. I'm a smoking crater with nothing around for miles." I bowed my head. "I am death."

"Wolfe was death," Zollers said, stern, "and you're nothing like him. You're like...like a fragile package. 'Handle with care'." He stood up and grabbed a blanket from the back of his couch. He threw it around me and hauled me up, wrapping his arms around me in a hug. I started to struggle but something stopped me.

"I just..." I choked out, "I just...want to be normal."

I could hear the Cheshire Cat-like smile in his voice. "You're seventeen years old and you feel like the world is ending around you." He pulled me tighter, and the gentle pressure was reassuring in a way that I had never known. "Sienna...this *is* normal."

21

"Gavrikov wants Kat Forrest." I stared across the desk at Old Man Winter, a few hours later. I felt better after talking to Zollers, more determined. I had some clarity. Old Man Winter watched me the same as always, but next to him, Ariadne seemed to study me with more suspicion, more wariness. "But you probably knew that, because you know her name's not Kat, not originally."

Ariadne's facade of wariness broke and she looked at Old Man Winter, then back to me. "What do you mean? What's her name?"

"Klementina Gavrikov," I said, forcing myself not to smile. It wasn't funny that Old Man Winter hadn't told his top lieutenant, who I liked to snark at, something of vital importance. Or at least that's what I told myself as I mashed my toe into my shoe and against the floor. Nope, didn't smile.

"She's his..." Ariadne blinked three times, then looked to Old Man Winter for confirmation.

"Clone," I said, "or at least that's what he thinks."

"He is incorrect," Old Man Winter said, his hands steepled in front of his face.

"Don't tell him that," I said. "I don't want to see what happens when a human bomb gets told he's wrong."

"She is his sister," Old Man Winter said, as though I had not interrupted. "Not a clone."

"Oh?" I cocked an eyebrow at him. "Gavrikov...Aleksandr,"

I said, softening my tone, "seemed to think she had died in 1908."

"She did not." He stared back coolly. He did everything coolly, dammit...I wished I had his glacial reserve. Half the time I was trembling beneath my badass exterior, just a scared kid. "She is as long-lived as any other powerful meta and as adaptable at healing. Whatever happened to her, she recovered." He hesitated. "Though there is a...cost to her power."

"There's a cost to any power, it seems." I breezed it out, way more than I really felt. "After all, if I used my power constantly, I'd end up with the mental equivalent of a clown car."

Ariadne didn't seem to find that amusing. "Her power, when used to excess, triggers almost the opposite."

"Personalities leave her?" I shrugged. "Explains a lot."

Old Man Winter spoke. "She loses her memory. If a Persephone-type reaches the end of their strength and continues to heal or grow a life, it is at the cost of their own faculties. They become a blank slate, new, fresh. Young again, as well, but at the cost of all they remember."

"Tabula rasa," I said with a breath.

"Indeed." Ariadne took her usual place by the window. "If Gavrikov is after her, it would be best if we hid her for a while."

Old Man Winter gave her a subtle nod. "You know where."

"The basement? You're gonna send her to the basement, right? Where you stuck me when I was hiding from Wolfe?" I shook my head. "Bet the flower girl will love that. Couldn't you send her to another campus?"

Old Man Winter's reaction was subtle, but not so subtle I missed it. "It would be best to have her close at hand."

"Why?" I was curious. "Because you can protect her better here?"

His answer was lacking in any kind of subtlety, and it rattled me. "Because it is not wise to deprive a man who can explode with the force of a nuclear bomb of the only thing he desires—the thing he would be willing to do anything to get."

I felt a pressure deep in my throat, this time less raw emotion and more...unsettling. "Yeah...that doesn't sound too wise."

22

I found myself in the cafeteria. The glass had been repaired from when Clary and I had our epic battle, but the kitchen looked as though it were closed. The options for meals appeared to have been carted in by caterers; the serving buffet (which we had destroyed) was gone, replaced by long tables, heating elements and silver devices designed to keep the food warm. Most of the cafeteria ladies were gone, but the few that were left gave me glares as I passed. Nothing new there.

Until I got to the end. I picked up a croissant and put it on my plate, ready to face the inevitable crowd to see if there was a place for me to sit by myself. "Excuse me?" The light voice jarred me and I looked up to see one of the cafeteria workers. She was young, a little older than me, but round of face and with big brown eyes. She smiled at me and I looked back at her. "Thank you. For warning us to get out of the kitchen before it happened."

I stared at her. "What?"

"When you and the big man fought into the kitchen?" She indicated with her eyes to the corner where M-Squad sat, Clary laughing his way through three plates piled high in front of him. "You warned us to get out right before it exploded." Her eyes were sincere and her smile was sad. "I just wanted to say thank you."

"I wouldn't have let you get caught in the middle of what was going to happen." I managed to croak the words out. In truth, I didn't even remember saying anything to them. If I had, it was an offhand comment, no more worthy of recognition than anything else you do without thinking about it.

Yet somewhere, deep inside, I felt Wolfe, almost buried, stir in revulsion. Zollers had given me a second dose of the drug after our session in his office, and the drowsy effects were considerably less (though I was still tired). I could feel him though, in there somewhere, upset at what I had done.

Naturally, it caused me to smile back at the girl. "You're welcome."

I walked across the cafeteria to where a guy sat at a table for two, all by his lonesome. He looked, honestly, like someone had stolen all his happy. I stopped in front of him. "Is this seat taken?"

"What do you want?" Scott Byerly's voice was worn resignation, all shot through with deadness.

"I want..." I took a deep breath. "I want to apologize." I swallowed my pride and went on as he looked up in surprise. "There may have been some other influences pushing me toward what I did to you, but it was still wrong and ultimately it was on me. I...I'm sorry."

He seemed to awaken, his glazed-over eyes darting back to life. His leg slid the chair out across from him and a nod of the head was all it took to convince me to sit down. "You know where Kat is?" He looked at me with a little hope.

I froze, mouth full of Swedish meatballs (they were awesome, way better than anything Mom made). "Yes," I said at last. "She's in the basement at Headquarters."

He leaned across the table and whispered to me. "Why is she there?"

"It's kind of a long story."

His eyes narrowed. "Maybe you'd prefer to talk about something else? Like, say, damned near killing me?"

I swallowed hard. "You didn't accept my apology, did you?"

"Not yet. Why is she down there?"

I looked around on all sides of us. Nobody seemed to be very interested, and no one was in earshot. "She didn't tell you?" I waited until he nodded before I looked around one final time. "The exploding guy, the one that trashed the Science Building—he's after her. Wants her released from here."

His face flushed. "She's not a prisoner. She's here because she wants to be."

"That's not how he sees it."

His hand slammed the metal table and left an indentation. "It doesn't matter how he sees it; she's not going anywhere with him!"

"Take it easy. I'm not arguing with you, just telling you the why."

He stared off into space and then his eyes came back to me. "You're a succubus?"

I chewed on the next Swedish meatball, almost afraid to answer. "Yeah."

"They don't have the greatest rep among metas."

I laughed. "Hard to see why that could be; we touch people and they die."

"'I'm death'." He shook his head. "That's what you meant when you said you were Kat's opposite."

"She can give life," I speared another meatball with particular violence, "all I can do is take it away."

"Hm." His eyes were sad. "You haven't asked me about my power yet."

"Huh?" I looked back at him. "Oh, yeah. Well, can you blame me? Until now, I was afraid a mutual discussion of powers might out me for the weirdo I am." I turned my gaze back to my plate. "Besides, I didn't really want to...um..."

"Be civil?"

I didn't glare, but it was close. "Connect...with others until now. I didn't want to be disappointed or burned or let down." I gritted my teeth. "In case I had to leave abruptly."

"Leave, huh?" He picked at his food. "I could see that, if I was in your shoes. So why weren't you more pissed when you found out I wrote that note?"

I flicked my eyes away from him but allowed a slight smile. "With as many real, legit, scary enemies as I've got, it seemed like a waste of time to worry about one more person trying

312

to take a shot at me for something I already blamed myself for."

"Yeah, well, that's kinda dumb as far as reasons go, but I'll take it, I guess. I took a cheap shot at you, you took one at me, we're square."

I frowned. "Yours helped drive me into a confrontation with a maniac that nearly killed me."

"Yeah, well yours almost ended up taking my soul."

"Touche."

"It's all a wash—" He stopped, looking past me then nodded slightly. "Here come Zack and Kurt."

They stopped at our table, Zack looking a little haggard and Kurt looking like a blowfish ready to explode (I saw a nature documentary once). "Hey, guys." Zack started talking, a little wan and more pale than usual.

"What's the matter?" I leaned back in my chair, arm draped over the back as I looked up at them. "You look like you've had a rough day," I nodded to Zack, "and you look like you were forced to skip breakfast, lunch and dinner." I smiled at Kurt.

"Byerly," Zack said as Kurt glared at me, "Old Man Winter and Ariadne want to see you."

"Oh?" Scott pushed his tray away. "Might as well go see what that's about."

He stood and left, with a nod to Kurt. Zack watched his receding back for a minute then turned to Kurt. "Can you give us a few minutes?"

Kurt didn't look amused. "Keep your hands to yourself," he said to me.

"You sure?" I shot him a dazzling smile. "I could goose him a little bit, then maybe you'd look smart and commanding by comparison." Kurt emitted a grunt and stomped off toward the serving line. "Don't eat too much! You don't want to mess up your girlish figure!" I turned back to Zack with a smile. "I just love antagonizing him. It's like having a little piggy whose tail I can twist any time I want."

He looked at me warily. "You feel better after making him feel worse?"

I ate another Swedish meatball. "Always."

"Did Dr. Zollers give you a psychological explanation for why you do that?"

"Don't need one. It's because I have time and wit to spare."

He sighed, his body uncomfortable. "There's things you haven't been telling me."

I put my fork down. "In fairness, there are things I haven't been telling anyone. It's not like I've been looking forward to admitting I have Wolfe rattling 'round up here." I pointed to my head.

"And that you can touch other people's dreams," he said, quiet. He wouldn't meet my eyes, but I thought I recognized his posture. He looked like he'd been betrayed.

"Not something I really wanted to brag about; first because I didn't know I could trust you guys, then later, because I forgot."

His eyes were accusatory. "You should have told us."

"I did." I felt a little guilt burning at me. "It just took me a little while."

He stood. "That's not fair, Sienna. We've been square with you since the word go and you've been holding out." He shook his head. "I guess I expected more."

"More what?" I snapped the words back at him. "You broke into my house, remember? I didn't come looking for you guys, you stepped into my room with a tranquilizer gun, not vice versa. You talk about trust but you act all surprised that it's been two weeks and I'm not ready to sign on and be a member of the team. Forgive me for not jumping in and telling you all my dirty little secrets yet."

He stared at me evenly. "Feel better?"

"A little." I sighed. "Seriously, though. I've been through the ringer with Perugini, Zollers, and now you. Can we just...talk about this later?"

"Yeah." He looked down at his feet. "Ariadne wanted me to tell you that they assigned you a different room and moved your stuff."

I took a slip of paper from his proffered hand. "Good timing, actually. This drug Zollers has me on to suppress Wolfe really takes it out of me."

"Sleep tight," he said. "I gotta get back to guard duty."

"Zack," I called after him when he started to leave. "I'm sorry."

He nodded his head, just slightly, causing it to bob as he looked back to his shoes. "I know."

"But it's all out there now." I looked at him hopefully. "I don't think there's anything else. No more secrets." I smiled. "Now it's just decisions to make."

He smiled. "Get to making 'em, will you? Kinda curious if I'm gonna be working with you or not."

"You think you could handle that?" I smiled at him impishly. "You might have to partner with me someday."

He looked up as though he were thinking about it, then slowly nodded, only a hint of a smile visible, arching his lips up. "I think I could handle that. You know, for the good of the team."

I flung my napkin at him in mock outrage. "For the good of the team, eh?" He laughed, retreating. "Keep yourself out of trouble, will you? Watch out for men on fire." I looked at my hand, now covered in a glove and felt the itching that was coming from the last layer of skin returning. "They tend to leave a mark."

He nodded and gave me a playful salute as he left the cafeteria, Kurt trailing behind him. I rubbed my eyes. Zollers' drug was putting me down. I looked out one of the windows; it was probably midday, the cloud cover overhead still masking the sun from my sight. I walked back to my room across the grounds, the white blankets of snow still covering to the horizon. It wasn't quite as oppressive today, for some reason.

I followed room numbers in the dormitory to the one on the paper Zack had given me. I opened the door, feeling like I was ready to collapse. I found a room inside that was the same as the one I'd had before, which gave me a moment's pause. I unlaced and then kicked off my boots, pulled off my shirt, throwing it straight to the garbage, then stripped off my jeans.

I fell on the bed, on my back, not bothering with the covers. The cool air tickled my exposed skin and below me I felt the silky smoothness of the bedspread. The slight smell of construction was in the air; my old room was just down the hall, after all. I still had the faint aftertaste of Swedish meatballs lingering in my mouth and I hoped that when I woke up there would be more in the cafeteria. If there weren't, maybe I could order them directly from the caterer. Or that nice girl in the cafeteria who thanked me. Saving her life had to be worth a few Swedish meatballs.

I stared up at the lightbulb above me as my eyes started to shut. They squinted as I tried to force them open one last time, but it didn't work. I saw the light and it distorted and glared, reminding me of the rising flame in the darkness that was Aleksandr Gavrikov, hovering above me like what the sun must look like, lighting up everything around.

I closed my eyes, and he was there, on fire, just like all the times I had seen him but one. The flames flickered where his skin should have been, an inferno in place of flesh. I could almost smell the burning, taste the ash that should have been in the air. He edged closer to me but there was no heat, and for a bare moment I couldn't figure it out, then I did. "Dreamwalking," I whispered.

He floated closer, and I watched the fire recede from his hands, from his face. His dark hair appeared, then his nose and eyes. He looked less pallid than he had when I'd seen him in real life, and the world around us coalesced into my old room. Fire crawled up the walls, slowly burning around us as his feet touched the ground. The silence consumed me like the flames, surrounded me. He stood in front of me, staring into my eyes. "You said you would help me."

I felt the burn of his almost accusatory stare. "I was trying to save your life." I looked away, walked a few feet in the other direction, as though placing distance between us could absolve me of my promise. "Not to mention the lives of the others."

His voice came back to me, cold and empty. "Did you tell them? Do they know what I want?"

"I did." I turned back to him. "They're not going to release her. They think you're a dire threat."

I saw the haunting in his eyes, the guilt in his face. "I am a dire threat. I am more than that. I am death; more death than they can handle."

I didn't blink away from him as he said it, but a part of it hit home. "Sounds familiar. I don't think they're going to just give her up on your say so, though."

He took a deep breath, in and out, closed his eyes and smiled. "Then I'll convince them. I'm in Glencoe. It's only about fifteen minutes west of you. Tell them to come and see me and we'll talk."

Something about how he said it raised the little hairs on the back of my neck. "You just want to talk? Why do I doubt that?"

"I have a message for them," he said with an icy calm. "Tell them. I'll be waiting in the middle of town. Bring as many of their men as they'd like."

I felt a chill of fear. "I don't love the way you're saying that."

He burst into flames again, his brown eyes replaced by soulless, dancing fire. "Tell them. Tell them to come to me. I'll be waiting." He remained afire, but dimmed in my sight until he was gone, replaced by the light over my bed.

23

Less than an hour later I was cruising west along a highway with Zack and Kurt. In front and behind us were vans, one filled with agents and the other carrying M-Squad. It was early evening, the sun was already down and a bitter cold had followed with the darkness. The thermometer on the rearview mirror said that it was already -4 degrees and I had to guess it was falling. We had streaked through a small town already and now there were snowy fields to either side as we chugged along the highway. I could see the lights of another town in the distance, and as we drew closer the car slowed.

"He said he's waiting there for us?" Kurt looked back at me, nerves plain on the older man's pudgy face.

"Yeah. You scared?" I didn't put much venom into it, but I didn't need to. His gave me a nasty look anyway.

"If you're not, you're stupid." He turned forward again. "In case you missed it, he burned your damned hand off."

"I can see why you're worried; that'd be a fatal blow to your sex life."

I heard the seething noise he made in the front seat, but he didn't turn back around. Zack let out a soft chuckle and when Kurt turned on him, he said, "What? It was funny."

We turned off the main highway at an intersection. After passing a few cross streets, we turned left onto the main street of the town. There was a bank across from a flower shop and a jewelry store. It looked idyllic as we pulled into the empty parallel parking spaces. I stepped out onto the curb, over the small mountain of accumulated snow, onto the sidewalk.

I felt my breath catch in my throat. My coat was buttoned, my hands were covered with gloves, but I could still feel the frigid air creeping in. I felt like I was going to turn to ice. I looked down the sidewalk, but it was empty, the streetlights shedding the only illumination. There was not another running car in sight. Agents exited the van behind us, their weapons concealed under heavy coats. Clary stretched as he got out of the vehicle in front of us, Parks and Kappler joining him as Bastian walked around from the driver's side.

The agents huddled around Bastian, who didn't order anyone to come over to him; they just did it automatically. I watched and nudged my way into the circle next to Zack as Roberto started to speak. "We're gonna sweep Main Street. If you find him, do not engage. Keep eyes on target and maintain a healthy distance." I watched him touch his ear and realized he had some kind of miniature microphone in it. I looked around the circle and saw the others with the same and felt a little irritation that I hadn't been offered one. "We're sticking with the same strategy. This guy can kill any of you faster than you can pull a trigger, so Clary is our point man when we find the target."

They were all so focused, they didn't notice a familiar (to me, anyway) figure step out of an alley across the street. "Uh, guys?" I felt the pressure of so many sets of eyeballs lock onto me, but I kept watching Gavrikov as he stepped onto the road, heading toward us. "I have eyes on target," I said, prompting them all to swivel.

"Scatter!" Bastian's words echoed through the night as Gavrikov burst into flames in the middle of the street and shot twenty feet into the air. Three fireballs lanced out from his hand and destroyed the front van in an explosion that sent me to my knees. He sent another blast at the jewelry store behind us, a bigger one that caused the storefront to burst into flames.

Zack was huddled behind the car, along with Kurt. One agent was down after the explosion of the van and I couldn't tell from where I was whether he was hurt badly or not.

Disregarding most of my good sense, I stuck my head up over the top of the car and yelled to Aleksandr. "Is this the message you wanted to send?"

"Hardly," came back his reply. "That was to get your attention. You have two minutes to get back in your cars and leave this town. After that, you have until tomorrow morning at six A.M. to bring Klementina to me at the top of the IDS tower in Minneapolis. After that..." He let his voice trail off and even from where I was behind the car, I could see a smile. "Well...you'll see in two minutes. Let us call this town...a warning. For what will happen if you don't deliver."

I heard Bastian scream behind me. "Back in the cars! Move out!"

I ignored the frenzied action around me and focused on Gavrikov. "Aleksandr...this isn't the way."

He drifted to the ground as the first van shot out of its parking place. Agents were hanging from the side and I looked back to see the one still left on the sidewalk. He was not moving. I heard Zack shout my name from the car. His hand extended toward me, fingers dangling in the air between us. Kurt was struggling with him, trying to pull him into the vehicle. One of the agents in the back punched Zack in the back of the head and he crumpled forward, slumping against the dashboard as the car pulled away, slinging snow and mud.

"They left you behind." His words were calm, icy even, as his burning eyes continued to stare at me.

"Yeah," I said. "They didn't try to shoot you, either. I'm guessing they took your threat seriously."

"They should." The flames around his hand died, revealing his fingers, then his arm. He took hold of my hand, and I let him. "These are men who understand nothing but force. They are weapons, turned loose when necessary, meant only for destruction." He sounded weary, bitter even. "I know these men. I was one of them, but on a grander scale."

"Should I be afraid?" I said it without fear, but I had the beginnings deep inside, the smallest well of concern.

"You have nothing to fear from me; you are not one of them." He pulled the glove from my hand as he said it, twisting the leather in his grasp. The cold in my hand didn't bother me. "There is only one thing that matters to me now. I want her; she is my penance. Freeing her is all I have left. Everything else..." He grasped the glove and it burned in his hand, turning to cinders and slipping from his fingers into the wind. "...is ashes. Those who stand between us have everything to fear."

He stepped closer and I blanched. "Not to worry, little *matryushka*. You could not run fast enough to escape what is coming to this town if you had to." His hands, now flesh, reached out and enfolded me and I felt the ground lift away under my feet. "I will help you." I was flying, the wind whipping my hair, the freezing cold streaking in my eyes, drawing tears and an exclamation of joy from me. The fresh, cold air hurt my nose and lungs as I breathed it in. He held me tight, carrying me through the night, his flames gone and his body pressed against me.

I felt us slow as the ground approached, and my feet touched solid pavement. I felt his arms let loose of me and his face drifted away. My teeth chattered involuntarily, and I looked behind him to see the town of Glencoe, the faint city lights glowing against the clouds above. "Remember my words," he said, hovering in front of me. "Six in the morning—less than twelve hours, on top of the IDS Center in downtown Minneapolis. Otherwise..." He burst into flames again and streaked into the sky, headed back toward the town.

Headlights on the highway raced at me, slowing at the last possible second. A van rolled up and the passenger window came down. "Girl!" Clary opened the door before the car even came to a stop. "Get in here! Old Man Winter will have all our asses if you get left behind."

My eyes were transfixed on the distance. Glencoe sat, still shining into the winter sky, a little beacon of light in the middle of the nothingness of snowy fields. "Hey!" Clary reached out and started to grab my arm, then must have thought better of it, because he waved his hand in front of my face. "We gotta go!"

"We're fine," I said. "Just wait." The second car full of

agents came to a skidding stop behind the van and Kurt popped his head out, eyes bulging in shock at the sight of me.

I couldn't take my eyes off the town. I knew there were people there; there had to be. It wasn't just some ghost town, some empty place...

A light glowed in the middle of town like a cigarette lighter sparking, then there was a flash that blotted out my vision. A wave of force came rushing toward us and the only thing that kept me on my feet was that I reached out and grabbed Clary's arm as he turned to steel, anchoring me in place as the shockwave hit. I turned my eyes back to Glencoe as a mushroom cloud of fire and smoke blossomed into the sky.

The smell was what hit me first, the awful smell of something burning. I could hear the rumble still in the distance as the cloud drifted up into the sky, mingling with those already hanging above Glencoe. Little pieces of ash began to rain down around me like a falling snow and my hands were numb, along with my nose, followed by the rest of me.

Zack opened the door to his car and staggered out, his hand clutching the back of his head, stumbling over to me. "You okay?" He asked the question while I still stood transfixed, staring at the remains of the small town where I had been only minutes before—and which was now wreathed in flame and smoke, the last resting place of its occupants. "Are you all right?"

His glove brushed my cheek, stirring me back to reality. The explosion had died down, but the light of the fires still burning in Glencoe reflected off the clouds, casting the night in the most surreal light. "I'm fine," I said, barely managing to get the words out. "How many people lived in that town?"

Zack's hand was still on the back of his head, but his gaze fell. "I don't know. Several thousand."

I spoke in a voice of awe. "He killed them all. He'll do it again, Zack, he's going to do it again in less than twelve hours if he doesn't get what he wants. He said this was his warning—his only warning."

322

"Even Gavrikov wouldn't be so insane as to..." He didn't finish his sentence. His eyes stared back into the distance, to the fires that still burned. "He wouldn't. He just wouldn't."

"He would," I whispered. "He will," I said, this time with firmness. "Unless we bring Kat to the tower tomorrow morning, he absolutely will.

"And you can kiss the city of Minneapolis goodbye."

24

We stood arrayed around Old Man Winter's office, Zack glaring at Kurt, Ariadne leaning against the wall looking faint, the four members of M-Squad situated behind me and Kappler. Ostensibly because we were women, we were the ones that got the chairs. I didn't care; I was tired. Old Man Winter sat behind the desk, his usual inscrutable self.

"Why's the girl in here for this?" Clary's words came out in a kind of low whine. "She ain't an agent or one of us."

"She's here because she's got more experience dealing with the hostile than any one of us," Bastian said in a clipped tone. "He spared her life from the explosion, after all."

"He did more than that," Kappler said in a heavy, Germanic accent. "He picked her up and carried her clear." Her eyes were narrow by nature, now they were slitted, her thin face looking like nothing so much as a snake. "I think a good question would be 'Why'?"

"He perceives me as the only one who will reliably deliver his message." I was so tired, I didn't care if they thought I was in league with Gavrikov. I guess technically I had let him loose.

"I figured it was because he was sweet on you." Clary said it with a suggestiveness that made me assign him once more to the category of "idiot" in my head. Thank God Wolfe was quiet.

"He's gonna do it," I said. "You don't get Kat to the top of the IDS Center, he's going to send you another message and

324

this one will be a hundred square blocks of flattened buildings and an inferno at the middle of it."

"He won't do it," Ariadne said, quiet.

An uneasy silence settled over the room, broken by me. "Um, yes he will. He's already done it once tonight just to prove his point. If you've already killed several thousand to make a point, why not a few hundred thousand to actually get what you want? Just because you hope he doesn't, don't think that bears any resemblance to what will actually happen."

"He will do it," Old Man Winter said, quieting the whispers I heard from M-Squad. "Let there be no doubt. But equally certain is the fact that we cannot turn Kat over to him. She is an innocent and he is...unstable to say the least."

"Sir, we'll do as you order," Bastian said, "but the girl compared to a several hundred thousand lives..."

"You will eliminate him," Winter said.

"I'm sorry," I interrupted again. "But you guys had a chance to go a few rounds with him down in South America, as I recall, and it's all well and good that you captured him, but it seems like the nuclear option wasn't on the table for him back then, for whatever reason. Now it is." I turned around to find Bastian staring at me, along with Parks, while Kappler glared and Clary looked on with a kind of cluelessness. "If you couldn't take him down then, when he wasn't up to using his full power, how are you going to do it now?"

Bastian turned to Parks, the wizened guy with his long, gray hair and goatee that looked like it was almost white. "This time," he said in a gruff voice, "we get to kill him instead of playing the capture game, ma'am."

"Oh, good," I said, "you get to try and kill the walking nuclear bomb. That won't piss him off at all."

"We'll kill him, ma'am." Bastian's voice was filled with conviction. Too bad it didn't convince me. "With the kid gloves off, my team can take him down."

"Glorious." I'm pretty sure the wearying effect of the drug I'd been taking leeched any chance of me pulling off false sincerity, so I didn't bother. "Couldn't you maybe...I don't know, lay the situation out for Kat and see what she thinks? She might consider it an acceptable risk to jump through his hoops for a bit to keep him from blasting the city into rubble."

Old Man Winter's reply was like a crack of thunder. "Placing her into that situation is unacceptably risky."

"For her? Or for the city of Minneapolis?" I leaned forward, tossing all caution aside. "You're playing a hell of a game here. You're placing the survival of an entire city on the idea that these guys—no offense," I waved vaguely at Kappler, who was still glaring at me, and the rest, sitting behind me, "can kill him before he can go critical. That's a pretty big risk considering he dropped me off in the countryside, flew back to the detonation site and I bet he wasn't there for more than ten seconds before he went off. That means if they err even slightly, a lot of people die." I saw no change in any of the faces around me, except maybe Ariadne, who had grown slightly paler. "More than I let die, that's for sure."

Old Man Winter's cold gaze burned over my head to Bastian. "You have your orders."

I bit my lip and wrenched myself to my feet. "I sense my presence is no longer needed here. If you'll excuse me, I'm going to go find a quiet place to hide until the atomic apocalypse is over." I didn't exactly storm out, but I did break the door behind me. Because of my super-strength, not because I was in a snit. Well...maybe a little bit of both.

I seethed in the hallway and all the way down to the lobby, which was quiet save for a few guards standing around. Different than agents, they wore tactical vests and held submachine guns slung across their chests. A few of them had stood guard outside my door back when they held me in the basement room where Kat was currently residing. I wondered where they recruited all these yahoos. They should have given them all red shirts.

I started toward the front doors, intent on leaving, on running far, far away, wanting to go someplace where I'd never again have to be put in a position where all I could do was sit back and watch a massacre take place. I slammed into the glass doors at the front of Headquarters, sending them rattling open on their hinges. I would have been far more satisfied if they had broken, but apparently they were designed to be abused by metas, because they started to pull shut on their own.

I stood outside, sucking in the cold air. It all came down to power—it always did. With Wolfe, I didn't think I had the power to face him, to beat him. It turned out I did, but I didn't know that at the time. Now, with Gavrikov...I was really unsure. It wouldn't take him much to vaporize me if he got pissed, that was certain after what I saw him do in Glencoe.

But what if Kat was with me? I thought about it a little harder. He wanted to save her, to keep her safe, more than anything. If I took her to the rendezvous point, I could get close to him, maybe stop him. I stared at my hands. It didn't have to be for good, just long enough to get him contained again. I cringed. In another one of those boxes. Surely I could keep him out of sorts until the Directorate could find a way to crate him up again. I didn't like that option, but I liked it better than the thought of him waltzing away with Kat, who didn't even know him, or letting M-Squad and that assclown Clary take a crack at him, or worse, letting him level Minneapolis.

To save the city, to make amends for what I had let happen with Wolfe, I was going to have to consign Aleksandr Gavrikov to a fate I was all too familiar with—confinement in a coffin-like containment chamber. A box of his very own.

I cursed the irony of the whole situation, of how it had all played out. I turned back to Headquarters, studying it and wondering how I was going to make this work, when I heard the scuff of a shoe behind me and turned, ready to strike—

Scott Byerly stood there, hands in front of him. "Whoa, I'm just here to visit Kat," he said, circling around me toward the Headquarters building.

What was it he had said about writing me that note? "Hey," I said. "You have family in Minneapolis?"

He stopped, turned back to me. "Yeah, my whole family is from around here. Why?"

I steeled myself for what I was about to have to do. "Just thought you might want to know—the guy that blew up the science lab?"

He furrowed his brow. "Gavrikov, wasn't it? Russian guy?"

"Yeah," I said. "He just nuked Glencoe, you know, that town west of here."

Scott's face paled, his dark complexion going white. "I heard about that earlier. I didn't know it was him."

"Yeah, well…" I tried not to belabor the point, but I wanted to draw him in a little, "…I was there when it happened. He did it as a warning to us—to show us what would happen to Minneapolis if we didn't bring Kat to him by tomorrow morning at six."

"Excuse me?" The reaction was immediate. His jaw clenched, he took a step toward me, his fist balled up. "He threatened the city?"

"Said he'd nuke it to the ground," I said. "Bye-bye, City of Lakes."

He turned without saying anything else, started to stalk off. "Where are you going?" I asked.

"To stop him," he tossed back.

I ran after him. "Wait. You can't just attack the guy, he'd turn you into the stuff you find in the bottom of a microwave."

Byerly stopped, but the fury was still evident on his face. "What, then?"

"Well," I said, "M-Squad and the boys have a kill order—"

"Not good enough," he said and started to walk again. I reached out and grabbed his arm, keeping my grip firm enough to catch his attention but not enough to spin him around. He did that on his own, looking like he was ready to explode on me, his face red, his eyebrows locked into forty-five degree angles, and his mouth in a thin, downturned line.

"Whoa!" I held my hands out in a gesture of peace. "I'm with you on this one. I think M-Squad is gonna foul it, big time. I mean, if you heard about how things went for them in South America, or you've had five minutes to consider that Clary is the linchpin of their strategy, you recognize that giving them this shot means that you're basically comfortable with turning Minneapolis into a burning wasteland. Which I am not," I said, trying to reassure him and dislodge his angry face. "But you can't just charge after him without a strategy."

"I have a strategy," he said in a kind of roar. I took a step back, more out of concern for his safety than mine. "I find Gavrikov and I drown his ass."

"And a fine strategy that would be," I said, suppressing all my smartass instincts for the sake of my penance, "but may I suggest one that's got a better chance of success?"

He drew up to his full height, arms folded in front of him and said, "I'm listening." His posture said he was not, but I was desperate enough to try anyway.

"The thing you have to understand about Gavrikov is that he thinks Kat is a clone of his sister," I started.

"Why the hell would he think that?"

"Because she actually is his sister," I said, "and don't interrupt me. He feels guilty because he thinks she died or something, back in the early 1900s, and the only thing he cares about is giving her spiritual successor a chance at freedom." I paused, taking a breath. He looked at me with less rage, but also a look that told me he didn't totally understand. "Because he thinks the Directorate is keeping her imprisoned here."

He frowned. "They are."

"Yeah, but not totally," I said. "I mean, if she really wanted to, she could probably get out—speaking from personal experience."

He looked at me with skepticism. "I have my doubts. Kat doesn't strike me as much of a fighter."

"Doesn't matter. Anyway, if she's with me, he won't go nuclear because he doesn't want to hurt her. That gives me a chance to neutralize him without anyone having to get hurt. I can bring Kat back here, safe and sound, and keep Gavrikov down." I stared him in the eyes. "You know I can."

He blinked, then his eyes clouded with suspicion. "Why are you telling me this?"

I took a deep breath. "Because I don't know how to drive. And I don't exactly know where I'd be going. And Kat...well..." I hesitated. "I don't think she's going to come willingly just on my say so."

He held his hand up to his head. "So you want my help convincing her, too?"

"I do. I really, really do." I added a note of pleading to my voice. "Look, if we leave this up to the so-called pros, I don't know how it's going to turn out, but I suspect bad. Really bad. And I mean, yeah, we could hide here, we're probably safe from the blast radius, but..." I didn't know what else to say.

Scott Byerly just stared at me, with those eyes, those cool blue eyes. "One question. If you answer it honestly, I'm in."

I smacked my lips. Why did my mouth always dry out at dramatic moments? "What is it?"

He stared so hard I almost felt his gaze burn through me. "Why are you doing this?"

It felt like he'd wound up a swing with a sword and punched it straight through the middle of me. "You know why," I said, my mouth even drier than it had been a moment earlier.

He shook his head, impassive. "I really don't. Why?"

"Because..." I swallowed, trying to get the taste of ashes out of my mouth. I felt like I could taste them, like I had been on the main street in Glencoe after the detonation, and it reminded me of blood. Blood in my mouth, from fighting with Wolfe. "Because the last time someone super-powerful held people hostage I let the clock tick down and a lot of people died." My hand came up, brushing the hair out of my eyes where the wind had tossed it. "I felt helpless, weak, like I couldn't do anything. I can't ever undo the consequences of my inaction. But this..." I tightened my hand into a fist in front of me, "putting down Gavrikov...this I can do."

He looked left, then right, then back at me. "I'd shake hands with you, but I know what that would do to me. I'm in. Let's go get Kat."

25

We took out the guards with minimal effort. We did it fast because I was afraid Old Man Winter would get wise to our idea and send M-Squad to protect Kat. Fortunately, he must have had them working on the plan to take out Gavrikov, because there was no siren, no klaxon as the last guard slipped from my grasp, unconscious. I cracked the knuckles of my right hand, the one that had been burned off just yesterday.

Scott raised an eyebrow at me. "Feeling okay?"

"Better than him." I picked up the card key looped to the guard's belt and ran it through the reader on Kat's door. It slid open and she jumped up from the bed, looking a bit haggard. Her hair was tangled, as though it hadn't been washed for a few days, and she wore a tank top and sweatpants. I started to crack wise about the way she looked but remembered a similar visit I had in this room from Zack and wisely shut my mouth. "Check out time," I said, drawing a look of surprise from her.

"What are you doing here?" She looked to Scott. "Both of you."

"He was coming to visit," I chucked a thumb to indicate him. "I was coming to give you a choice. Did they explain why you're down here?"

She nodded. "The man who blew up the science building thinks I'm his sister, and he's after me."

"I'm told you actually are his sister," I said, "but the point

331

is, he doesn't want to hurt you. He thinks you're being imprisoned and he wants you set free."

She looked around her gilded cage, with its wide-screen TV and luxurious private bathroom. "Um, I am being imprisoned."

"Perfect, let's escape," I said and started to turn.

"Wait!" The alarm was urgent in her voice. "I don't want to go to him, either!"

"He's going to blow up the city of Minneapolis if we don't turn you loose and bring you to him. He already blew up a town west of here to prove he'd do it." Scott delivered the news I didn't want to.

I watched Kat as she took it in. She was always pretty; enough to make me jealous, at least. She was like the cheerleader everybody loved because she was just so sweet and perky and innocent. Even despite her somewhat unwashed appearance, she was still pretty. That annoyed me.

But I watched her face crumple as Scott's news hit her. Her green eyes lost their glow immediately, turned hollow. Her face fell, her eyes dropped to the floor and her shoulders slumped. She took a step back, staggered, as if she had been punched in the stomach, and she dropped back to the bed. When her voice came, it was no more than a whisper. "He did that...? For me? Because...because of me?" She looked younger than eighteen years old, and as I watched the emotions played across her fine features like the ravages of age. I felt a tightness inside that I didn't really care to explain. It was all too familiar.

"He's going to blow up Minneapolis if we don't get you to him." Scott closed the distance between them and knelt down. "But it's okay. Sienna and I will protect you from him." He looked at me. "He doesn't want to hurt you, Kat. Sienna can take him out; you've seen what she can do." He smiled. "And you know what I can do. He's not going to try and hurt you, but even if he did, we can protect you—we can stop him."

"I...I don't want to go." Her words were choked. "I don't want anybody to die, but I...I don't want to go."

"It'll be okay," he said. I watched her eyes; the soothing

wasn't working. "We can stop it."

"It may not be okay." I said the words before I could stop myself, drawing a startled look from her and a venomous one from him. "Aleksandr Gavrikov just killed thousands of people to convince us to bring you to him." I took a deep breath, and watched the horror in her eyes. "He's a monster in his way, but I know him—or rather, I've gotten to know him. You're the only thing that matters to him. He thinks you're caged, tortured, and he wants you free. There's something in the past between the two of you that happened that he desperately wants to make amends for. I think he needs you to forgive him for something. It's all he cares about."

"Why would you tell me this?" The first hint of tears broke through onto her face, sliding down her cheeks, sparkling in the overhead light. "I don't want to face him, he's a monster!"

"He is. But if you don't, a whole city of people will die." I took two steps forward and reached out to Kat, putting my gloved hand on hers. "When Wolfe was tearing up the city, I sat back because I was afraid, because no one could fight him, no one could face him, and I didn't think there was anyone that could stop him. I was wrong. I could stop him the entire time, but it required a sacrifice that I wasn't willing to make. I sat by as more and more people died until I couldn't stomach it anymore." I saw the emotion flicker behind her eyes. "People are already dead, and it's not your fault, and there's nothing you can do about it. I don't blame you for not wanting to go. I wouldn't blame you if you wanted to run and hide, because Aleksandr is broken inside, and powerful, and that is a dangerous combination.

"But I'm going to fight him," I said. "Whether you go or not, I'm going to try and stop him. I doubt I'll be able to do much because he's fast, and could vaporize me from about a mile away before I even got a chance to take a shot at him. But I'll be there." I set my chin. "Because I know what it's like to stand by, to hide and to have people die, to have those deaths on my conscience. And I won't do it again."

She stared me down, her eyes brimming, full of emotion

and the flickers of guilt and fear, and I wasn't jealous of her any more. All I felt was sorry for her, sorry that she had to experience the same hell that I had, but with even larger consequences. "But..." her voice trembled. "...you..." she looked to Scott, then back to me, "you'll be there? I won't have to go alone?"

I squeezed her hand in mine, felt the depth of her plea all the way through me, tingling my emotions and bringing me back to a morning in the basement of my house where I was forced to confront all my fears. Alone. "We'll be with you every bit of the way."

She looked ghostly, but her eyes came back to life and she stared back at me. "Okay." Her voice gained strength. "All right."

Byerly gestured toward the door as he swiped the card I'd handed him from the guard and it slid open. He and I led the way after giving Kat a minute to change into something more protective than a tank top. She came out wearing a black turtleneck, black leather gloves, jeans and a black wool coat that looked terribly familiar. I frowned at my "twin" and she shrugged. "They brought me here and didn't bring any clothes. This was all that was left in the closet." She looked down at her pants. "The jeans are kinda loose on me, though. And short."

Instead of smacking her, I started toward the stairs, the two of them in tow. I rounded a corner and a guard stood in front of me. I chopped him with a hand to his throat, causing him to gag, then slammed him in the side of the head with a punch that put out his lights. I turned to tell them to watch out for any other guards, but I found Scott letting loose of a guard of his own and Kat pummeling another with a flurry of punches that sent the man reeling, finishing him with a reverse side kick that caused him to ricochet off a wall. When she caught my surprised gaze, she smiled. "What? Everyone always thinks I'm so delicate because my powers are healing. I'm a meta; I've got strength too."

"And moves," I said. "Where'd you learn those?"

She shook her head as we started toward the lobby doors. "I don't know. My memory is pretty fuzzy before Arizona. I don't know if you're aware of this, but Persephone-types have limits on our powers. We can only heal—"

"Until you run out of strength, then it starts leeching your memory. So you don't remember anything?"

"I still have skills, abilities," she said as we brushed out of the double doors, Scott looking skittish as he trailed behind us. "I can understand other languages, I can fight some." She frowned. "I can farm. Don't remember how I learned that."

"Memory loss isn't cool," I said, "but every time I kill someone with my power, I absorb their personality into mine."

"Eep!" She blanched. "So does that mean that the psycho you killed..." She paled.

"Yep," I said, pointing to my skull. "I've got Cujo panting in my brain. The good news is Doc Zollers seems to have found a way to keep him under wraps." I yawned. "Unfortunately, there do seem to be some adverse effects."

We ran to the garage, which was unlocked. Scott grabbed keys from a box that held a bunch of them, and I knocked out the guy in charge of watching them and stuffed him under the desk he sat behind. We made our way through the garage as Scott pressed the button on the key fob until he found the right car, a nice little SUV. I sat up front with him and Kat took the back seat. She looked nervous as we pulled out and headed for the front gate. Scott pushed a remote on the visor and the gate opened, fast.

We shot out and took a quick turn, zipping down the road at about sixty. "I'm not exactly an experienced driver," I said, "but I'm pretty sure there are speed limits."

"I'll keep that in mind," he said, mumbling.

The night was black, and up ahead there was a van pulled off to the side of the road. Scott slowed as we drove by and I caught a glimpse of the logo—a local telecommunications company—and saw, very briefly, the worker jump out of the way for us as Scott screamed by. "You know, saving the city isn't going to do us a ton of good if we end up killing a hundred people on the drive there."

He rolled his eyes, but I saw him slow the car a little. We passed through Eden Prairie as the clock on the dashboard flashed 4:30 A.M. Traffic was almost nil, a few cars as we got on the interstate. Kat was a silent hole in the backseat, and I cast frequent looks back to make sure she was still there. Scott gripped the wheel, white-knuckling it, the tension evident on his face as he steered us onto another major freeway. As he angled the vehicle onto it, I could see the lights of downtown Minneapolis in the distance.

The outline of the skyscrapers was pressed against the horizon, lighted shapes that gave form and substance to my thoughts of a city and what it should look like. A thousand windows gleamed and shone out at me, and some sort of lighted display shimmered in a rainbow of colors atop one of the buildings. They grew closer slowly as the distance between us and the city faded. We passed a few cars here and there, and soon enough the skyscrapers towered above us. "Which one is the IDS building?" I asked.

Scott craned his neck to look up and he pointed at the tallest one, made all of glass and jutting up into the sky. "That one."

I studied it. "He picked the biggest. I bet he didn't want a sniper shooting down at him."

Scott cast me a glance. "Really?"

I shrugged. "If you think about it, it's probably the only way he's vulnerable. I'd bet most low caliber rounds would melt before they hit him. Anyone attacks him physically, he can keep them at bay long enough to explode. But it's hard to concentrate enough to blow up when your brains got sent out the other side of your head."

"Good point. Wonder why they didn't do that to him in Glencoe?"

I kept my eyes on the building that dominated the skyline above us. "I think they were going to try, but they didn't get a chance to set it up. Which reminds me, M-Squad will be here in an hour or less. Best we're done by the time they show."

Scott eased the car onto a side street and found a parking garage. I heard the noise of another vehicle somewhere below us as we stepped onto the street. I watched another telecommunications truck pass us and I felt a tingle of nerves. It was the cable company for the entire Twin Cities, after all. Not unusual to see a couple of their trucks out, even at this time of morning. "Let's go," I said as we entered the glass lobby.

All around us was a dramatic promenade with trees, restaurants and shops. I was a little surprised, but I kept my focus as Scott led us up escalators to a bank of elevators. I stood looking at him and Kat, watched him take her hand and squeeze it with encouragement. I felt a pang of jealousy that turned to sadness by the time the elevator dinged and the doors opened. I shuffled in after them and watched them hold hands. I tried to feel good for them, really I did. Kat needed comfort right now. So did Scott, surely. So did I, when it all came down to it. But as per usual, there was no one there to hold me.

We reached the top floor and stepped off the elevator. I saw a sign for the stairs and headed toward them, Scott and Kat trailing behind. I looked up, and sure enough, there were steps leading up to a locked door. I broke it with ease and we stepped out onto the roof, the winter air chilling me as I led them out under the open night sky.

Snow was piled in drifts around edges and corners, but it looked as though someone had shoveled the roof to keep it mostly clear of snow. A few shacks and some ducts and machinery sat atop the flat surface, but most of it was empty space. I walked across to the far side, wondering if Aleksandr was here yet.

I heard Kat and Scott's footsteps behind me, soft and even as we padded our way across the roof. "Aleksandr," I said. The wind carried my words away. I had not bothered to shout it.

"Here." A small voice reached me and I saw him step out of the shadow of one of the boxy structures. He wasn't in flames and he wore different clothes since the last time I'd seen him. "You brought her..." He said with something approaching joy, then his eyes alighted on Scott and they narrowed. "And another."

"Precaution," I said. "I had to break her out of the Directorate myself. I needed help." I glanced back to Kat and then to Aleksandr. "There's something you should know; this isn't a clone of your sister. It's actually her."

His face wrinkled in confusion. "How is that possible?"

I shrugged at him. "How are you possible? She's a meta, like us. She's what they call a 'Persephone-type—'"

"I am familiar with them." He said it brusquely and then took a couple tentative steps closer to her. "You presume her memory is gone, then?"

I looked back at Kat and gave her as reassuring a smile as I could muster. "Ask her yourself."

He took another step and stopped, still a dozen paces from her, as if he were afraid she would disappear like a mirage when he got closer. "I was sure I lost you." He took another step, cocking his head to the side, examining her from all angles. "I watched you burn, watched your skin flake off in the fire." He swallowed and his cracked lips brushed together. "It was an accident. I am...so sorry. It was my first time...to learn my power, and you thought I was hurt, and tried to help me...and I couldn't...couldn't stop it in time—" He choked on the last bit. "I am so sorry, Klementina."

"My name is Kat," she said, her voice faint. "Katrina. Or at least that's what they've called me for as long as I can remember."

He hesitated, then stepped again, now only a couple arm's lengths away from her. "Your name was Klementina. You are my older sister."

"I don't remember." She held tight to Scott's hand, but didn't step back. "You said you last saw me when?"

"1908." Another step closer. I knew I was going to have to act soon, but I almost couldn't bring myself to break up the reunion. Gavrikov was so fixated on her, little pieces of his joy at seeing her were breaking through his normally impassive mask. "We grew up together on our father's farm outside Kirensk."

"I see." Her words were soft, contemplative. "Is he still alive, like us? Or our mother?"

Aleksandr seemed to shudder. "Mother died giving birth to me. Father..." He hesitated, looked away, then turned his face back to her but the joy was gone. "Father died on the same day I thought you did."

There was a cold silence, broken only by the howl of the wind around us. When Kat spoke, it was with more chill than the tempest around us. "Did you...kill him too?"

I cringed and waited for Aleksandr to respond. He did, but not as I expected. "I did," he said with a glint of pride. "He was not kind to you, Klementina, nor me. He...tortured us. You would come to me, to help salve my wounds after he beat me. And I would console you, after..." He broke off, unable to finish his sentence. "You remember nothing?"

Kat licked her lips and looked to Scott for reassurance. "Before the lab, I can't really remember anything concrete. I remember a light. I remember...burning. Some other things...a baby crying. But it all seems very far off, so long ago."

"But not what he..." Aleksandr shuddered, emotions tearing through the formerly seamless mask of his face. "Not the nights, not...what he did...?"

"I don't—" Kat looked away, to Scott, then to me, then stopped mid-sentence and screamed, but it was too late.

I didn't see the fist come at me, didn't sense it coming in all the air rushing past us on top of the tower and by the time I reacted to Kat's warning, it was too late. I felt my legs buckle as the fist hit the side of my head and I went flying, smashing into the metal ducting that ran across the roof. It collapsed on impact with my shoulders and back and I came to rest, blood dripping down the side of my head to my cheek. I blinked, trying to assess the damage. It hurt. A lot.

I tried to rise to my feet but before I could move, he was on me, hand around my neck, suffocating me. David Henderschott, his armor now all black, clutched me in his metal-clad hand, his cold mask blacked even to the eyeholes, not a trace of remorse or humanity visible as I started to pass out.

26

A fireball exploded behind Henderschott, causing him to stagger and drop me. I would have been thankful, but one of his armored feet caught me as he stumbled and tread on my midsection. I felt pain in my guts like I hadn't experienced since Wolfe stuck his finger in my belly and started ripping. I tensed my abdomen and heaved, knocking him off balance and sending him clattering to the ground. I clutched at my stomach, fighting for a breath and left with a perfect view of Kat, Scott and Gavrikov.

"She's not coming with you," Scott said, holding his hand out, palm facing Gavrikov, who had already burst into flames.

"Do not stand in my way," Aleksandr said, that lifeless rumble in his voice again, the guttural horror that he sounded like when he was an inferno. His hands were out, one beckoning to Kat, the fire put out of it, the other pointed at Scott. "I will not warn you again."

From where I was, rolling in agony, cursing the day I left my house, it looked like Scott smiled. "Do you know what I am?" He seemed to be asking Gavrikov. "Ever heard of a Poseidon-type?"

I didn't have time to connect the dots before water rushed out of Scott's extended hand, a pressurized force that knocked Gavrikov back thirty feet into a radio transmitter. I heard the impact; I compared it to the blow I'd taken when Henderschott hit me and thought myself the lucky one.

I started to pull myself up, trying to ignore the pain as I hoped it would subside, but Henderschott was faster. He was on his feet and reached me as I got to one knee. His armor had been painted, all black, causing a bizarre contrast against the night sky, a shadow in the dark. He grasped at me and I lunged. My shoulder hurt as I caught him under the arm, knocking him off his feet with a tackle that I rolled out of. He landed on his back, once more looking like a turtle.

I leaned against some ductwork as I tried to stand up straight. His foot had done some damage to my insides, of that I was certain. I grunted at him as he stood up. "First you were obsessed with Iron Man. Now what?" I stared at his black armor. "You a Darth Vader wannabe? Or just a big Johnny Cash fan?"

He took a swing at me and I dodged, falling to my knees and rolling away. Not my preferred method of avoidance, but it worked. His fist caved in the ductwork I had been leaning on, burying his arm up to the elbow. His metal mask swiveled to look at me and I dodged his other hand, wrapping my arm around his neck, trying to get my upper arm between the metal plates to choke him out.

It was a stupid move on my part. He brought his helmet down and pinned my wrist between his chestplate and the metal that protected his chin. I heard the bone break and I cried out as he grabbed me by the arm and tossed me through the air like I weighed nothing. For the few seconds I was aloft, it was like flying with Aleksandr again.

I landed, skidding and bouncing until I hit a wall. My arm screamed at me where he'd broken it, and I was gritting my teeth. I caught a flash as Gavrikov flew nearby, a thick burst of fire shooting forth from his hands in a continuous stream like he was holding a flame thrower. I saw it meet a similar burst of water on the other side and saw Scott Byerly with a cocky smile on his face, pushing Gavrikov back while keeping Kat behind him. Gavrikov shifted directions and Byerly countered, a jet of water hitting Aleksandr across the chest, snuffing out the flames and revealing his bare chest beneath before it ignited again.

Full Metal Jackass came hammering across the roof at a

run, and I had only seconds to move out of the way. He clipped me with a clothesline that caught my good wrist and shoulder and flipped me. I landed on my back and all the breath rushed out of my lungs. I watched him lift a foot to stomp and I had the presence of mind to reach up and catch his foot, pushing and sending him teetering off balance as he fell again to his back. It was one of the only weaknesses I saw from him, the fact that it took him a minute or so to get up. Like a turtle.

I got to my feet, clutching my injured wrist to my side and ran away from him. It wasn't my best plan but I was hurt badly, and needed time to recover. Or formulate a strategy. Or hurl myself over the edge to end the aches and pains. Maybe the last one, actually.

I slumped behind one of the outcroppings on the roof, trying to catch my breath and assess the damage, and remembered my last fight with Henderschott. It brought a little smile to my face because it had gone so much better than this one. And it was all predicated on the fact that in both fights when he sucker punched me, I ended up dancing to his tune, to my detriment. Then the question became how to get him to dance to my tune, how to beat him, get the Full Metal Jackass out of his armor. Or kill him. I looked out over the edge of the building and realized it was a long way down. One question was answered.

I heard him behind me over the dull roar of the fight between Scott and Gavrikov, the weight of his footsteps causing the roof to tremble. He sounded like he was heading in the wrong direction, and I breathed a sigh of relief as I worked out how I could get him to the edge and fling his sorry metal ass over it. I hoped that would kill him; I thought it would. If it didn't, I'd have to find something else, but as far as strategies went, it was the best I had with the little I had to work with.

I peeked over the top of the little radio shack I was hiding behind and saw Henderschott moving parallel to me. With ease I got to my feet and stayed low, trying to creep up behind him. I had an idea, but it was based on stealth, on being able to sneak up and turn the momentum of the fight.

Making my way around one of the ducts, I slid through the snow beneath to come out a little behind him. I kept low, almost walking hunched over, creeping up behind the armored man. I took a last step and started to reach up. I planned to grab him by the helmet, drag him down with a horse-collar tackle, pull him to the edge of the roof and send him flying. I didn't want to kill him, but I had a feeling it was down to him or me, and I wanted to live. Really, truly, down to my bones, I wanted to.

My last step led me to a small patch of ice that wasn't visible. My boot found it and I went down with a loud cry as the landing jarred my already hurt innards. Henderschott swiveled and was on me before I could recover, one hand on my neck and the other on my broken wrist, pinning me against the rooftop. He wrenched hard on my hand, drawing a scream of pain from me, then another. I hit him with my free hand, right on the head, doing no damage to him but causing him to yank my wrist so hard my vision blurred and I started to black out.

I thought I was crying but I couldn't tell through the pain. All I could feel was the anguish from the damage he'd already done and the screaming of the nerves through my forearm as he bent it back. A thrumming sound in the back of my consciousness made its way through my ears, the blood rushing and making a connection for me.

The cable company truck I'd seen at the Directorate and outside the tower were the same. He'd followed us. Somehow he'd found the Directorate and watched. Sure, Scott nearly ran him over, but he'd recovered and managed to tail us all the way here, follow us up the elevator and show up when we least needed him to.

I saw Gavrikov and Scott, still facing off in the distance. I complimented myself on my knowledge of how Aleksandr would react; he hadn't exploded yet. Then I felt the squeeze of Henderschott's iron grip on my neck and wrist again and I realized that was of little consolation as he hauled me into the air and dangled my feet over the edge of the tower. I felt the brush of the freezing wind as it rushed past my face and then felt the push as his hand let go and I started to drop.

27

My broken arm reached full extension and his grip on my wrist stopped me. I screamed again, the surge of pain down my arm dragging cries from my lips. The sound of blood in my ears had gotten worse, so bad that I could tell that Henderschott was talking to me, but I couldn't tell what he was saying, only hearing fragments. "Submit...do not resist..."

I twisted and dangled, hanging by my broken wrist and staring fifty-something floors down to the plaza below where we had entered, the atrium lit up like a light with spiderwebs of darkness running through it. There were no clouds for the first time I could remember since leaving my house, and the first strains of light on the horizon told me it was close to sun up. The noise in my ears was getting worse, and finally I realized that it wasn't the blood rushing through them, or the wind.

A Black Hawk helicopter dropped into view from above. Henderschott looked up and froze, almost as if he were shocked at its appearance. I could see the members of M-Squad inside, the door was open and someone wearing a tactical vest was hanging out as it swooped low over the rooftop. It didn't slow down and I saw the person jump out about ten feet above the roof as the helicopter started to pull up and gain altitude. I saw an M16 with an underslung grenade launcher go skittering as they landed rather badly.

Henderschott dragged me in from the edge and tossed me to the ground, then placed his boot on my chest. I felt the pressure of his weight lean onto me and I couldn't breathe. "Don't...go...anywhere." His words came out in low gutturals but I understood every one of them.

"Why...would I go anywhere?" I put my good hand on his foot. "I like this...spot," I said, fighting for breath. "It's you who...needs to move!" I lashed out at the last, rocking my hips and pushing my legs up so my heels hit him in the chest, sending him teetering off balance. I pulled in my leg again and then kicked him, knocking his feet out from underneath and sending him toppling.

I stood, ignoring the fire in my side. "You know," I said, "I used to spend hours encased in metal too. Probably wasn't as pleasant as how you're doing it." I tried to grab him by the leg but got a metal boot to the chest for my troubles. If possible, the already painful injury to my stomach multiplied and moved north. I suspected he had broken some ribs. I curled up into a little ball and tried to catch my breath, then attempted to force myself to stand. I watched as Henderschott got to his feet and I backed away from him, taking one hobbling step at a time.

"Hey!" The shout caught my attention, forcing me to look back and see Zack, holding the M16 with the barrel slightly elevated, pointed at Henderschott. I covered my ears and dived to the ground as I watched Henderschott's metal head tilt in confusion (or maybe amusement) at the sight of Zack. He didn't stay confused (or amused or whatever) for long. A low, whumping noise cut across the roof as the grenade launcher on the bottom of Zack's weapon fired and it caught Henderschott right in the armored chest and exploded, sending him backward, arms pinwheeling, over the edge of the building.

I got to my feet and lurched over to Zack, still holding my chest and side. "Big strong man, come to save me," I said, cringing from the pain.

"You looked like you needed some help." He pointed his gun in the air.

"He sucker punched me," I said. "Again."

"Yeah?" He looked at me with a little acrimony. "Maybe this wouldn't have happened if you hadn't totally disregarded what Old Man Winter told you—"

"Yeah, yeah," I said, mocking. "I don't see the city leveled, so don't count my strategy out yet."

"What was your strategy again?" He looked at me. "Get pummeled by the man in black while Scotty and Kat tried to avoid getting toasted?"

"You should talk." I took a deep breath and cringed at the pain from it. "If I'd had a helicopter, none of this would have happened. That armored assclown followed us from outside the campus." I looked back at the helicopter, which was swinging around for another pass. "Besides, what was your strategy?"

"Parks is up there with a sniper rifle," he said, pointing to the Black Hawk. "Clary's jumping down on their next pass, but if we get even a sign that Gavrikov means to explode, Parks will drop him."

"Why didn't Clary jump the first time?" I looked at him. "You know, with you?"

He looked a little hesitant, almost embarrassed. "I uh...I wasn't supposed to."

"You fell out?" I tried to hide my amusement.

"I jumped out," he said, "to save you. Clary was tasked to Gavrikov, he wouldn't have helped you in time, so I forced the issue. The crosswinds are a real bitch up here, though, and it wasn't the best moment to jump. Bastian is having a hell of a time keeping the chopper steady."

"Makes me wonder how Parks is gonna pull off his shot," I said, starting to limp toward the other side of the roof. I could see Gavrikov and Scott still going at each other, the flame versus the water.

"He'll pull it off," Zack said. "But honestly, we don't really need him to." He pulled his gun up and stared down the sights. "I can riddle him with holes if we get closer."

The helicopter swooped overhead and Clary appeared at the door. It looked like Bastian was trying to keep it level but there was serious chop and the helicopter was swaying in the wind. I watched Clyde yell out something that sounded like "Geronimo!" and jump, his skin turning to darkened steel on the fall. He was aimed perfectly, and hit the roof only a few feet to Gavrikov's left, causing the flaming man to look up from his battle with Byerly. I watched Clary land—

And disappear, falling through the roof. I turned to Zack. "Boy, am I glad we amateurs left this crack mission in the hands of you professionals. Marvelous work."

He shot me a pained look. "I'm sorry, I gotta—"

"Go," I said. "Do what you have to in order to stop him." I started to say more but a black metal glove hit Zack across the back and he went flying, his gun skittering off the roof, his body stopping just before the edge. I wheeled and threw myself back in time to dodge Henderschott's next assault. "Next time we throw you over I suppose I'll have to make sure you really fall." He swung at me again and I started to panic; I couldn't evade him like this forever.

Something stirred inside me as the fear took over. He had beaten and pummeled me, hurt me again in a way I would never get used to. Whatever it was came from deep inside, was primal, destructive, awakened by my purest survival drive. It was familiar, a feeling and a consciousness that had been suppressed by the drugs that I hadn't taken in...I glanced at the lightening sky...over 24 hours.

"You've got more lives than a cat, Henderschott." I shouted as I dodged another attack. The pain started to fade and it felt like it had in the cafeteria when I had attacked Scott; I was there, but parts of me were starting to respond to someone else's command. I vaulted over him, the pain in my side masked from my feeling it, and I grabbed hold of him before he could turn to face me, somehow gripping him with both hands. This was going to hurt tomorrow. A voice, deep and sinister, something absolutely nothing like my own, filled my ears with a hissing, lustful sound. "But not as many as Wolfe."

My good hand grabbed at his helmet and pulled, ripping at it with a strength far beyond my own. I twisted, dragging him off his feet, tearing at the metal surrounding his head, knowing it was attached to his skin and ripping as hard as I could. I could hear him screaming inside his suit and his hands reached up for me but I fended them off, turning him over, stretching out of their reach even as he hammered at my wrists and I ignored it, blind to any sort of pain at all.

With a last, wrenching tear the helmet came off, filling the world with Henderschott's scream. His face dripped blood as the helmet came off and my hands brought it down across the back of his head. I heard a sickening crunch of metal on bone. Henderschott went limp, but I wasn't the one who brought the helmet down again and again. My hands did it while I watched, dumbstruck, his head turning to little fragments of flesh and bone before my eyes.

"Wolfe," I said, whispering, "enough." But he was in control and I had none. My hands grasped Henderschott by the remains of his head and dragged him across the roof to the edge. I lifted him up in one hand, his eyes dead and rolling, but they found mine for a second and the awful, hissing voice of Wolfe came back. "Wolfe should have done this a long time ago, but Wolfe showed you mercy. Now there is only the mercy of gravity."

Henderschott spoke, but it was hard to hear. "They'll keep coming for you." His eyes were locked on mine, even as his head lolled back at a sick angle.

I wanted to ask who, and I fought, fought for control of my voice. "Who...?" I said it, and it came out as a whisper.

He blinked his eyes, the blood trickling down from the top of his head falling into the lids, turning them red, as though he were crying tears of blood. "Omega."

Before I could ask him anything else, my hands drew him back and heaved Henderschott off the side of the tower. I saw his eyes look at me as he passed, and they were haunted, horrible. He flew out in a lazy arc and started to fall. I watched him sail downward, but it took an impossibly long time for him to finally land on the street below.

When he did, a scream tore through my head and I realized it was my own. I dropped to my knees at the edge of the tower, Wolfe receding to the back of my consciousness. I cried out, again, tears freezing on my cheeks as I stared down, far below to where Henderschott had landed; the second person I had killed with my own hands.

I wanted to cry, wanted to scream, but I heard both from behind me before I could let out my own. I lurched to my feet and started back toward the far side of the roof. Gavrikov hovered, bursts of flame flying through the air, balls of fire aimed at the helicopter above, forcing it into motion.

Kat was kneeling next to Scott, whose body was burned horribly. Her hands were already on him and his skin was returning as I stepped onto the long, empty section of roof where they were. Gavrikov turned to them from where he hurled another bolt of fire at the helicopter and his face changed, even beneath the flames. "What are you *doing*?" He threw a small fireball at Kat, forcing her away from Byerly. "I save you from them and this is the thanks I get?" The Black Hawk shifted and flew off, coming around in the distance angling to approach the tower.

"I don't need saving!" Her words came out as a cry. I was still a good many paces away from them, but I could see Aleksandr's skin begin to glow brighter. "I don't even know who you are! I don't want to go anywhere with you, I want to go back to the Directorate—it's my home!"

Gavrikov was quiet for a moment, but he hovered only a foot or so off the ground. "I tried to save Klementina. My penance for failures, for crimes—for murder. For the murder I did when I was too young to know how to control myself." He edged closer to her.

She skidded away from him, sliding across the roof, almost on her back. "I didn't ask for this—not for you to help me, not for any of this!"

Gavrikov drifted closer to the ground. "I see how it has become. Things are not so different from the world we grew up in. Family betrays you at every turn, it is cold and dark and miserable and bereft of light. Everything Father did to us was nothing compared to what the world will do, with its cheap brutality and meanness." He let out a tortured howl that shook me inside. His skin glowed all the brighter, but he had stopped advancing on Kat. "You'll see soon enough."

There was a crack of gunfire and a bullet whistling through the air. I saw it hit Gavrikov and he dropped to a knee, the flames around his shoulder dissipating to show puckered flesh, blood squirting out in short intervals. He seemed like he was going to fall over but steadied himself. "Thank you," he said, "for proving my point." He heaved the largest fireball yet at the Black Hawk and I watched it sway as Bastian tried to dodge, sending the chopper into a dive beyond the edge of the rooftop and out of our view.

I was only a few feet away now and Gavrikov saw me but didn't react. I stopped, my chest heaving from the effort of crossing the roof. "And you too, *matryushka*? You are more like the sister I remember than this one is." His hand reached out, the flaming fingers extended to indicate Kat, who quailed away from him. "You know the pain she has forgotten. You have tasted the rich inequities of life." He smiled, but it was rueful. "You have fought, been hurt, been beaten down."

I stared back at him, exhausted. "What of it?"

He smiled and his chest burst back into flame. "I will give you the greatest gift I can." He rose into the air a foot. "Life doesn't get better from here, it gets worse." His hands came up at his sides, giving him the rough look of a human cross and he started to grow brighter. "I will give you the only gift I can. The same gift I will give all these people." His hand waved to indicate the city spread out before us. "Peace. True peace, lasting and final."

"You say peace," I said, drawing closer to him, "but I kinda think you mean death."

Even through the fire that engulfed his face, I could see the line that was his mouth twist into a rough smile. "Death is the only peace in this world."

The flames leapt all around him, the glow encompassing him like what I imagined the rising sun to look like. "I'm sorry, Aleksandr." I peeled off my gloves and let them fall to the ground. "I can't let you do that."

His burning eyes looked down at me and he drifted closer, the flames receding from his face so that he could look at me with his own eyes. He glowed ever brighter and I knew I had only seconds. "What will you do?"

My mouth was dry. "Give you peace," I whispered and brought my hands up to touch his face. I felt the skin singe as I touched him, the fire from his body so hot that it started to burn me. I ignored it and looked into his eyes, saw through the pain, the anger, saw the wounded soul beneath. He smiled when I touched him, and closed his eyes. His face went slack, even though I knew he hadn't felt the effects yet. He jerked for the first time a few seconds later, and the fire around his body started to gutter out.

"A metal box to spend the rest of your life in would do you no favors," I whispered as he sagged to the ground, then fell to his knees. I held his cheeks clenched in my fingers and he jerked again, the fire now out. Tears streamed down my face as I felt him heave for the last time and I let go, staggering back and falling over, my brain on fire with memories and visions, whirling in my skull. I looked over and saw his body start to blacken, then turn to ash that was carried away by the wind.

My head was pounding but I forced myself to turn over and sit up. Kat passed me and knelt next to Scott, putting her hands on him. He started to stir, a few moments later, his skin rejuvenated, coming back to life. I felt a hand land heavily on my shoulder and turned to see Zack. I tried to force words through the jumble of thoughts clogging my head as my brain made way for Gavrikov inside it. "Are you okay?"

"I feel like I just spent an intimate evening on the freeway being made love to by a Mack truck." Zack's face was bruised.

"Is that better or worse than spending the evening being made love to by a trucker named Mack?" I said it, huffing as I tried to stop the spinning in my head. I started to shake my head, but it felt impossibly heavy, like it would roll off my shoulders at any minute.

"What happened to Gavrikov?" Zack reached out and tugged at my arm, helping me to my feet.

"He wanted...peace." I stared over the edge of the roof to the east. "I gave it to him...as best I could."

"So he's..." He looked around. "Gone?"

"No," I said and pointed to my head. "He's in here, now. With the other one."

"Oh, I'm sure that'll end well," he said as I caught sight of

Clary hobbling toward us from the stairs. I could hear the blades of the chopper as it hovered above us and Bastian drifted her down, using the wind to steer his approach. He brought the helicopter down to a mere foot off the roof, resting the front wheel as Kat and Clary helped Scott into the side of the chopper.

I paused as Zack pulled me toward the door and turned around. The sun was rising in the cloudless sky, a bright red disc slipping over the horizon, the sky lighting up gold around it, with the first strains of blue transitioning to a deep indigo in the west. I stared at it, trying to savor the moment. I stopped resisting Zack's tugs and let him guide me into the helicopter and I watched the roof drop away beneath us as the Black Hawk turned and we headed west. I craned my neck in my seat, trying to watch the elusive sun as it cast a light on us.

"It does get better," I whispered so low no one could hear it over the chopper noise but the one I intended it for, nestled as he was in mind. "It has to." I watched the light as we raced the sunrise back to the Directorate.

28

Our first stop once we landed was the medical unit. I saw Dr. Perugini waiting along with Old Man Winter, Ariadne, and Dr. Zollers as the helicopter came in for a landing. I thought about bracing myself for the inevitable onslaught, but instead I just soaked up the rays of the sun, beaming down from outside. When the blades spun down and the doors opened, Scott was the first out. He looked a little discombobulated, but his skin was pink and fresh, like I suspected a newborn's would look. He caught my eye as he passed and nodded.

Roberto Bastian and Eve Kappler were in the cockpit but Parks and Clary were in the back with us. The whole way back, Clary had a look on his face like he was pissed off he missed the fight or something. Parks, on the other hand, stared out the window, like me. Zack had been on his headset pretty much the whole time, except for firing a reassuring smile at me now and again.

I waited until Clary had cleared the door and then Parks gestured that I should go next. Ariadne looked especially stiff, standing with her arms crossed, stern, head held high. Old Man Winter still dwarfed her, his hands relaxed at his sides. I felt Zack behind me as I walked across the helipad cradling my wrist. It didn't seem to hurt anymore.

Dr. Perugini looked up from where she already had Scott on a gurney, wrapped in a blanket, and gave my arm a cursory glance. "Might be fractured. Let's get it set before you do anything else."

Dr. Zollers caught my arm as I started to go by. "We're gonna have a long conversation later, I'm sure." He didn't look mad, just...knowing, or something. Like he was sharing a secret only I could know about. He pulled a needle out of his lab coat and pointed to my arm. I rolled up my sleeve and he gave me a quick shot. I felt the drug start to work in less than thirty seconds as the cacophony that had been present in the back of my head began to die down and I started to feel drowsy.

I followed Dr. Perugini as Clary pushed the gurney into the Headquarters building. We navigated the corridors to the medical unit quickly and were settled in within minutes. Dr. Zollers began monitoring Scott's condition, more as a precaution, it seemed, while Perugini found her way over to me.

She poked and prodded at my hand and wrist. She reached under the cart she had slid over with her and pulled out a brace. "No point in doing a cast since you'll be healed by tomorrow, but it will be best if we control the direction of the healing." She took the brace out of the box and began to wrap it around my wrist. "Got into trouble again, eh?"

"See it however you'd like," I said to her, inflectionless.

She didn't bite immediately, but after a moment she did. "How do you see it?"

I thought about it before answering. "I made amends for some bad decisions in my past."

She stopped and looked up from what she was doing, as though she were trying to smoke out the truth by looking in my eyes. Whatever she found, she kept to herself. "Good for you," she said, and finished tightening the brace before she turned her attention to Zack, who was talking to Scott. "You! You're next." He protested, but she didn't let him sway her. She had him take off his tactical vest and then his shirt, examining some bruising on his shoulders from where he jumped out of the helicopter. I watched.

Kat made her way over to me as I lay on the bed, trying to work up the motivation to move. "You saved my life," she said with a little smile.

"You're welcome." Her eyes clouded over and she looked troubled, as though she were trying to find a way to say what was on her mind. "Spit it out," I said with an air of impatience.

"I was thinking about the rooftop." She fumbled with her hands, gripping the rail of the bed. "When you faced that maniac in your basement, you were the only one there."

"Yeah, and?"

"So...I mean, you faced someone as bad or worse than..." she tried to say it but it didn't come out as anything but a pronoun. "...Him. But you faced Wolfe alone, all by yourself. And on the rooftop, you didn't have to be there. You had no reason to stay, you don't know anybody in Minneapolis. Scott has family in the area and Gavrikov would have chased me around the planet...but you didn't have any reason to be there."

"I told you before." I crossed my gloveless hands in my lap. "I had my reasons."

"Well...thank you." She smiled at me, and I still felt bad for her.

She started to shuffle back to Scott's bedside but I called out to her. "Wait!" She turned, almost expectant. "Do you know if there were anymore of those turtlenecks and jeans in the closet down in the room you were being held captive in?" I fingered my shirt, which was once again tattered around the arms and shoulders and my jeans were wet and caked with dirt and blood from the rooftop battle. "I think the rest of my clothes got lost in the fire."

"Yeah, there were a few of them," she said. "Coats and gloves, too."

"Oh, good." I looked back down at my bare hands.

She walked back to Scott's bedside and I looked around the room once. Zollers and Perugini were consulting in the corner, Zack and Kat were talking to Scott. I presumed M-Squad was with Ariadne and Old Man Winter. I tried to decide if I wanted to talk to them today or tomorrow and realized I didn't really care which, so long as I got some fresh clothes.

I left the medical unit without saying anything to anyone. I didn't sneak out; I didn't have to. Everyone was occupied and no one saw me leave except Zollers, who caught me with a sly smile that told me I'd see him later. That was fine, so long as it wasn't now.

I went to the staircase and found my way to the basement. The confinement room that they'd kept Kat in was unlocked now, no key card necessary. I walked in and went to the closet, finding exactly what she had promised inside. I grabbed a change of clothes, along with some undergarments that also fit me and went into the bathroom.

I took maybe the longest shower ever known to man, taking care to keep my wounded arm out of the spray but drowning every other inch of my skin in hot water. I scrubbed off the dried blood, the caked-on grit from the roof, and afterward I combed all the tangles out of my hair. I stared at myself in the mirror. I was the same girl I had seen a thousand times before, in the mirror of my own bathroom, back home, before all this happened.

Except I wasn't. The blue-green eyes were different. Not weary, but aged. I'd aged even in the weeks since I left home.

I heard a noise outside and dressed quickly. I didn't slide my gloves on until after I opened the door to find Zack waiting. I let out a breath I didn't know I had been holding and rolled my eyes. "What are you doing here?"

He looked at me innocently. "Came to check on you. Kat told me you were coming for clothes but I didn't realize you were going to shower too." He nodded at my wet hair. "I can wait if you want to dry off first."

I shook my head. "No big deal. I'm fine. I might sleep down here; it's as good as anywhere else and I don't know if I have it in me to walk all the way back to the dormitory building tonight. Besides, I'm sure Ariadne and Old Man Winter will be looking for me tomorrow morning."

"I wouldn't worry about that." He said it with more assurance than I would have expected.

"I'm not worried." I blinked my eyes, as though I could just shed the tiredness out of them with that little effort. "Worst comes to worst, I move along on my own." I felt a strength in those words that wouldn't have been possible a week earlier. "I'm okay with that, really. Maybe for the first time."

"I don't think they're going to ask you to leave," he said. "But why the change? Not that you showed much sign you were feeling all dependent before, but what triggered the shift?"

I took a deep breath. "I don't know. I guess I've been so busy feeling sorry for myself for all that's happened, for all the tough breaks—literal, in some cases," I held up my wrist, the brace still snug around it. "I've been jonesing so hard to be normal, whatever that is, that all I could think about was myself, about how I'd have to live a life where I had walls up all the time, where I couldn't really connect with anybody." I held up my hands as I slipped the gloves on. "Where I'd live untouched by people or emotion or life."

He nodded slowly. "It's up to you whether you connect with people or not. And I hate to break it to you, but your own little world is not the center of the universe."

I cocked my head at him and shot him a "duh" look. "Thanks, Galileo. You're a little late to the party on that one. And not fashionably so, like...party's over, GTFO. I figured it out, thanks."

"How?" He took a step closer to me, reminding me for some reason of Gavrikov as he took the first steps toward Kat.

"It was Aleksandr," I said, thinking about it. "He lived over a hundred years with his flames up all the time, by choice, ever since...whatever happened with his sister. He chose to live that way, isolated, alone. I think..." I felt the loneliness creep over me, the walls start to rise, and pushed them away, "...I would give anything to be able to take the barriers down and just live. And I can do that for most of them." I held up my hands, uselessly, showing him the gloves once more, the things that separated me from everyone. "All but one, anyway. It's not normal, but it's all I can do—"

He interrupted me by taking two strides to close the distance between us and before I could say anything his arms wrapped around my back, enveloping me, and he pressed his lips to mine. My eyes closed; the touch was magnificent, warm and sweet, and he pulled away just as I felt the first stirrings of my power start to work. I took a breath and opened my eyes, and his were staring back at me, brown and big and with his smile reflected in them. He had a really nice smile.

He didn't say anything else, just pulled away, leaving me speechless, standing there with my wet hair, and walked to the door. "See you tomorrow," he said, and the door shut before I could answer.

29

I sat across from Old Man Winter, playing the staring game. Oddly, my eyes didn't seem to burn this time, so I just kept going.

Ariadne was there, of course. "We've already gotten M-Squad's report and spoken with Scott and Kat, so we have a general idea of how everything went, for the most part. Zack said that Henderschott showed up?" She flipped through the file in her hands as if looking for confirmation.

"Yeah. He had the campus under surveillance and picked us up as we left. He must have followed us all the way to the IDS tower, because I saw the cable truck he was driving pass us as we went into the lobby. Didn't really put it together until he hit me, but that's the only way it could have happened unless someone tipped him off we were going to be there."

Ariadne closed the file. "Makes sense. Would you like to explain your actions?"

I was still locked on Old Man Winter's ice blue eyes. "Which ones?"

Ariadne coughed. "Taking two untrained metas and yourself into combat with not one, but two, extremely deadly foes, stealing a Directorate car, assaulting our guards, interfering in our efforts to contain the situation—"

"Your containment strategy sucked," I said, still not breaking my gaze away. Ariadne's jaw dropped and she took a step back. Old Man Winter didn't look away from my gaze.

"It would have resulted in about a million deaths; the crosswinds on top of the tower made a clean shot against Gavrikov near impossible without a stable platform to shoot from. Hell, I'm amazed Parks even hit him."

"And your plan was better?" she said with an air of snottiness. "Byerly almost got burned to death, Forrest was cornered—"

"But I saved her," I said.

"—Zack jumped from a helicopter, injuring himself, and Clary ended up going through the roof—"

"That was his own fault, you can't blame me for Clary being stupid."

"And then there's you." She came around and sat on the edge of the desk, just to the side of my staring contest with Old Man Winter. "You disobeyed our explicit commands and substituted your own judgment for ours."

"You're right," I said, firm. "Based on my experience with Gavrikov, I handled the situation as I thought best. None of the rest of you knew him personally or knew what to expect from him. Don't put me in a position where I have to watch countless people die. Let me take the responsibility a thousand times before you hand it off to someone else who will screw it up. I won't stand by and take dumb orders. I did what I thought—what I *knew* was right. And if you expect anything less from me as an agent or a retriever or a whatever you wanted me to do, you need to find someone else for the job."

There was a freezing effect in the room, as though all particle motion had halted, and Ariadne spoke first. "I'm sorry, what?"

I still didn't look away from Old Man Winter. "The job offer you extended. If it's off the table in the wake of this incident, I understand. But I figured you ought to know that if it was still open, that I'm not some brainless shell that you get to use just for my powers."

Ariadne shifted from where she was sitting on the desk. "I...don't think we would ever expect anything less than your full opinion at any time. And..." She looked to Old Man Winter, who finally broke his gaze away from me to look to her. I mentally declared victory and pumped my fist. They pretended not to notice. She turned back after a look was shared between them. "The offer is still on the table."

"Then you have a trainee," I said. "And I have a signing bonus, I believe." I looked at her. "Do I get paid with checks or cash? Because I don't have a bank account. Yet."

"I'll...have someone cut you a check," she said, standing. "I'm sure we can find someone to take you into town to make banking arrangements."

"I'd like to go to the mall." I stood. "I need some clothes." I pulled on the shoulder of the black turtleneck, the thousandth I'd worn since arriving at the Directorate. "Nothing personal, but I'm kind of sick of wearing black all the time. Who does that?"

She nodded. "Anything else?"

I thought for a moment and remembered something. "One last thing. Henderschott, before he died—"

"Ah, yes." Ariadne opened the file. "Rather spectacular, that. A 57-storey plunge to the street?" She looked away from the photograph I could see in the folder. "Not a pleasant way to go, especially when strapped into a tin can as he was."

"He said something before he died, about his employer." The silence in the room became oppressive in an instant. Old Man Winter seemed to perk up and Ariadne had a wide-eyed look on her face. "He said they'd keep coming after me. I asked him who, and he gave me their name—Omega." I looked at the two of them as they exchanged a look. "That mean anything to you?"

"No," Ariadne said after appearing to consider it for a moment. "So we have a name for this new threat—"

Old Man Winter cut her off. "No. Not a new threat at all. Not Omega." His blue eyes glowed, shining in the dimness of the tinted office. "An old one, rather. A very, very old one." The office was warm enough, and I was already wearing my coat. But the way he said it, the timbre of his voice, the delivery—gave me a very real shudder that was absolutely unrelated to the cold.

30

It was a Monday, I think. I let the nice agent (he didn't sneer or get pissy at all with me, a rarity for people from the Directorate in my experience) drive me to the bank. They were very pleasant and understanding, having had a long relationship with the Directorate, and so I opened an account and the money was in it within just a few minutes. Which was fortunate, because I didn't have a driver's license. Somehow, Ariadne had gotten copies of my Social Security Card and Birth Certificate, which made things easier.

I left the bank with a temporary checkbook and a debit card, walking across the parking lot back to the car where the agent was waiting for me, the heat from the exhaust causing the tail pipe to steam in the cold. And it was cold, cold but beautiful, the sunlight streaming down from above, shining off all the ice and snow. I looked up, just to make sure the sun was still there. It was, seated in the middle of the blue sky. I smiled and got in the car.

The drive to Eden Prairie Center only took a few minutes. I entered through the same entrance by the food court that I had fairly destroyed last time I was there. There was still a hole in the wall where I'd thrown Henderschott through, though they had workmen patching the damage. I passed by without paying too much attention, trying to appear innocent.

I stopped at a lot of different stores, and I bought a few things. I had decided before I walked in that I was going to

362

try and spend less than five hundred dollars, because even though I had ten thousand, I didn't ever want to be stuck in a situation where I needed money and didn't have it. I tried to find the bargain tables, checked the prices on everything before I bought it, and did the math in my head. It all worked out well and I found some very nice things (all of which were long sleeved and didn't show much in the way of flesh, because every inch of it I exposed was an inch that could kill someone) but that took my wardrobe beyond the dullness of Ariadne's. Not that it would take much.

I walked out of the store I was in, having stocked up on some professional-looking outfits and started to make my way back to the car. By my estimate, I was a couple hundred under my limit and quite content with that until I passed the store I'd gone by with Zack only a week earlier. The dress was still in the window, the red one that I had seen on the woman I had thought was my mom. I hesitated outside, staring. It was impractical. It wasn't for me. But I went inside, and they had it in my size.

I tried it on and stood in front of a mirror, staring at myself again. I looked...so different, now. I bought it and I couldn't define exactly why. Call it recklessness (even though I questioned whether I'd ever wear it in public), call it desperation (because to be able to wear it meant consequences that could be quite dire) or you could call it...hope. That things would change somehow, get better.

I was walking out of the store, lost in thought when a flash of red drew my attention to someone standing in my path. I looked up and found her staring at me, the woman from before. She still wore red, but it was a different dress this time. This one was cut to the knee, a little more conservative but not much. I could still see every curve she clearly wanted displayed, and it made me want to shrink away in envy. I tried to smile and go around her, but she stepped into my path. "Hi there," she said.

"Hello." I didn't know quite what to say. I could feel the hint of flush on my cheeks. "I'm sorry about last time, I didn't mean to scare you. I just...saw you from a distance and thought you were my mom." She stared back at me, impassive.

"She's missing, so...anyway, sorry." I half-expected some soft, cooing sound of sympathy like I had heard from the women on TV. She didn't make a noise like that.

She laughed. "Don't worry about it, although you have to admit, it was kind of a foolish mistake to make." I feigned a smile and as I started to leave she blocked me again. "It's hardly the first time it's happened, though. I mean, growing up in the shadow of Sierra Nealon wasn't the easiest experience." My blood turned to ice at the mention of my mother's name and I locked my gaze on hers and noticed for the first time that her eyes were blue but flecked with green. She laughed again. "I had to find some ways to stand out from big sister." She ran a hand down the side of her dress. "See what I mean? Your mother would never wear this."

I froze and my shopping bags slipped from my fingers one by one. I knew the look on my face was pure shock and she reached out for me, grasping my arm, hooking it in hers and angling it so I didn't drop my bags. "You look surprised. I take it mommy dearest never told you about her little sister? That's all right. We're three of a kind—you, me and her." Her hand found its way to her chest. "But where are my manners? I'm your aunt, Charlene—but you can call me Charlie." Her smile was ten thousand watts, bright and vibrant. "I'm here to help you."

ACKNOWLEDGMENTS

Who's in charge of this mad house of literary achievement (or mediocrity, depending on your perspective)? Well, technically, as the author, I am. But that's not the whole story.

Shannon Garza once more gave me her whole-hearted effort at making sure my characters didn't jump the emotional shark, as it were. She gave detailed feedback and commentary that allowed me to keep a pulse on how everyone was feeling, what everyone was doing, and how it all fit together to create a reading experience, and for that, I owe her my thanks.

Debra Wesley once more came to the rescue with countless technical details and thought of things I didn't even consider.

More thanks also to Calvin Sams, who once more read the draft and provided some additional critique.

We also had a new addition this round, the great Robin McDermott, who took time away from her busy life as a new mommy to parse the book, and she found some insights that no one else did.

Lastly in the editorial department, but certainly not leastly, muchas gracias to my esteemed Editor-in-Chief, Heather Rodefer, who not only finds my errors and corrects my grammar, but also found the flaming man in the cover art for this work! That's why she's the Editor-in-Chief.

The cover was put together by Karri Klawiter (artbykarri.com).

My apologies to the city of Glencoe, Minnesota. It was nothing personal; it was down to either you or Norwood Young America, Minnesota, and frankly, look at the name on them! You expect me to type that over and over? Simplicity was your undoing. Accept it with grace and move on.

My mom marvels at my ability to churn out books (frankly, so do I, but let's not look gift equines in the oral cavity, okay?) and recently asked me how it came to be, since neither she nor my father have even the remotest interest in writing. The answer is this - my mom has read more books than any other person I've ever met. If she ever created a

Goodreads profile and plugged in all the books she's read, it'd crash the site (thanks for not doing that, mom). My father, on the other hand, is not much of a reader, but is quite the wordsmith. He makes up rhymes and turns phrases just for the fun of it. Nothing narrative, just idle amusement. But when you combine my mother's love of story and my dad's enjoyment of messing around with words...well, you get me. Someone who wants to write a lot of novels. For their respective contributions to my career path, I owe them my thanks.

Finally, we come to my wife and kids. Once more, I owe them everything, because without them, I wouldn't be doing this.

BOOK 3
SOULLESS

1

Someone Else

I wondered how many cops were within a hundred miles of me as I slammed the convenience store clerk's head into the counter. It made a satisfying thump and rebounded as he spiraled to the ground, his head hitting the shelf behind him before it made contact with the tile floor. He didn't move, which was fortunate more for his sake than mine, as I took the bills out of the register and stuffed them in a plastic bag. I fiddled around behind the counter for a minute, tidying up loose ends, then broke his cell phone and the landline, smashing the plastic into pieces. It'd be a long walk to the next one.

The smell of day-old hot dogs wafted around me as I walked past trinkets and tourist shirts that proclaimed *See South Dakota!* The slow hum of the air conditioner working overtime to keep the building cool in the prairie summer heat thrummed around me. I ripped open a candy bar and took a bite, savoring the sweet taste of the caramel and chocolate mingled with the salt from the peanuts. It was the first thing I'd eaten since I made a stop outside Gillette, Wyoming a few hours after sundown. I wondered if the clerk at that store had woken up yet. Probably. He wouldn't remember anything. Just like this one.

I walked to the back of the store and paused when I opened the cooler to grab a drink. The bitter chill of the freezer air overpowered the air conditioning, sending goosebumps up and down my arms. I threw three bottles of soda on top of the piddling amount of money I'd taken from the till; I'd thought it would be more. I considered trying to wake up the attendant to get him to open the safe but decided he'd had enough excitement for one night.

I stepped up to the door that led to the space behind the freezers. Locked. I rolled my eyes and kicked, sending it off its hinges and into the room. It wedged in the back wall, sticking out as though it was a tombstone buried in the brick. The symbolism was obvious, at least to me. I reached over and ejected the DVD that was recording from the camera feeds all over the station, put it into my plastic bag and pondered the safe in the corner. Wasn't worth the time. I only needed petty cash for this trip and it was better to remain as off the radar as I could. Not that robbing convenience stores was going to keep me off the radar, but let's face it: it was a means to an end, not an end itself.

And the end was ahead. Far, far ahead.

Everything on the shelves looked good as I wandered back out into the store, but I didn't need much. I threw a couple packages of chips into the bag and three boxes of white powdered donuts. Way better than the chocolate ones. I took one last look around and decided to try one of the hot dogs. Sure, they looked old, but I'd been eating food that came in a plastic wrapper since I left Casper, Wyoming yesterday. And before that, other canned and plasticized food. Laying low wasn't pleasant, but living off gas station food wasn't much better.

After I finished fixing my hot dog, I took a bite and stepped outside, the flavor of the ketchup and mustard masking the chewy, rubbery consistency of the meat. The convenience store was right off Interstate 90. The nearest town, Draper, South Dakota, was a few miles away and probably deader than a prairie dog on the freeway by this time of night.

I felt the hot summer air of the plains, my little bag in one hand, and a half eaten hotdog in the other, as I walked back to my car, an older model Honda. I'd stolen it before I left

Casper, but I acquired some new license plates in Rapid City so I wasn't real worried about the cops taking an interest in me. By the time the sun came up tomorrow I'd be in southern Minnesota. I could melt away onto the back roads, pick up some new tags, maybe even a new car. This one smelled like the previous owner had a problem with Mary Jane. Actually, not so much a problem as a deeply troubling relationship.

I watched another car pull into the parking space just down from me. I caught sight of the lights mounted on the roof and realized my earlier question about cops was answered: there was one here, now. The lights weren't on, no siren was blaring and once the officer parked his car he sat there, looking at a clipboard in his lap. I sighed; the minute he walked inside he'd discover what had happened and I'd have the cops after me. I needed time.

I walked to his window and rapped on the glass with my knuckle. He made a motion for me to step back, which I did, and he opened the door. Tall, heavily built, and in his early forties, he clicked on his big, heavy flashlight before he started to speak. "Is there a problem—"

He didn't have a chance to see it coming. It wasn't his fault; he followed procedure flawlessly, but I was possessed of strength and speed far beyond a normal person. His hand had reached his holster when mine broke his nose. I brought his head to my knee, giving him something else unpleasant to deal with when he woke up. He hit the ground and I stooped over him. After I was done, I grabbed his pistol, his pepper spray and taser. I smashed his cell phone to pieces, broke his radio, then picked him up and stuffed him back in his car. He'd live, but suffer for the inconvenience he'd placed on me by driving up at this particular moment.

I got back in the Honda and caught another whiff of the reefer that permeated the seats, the upholstery, the dashboard, everything. I looked at the map sitting on my passenger seat and traced my finger along the line I'd drawn to my destination. From the money I stole this time, I might actually be able to pay at the next convenience store. That'd throw 'em off the trail.

I stepped on the accelerator and took off, back to the freeway, back to the long ride. I was over five hundred miles from where I was going and it'd take me at least a couple more days to get there. But it'd be worth it; I'd show them all. I let a little smile of triumph float onto my face as I broke open the pack of donuts and pulled out the first powdered. I took a bite then spit it out the broken window.

Stale. I felt a flash of rage and had a fantasy about killing the convenience store clerk instead of letting him live. I threw the rest of the package out as I hit seventy, not a car on the road ahead of me. This time...this time they couldn't stop me.

2

Sienna Nealon

My heart thudded in my ears as I ran, the green of the woods surrounding me. My breath caught in my throat; I was gasping from the exertion of running, and that wasn't easy for me. I'm a metahuman, with powers that include far more strength, speed and agility than humans. But apparently I needed more cardio in my workout.

I heard the footsteps behind me, pounding against the hard ground. I stopped, pressing my back against a tree. Scott Byerly ran past and did the same while Kat Forrest trailed a little behind him.

"Thanks for slowing down," Kat said, huffing as she came to a stop. She was taller than me, with long blond hair and green eyes. Her face was usually tanned but it was red now, spots of color standing out on her cheeks. She wore a simple T-shirt and gym shorts which seemed far too short, and socks and tennis shoes far too low for my tastes. Her long, smooth, tanned legs almost blended in with the backdrop of old pine needles on the forest floor. "Thought you were gonna leave me behind."

I grunted. It wasn't for lack of trying; we were on the run for a reason, and I had no intention of getting caught because Kat couldn't keep pace.

"Any sign of him?" Scott didn't bother to complain. He was tall, with short dark hair and a nose that was a little rounded. Kinda good-looking. Like me, his eyes were scanning through the trees around us, watching for the unseen threat that was somewhere out there. His eyes halted for a second on Kat's legs, causing me to snort, then they kept going. He wasn't breathing as hard as she was, but close.

"Not that I can see." I pushed off the tree, trying to steady myself. We had been running for over an hour before this, full tilt. I was tired; my legs hurt, my lungs hurt, and I was cranky. "But the way the three of us are gasping for air, a tractor trailer could sneak up on us and we wouldn't know it until we felt the treads on our backs."

"I'm exhausted." Kat stood up straight and her hair hung in strings over her shoulders as she joined us in looking around. "I'm in no condition for a fight; I'm not sure they're paying me enough for this."

Scott shot her a half-smile. "You don't think it's worth it to be the next generation of M-Squad recruits?"

"Not sure I wanna be an M-Squad anything," Kat said under her breath.

I had been offered a position as a trainee with the Directorate, an organization that helps track and police metahumans – metas – like me. They hoped to position me to help their agents in hunting down dangerous metas. Shortly after I'd gotten an offer, so had Scott and Kat. Their offers might have had something to do with the fact that the three of us almost single-handedly stopped a very dangerous meta who had threatened to blow up Minneapolis. I thought it was a signal that the Directorate was looking to expand their reach because of some growing threats.

"So are we gonna keep moving or wh—" Kat got cut off mid-sentence as something hit her from behind. I saw a flash of white fur, heard the WHUMP! as she went down, her hair a solid streak of blond. I was already in motion. My foot lashed out at the ball of white as she hit the ground, her shriek drowned out and muffled. I missed clean; the creature that attacked her rolled through and landed on all fours, ready to strike. I was off balance and it was impossibly fast. I stared at it, the red eyes of a wolf glaring back at me as I tried to recapture my footing.

It was long, bigger than the dogs I had seen, and the fur was stark white, the faintest reminder of the last winter, when snow blanketed the ground in the same shade. I saw it tense, watched it shift weight from its hind legs to its front as it moved to pounce again. I had no easy defense; my leg was almost down when it left the ground and I flinched, already anticipating the pain as I saw it leap, mouth open and focused on my neck.

A solid wall of water hit the animal, causing it to yelp and hurtle sideways, knocked off course by the pressure of the blast. It slammed into a tree trunk and I lunged, foot extended in a running jump sidekick. I aimed at the neck, hoping to put the beast out of the fight. When I was a foot away from my target the hair changed color, shifting in a ripple down the fur like the summer wind had stirred it, and as it went brown the neck grew wider and longer and the shape of the creature began to change.

It stood on its hind legs, leaving all fours behind as its limbs grew longer, paws sprouting long claws. My foot hit it behind the shoulder and I heard bones cracking; a roar came from the mouth of what was now a bear. The brown mass twisted and batted at me with a paw and I dived, trying to avoid the swipe. I felt one claw hit me, raking behind my ear and drawing blood.

"Let's coordinate our attack," Scott said from my left, loosing a stream of water that missed the bear wide.

I ignored him as I rolled to my feet, already in a defensive stance. The bear reared up on its hind legs, standing an easy four or five feet taller than me. I glared at it, my hands raised, ready to try and counter whatever it tried. "You got blood in my hair."

The bear cocked its head at me, distracted, for just a second. Long enough for the blast of water to knock it over again, taking it off its hind legs and down to all fours.

"I had him!" I said. A hot flush of irritation ran through me as I watched the bear stagger from the stream.

Scott had both hands out, the air around him shimmering as he drained the humidity from it. It was Minnesota in July;

he had plenty to work with. A jet of liquid shot from his fingertips in a pressurized burst, splattering against the brown fur and driving the bear back. I'd been on the receiving end of it before; he could make it hurt, if he wanted to. "Sorry, I thought we were supposed to work as a team."

I ignored his jab and pounced while the bear was distracted, jumping on its back. I didn't pull my punches, and I landed three of them in rapid succession behind the ears. If it'd been a human, it would have been dead, I think. The bear, with its thicker skull, started to wobble and tried to bring up a paw to bat me off. I slid lower and wrapped an arm around its throat, locking it in tight while I hit it thrice more. It collapsed under my weight and fell to the ground. I hit it again and watched the tongue fall out of its mouth, unrolling on the ground as it went limp in my grasp.

"Is it over?" Kat brushed herself off as she got to her knees. "Can I get up now?"

I stared at the bear underneath me. "I don't think s—" I stopped when I heard a whizzing noise; something was coming toward us, something fast. I felt something brush past me and threw myself down. Something soft grazed my cheek and pulled at my arm as it passed. I caught a glimpse of Scott out of the corner of my eye; he went down hard, something pulling him off his feet, a net made of beams of light, shining and intertwined. It pinned him to the ground, the energy forcing his hands and arms down, mashing his face as it cut into him. Kat was similarly pinned to a tree in a sitting position; I could see her feet sticking out the bottom of the net as she hung there, limp, a foot off the ground.

"You think it's over?" A blond woman hovered in the clearing above me, her outfit a kind of shameless riff on things I'd seen people wear when riding bicycles, minus the helmet. Her hand extended, pointing at me, and I lunged as I felt another net fly past me, disturbing my hair as it missed, passing down my back. It stretched in a four foot square, holding tight to the earth like a web made of light.

My shoulder hit the ground, little pieces of rock pushing up into my clothes and skin as I rolled back to my feet. I ran, not bothering to look back as I made for the cover of the forest. I heard a laugh from behind me, heard the air move around her as she pursued me. I dodged around a tree and chanced a look back; she was lower now, only a few feet off the ground, and not far behind me.

I could smell the fresh air, feel the sun on the back of my neck as I ran, dodging past the trunks of trees and hearing the whoosh of the little nets she was sending my way. Scott and Kat were both down; they'd be okay. I just had to get away long enough to turn the tables. I had to beat her, had to win, more than anything.

I came upon a small ravine and let myself drop. I hit the ground, absorbing the impact along my legs. I had fallen next to a huge rock, at least three feet across. I smiled as I hefted it in both hands and readied it to throw. A normal person couldn't have done this; the rock was huge, almost a boulder – the kind you'd use for decoration in a garden.

I heard sound overhead as she overflew me. I watched her disappear past, and waited, my muscles straining as I held the rock at the ready. I could hear the flutter of wings, and she came back around, her head visible through the boughs above me. I waited until I had a clear view and I let the stone fly. It soared and hit her in the chest with an awful cracking noise. I pumped my fist in victory until I saw her flip over and fall from the sky.

I felt a sick sensation in my stomach as I watched her drop. She followed a lazy arc as she fell; I heard her body hit the ground, the impact reminding me of the time I'd dropped a steak on a counter; a kind of wet slap.

I ran over uneven ground, feeling the dirt kick up as I raced toward the place where she had landed. I pushed aside tree branches to find her in a creek, the water running over her. I cringed and hurried over. I felt the cool water splash into my boot (black, pleather, fairly nice until I got them wet) and soak my socks, felt the chill of it on my hands as I reached down and grabbed her under the arms to drag her to the bank. My gloves were leather and not meant to get soaked, but I dared not take them off; her shirt was sleeveless and her pants were short. My touch as I pulled her out of the water would be much worse than the damage she'd already taken.

Her hair was wet with water and just a little blood, I noticed as I pulled her onto the stony bank of the creek. She snorted and choked out clear liquid and bile as I pulled her onto the rocks. I felt the dampness make its way through my jeans and my long sleeved shirt. It was desperately hot, I was sweating, and the cool wetness was a kind of sweet relief from the heat.

"Woo hoo hoo," came a catcall from the other side of the creek. "Look at that; Sienna and Eve, getting all wet and clingy." A low guffaw came after it and I felt a bitter pang of annoyance. The speaker was a little taller than me but still short for a man. He wore a cutoff tank top and ragged blue jeans, and his hair was thinning on top, obvious since he wasn't wearing his usual baseball cap to cover it.

"She's hurt pretty bad, Clary," I said. I looked down at her and her eyes fluttered. A thin trickle of blood ran down her forehead.

"She'll be fine." He dismissed us with a wave, turning his head away and puckering his lips in amusement. "It's not every day I get to see the two of you rubbing up against each other. I might have to watch for a bit."

I picked her up and carried her off the rocks to the trail. She was wet, an unconscious, dead weight that wasn't fighting back. I set her on the dirt, long strings of her hair tangled. They touched the ground and I saw the little granules of sand cling to them. I felt guilty; she was going to be super pissed when she woke up.

I heard Clary splash through the creek behind me as I knelt next to Eve. Her hair had gotten long; it was short when I first met her. She was very thin, her chest flat, heaving up and down with great effort; her breathing was ragged. When I pulled her shirt back to look at the damage, I heard a moan of pain from her and a deep breath of interest from Clary. I shot him a dirty look and turned back to Eve.

Her sternum was broken, a hideous blackish blue bruise had begun to spread from the center of her chest. I didn't dare unzip her shirt to look closer (especially with that pervert Clary behind me) but I knew enough that I was certain I'd have to call—

"Dr. Perugini is on the way," came the voice from in front of me. Roberto Bastian came toward us at a jog, his buzzed black hair dripping with sweat. "She'll be here in five or less. Until then, let's just assess the damage—" He halted and dropped to a knee next to Kappler. "Damn." He shot a look at me, but there was a surprising lack of guilt in it. "You're playing a little rough for a training exercise, Nealon."

"The rock kinda got away from me," I said. "It's not exactly easy for us ground-based types to take down a flyer. She was throwing her nets at me and I just..." I searched my memory, trying to make my vicious ambush seem not quite so vicious. "...figured out a way to take her down and did it."

"Boy, did you," said Glen Parks, splashing across the creek with Scott and Kat in tow. Parks was an older man, his long hair gray, mustache and beard matching it perfectly; not quite ZZ Top length, but close. He brushed the beard to the side and I could see a contusion across his neck that looked like my wristwatch. "I'm not upset that you took this exercise seriously, but next time be more careful with the neck. Even as a bear I'm not immune to your strength."

"Sorry," I said, somewhat abrupt. I turned my attention back to Eve as Kat eased down beside me, her hands already brushing against Eve's neck. The German woman was rasping and her eyes were still rolled back in her head. "I was just trying to win."

"Damn, you sure were, girl," Clary said. "But you're gonna catch all kinds of hell from—"

"What is going on here?" The crackling of an Italian accent was laced with thunderous irritation. I blanched at the sound of it, and after examination, wondered why I was more afraid of the reaction of a human doctor than the metahumans I had been sparring with only minutes before.

Dr Isabella Perugini stopped on the bank opposite us, her dark hair pulled back in a ponytail, her white lab coat falling below her knees. She slid off her high heeled shoes and began to pick her way across the stream, trying to balance on the rocks jutting out of the water. Her dark complexion was more flushed than usual, her eyes narrowed at me. "You again?" She said it as she executed a hop from one rock to another. "I thought I sorted you out!"

"I got carried away," I said.

She made her last jump and flinched as her foot caught the edge of the rock she landed on. She cursed loudly, then covered the ground to get to us. She knelt and looked to Kat, who had unzipped Eve's shirt to expose her bruised and misshapen sternum. "How is she?" the doctor said to Kat.

"All the problems you'd expect her to have." Kat ran a hand through Eve's hair. "Fractured skull, presumably from the landing, broken sternum." She gave the doctor a wan smile. "I'm working on it. The broken bones will be mended in just a minute."

Perugini turned back to me, one eye cocked and twitching, the other narrowed. She didn't say anything. She didn't have to.

"Training's rough," Bastian said as I avoided her gaze. He looked at me, expression neutral. "It's gonna be fine. We've got Forrest; she'll fix it."

Perugini's mouth became a thin line. "What happens on the day she isn't around?"

Kat let out a sharp exhalation and fell back on her haunches, then lay down on the rocky shore. "That day is not today," she said with a gasp as I watched little blades of grass and weeds spring up from between the rocks she lay on, reaching up to stroke her exposed skin. "She'll be fine." Kat lifted her head to look at Dr. Perugini. "I might need a minute, though."

I heard the sound of feet splashing in the water and looked up to see Ariadne Fraser making her way across the water. She held her high-heeled shoes in her hands, and her black jacket and skirt were taxing her balance. I raised an eyebrow in surprise when she made it across the bank, her pantyhose having developed three runs along her thighs and two holes in the toes from her crossing. Her red hair was the only splash of color visible on her as she made her way over to us, serious as ever. "Situation?"

Perugini answered, frost under her words. "She'll be fine. Training exercise got out of hand."

Ariadne dropped to her knees next to Eve, looking down at the German woman, who was still unconscious but now breathing easily. "Why is she out?"

"She landed on her head," Perugini said, her eyes glancing at me for a brief second. "Kat has healed her skull fracture but I suspect she won't be awake for several minutes, possibly an hour." The doctor put on her stethoscope and placed the metal end on Eve's chest. "There doesn't appear to be any lasting damage but I'd like to do an MRI just the same."

"You're sure she's all right?" Ariadne looked back up at the doctor, her eyes slitted, her hand clutching Eve's in a way that caught my attention. I looked up and saw Clary looking back at me. He gave me a subtle nod, a wide grin on his face.

"I'm sure." Perugini wrapped her stethoscope around her neck. "Have someone come out here with a Humvee to pick us up with a stretcher. I want to get her back to the medical unit for tests and observation until we're certain she's fine."

Ariadne hadn't taken her eyes off Eve the entire time Perugini was speaking. "Okay. Bastian, do it."

"Yes, ma'am." Roberto stood up and took a few steps away, speaking with his hand up to his ear.

"How did this happen?" Ariadne's voice was quiet, but it crackled with accusation and left a silence no one seemed eager to fill, least of all me. I started to speak, but was interrupted by Clary.

"Sienna hit her with rock while she was flying and she came crashing down into the creek." Clary's tone was purest joy, as though he were a kid tattling on his wicked sister. "She put some heat on it, too, took Eve right outta the sky like a friggin' plane comin' down—"

"Thank you, Clary." I don't want to say I was frightened of the icy edge in Ariadne's voice, but it was probably the harshest I had ever heard her sound. I didn't back away, but my eyes locked onto hers and I caught an undefinable hint of something that made my heart beat a little faster. Ariadne let go of Kappler's hand and stood. "You're all dismissed." She locked eyes with me. "You too. We'll discuss this tomorrow."

"I'm sorry," I said. "It was an accident—"

"Did you intentionally knock her out of the air with a boulder?" Ariadne's voice came out low, almost whispered. When I nodded, she followed with, "Then that tends to rule out the possibility of it being an accident." Her eyes were dark and they watched me. "We'll discuss it tomorrow. Just go."

I paused and started to reply – something about them pitting me against unfair odds, since Eve could fly and had been a member of M-Squad dealing with dangerous metas long before I even showed up, about how maybe I was doing her a favor by pointing out a pretty big vulnerability in the way she did battle – but every one of those arguments died on my tongue. I nodded and turned away, forcing one foot in front of the other as I walked out of the clearing and into the trees.

3

I heard the sounds of conversation die down behind me as I grew further and further from them. The heat in the woods was oppressive, even under the shade of the trees. The air didn't feel like it was moving, even when a brief gust of wind shifted more hot air in my direction, turning the sweat that was already trickling down my back into a tepid river that slid down the crease of my spine. I took a deep breath, sucking in the warm air, feeling it seem to stick in my nose and mouth, felt the perspiration drip from my forehead into my eyes, mixing with a little of the moisture already there.

Dammit. I got so caught up in the training exercise, in winning, in beating the others, that I let myself get carried away. For years I'd had no one but Mom to spar against, and now, only a few months out in the world, was testing myself against people that tracked and caught metas for a living. I felt a twinge of relief at the knowledge that Eve Kappler was going to be all right, and a little bit of pride knowing that I'd knocked her out of the sky.

Kappler was a severe woman by nature: she was thin, austere, too dry in personality and reserved in her manner to draw much attention. She had never really been nice to me (not that I'd smite her for that; there were a lot of people in the Directorate that had never shown me kindness; I'd be smiting for a long time to get to them all) but that didn't mean I wanted to hurt her. It was practice. Mom had never intentionally hurt me during practice. Well, most of the time, anyway.

I ran my sleeve along my cheek, slopping off the salty mix of sweat and the first annoying hint of tears. I wanted to believe they were from all the perspiration that was in my eyes, but I suspected they might also have been from the pride stuck in my throat, that burning feeling that I couldn't swallow away even though I wanted to. I had just gotten called out on my performance in the midst of my peers and fellow trainees. I hated that.

I took another breath, in and out, then another. I had stopped walking and was just standing, feeling the hot air gathered around me in a wall, like some sort of fortress of heat that had enshrouded my body. My long sleeves, gloves and pants didn't help, and even though I wore tennis shoes, my socks were long. They were all soaked, some from sweat but most from wading into the creek to recover Eve. Every single article of my clothing was starting to stick to me, even as the water that had taken up residence within had matched my body temperature; only a little dash of coolness was running down and surprising me every once in a while. The rest just felt like sweat.

The first days of brutal summer had started only a couple weeks ago; before that it had been a beautiful, sunny-skied and cool-aired spring, all the way to the last of June. Since then, it was as though the weather had decided to get hostile. I had to say I preferred winter as a season to summer; it was colder, but even factoring in the number of times I'd landed in the snow while fighting, I didn't get as wet as I did sweating during these training exercises, which were an everyday thing, in one form or another.

"Hey." I had missed the footfalls behind me, caught up in my own thoughts. I turned without drying my eyes, hoping that the sweat would mask the other, marginally less stinging liquid. I doubted it would. Scott was there, along with Kat, who was leaning on him. They walked like I envisioned a couple would, her arm around his waist, her face looking more drawn than it had a few minutes ago. She rested against him, leaning her weight against his muscular chest. If we had been in a different place, and different people, she could have been a drunken sorority girl, leaning on her boyfriend for support.

And I could have been a...I dunno. Something else.

"You took down Eve pretty hard." Scott stopped, repositioning himself as Kat pushed off him to stand on her own two wobbly feet.

My hands came up to cover my mouth as I wiped the sweat that was beading on my upper lip. "Yep." I let them rest there, as though I could cover the lies that were bound to drip out when he asked the inevitable question.

"Why?" It was Kat who asked it, her hair looking stringy because of the humidity, but without a hint of the frizz that was afflicting mine. Thanks, humidity. It'd take a miracle and an hour with the flat iron later to get the kinks out.

I didn't move my hands away from my mouth. "Why what?"

"Why'd you take her down so hard that I had to fix a skull fracture, a broken sternum and three ribs?" Kat let go of Scott and dropped to her rump, sitting with her legs in front of her. "I know we don't do these kind exercises where we beat the hell out of each other for real very often, but we've done it enough to know you don't lose control like that." She laughed and tossed a blond lock over her shoulder. "I mean, when it comes to the training, you're like the queen of control; it's why you're Parks' favorite—"

"I just didn't think." I was sweating even harder now, my lip pressed up against my hand, more perspiration trailing down my forehead from my hairline. I felt my shirt sticking to me and all I wanted was a shower. "It got away from me, the rock. The adrenaline was pumping after we took down Parks—"

"After you took down Parks, you mean? When you left us behind?" The accusation came out of Scott, his arms folded but his manner cool.

"I drew her away from you," I said. "I don't know what else I could have done to help you. I wanted to win, and it was just..." I pulled my hands away from my mouth and licked my lip, tasted the salty residue of sweat.

"It's not Wolfe, is it?" Scott stared me down. His T-shirt

had been white when we started, but now it was gray in the places where he had sweated through, and bore the stains of dirt and grime from where he'd been pinned to the ground. "He's not breaking out or whatever—"

"He's not," I said. "I haven't heard from the rogues' gallery in my head in months. I think Zollers and I have that under control." That was mostly true. The medication Zollers had given me was working, but I had other help as well.

"I guess it was hard for us to tell by the way you acted back there," Kat said, sarcasm oozing through her words, which were laced with a kind of bone-weariness. Her eyes flicked down, and they were lacking the brightness that was ever-present in them. "I didn't mean that. Accidents happen, especially when they're trying to train us for all the possibilities that could happen out there. It's just not like you."

"It happens." Another voice joined our conversation. My head swiveled and I saw Glen Parks, shifting out of the shape of a wolf again. "You get reckless after playing this like it's a game for too long." He got taller as he walked, leaving behind all fours as his fur receded into the long beard and hair that I was accustomed to seeing. "Too much of this type of training's not good. We need some real world experience for you three." He halted behind me. I didn't look away, even though my eyes were burning, this time from the sweat. "Especially for you, before your killer instinct gets away from you."

I felt a burning again in the back of my throat. "I...do not...have a killer instinct."

Scott coughed. "Um...haven't you already killed three people?"

My tongue seemed to stick to the roof of my mouth and my jaw fell open. "I didn't...I mean, Wolfe was unintentional and Gavrikov...he was gonna nuke Minneapolis."

"And the other guy?" Scott stared back at me. "Henderschott? The one you tried to teach to fly?"

The angry red settled in my cheeks, burning me as I took a breath before answering. "That wasn't me."

Scott looked back the way we had come, back toward the creek, which I could still hear running in the distance. "Yeah, well *that* was all you. And Eve wasn't an enemy."

"This is a pointless discussion." Parks' voice was rough, like a flint striking a rock or a knife running over a sharpening stone. "Byerly, help Forrest back to her room. And let her rest, will you? You know how using her power takes it out of her."

The burning in my cheeks got a little worse; I was pretty sure that Scott and Kat were sleeping together, but I didn't really want to know for fact if it was true. Most of that was because there was someone I wished I could be sleeping with, but it wasn't possible for me to touch him for more than three seconds without causing him excruciating pain followed by death. They walked away, Scott half-carrying Kat toward the dormitory building, which was quite a distance.

"What's your problem, Sienna?" My head snapped back around to find Parks still looking at me, the rough, wrinkled skin around his eyes folded more than usual. They weren't quite slitted, but they were a lot closer to closed than normal. It was the same look he got when we'd go to the firing range for weapons practice and he had to focus on a target at some distance. Parks was blunt to a fault, but he didn't mean anything bad by it. He just said what he thought and let you sort it out.

"I'm just tired." I couldn't get a hand up to cover my mouth without Parks knowing I was lying. Hell, he probably knew anyway because his eyes grew more closed and he nodded. For the last six months he'd watched me as he trained all of us. We were a class of three, so it's not like he had a ton of people to pay attention to. "We've been at a higher tempo of training lately, early mornings, late nights, all that. Like you said, it just wears on me. I'm ready to get to it." I tried to hold my head higher, look him in the eyes, all that point-the-chin-in-defiance stuff. "I've had enough of the games. I want to get out in the field and go to work chasing down rogues."

His gaze softened, the wrinkles spreading out. "Ariadne says you're not ready."

"That would matter to me if Ariadne was my training officer and worked with me every day." I found I no longer needed to fake the defiance, the chin jutting. "I'm ready. Like it or not, me and the Junior League just took out two members of M-Squad. What do you think?"

He played it cool, too damned cool, not looking away but not registering a thing until he kicked his old, brown cowboy boot into the dusty ground. "We'll find out soon enough if you're ready. I must be getting old and senile to have taken down Kat first instead of you."

"She's easier to sneak up on."

"Don't get cocky." His eyes found me again, his fingers stuck in the loops of his old jeans. "Fast way to get yourself killed, underestimating the people you're fighting – or did you not learn from my example today?"

"I got it." I cleared my throat. "I won't underestimate anybody."

"Bold statement to make. Hope you're right about that. You need to trust your teammates though, watch their backs, because they'll be the ones watching yours, not anyone else." He got a sour look and turned away from me for a second. "Get on home, then. Looks like you got the rest of the day off; might want to take your liberty when you can get it. Not much time off around here, you know."

"I know." Believe me, I knew. It'd been six months since I had a day off. I walked back to the dormitory thinking about how different training to be an agent of the Directorate had been from what I thought it would be when I started. Looking back, I felt naive, like I was a kid when I began, wandering in because I had no idea what else I should do with myself. I had, after all, been cast out into the world after the ultimate sheltered life. Sort of.

It was only a couple weeks after first leaving my house (for the first time in over ten years) that I decided to enter the training program. I hadn't even come close to living a normal teenage life when I decided to really leave normal behind and become what amounted to a paranormal cop. The Directorate paid me a lot of money to do this, all in hopes that someday I'd be a useful member of their policing force. And I was good, at least if we went by the training results. I put Scott to shame and made Kat look like a helpless little girl by comparison in every exercise they threw at us, from martial arts to weapons to chase and apprehension.

It was the "soft skills" that I lacked. Diplomacy, presenting a kind face and sympathetic ear to a metahuman who has just manifested their powers or to a human witness, freaked out by something they've seen that defies explanation. That was part of the job I was training for, being what they called a "Retriever" – trying to convince the newly powerful to come to the Directorate to get some purpose and direction in their abnormal lives. I sucked at that. Probably because it was foreign to me.

Maybe it was because I left home at a dead run with only the clothes on my back, being chased by two guys with guns and then, shortly thereafter, a crazed homicidal meta who nearly killed me. I guess after my own experience, it was hard for me to feel a ton of empathy for someone who gets a gentle knock on their door from someone without a gun who explains that they're different, they're special, and that there's a place for them, then offers them a chance to join a training program to channel their powers. It's a little different than my first real encounter with powers, which involved me being nearly choked to death in a grocery store parking lot after watching a maniac kill two innocent people.

I entered the dormitory building and felt the beautiful bliss of the air conditioner unit working overtime, sending a sweet chill across my body. The smell of the air was even different in the dormitory than it was outside, holding some kind of magical scent, like the processed and machined smell of the indoors, so much different than the overpowering, heated and wet atmosphere of the outside. By the time I got to my dorm room all the sweat on my body had congealed, evaporated or turned to a freezing layer of moisture.

I closed the door behind me and peeled off the layers of sticky clothes. I grabbed a bottle of water out of the mini fridge by the desk and drained it on the way to the bathroom. As I stepped under the shower head I reflected that this wasn't so bad; the cool water washed down, rejuvenating me. I was in there for about thirty minutes, which was a short shower for me. When I stepped out I heard someone out in the room, and brushed open the door.

Zack was standing in front of the windows, looking out on the sun-beaten grounds. The sprinklers were going just outside, spraying the thirsty grass with water. I leaned against the bathroom door when I saw him, a smile spreading wide across my lips as I felt the wood of the frame through my bathrobe. "You're watching sprinklers water the lawn instead of me in the shower?" My smile turned wicked as he spun to face me.

Zack was tall, at least six feet, which was a bit of a stretch for me. His hair was a darkish blond, and he usually wore a self-aware smile. He was impassive now, though, with a hint of hesitation. I didn't like it when he wore that expression; it meant he had bad news. "I didn't want to gawk." I knew him pretty well by this point; he was my boyfriend, after all.

"You've got bad news?" I stepped out of the bathroom door, taking a couple steps closer to him, waiting for him to break it to me.

"I'd call it 'disappointing', not 'bad'," he said, crossing the distance between us and carefully placing his hands on my hips as he pulled me closer. He kissed me, but only for two seconds. After three, he'd stagger and get lightheaded. At five seconds, it'd start to burn. He broke away, but kept his hands where they were, avoiding any other flesh-to-flesh contact. The effect of my powers is cumulative, so if I kissed him again, it would start to drain him. "I have to cancel our date tonight."

"Oh." I tried not to show my disappointment, but it was definitely there. We had planned to go into Eden Prairie to eat at my favorite Greek restaurant, and after that see a movie. It was my favorite kind of date night.

"Kurt and I have to go to Michigan to track down a meta that's causing a stir in Detroit." He looked pained as he said it, his handsome face pinched with the regret of having to tell me. "Not sure when I'll be back."

"Hopefully soon?" He rested a hand on my shoulder and I wished I could pull him closer, kiss him again. And again. "Maybe tomorrow?"

He grimaced. "Maybe, but I doubt it. This one sounds complicated – a couple of assaults, a robbery. Might not be that quick."

I rested my head on his shoulder for a second, smelling his cologne, then remembered my hair was wet and pulled away, my hand feeling the cloth of his black suit, where I'd left a damp spot. "I'm sorry."

There was a twinkle in his eye as he laughed. "It'll dry on the way to the airport, and if it doesn't, I'll probably be glad when Kurt and I have to haul our bags through the parking garage to the terminal. I don't know if you noticed, but it's kinda hot out there."

I ran a hand through my hair, trying to untangle it. "I noticed. The most comfortable part of my training exercise was when I ended up having to drag Eve out of the creek."

His brow lowered as he frowned. "Out of the creek? What happened?"

I felt my teeth click together and my jaw tighten. "I...um...kinda knocked her out of the air with a rock."

"That must have been a helluva a rock."

"It was a helluva throw, actually. The rock was just average."

"It's always a helluva throw if you're doing it, Miss Meta." He found his way back to a smile. "Why did you have to pull her out of the creek, though?"

I flinched at the memory of Eve, broken, lying on the rocky shore of the stream. "I kind of...broke her sternum...and ribs...and maybe fractured her skull a little."

His right eyebrow crept up until it was an inch higher than the other. "A little? I've had a fractured skull before. It's not a minor injury."

"It was an accident. Things just got a little out of hand." I took a deep breath.

He chewed his lip, opened his mouth and started to say something, then stopped. He blinked, then started again. "It wasn't Wolfe?"

"Ugh." I turned away from him, exhaling sharply. "Why does everyone keep asking me that? It's not Wolfe, okay? He's buried, safe and sound, way in the back. It was just me, slipping the leash a little, sick of training and thinking I was actually fighting someone. It's kinda been a while since I felt a real threat and peril, you know."

"Yeah, I know." I felt his hand on my shoulder and it took everything I had not to put mine on top of his. Passing out on my floor wasn't something that would make him very happy. "Not much longer and you'll be done with training and into the real world." I turned to look at him over my shoulder. "Then you'll long for the good ol' days of training."

I hung my head. "I doubt it. I just wish things were easier sometimes."

His eyes watched me. "With training?"

"Like...with everything. With training, with us...everything."

"With us?" His hand dropped to his side and he cocked his head. "What's wrong with us?"

"Let's see...I'd like to be able to touch my boyfriend for more than two seconds without stealing his very soul." I spat the words out like they were some kind of foul venom. He took a step back and I closed my eyes and took a breath. "I'm sorry. That's my issue, not yours."

He stared at me, almost a blank look, and I caught the subtle calm of his gaze. "No, it's an issue for both of us."

"Yeah, but it's my fault." The full meaning of his last sentence made its way through my warring emotions and I felt a sharp drop in my stomach. "What do you mean by that?"

He perked up, his mouth forming an oblong "o" as he recoiled slightly. "I...nothing."

"It meant something." I could feel the tension in my face. "It's because we can't—"

"No, I told you, that doesn't matter—"

"It matters to you like it matters to every guy—"

"—there's more to us than just—"

"*It matters!*" My shout ended his protest and he took another step back, as though he were afraid of me unleashing Wolfe on him. "It matters. I know it matters to you. I may have to wear heavy clothing but it doesn't mean I can't *feel* anything through them—"

"I was out of line." He held up his hands. "We knew getting into this that it was going to be different, because you're different. That's not bad, it's just..." His eyes went to the side as he searched for the word. "...really inconvenient at the end of the night."

"Yeah. Well." I looked at the floor. "You're not the only one it's inconvenient for."

"I just meant that—"

"You think I don't want to?" I was back on his eyes again and he grimaced, balled up a fist and looked away. "You think I don't think about it all the time? You're not the only one that feels the effects after a date. We can't even sleep in the same bed without worrying that I'll roll over and press my cheek against you in the middle of the night, making you another ghost in my head."

"I didn't come here to fight." He was focused on me, his eyes earnest, face oddly blank. "I came to say goodbye. I have a plane to catch in an hour and a half."

"Well, you better get moving, because the airport's at least a half-hour away at this time of day." I pulled my arms tighter against me and narrowed my eyes at him.

He started toward the door and I watched him go. He stopped and started to say something, his fingers and knuckles white as they held the edge. He made it through a half-spin and halted, and I heard him breathe deep as his head dipped down. Whatever he had on his mind didn't come out, though, and after a minute he turned back and walked out the door, closing it much gentler than I would have expected.

My hand went to my forehead and covered my eyes from the light. I hoped he'd be all right on his trip, but I didn't have the guts to call him and tell him that. I heard my smartphone beep – the one the Directorate had given me – and felt a thrill as I ran to where I'd left it on the desk next to the computer. I turned it on and swiped the screen to find I had a text message waiting. It appeared and I sighed – it wasn't him. My eyes played across the words and my hand went back to my forehead, blotting out the light, as if that could make the world, all my troubles, and that damned text message go away.

I'm back in town. Come over so we can talk. – Charlie

4

About an hour later I shifted my car into park in the driveway of my house. The tree-lined streets provided a little shade, but when I opened the car door, I felt the blast of warmth and hurried to get inside. The soles of my shoes seemed to stick on the driveway as I walked to the front door, pausing in the closed-off porch to shut the outside door before I opened the door to the house. The light was dim and mostly came in from gaps in the boards that covered all the windows, just the way Mom had set them up, screening me, the girl in the house, from the world outside every time she left.

I took a deep breath and slid my key in the lock. While Mom had been missing for the past six months, Ariadne had checked the records and told me that there wasn't a mortgage on the place. I had used my ample earnings to keep the property taxes and homeowner's insurance paid and a lawn and maintenance service helped keep the place up for me. I stopped by every week or so, just to make sure everything was okay, but otherwise the house was empty.

Except when Charlie came to town.

The smell of something cooking on the stove hit me as I shut the door. The air conditioner was running and I felt the effects, the cool air filtering in like a sigh of relief after holding my breath. The alarm was deactivated; no reason to keep it active since no one was living here. When last I had left, the place was clean, a little musty, but otherwise all right.

I had left all Mom's clothes in her closet, the dishes in the cupboards, but cleaned most of the food out save for the things like Ramen Noodles that didn't have an expiration date looming.

I heard her clanging some pots in the kitchen before I saw her. She peeked a head around the wall and flashed me a smile. Her hair was dark, long, and stood out against her tanned skin and white teeth. Her lips were curled, and painted the deepest shade of red the cosmetics companies made. "Hey there." She emerged from the kitchen and I almost blinked in surprise. I shouldn't have; nothing about my aunt Charlene – Charlie, she liked to be called – should have surprised me by now.

She wore a white tank top that was partially sweated through, and jean shorts that were cut off way too short. Her bare feet were leaving moisture spots on the linoleum floors as she stepped, walking delicately on her toes over to me. Her midriff was bare where her shirt didn't quite reach the waistband of her shorts, which was frayed badly and washed out, white threads where there might once have been blue, the button at the top of her fly a clash against her belly. I shook my head and she smiled wider. "Your mom didn't like how I dress, either."

"I don't care how you dress." I walked toward her, suddenly self-conscious in my heavy jeans and t-shirt that covered me to the neck.

She spread her arms wide, prompting me to give her a careful hug, avoiding the prodigious amount of skin she had exposed. "Be careful," she said in whispered caution, "you know the stronger succubus will drain the weaker." I pulled back and she made to muss my hair, but I pushed her away with a gloved hand, drawing a laugh from her.

"What brings you back to the Cities?" I asked, using the local slang for the Twin Cities of Minneapolis and St. Paul. I walked my way to the couch as she leaned against the pillar at the edge of the kitchen.

"Just passing though." She said it breezily, like she did almost everything, not a care in her world. She smiled. "Figured I'd drop in on my favorite niece."

"Your only niece, to hear you tell it."

"That too. You know, you could do a better job of stocking this place. All I found was Ramen."

"Want to go out to eat?"

"No plans with your boyfriend, the agent, for tonight?" Her leer was suggestive, in a way that if my mom had ever let slip onto her face, would have freaked me out. They were so different.

"No." I didn't look away, exactly, but neither did I look toward her.

"Uh huh." She bored in on me and stepped back into the kitchen, peering through the tiny pass-through that looked out into the living room. "You guys break up?"

I sat down and tugged at my jeans, which felt tight, restrictive and hotter than they had any right to be considering how low the air conditioner had been set in here. I'd feel the electricity bill this month, I bet. "No. Not exactly." She stared through the little square hole at me, not looking away. "We had a fight."

Her face disappeared, but her voice was still loud. "Lemme guess: about touching."

I felt my lower lip jut out, puckering. "What else would we fight about?"

"Couples fight about lots of things, sweetie." Her voice came from the kitchen, over the clanging of a pan. "But succubi tend to argue about one, if they're crazy enough to be part of a couple."

"You calling me crazy?" I said it with an air of amusement.

"Little bit. You are just like me, after all." I caught a grin through the pass-through and then I heard water pouring down the drain in the sink. A minute later Charlie emerged from the kitchen. "I mean, there's a whole world of men out there. You don't really have the luxury of sleeping with the ones you like and expecting them to be alive in the morning, so..."

I looked away from her. "Yeah. I know it, he knows it, but it still makes us both crazy." She sat down on the couch next to me, splaying out and putting her bare feet on the glass coffee table I'd bought as a replacement for the one broken months ago. "How do you deal with that?"

She had her mouth open, her tongue rolling over her molars, the very picture of disinterest. "You don't sleep with the ones you don't want to die, and you don't get close enough to anybody to have it matter."

"I just...I'm sick of being the world's greatest tease to my boyfriend. He's a good guy, and..." I stopped as her chest jerked in a case of the giggles. "What?"

"You don't have to be a tease. I mean, there are other ways to—"

"Well, yeah, I mean, I know but—" I stuttered as I answered her.

"Just making sure. I wouldn't have expected your mom to teach you anything."

I blushed. "She didn't. But I mean, I know stuff—"

"Sure you do, sweets. Sure you do." Charlie slapped me on the thigh and clicked her tongue against her teeth. "So are we going out to eat or what? 'Cause I'm starving and I poured the Ramen down the sink."

"What?" I blinked, still thinking about what we'd been talking about a sentence before. "Oh, sure."

"Your treat, right?" She gave me a wide grin. "Not all of us have high-paying gigs with the meta cops. The rest of us have to make our money honestly, and I blew the last of my cash getting back into town. Haven't had a chance to stop by the...ATM...yet."

"Sure." I nodded at her and reached for my purse, which was hanging at my side. "My treat. There's a Greek place over in Eden Prairie that's really good—" My attention was caught by the sudden ringing from my bag. "Sorry." I grabbed my cell phone and answered it while Charlie looked on with an eyebrow raised. "Hello?"

"Are you off-campus?" Ariadne's voice was clipped, urgent, washed out slightly by the connection.

"Yeah." I looked around the living room. "I'm just at my house, checking to make sure everything's still all right."

"I need you at Headquarters immediately." Her voice was pinched, more hurried than usual. "The Director and I need to speak with you."

"Umm." I swallowed, heavy. "Is this about—"

"I'm not going to discuss it on an open line. Report to the Director's office in forty-five minutes." I heard a click and looked at the screen of my phone. She'd hung up on me.

I looked up to see Charlie staring at me, her head slanted to the side. "About this Greek place?"

I felt the tension in my guts and wondered if I was about to get a thorough ass-chewing back at the Directorate. "I can't. I just got called back to work."

Charlie's jaw dropped slightly and then twisted to a kind of cold disbelief. "I just threw out the Ramen."

"I'm sorry." I put my phone back in my purse and my hand pushed my hair behind my ears before it fell over my eyes. "I have to go." My hand came out with ten crisp twenty-dollar bills and I handed them to her. "This should cover dinner and a little more. I'm sorry to leave so abruptly, but—"

Her eyes lit up and she took the money a little quicker than I would have thought. "It happens." She tossed her hair over her shoulder and bit her lip as she counted the bills.

"How long are you in town this time?" I tried to catch her eyes, but they were on the money still.

"Not sure." Casual indifference. Great. "A day or two, maybe more, maybe less." She smiled, oddly infuriating me. "You know how it is. Sometimes I get the call and I have to get outta town."

"Yeah, maybe you can explain how that works to me sometime." I laced it with irony. "I need some help, when we get a chance, you know, keeping them under wraps—"

"Pfffff." She turned her exhalation into a full-blown insult by rolling her eyes at the same time. "We've been over this. You absorbed them, not vice versa. It's not that hard. You just make them do what you want them to do. It's your body, not theirs. If they give you any flack, tell them to sit down and shut up, that it's your head and you'll run it however you please."

I pondered how to explain to her how powerful Wolfe could be when he wanted to assert himself. The drug that Dr. Zollers had put me on helped keep him on a leash, along with some other pointers about building a wall in my head that Charlie had given me over the last few months, but I didn't feel like it was enough. He was still back there; I could feel him sometimes, and I hated it. "All right. I gotta go."

"Call me, kiddo. We'll do lunch sometime." She winked at me and started toward the bedroom.

"Just make sure you do the dishes before you leave." She stopped in the hallway and shot a look back at me, a little frown with a slanted down eye that made me wish I hadn't said anything. "You left them in the sink last time and I didn't find them for a week."

"Ugh, fine, yes, Mom." She said it with a laugh and another roll of the eyes. "Tell your bosses I said hi."

"Yeah, right. Because you want the Directorate to know about you."

"Hell no. I'd like to remain far off their radar, if you please." She tugged on her waistband. "They've probably got a file on me. You should check sometime."

"I don't think so," I said. "They don't have any record of my mom having a sister."

"Uh huh. If you were the suspicious sort, you might think something of that – like I was lying?"

I started toward the door. "I don't think you're lying, Charlie."

"Why's that? Doesn't everyone in the meta world want a piece of you? Having someone pretend to be your aunt when you still don't totally know who to trust? Seems like kind of a winning strategy to get close to you, if it worked." She was stock still, waiting for me to respond.

"You're right." I opened the door. "But that's the problem, isn't it?" I smiled at her and a puzzled look crossed her face. "You may be my aunt, but I don't trust anybody."

I caught a flash of a smile from her as I backed out the door. "Heh. You really are just like me. See ya later."

I closed it behind me, stepping out onto the warmth of the porch, and felt the heat pervade me again. "Guess it runs in the family."

5

I wondered if I was in trouble the whole way back to the Directorate, pondering if the man in charge (Old Man Winter, we called him, because he was old, a frost giant, and his name was Erich Winter) was going to run me through the mill for what I'd done to one of his stars. I parked in the Headquarters building and took the elevator straight from the garage to the top floor, where his office was. It was still sunny out when I arrived, in spite of the fact that it was nine o'clock at night. And ninety degrees. I love Minnesota.

It was damned quiet when I knocked on the door, and a muffled call of "Come in," was followed by the door swinging open to reveal Glen Parks, his gray hair pulled back in a ponytail. I checked to make sure I was in the right place. Old Man Winter was sitting at his desk, his back to the window, gray hair and cold blue eyes visible even at this distance. Ariadne was at his shoulder, but her clothing had changed since I had seen her on the grounds earlier. Her red hair was pulled back and her blouse was white.

Parks moved aside for me to enter and I blinked as I stepped into the office. Scott Byerly and Kat Forrest were seated in the chairs in front of Old Man Winter's desk, Kat still looking slightly washed out, and Scott was quiet, his fingers resting on his chin, eyes forward. "Looks like the party started without me." I clutched the strap of my purse a little tighter, wondering if I was about to get smacked down. No one said anything.

Scott stood as I approached the desk, offering me his seat. I smiled and shook my head, then turned my concentration back to Ariadne and Old Man Winter, who both stared at me, Old Man Winter with his usual stoic calm, Ariadne intense, her eyes almost on fire. Scott found his way back into the seat and the silence continued, unabated, as I shifted my weight between my feet for the next thirty seconds or so, hoping someone would say something before I had to resort to small talk.

"I suppose you're wondering why we called you all here." Ariadne was the one that spoke, the lines visible at the corners of her eyes.

Kat and Scott exchanged a look with each other. Kat sat up straighter in her seat, her eyes a little wide. "Um...because Sienna nearly killed Eve?"

"I didn't..." I stopped myself just in time. I didn't look at Old Man Winter. "It was an accident."

"Unfortunately, we don't have time to hash over training accidents at the moment." Did I detect a note of regret and acrimony in Ariadne's voice on that one? Her mouth remained a severe line. "We have other business." She looked over Kat's shoulder to Parks.

I turned to look at our trainer and he stepped forward, a folder in his hand. "In the last twenty-four hours there were a string of convenience store robberies from Gillette, Wyoming across the Interstate 90 corridor in South Dakota that have caught our attention."

Scott snorted, and when we all looked at him, his face went red. "Sorry. It's just funny to hear I-90 described as a corridor. It's a big, long stretch of dusty plains and nothing."

Parks stepped between us and set the folder on the desk, opening it to reveal some photos. "Corridor or not, this could be a problem. No fatalities so far, but there were assaults during each of the robberies. The one in South Dakota included an assault on a local police officer. Several concussions for the store clerks, some trouble remembering what happened, including the assailant, who," he coughed, "appears to have overpowered all the victims without a weapon." He pointed to one of the photos. "This clerk was lucky: his head nearly went through the counter, but he lived."

I stared at the picture he indicated. The shelves behind the counter were trashed, the glass broken, and blood stains ran in a circular splatter down the surface. It looked like whatever had happened had been painful. "You think it's a meta."

Parks paused before answering. "Yeah. It's the Sherriff's Deputy in Draper that puts it over the top for us. He was knocked out before he could draw a weapon or react. That's not normal. Assuming he was following procedure, he wouldn't have let someone get so close to him." He looked at each of us in turn. "We've seen this sort of pattern before. It's probably a young meta, a junior hellion who's getting hold of his oats, thinks he's a badass, not quite ready to cross into the realm of killing just yet, but getting there."

"Probably dangerous if cornered," Ariadne said, leaning on the desk with both hands. "M-Squad is being dispatched to help some of our agents from the Texas branch deal with a severely dangerous meta that's wreaking havoc in western Kansas, and our other agents are on assignments, which leaves us with no one to follow up on these incidents."

I perked up and saw Scott and Kat do the same. "No one?" My question was tentative, and I was reminded of the times when I would get Mom to break her rigid and inflexible rules. I called those occasions miracles, because they didn't happen very often.

Ariadne's mouth became a thin line. "We're strained. Meta activity is up – way up. We're spending a lot of time chasing ghosts lately – things that don't pan out." She brought a hand up to push her hair back and I caught a glimpse of something, written hard across the faded lines of her face. Ariadne wasn't old, more like middle age, but in that moment she sure as hell looked it. "We have no one else to send, and this needs to be followed up on. Congratulations." Her eyes bored into each of us in turn. "You're up."

"This is serious business," Parks said, his arms folded as he stood apart from Ariadne and Old Man Winter. "You're not kids anymore and I vouched for you, told 'em you're ready to give it hell. Don't take any stupid chances, and watch each other's backs."

I swallowed my excitement. "What do you want us to do, exactly?"

Ariadne exchanged a look with Parks. "The last robbery was about three hundred miles south of the Twin Cities, at six o'clock this morning, in Owatonna, Minnesota."

"I know where that is." Scott was awake with a little excitement. "They've got an awesome outdoors store down there—"

"You're not going down there to go shopping." Ariadne cut him off without mercy. "You're going down there to ask questions and establish a direction to head." She opened a packet and slid the contents across the desk to us. I saw my face on a driver's license, as well as one for Scott and Kat. There were also three leather holders that looked a lot like wallets, but when I picked one up and flipped it open it held the credentials of an FBI Agent named Katrina Ahern, with a picture of Kat.

I held it up and dangled it in the air in mild surprise. "Impersonating a federal agent is a felony."

Ariadne met my stare, grim and serious. "It's real. Your names and pictures are in the FBI database and you'll pass muster unless you do something deeply stupid. My advice?" She let a little half-smile loose as she said it.

"Don't do anything deeply stupid," I said, staring at the FBI ID with my picture in it. "You said these are real—"

"They'll even get you into an FBI field office if you had some reason to go there," Parks said. "I wouldn't recommend it, though, because you'll likely have to answer questions you won't want to. These are so you can bypass local law enforcement if they give you any guff, and to get civilians to answer your questions. Now, you all look like friggin' kids, but we'll dress you up professionally and that oughta take care of most of the problem."

I stared at the Driver's License with my picture on it. I wondered idly why I'd been given it, then realized it fit my new name, Sienna Clarke. I also noticed it added about five years onto my birthdate. I tried not to think about the implications of being twenty-three years old in a single stroke.

"All this is part of your cover story." Ariadne's voice snapped me out of my thoughts. "You're rookie agents, chasing down leads on a robber that's crossed interstate lines."

"What happens if we run across the real agents who are investigating it?" I asked because I was curious. I had a feeling it would be bad.

Parks smiled. "According to the FBI's computers, agents Clarke, Green and Ahern," he nodded at each of us in turn, "are the only ones assigned to this case. Your only issues will be the ones you make for yourselves, which is why Ariadne was cautioning you not to make a spectacle."

"So you want us to track this guy down?" Kat looked a little confused. "Catch him or kill him...?"

"Capture, please." Ariadne's tone turned to ice. "If things escalate, we'll examine other options, but for now it's capture only. While the robber has used brutal means, as yet he or she hasn't caused serious, lasting harm to any of the victims. Like Parks said, we suspect a teenager, manifesting their powers and getting out of control with the taste of freedom they're experiencing."

She drew herself up, removing her hands from the desk and tucking them behind her back. "This is their tipping point. If we act quickly, we can save them and bring them back here. If you screw it up, they go the other way, become a criminal for life and either spend time in our Arizona facility or end up dead."

"You'll draw weapons from the armory in case things get out of hand." Parks was stern as he said it. "Just make sure you aren't the ones who make it go that way."

Ariadne shot a look at Parks. "They're all qualified to carry a sidearm?" After he nodded, she went on. "Remember that your best weapon is yourselves. You'll leave within the hour. Pack a bag and be prepared to be gone for a week or more. Any questions?" She waited for us to ask anything, but none of us did. "Keep your cell phones on you at all times. I expect progress reports every three hours while you're awake, even if it's only something as mundane as 'We stopped to pee at a gas station'. If we suffer from anything on this excursion, it will be overcommunication, not under." She glared at each of us in turn. "And no fighting amongst yourselves."

"It's been like...months, since any of us fought," I said.

"And keep your temper in check." Ariadne looked daggers at me. "Are we clear?"

"Like Saran wrap, but without the flexibility." I smiled at her.

"You are being entrusted with a responsibility that is most serious." Old Man Winter finally broke his silence, leaving behind the role of set piece that he so often cultivated during meetings and gracing us with his deep, thickly accented voice. It was so smooth he could have been on the radio, but it was intimidating too, the way it spilled out, with more authority than anyone else I'd met. "This is your first step out of training. Agent Parks has assured us that the three of you are ready, but remember that you are still being tested, that you are not yet agents. Succeed and follow the rules and this can be a significant mark in your favor; fail and we will have to evaluate how effective your training has been."

His ice cold gaze fell on Kat first, causing her to shudder, then on Scott. "Be careful and achieve your objective. This is your chance." His eyes fell on me last of all, and I felt a freezing chill as he looked through me. "Do not fail us."

6

"Can you believe this?" Scott slapped the steering wheel as we cruised out the front gate of the Directorate an hour or so later. "This is it! Finally, the big time!"

Kat gave him a weak smile from the passenger seat, but she didn't say anything. I was stretched out across the seat behind them, supposed to sleep first so I could drive later if need be. It had been a long day, filled with more emotion than I had wanted it to contain. I checked my phone for the thousandth time since Zack had left. Still not a word, a text message, anything. We'd had fights before, but this one was different. He'd never not talked to me afterward. I chalked it up to him catching a flight and hoped he'd call me when he landed.

"Isn't anybody else as excited about this as I am?" Scott's disbelief was edging into his enthusiasm. He looked at Kat, who shrugged, then turned to me. "What about you?"

I yawned. "It's a hell of an opportunity. Let's not screw it up, lest we get six more months of running around the woods, trying to subdue members of M-Squad without hurting them badly."

"About that," Kat said, turning to face me. "You got your head on straight? Not gonna go crazy and flatten this meta we're chasing, are you?"

"Let's catch him first," I said, "then I'll worry about whether I'm gonna put the severe hurt on him or not. After all, we're basically heading to some town in the middle of nowhere hoping there's a clue that will lead us on to the next place this person's gonna strike."

"Criminals are dumb." Scott turned the SUV onto US Highway 212, heading east. "It wouldn't surprise me."

"You think he left a note that says, 'Next I turn south and drive 400 miles to Ankeny, Iowa, where I will rob a convenience store and stop to use the potty'?" I rolled my eyes.

"Why do you think they're sending us to Owatonna if there's not going to be any clues as to where he's going next?"

"He or she," Kat said.

I yawned again. "Because half of what the Directorate does is gather evidence so they can justify locking these criminal metas up when they actually catch them. I've seen the files. We'll pick up the evidence and get whatever info the locals have, and when the Directorate hears about the next attack, we'll haul ass to catch up."

Kat and Scott exchanged a look and then she turned back to me. "Wow, you've given this some thought. But what makes you think that the, uh...the meta...the criminal—"

"Suspect." Scott said it businesslike, as though he were trying to play the part of a real FBI agent. "Or perp. That's what they call them on the TV shows."

"Anyway," Kat said, "what makes you think the perp will have a destination? Couldn't they just be on a drive, or maybe running from something?"

"Maybe." I felt the cool air from the AC, slowly flushing out the humid heat that lingered even now, after the sun was down for a couple hours. The temperature display for outside still read 83 degrees. "It could be a Bonnie and Clyde-type situation, where they're just bopping around from place to place, but it seems a little odd. I'm kinda surprised there's not more information on who the perp is."

"We'll ask some questions when we interview the victim." Scott sounded self-assured.

I looked over at Kat. "You have the details on this one?"

"Um..." She fumbled for her phone and clicked it on. Peering at the screen, she tapped it a few times and then started to read. "Yes, okay. Daniel Lideen, age twenty-five, of Waseca, Minnesota. Looks like he's worked at the store for about six years, assistant manager, was alone on the night shift...a patron found him at around 6 A.M., looked to have been knocked out for a while before he got rousted by this customer, who's a regular." She looked up. "Nothing spectacular there. Multiple contusions to the head from getting slammed into the counter, maybe a concussion or brain injury; the last report indicates they weren't sure."

"Hm." I got lost in my thoughts. "You can take a peek inside, though, right? Figure out what's wrong with him?"

She nodded. "I can probably take care of any memory loss. Was that what you were thinking?"

I smiled. "I was thinking it'd be nice to help the poor guy out since he got the crap kicked out of him, but that's not a bad idea either. After all, if he can give us a description of the perpetrator, that would make our job easier."

It got quiet for a while after that. I sat with my head leaned against the window, staring out at the darkened fields passing us by until we got into the suburbs. I recognized the familiar lights of Eden Prairie as we passed through and got onto the 494 loop, skirting the southern edge of the city. I could tell Scott was still excited, and he chattered occasionally about how great the assignment was going to go and his certainty we'd achieve success and start building a reputation within the Directorate. I was sure he was right, but was privately hoping that it would be a good reputation rather than a bad one.

We caught Interstate 35 and headed south as the clock clicked 11 P.M. The traffic on the road was light and Scott kept us well above the speed limit. Parks had mentioned before we left the Directorate that the plates for the SUV were flagged as an FBI vehicle, and there were flashing lights and a siren in case we needed them.

The land flattened out and the buildings became more scattered as we passed out of the southern suburb of Burnsville. Shopping centers gave way to fields and forests, the trees becoming havens for shadow as the headlights of our SUV chased the blackness off the road ahead. Forty miles passed in the blink of an eye – I closed my eyes and was jarred awake what felt like seconds later, but I knew wasn't after I smacked my mouth and it was dry, my tongue finding a layer of film over my teeth.

I rubbed my eyes as I pushed myself off the window. Kat and Scott were talking in hushed voices in front of me. I heard him chuckle, saw her giggle and bat her eyes, watched her hand reach out and stroke his forearm. I started to ask them where we were but stopped myself. There was no reason for me to interrupt their moment.

I watched a sign pass that indicated that Owatonna was only a few miles away. I quietly pulled the water bottle I had left in the cup holder and drained it, rehydrating my mouth. Kat and Scott took no notice of me, still chatting in low voices. I could have heard them if I tried, but I made an effort to tune them out. I focused on Zack and checked my phone again. Not a text message, a missed call, a voicemail, nothing.

"You're awake." Kat's voice contained a hint of surprise and I looked up from my phone to find her tight smile looking back at me. Her eyes were slightly squinted and she appeared to be chewing on her lower lip. I felt a little bad for her, because it was obvious nerves were working on her at least a little. "The GPS says we'll be there in less than five."

I nodded as I took another drink of water and popped a piece of gum in my mouth. I had left the purse behind when I changed into a gray suit with a white blouse underneath, placing my wallet and FBI ID into the pockets of my suit jacket. I could feel the lump that was my pistol under my left arm, the weight of it against my side in my shoulder holster. I knew Kat and Scott were carrying as well, but I doubted that they knew I was carrying a backup in an ankle holster on the recommendation of Parks. The two of them had been uncomfortable with the firearms portion of our training. I reveled in it, like I did all the other parts that involved fighting.

Parks drilled it into our head over and over to use every tool at our disposal. "Your powers set you apart from others," he'd said. "In ancient times, people with your powers could rule entire countries. In modern times, one man with a gun can hurt you more than an ancient army. The gun is mankind's great equalizer and you're a fool if you don't recognize it." He talked like a drill sergeant when he was training us. I knew he'd done a stint in the army because he'd told me so. Parks knew his stuff. He'd been with M-Squad for almost ten years, since he and Bastian had basically built the unit from the ground up.

I also carried a knife strapped to my calf on his recommendation, but that was another thing I wasn't likely to mention to the squeamish Kat especially, nor Scott. No use making them edgy. I was glad Scott was excited. I was skeptical. I hadn't done this before, and I didn't want to get into a situation I might not be prepared for while hunting down a meta I had no knowledge of.

Scott guided the car onto the exit ramp as the gentle voice of the GPS told him to turn. I could see the Kwik Trip lit up just off the freeway, a fifty foot sign out front with the price of gas in red as an enticement to save a cent over their competitors across the street. We turned into the parking lot and stopped in front of the pump. Kat and I both looked at Scott, questioning, until he shrugged. "We need gas. We can look around here and then head out to the hospital to interview Lideen, if he's awake."

Kat walked alongside me toward the door while Scott pulled out his Directorate issued credit card to swipe it in the gas pump. "Talk to the clerk while I go to the bathroom?" She said this to me as I pulled open the glass door so she could go in.

"Uh, okay." I shook my head as she veered toward the back of the store. I watched her pass a bakery case with a wide selection of donuts. I felt my stomach rumble and realized I never did get my dinner, but I shook it off. It felt like my metabolism had slowed in the last few months, in spite of the training routine. I had to watch what I ate.

I approached the counter as the Asian kid behind it stared at me, the only person in the store. I reached for my FBI ID and flipped it open, trying not to feel nervous. After all, he was most likely going to be paying attention to the ID, not me. "Sienna Clarke," I said, just barely remembering my assumed name. "FBI. I'm here to ask some questions about the robbery."

"Uh, yeah." He nodded, his acne seeming to have reddened. "I wasn't here when it happened."

"I know that." I pulled out a small notepad and pen I was carrying in my pocket. "The victim was a Daniel Lideen, right?" He nodded at me. "You work with Dan very often?"

"Nah," he said. "He was usually mornings or overnights. I work evenings; this is only part-time for me. Dan's a full-timer. I was here before he took over last night at eleven, though."

"See anything unusual?" I was asking mostly out of general interest. I wasn't planning on spending a lot of time interviewing this kid, since he hadn't been around for the robbery, and based on our information, the perp had been in South Dakota during his last shift.

"Not really." He shrugged. "We get a lot of traffic from the interstate, so there's more strangers that come in here than regulars."

"All right, well, thanks for your help..." I looked down at his white nametag, standing out on his blue shirt. "...Shaun."

"Sure." He nodded again. He seemed to let out a deep breath and I suspected he might be a little nervous talking to the law. Couldn't imagine why.

"I'll take these." Kat appeared at my shoulder and plopped a plastic bag onto the counter. I looked down and saw she had filled it with a half dozen donuts from the bakery display against the far wall. She looked up at me innocently. "Want one?"

"I don't think I can," I said. "They go right to my hips."

She picked up one with white frosting and multicolored sprinkles and took a big bite. "You sure?" Her mouth was full, and the glorious smell of sugary dough was in the air. "It's really good."

I blinked and shook my head. "I can't." I looked down at the bag then back up at her with a suspicion. "Are you going to eat all of those?"

"Unless Scott wants one, yeah."

411

I sighed and pushed my way out the exit with a forced smile for Shaun, who blanched because I caught him checking out Kat. It figures; not only does she have a body that draws the attention of every man that crosses her path, but she doesn't have to work that hard to maintain it.

Scott was screwing the gas cap on when I got back to the car. "How'd it go?"

"Fine. Your girlfriend will be back in a minute; she's buying out their entire bakery."

He frowned. "I didn't expect to turn up much here, but I kinda hoped..." He let his words trail off.

"That we'd find the meta hiding out in front of the store, wearing a trench coat, a backward baseball cap, and rapping profanities?" I cast a look back toward the entrance as Kat made her way across the parking lot toward us, a donut in one hand and the bag hanging from her fingers in the other.

"Guess this is where the real detective work begins, huh?" He opened his door and climbed in while I got into the backseat behind him again. I watched him start to fiddle with the GPS. "Let's hope the victim or the local cops can shed some light on things for us, or else we're gonna be hanging out in this town until we pick up another incident. Hospital is an exit back, police station is east of here a little ways." He shrugged. "Hospital first?" I nodded and we were off.

When we arrived at the nurses' station and flashed IDs, a middle-aged overweight woman in pink scrubs showed us to Daniel Lideen's room. He was sleeping, his long face tilted to the side. The nurse left when Scott asked her to and I looked to Kat. "You should get a feel for his injuries before you wake him up."

She put her hand on his forehead, causing him to stir slightly. "Not a bad idea." She closed her eyes and her breathing slowed. A light glow appeared under her hand and the clerk's skin started to shine. A black and purple bruise under his eye began to fade along with a thin scab that ran the length of his cheek. I saw Scott shutting the door as Kat took her hand off the clerk's forehead and his eyes opened, blinking at the two of us. "That should do it," Kat said.

"Hello, Daniel," I said as I leaned over him. "My name is

Sienna Clarke and I'm with the FBI." I halted to give him a second to process that information. His eyes blinked a few times as he tried to focus on me. "I'm here to ask you some questions about your assailant."

"Oh...okay." His voice was a little scratchy, and I couldn't shake the feeling that he was more asleep than awake. "I already told the officers what I remember."

"I know." I tried to make my reply as soothing as possible. "But they're local cops and we're here to ask because the same thing that happened to you happened to some other folks in Wyoming and South Dakota. Can you tell me anything about the person that robbed you?"

He screwed up his face in intense concentration, staring over my shoulder, then went blank. "I don't...I can't remember."

I shot a look at Kat, whose eyes widened as she put her hand on his upper arm. I saw the glow from her as I asked him another question. "Tell me what you do remember."

"Um...I came into work at about eleven...and I did some restocking in the freezer." He squinted, as though he were trying to recall. "I remember eating my sandwich and drinking some coffee at about five." His face relaxed and he shook his head. "After that...I don't know."

I looked sidelong at Kat, who was taking long, ragged breaths and whose hand was at her side. She shook her head. "Can you tell me anything else, Dan? Anything could help."

His eyes were blank. "That's all. That's all I remember."

I gave him as warm of a fake smile as I could. "Excuse me while I talk to my associates." I beckoned to Kat, who followed me, shuffling along in slow steps to the hallway outside. I looked left and then right; the corridors were white, with dingy tile and little color, but empty. I honed in on Kat. "What's the matter with him? Has he got brain damage?"

"No!" She shook her head with more emphasis. "I checked him over again after the first time, and this guy is healed; he's in perfect condition. His skull is fixed, his scars are gone and it doesn't look like there was anything wrong with his brain even when I touched him the first time, let alone now."

Scott looked back at the door to the room, which was drawn. "Is it possible he's lying?"

"Possible." I nodded at him as I chewed that one over. "But I don't think so. I was looking in his eyes as he answered, and he didn't show any of the obvious signs. He was working last night, so it seems unlikely he's secretly the meta doing all this, unless he can somehow teleport to Wyoming and South Dakota on his breaks." I shook my head. "I don't think he's lying. I think there's a simpler explanation."

"What?" Scott looked at me. "You think he has some kind of neurological damage that Kat can't detect?"

I looked back at him, then to Kat, before I answered. "No. I think that whoever attacked him..." I took a step back and looked through the semi-open door to see the clerk sitting upright in bed, blinking, looking around the room, disoriented, even though he had just been healed by someone who could fix nearly any ailment. "...took his memory."

7

We cleared out of the hospital after some perfunctory goodbyes and thank-yous to Daniel, and checked in with Ariadne. We sat in the car, engine running to give us air conditioning to offset the heat (still almost eighty even though it was nearing midnight) while we listened to Ariadne.

"You think whoever attacked him is responsible for his memory loss?" There was a slight fuzzing in the speaker, probably the result of the air conditioner operating near full blast to keep the three of us from sweating through our suits, but otherwise it almost sounded like Ariadne was in the car with us.

"Which guarantees that it was a meta that attacked him." I was almost glum at the realization. I was kind of hoping it was going to be some petty criminal that we could slam dunk and leave to the local authorities. Part of that might be because I was checking my phone every few minutes for a call or message that I had yet to receive. I wasn't going to be the first to break the silence, that much I knew. "Any idea what kinds of metas can cause memory loss?"

"There are a few," Ariadne said. "Let me talk to Dr. Sessions and get back to you with a list."

"Any other incidents?" Scott cradled the phone in his hand, holding it just below his chin when he was talking, as though it were a tape recorder.

"Nothing at present. You still need to meet with the local

cops, but the Police Chief for Owatonna is out for the night, so it's best if you wait until tomorrow to make that stop." There was a pause and a hiss on the phone before Ariadne spoke again. "Check into a hotel and get some sleep. If there aren't any incidents tonight, check in tomorrow morning after you've stopped by the Owatonna PD."

"Understood." I tried to keep the fatigue out of my voice as Scott punched the end button on the phone after the two of them added their responses to my own. "I don't know about the rest of you, but I'm exhausted."

Scott grew a curious grin, one that cracked his ruddy face and made his eyes dance. "You can't go to sleep just yet."

"Pretty sure I can." I rubbed my eyes. "And will."

"No, no, no." The smile was getting kind of creepy. "Do you realize what we're carrying with us?"

"Guns and teenage angst?"

"Ha. No." He reached into his pocket and pulled out his wallet, dangling the new Directorate-issued driver's license in front of my face. "Fake IDs that aren't really fake."

I let my jaw drop in disbelief. "What are you thinking?"

He smiled again, then turned forward in his seat and fastened the seatbelt with one hand while fiddling with the GPS with the other. "I'm thinking we find a hotel with a bar."

I leaned back in my seat and draped my hand over my eyes. "Right. Because there's no possible way this could go horrendously wrong."

I kept my peace on the drive, even though I was questioning not only Scott's level of responsibility but also his sanity. We found a hotel (with a bar across the street) and I shook my head as we pulled up.

Scott must have sensed my discomfort. "We all agree that the meta who's doing this is probably far from here by now, right? If he keeps to the pattern?"

"Mighty big 'if,'" I said with a shake of the head. "But probably."

"So if we check into the hotel and then have maybe one or two drinks..."

I could tell by his smile he was already reveling in the

freedom and there was little I could do to sway him. Still, I had to try. "What if Ariadne calls us after we've been drinking with a lead we need to pursue immediately? We're screwed. We won't even be able to drive anywhere."

"I can drive." Kat spoke, turning to face me. "I'm pretty drained from healing that clerk; I don't think it'd be a great idea for me to drink right now. So if we get a call, I can drive while you guys sober up."

"See?" Scott gave me a shrug of unworry that did little to assuage my concerns. "Got it covered."

I grabbed my bag and opened the door. "Got it covered like what? Like you had Gavrikov covered?"

"You're never gonna let me forget that, are you?" He was following behind, and I caught a hint of annoyance in his voice.

"Not so long as he's stuck in my skull, no."

We checked in, getting two rooms. I started to suggest that Kat and I could stay in one room while Scott stayed in the other, but when I handed him the cards for his room he handed the other to her and I didn't bother to argue. I preferred to stay by myself anyway.

We went up to the third floor where our rooms were side by side. "Meet out here in five and we'll head down together," he said.

"I think I'll pass," I said. "You guys go have a good time. I'm just gonna turn in; might as well have one of us be rested for the morning."

"Come on, Sienna. We've been working our asses off for months, had Parks and Ariadne breathing down our necks, had all manner of shit go wrong, and now we have a chance to unwind. Don't be so uptight."

I took a deep breath before answering so I could avoid ripping his head off while we still had potentially weeks' worth of road tripping ahead of us. "I'm not being uptight. I just don't want to screw this up, okay?"

"I get it." He let the smile recede into a smug, almost taunting expression. "It's okay. I admire your restraint. You probably don't even wonder what it feels like."

I tensed, felt every muscle from my lower back up locking

into place. "Wonder what what feels like?"

"Drinking." His half-smile dissolved into a real one. "You haven't wondered what it's like? Your boyfriend goes out drinking sometimes, doesn't he?"

I felt myself relax, but only a tenth of a percent. Dammit, I had thought he was talking about something far different, and it had let a wave of acid loose in my stomach, sending it roiling. "Yeah, Zack goes out drinking every now and again." Usually when I'm busy, but he does it. Because he's old enough.

"And you never felt curious or left behind?" He smiled, a little too innocently.

Damn his smile. I knew what he was doing, what he was suggesting. Any other day, it might not have found its mark. After all, my boyfriend was mature, responsible, secure in his job, and if he went to the bar with his college buddies, he did it on his time off (and usually when I was training.) I'd never felt left behind, not really, because I was too busy doing other things. I pulled my cell phone out of my pocket and lit up the display. Still nothing. "Fine." I looked back up at him. "One drink."

"Attagirl." He shot a look at Kat. "This'll be fun. The three of us, on our first assignment, blowing off steam, hanging out at the bar." He draped a thick arm around Kat and drew her close, giving her a peck on the cheek. "It's kinda like..." He thought about it for a minute.

"Being grown-ups?" I offered it sarcastically, but it only widened his smile.

"Five minutes." He turned and his hand fell to grab Kat's, and they walked toward their door. "We'll head down together."

I nodded and slid the card key into my door and turned the handle. When I walked inside, I flipped the switch and waited for the lights to come on. The carpet was a deep maroon and it was a simple setup – two beds, desk, dresser and TV.

I threw my bag on the dresser and retreated to the bathroom. I looked in the mirror at myself. I looked older, mostly because of the suit, but also because I had my hair back in a ponytail. I held up a gloved hand and heard the leather stretch as I clenched a fist and then relaxed it. Grown-up indeed. I pulled the glove off and started to splash water on my face to help me wake up, but then remembered that it would probably destroy the careful amount of makeup I had applied earlier, before I left the Directorate. I rarely wore the stuff, but in this case it seemed important for the role I was playing.

I looked again at myself in the mirror and wondered what I was thinking. We were on a serious assignment, the first chance we had to prove ourselves, and we were going to a bar at midnight to have some drinks even though we weren't anywhere close to done with our assignment. I sighed and looked at the faceplate on my phone again. The LED indicator that let me know when I had messages or missed calls wasn't blinking. Screw it. Screw him. We'd been working our asses off for months, Kat was going to stay sober, and Scott and I would just have one or two and call it a night. An energy drink or coffee tomorrow and we'd be ready to keep going.

I tried to remember that reasoning as we walked in the doors to the bar. The light was orange in the room, with flatscreen TVs suspended from the ceiling around the bar itself. Tables were set up to the left and right of the bar area, with a small dance floor in the far corner. Music was playing, a modern pop tune, but not a soul was dancing. I scanned the room as we walked in and the place was only slightly packed, which surprised me given it was Saturday night.

We made our way to the bar, Scott leading us, his grin reaching an infectious stage. He bellied up and Kat sat next to him. I took the seat on the other side of him, mostly because he was more likely to talk than Kat. She was always tired and quiet after healing someone.

The bartender made his way over to us, a guy in his forties that had more than a few extra pounds. He had long brown hair in a ponytail and was happy enough after he checked our IDs. "Whaddya want?" he asked in an accent that was as far from midwestern as I could imagine.

Scott looked over to me first and I shrugged, so he turned

to Kat. "Just water for me," she said. "Designated driver."

"What's good here?" I picked up the mixed drinks menu that he had proffered and thumbed through it.

"Honestly? I got some strengths; I make a pretty good Whiskey Sour, Bloody Mary, Rusty Nail, Dirty Martini...my Fuzzy Navel is the stuff of local legend—"

"You don't need to show us that," Scott said.

The bartender smiled and his face split into jowls. "I also make a pretty good Cherry Bomb."

I shrugged, without a clue. "I'll try the Whiskey Sour."

"Straight up or over ice?"

He looked back at me and I felt the fatigue of the day edging in. "Surprise me."

The bartender nodded and Scott ordered a beer, a local brand, and went to the other end of the bar to prep our order. Once he was out of earshot, Scott turned to me. "What do you think so far?"

"He seems like a nice enough guy. Kinda big, though. You think that's glandular?"

"About the case." Scott shook his head.

"I think we should not screw it up." I tried to give him my most serious look. "Right?"

"Right." He looked back at Kat, who was resting her face on her palms. "Right?" She gave a lethargic shake of the head, pulling it off her hands to spread her palms with indifference. "It'll be fine. Just a drink or two, and we're off to bed for the night, and back to work tomorrow." He smiled again at me and I caught the first hint of nervousness. "But come on, admit it – we're out on our own, on the road, we're in charge of this thing, and we're sitting in a bar after a long day of chasing down a meta. Tell me this isn't how you imagined it."

I felt a charge of amusement. "First of all, it's been like four hours, not a day, and most of it we've been driving, so I don't know how hard it's been." I saw his nervous happiness start to evaporate and stopped myself. "Yeah, it's kinda how I imagined it. Freedom, right?" The bartender returned and set down a napkin and placed my drink on top of it, complete with a maraschino cherry, put a beer bottle in front of Scott and slid a water glass onto the bar beside Kat.

"I'll drink to that," Scott said, raising his beer up and angling it toward me. He waited for me to pick up my glass, which was a lot shorter than his; kind of a midget glass, I thought, like they didn't want me to have a grown-up's cup. I clinked it against his bottle as he said, "To us! To freedom!" and then reached around him to click my glass against Kat's. Even she was wearing a smile, as wan as it was.

"Pretty sure it's bad luck to toast with a water glass," I said to Kat as I took the first sip of my drink. Whatever she said in reply, I didn't hear. I felt my face contract as the full flavor of the whiskey hit my mouth. It was only mildly sour. What caused me to make a face like I'd swallowed battery acid was what I could only assume was the result of the alcohol. It was pungent, powerful, and I immediately wanted to spit it out and throw the cup far, far away from me. They had given me poison, I was sure of it.

"Are you all right?" Scott was looking at me with his brow furrowed. He took a swig and set his beer back down on the bar.

I swallowed the vile mixture and wondered where the barman had gone. I assumed he'd wanted to be as far away from me as possible when I discovered that his idea of a good drink was far removed from what I had thought it would be. "Is it...supposed to taste like I took a swig of household cleaners?"

Scott laughed and looked back at Kat, who feigned a smile of amusement as she rested her face on her hands. "A little strong, huh?"

"It's a little strong in the same way that compared to normal humans, we are a little strong."

He picked up my drink and took a sip. "Not bad. It'll probably take a little bit for you to get used to the flavor, that's all."

I wanted to tell him that the only way I could ever get used to the flavor would be to take a blowtorch to every taste bud in my head first, but I refrained. I stared down at the drink, looking at it like it was an adversary I was facing off with. "Acquired taste, huh?" I picked up my little kid's glass, suddenly thinking it was a lot bigger now. I didn't want to waste a lot of time on this, and it certainly didn't bear sipping, prolonging my disgust for an hour or more, a little shot of revolting nastiness at a time.

I threw it back like I'd seen on TV, trying to ignore the strong, nearly gag-worthy reflex it caused as it passed my tongue and drained down my throat. I felt the ice on my lips, and that was good, the last lingering aftertaste of the liquor still remaining on the cubes. I set the glass down on the bar and shook my head, as though I could rid myself of the tang that was still on my tongue.

The bartender made his way over, and just as I was about to ask him to make my next round a water, he set another Whiskey Sour in front of me. I looked up at him, frozen, like I had gotten caught flashing him a fake ID, except this was much worse. "The gentleman down there sent you this." I looked at the barman, and he lifted a pudgy finger to point to a man down the bar.

He had brown hair, spiked a little in front, with a thin face and intense eyes that caught my attention even from twenty feet away. He raised his glass to me and I could almost feel the ice cubes melt in mine as I picked it up and raised it in a silent toast across the distance between us. He took a drink of his and I took a deep sip of mine, taking care not to make the face that was struggling to get out, that mixture of putrid desire to spit and horror that drinking so vile a liquid was socially acceptable.

"Picked up an admirer, huh?" I turned back to Scott to find him with a second beer in front of him, and his words were drifting a bit as he talked, slurring. I looked past him at Kat, who was shaking her head as if to keep awake, not paying much attention to us.

"I guess." I looked back to the man to find he had turned back to the bar, nursing his drink, attention focused on a soccer game on the screen in front of him. "Or maybe he just figured I was the only unattached woman in the bar." I swiveled on my stool to look around and confirmed my suspicion; most of the people in the bar were plainly coupled up.

I looked to Scott and frowned. "Why didn't he assume I was your girlfriend and send a drink to Kat?" Scott got a blank look, then hemmed and hawed. "Never mind, it doesn't matter," I said. He took a breath and lifted his second beer, draining it.

"Take it easy." Kat leaned over, crossing Scott's body to weigh in over the blaring music that filled the bar, now a classic 80s rock tune that had more metal than an orthodontic patient's mouth. "You're not going for a third, are you?"

"I've been drinking beer and wine with my family since I was like...thirteen," Scott said, his words curling as he answered, his tongue sounding like it was getting heavy. "I can handle it."

"Uh huh." Kat looked from him to me, her eyes narrowed slightly. "How much does your family usually let you have?"

"One." He swayed on the stool. "We're social drinkers, not alcoholics." He laughed, as though it were the funniest thing in the world.

She rolled her eyes and then whispered something in his ear. He straightened on his stool and turned to me. "I think we're gonna turn in for the night." He pulled a wad of cash from his pocket and laid some on the bar. "You coming?"

I felt a flush of red as I imagined what Kat had said that got him to change direction so quickly. I didn't want to be in the room next to them, certainly not for the next half-hour. "I think I'll stay a little longer."

He grinned, a goofy one. "Heh. Well, you might wanna stop after that one." He pointed to my drink. "After all, if this is your first time drinking, you need to build up a tolerance."

I felt a sway of my own in my head. "I'll work on that." I shot him a dazzling smile. "Have fun."

Kat rolled her eyes at me but smiled, a weary look that I knew contained at least a grain of indulgence; her making an accommodation she normally might not have made when she was this tired, only for the purpose of getting him out of the bar before he became too trashed to walk.

As if to illustrate my point, Scott started to stand and his legs buckled. Kat caught him with an arm around his back and I could see her help him regain his balance, her meta strength enabling her to keep him upright. They walked to the door, her steering, him along for the ride. I chuckled under my breath and was dimly aware that the room had a gentle bob to it that could have been my head rocking back and forth. I knew that my best bet was to avoid drinking even one more drop of the suddenly much tastier drink in front of me.

When I turned back to the bar, I started because there was someone in the vacant seat to my left. He caught my eye, those intense blue eyes locked on mine, and he gave me a disarming smile that somehow got me to giggle, which came as a great shock to me. "Sorry," he said. "Didn't mean to startle you."

"I didn't mean to be startled." I took a deep breath and closed my eyes, shaking my head that I'd said that. "Sorry, I just didn't expect—"

"Do you mind some company?" He caught my gaze and held it, and his smile went beyond the realm of disarming and into charming. He was wearing a button-up shirt that was unbuttoned at the top, giving me a glimpse of the beginning of some well-defined chest muscles.

I caught my breath and it held for a minute before I could squeeze out my answer. "I don't mind."

"My name's James. James Fries." He held up his drink, a tall, clear glass with some sort of garnish being the only hint it wasn't water, and took a leisurely sip, not breaking eye contact the whole time he was drinking. "And you are?"

"Sienna." I thought about it for a second, remembering that my identification had a drastically different name on it than the one I'd grown up with. "Sienna Clarke."

"What brings you to the mighty town of Owatonna, Sienna Clarke?" He leaned against the bar, the angle of his body making him look very cool, his laid back attitude drawing my interest.

I took another breath and caught a whiff of a musk, something that left me wanting to take another breath so I could smell it again. "I'm here for work." I blinked a couple times and the room swayed pleasantly. "You?"

"The same." He took a sip and I admired his lips as they caressed the glass. "What do you do for work?"

"I'm..." It took me a second to remember my cover story. After all, I wouldn't have wanted him to think I was some sort of person with super strength and powers that defied reasonable explanation. "I'm with the FBI. I'm doing some...investigating."

"Investigating. How mysterious."

My hand found its way to my glass, which found its way to my lips for another sip. "I do like to keep a certain mystique about me." This time it didn't taste too bad. In fact, it was almost good. "Do you live around here, James?"

"No." I watched the sweat drip from his glass, leaving little blotches, like inkblots on the napkin as the dark wood of the bar bled through. His hand swirled his glass, slow. "I live in Minneapolis. I'm here for work."

"I see. What do you do for work?"

He smiled. "Recruiting."

I laughed, light, and I had no idea why. "That was vague."

There was a glimmer in his eyes. "I have a mystique to keep up, too, you know."

"Fair enough." I put my empty whiskey down and watched as the bartender slid by and snaked it, replacing it with another. I started to protest but he had a wide grin on his fat face and nodded at James as he headed back to the other end of the bar where someone waited with a hand raised in the air. I looked at the new drink and felt a certain pressure in my chest at the realization that this could not end well. "I can't drink this," I said to James and watched him half-smile.

"Why not?"

"I'm a lightweight." I said it with the air of someone making a confession. "And I have to work tomorrow morning, which means I kind of need to call it quits for tonight if I'm going to be at all able to think or drive tomorrow."

"Acetaminophen and ibuprofen are your friends," he said. "And lots of water."

"I think moderation might also be a swell idea."

"Much less fun." His hand moved, very casually, across the bar and came to rest on my own. I could feel the gentle weight of it through the glove, the very slight warmth, and it caused me to redden, a heat rising in my cheeks that might not have been noticeable had I not been drinking. He watched my reaction. "Is that too much, too fast?"

"What?" I had been in a little bit of a daze, staring at his hand on mine. "No. Not really."

"No?" He picked up my hand and cradled it in his, rubbing it. "Not this either?"

It felt strangely good, even through the glove. "No. That's fine." His eyes were on mine, staring, with a warmth that I found compelling, drawn to, and I couldn't quite explain it. I found myself leaning closer to him.

He leaned in and kissed me. It was sudden, and caught me by surprise. My eyes widened when he did it, but it felt so good, the pressure, the warmth of his hand as it touched my cheek, and rested there, his lips on mine. I kissed him back, the haze in my mind so agreeable, and I felt his tongue part my lips and swirl. I let him hold my face in his hands and he kept them there, pressing his lips on mine so firmly—

I opened my eyes in shock and with the realization that I couldn't, wasn't able to—

I pulled away, broke from him with sudden violence, standing so abruptly I knocked over both my stool and my drink, trying to get backward, away from him, him who didn't know what I was—

He looked at me with vague amusement. "So that was the line, huh?"

"What?" I looked around to see everyone in the bar staring at me, and turned back to him, still sitting on his stool, the same little smile crooking his lips. "No, it's fine, I just...can't..." I let out a breath in frustration. "Are you okay?"

His eyebrows arched upward. "I'm fine. Are you?"

"Yes. I'm fine. I'm sorry." I cocked my head and tried to give him my most regretful expression. "Thank you for the drinks, James. You're a really nice guy – and a fantastic kisser, by the way – but I have to go."

He stood and tossed some bills on the bar. "Why don't I walk you out?"

He took a step toward me but I held a gloved hand out and rested it on his chest. I let it linger there; damn, it was firm. "I don't think that's a good idea, for a lot of reasons."

He seemed to be suppressing his grin, but nodded. "Fair enough." He reached into the pocket of his pants and came back with a business card. "If you're ever in Minneapolis, give me a call."

I straightened my blazer and nodded, feeling the holster against my ribs. "I'll keep that in mind." I nodded toward his stool. "You might want to sit down for a few minutes." He gave me a quizzical look. "Just a suggestion. Nice to meet you, James."

I walked from the bar and tried really, really hard not to look at him as I pushed my way out the door. It didn't work, and he gave me a sizzling smile that made me want to go back to him, and kiss him until his eyes rolled back in his head and his face melted off. I shook my head in disgust at that thought and walked out into the parking lot. It felt like I was being weak when I thought it, weak and casual and flippant, endangering James's life so I could feel...something. I was lucky that the eternity that it felt like he kissed me was less than I thought it was, or he would have made a hell of a scene pitching over in the bar.

The parking lot lurched as I was about halfway across it. I stopped, regained my balance, and kept going. Once I reached the elevator after passing through the hotel lobby, I leaned against the wall and felt my head spin. Those Whiskey Sours weren't so bad.

When the elevator door dinged I opened my eyes to find the doors still closed. I heard another ding and stared, waiting for them to open. On the third ring I realized it wasn't the elevator: it was my phone, and I scrambled to grab it out of my pocket. I thrust it up to my ear after hitting the talk button, not even looking at the caller ID. "Hello?"

The elevator dinged, the door opened, and I heard Kat's voice on the other end of the line as well as in person. She stood in the hall and turned her head in surprise when she saw me stagger out of the elevator. "Get packed." She pulled her phone away from her ear and I got a good look at her face, which was still drawn, but now more serious, her blond locks twisted and mussed around her. "Ariadne called. There was another robbery."

I dropped the cell phone back in my pocket and my hand went out to the wall automatically to support me. "Where?"

"Red Wing, Minnesota." She started to hold out a hand to help me but I waved her off. "It's north of here, a little over an hour, on the Wisconsin state line. We need to move now." A little hint of a smile peeked at me, understated, on her tanned and pretty face. "If we hurry, we might be able to catch up with them."

8

A few minutes later our SUV was back on the highway, doing about a hundred miles an hour, barreling north on the interstate with the siren blazing. Kat was at the wheel and I was in the passenger seat. Scott was passed out in the back seat, his head against the window. We hit a bump and he didn't stir. I rolled my window down and let the warm night air blow in my face.

"How are you holding up?" Kat didn't take her eyes off the road. I could tell she was tense, white-knuckling the wheel. I would have been too. Scott had learned to drive years ago. Kat and I had learned in the last six months, with Parks as our instructor, in an intensive driving course that the Directorate gave us to teach us how to drive both offensively and defensively. Now I could run a car off the road at eighty miles an hour easier than I could parallel park.

"My world is in motion," I said, as I swallowed heavily. I didn't quite feel sick, but I certainly felt the first strains of it. "I could do with a little less of that."

A tight smile made its way onto her face and a few of her teeth peeked out from between her lips. "At least I didn't take the back roads route the GPS suggested. All those twists and turns..."

"Bleh." I shook my head. "Drinking is bad for you. Also, I think I came close to kissing a guy to death in the bar."

"What?" Her head snapped over to look at me.

"He's fine." My eyes pointed straight ahead, and I was

trying to watch the road in order to avoid getting motion sickness. "I mean, he seemed fine, so we must not have kissed for very long."

"Um, wow." Her eyes were not on the road, which became obvious a moment later when she had to swerve after the tires started bumping on the strips at the edge of the highway. "Sorry. Wait, so what happened? I mean, aren't you and Zack..."

"I don't know." I pulled out my phone and pushed the button again. The screen flared to life, giving me a perfect view of the background, but there were no missed calls or waiting text messages. "We kind of had a fight."

"Oh." She turned to look at me, then swiveled her gaze back to the road. "What about?"

"Pretty much about what you and Scott were doing just before we left."

"Sleeping?" She turned to me and then reddened. "Oh. Before that."

"Yeah."

She let the silence hang for a minute. "Because you guys can't...?"

"Yeah."

I think the edge in my response put her off, because she got quiet before she spoke again. "Not even a little? Like maybe being really careful, with some clothes on, and—"

"No." I tried to end her inquiries, but I felt my frustration bleed over. "I don't have much margin for error, Kat. A little unnoticed skin contact in the throes of passion and a few seconds later he's dead." I felt the breeze run through my hair. "That's not really how I would want it to go. It's not a turn-on, having impending death hanging over you during sex. Especially..." I swallowed heavily again, this time unrelated to that slightly sick feeling that was growing in me. "...you know. The first time. Or hell, any time."

"I guess it sort of kills the romance, huh?" She looked at me again, and her face turned sympathetic, her eyebrows arched in concern. I found it annoying, especially since I knew she and Scott were having plenty of sex; scads of it, loads of it, probably every single night of the week, and I couldn't even get a kiss in without worrying about hurting someone. "So, did you and Zack break up?"

"I don't know." I frowned. "We didn't really resolve anything, and he hasn't tried to talk to me since we fought, so maybe." I looked over at her. "Why?"

She didn't look at me, just shook her head, and when she answered, her tone was completely casual. "No reason. Just wondering." She chanced a glance at me, then half-shrugged. "Well...you were kissing some other guy in a bar..."

"Oh." I felt a dull pain in my head, and then I slapped myself right on the forehead. "Oh, damn." How could I have been so stupid? "I didn't even...it didn't even occur to me about Zack. Damn, I have a boyfriend. Damn damn damn."

"Well, maybe." Kat wasn't exactly reassuring, even though I knew she meant well, so I spared her the glare.

The trip passed uneventfully, though by the time we reached the sign indicating Red Wing's city limits, I was feeling a little more ill and had the beginnings of a headache. We pulled up in front of a gas station that had a police car parked outside, lights still flaring. My feet hit the pavement and I steadied myself, my FBI ID already in my hand as I crossed the pavement to talk to the two cops that were standing behind the yellow tape that cordoned off the door.

"I'm Agent Clark and this is Agent Ahern," I said, my ID wallet unfolded as I ducked under the tape and joined the officers behind the line. "What can you tell us about what happened here, Officer..." I let my eyes find the silver nameplate of one of them. "...Olmstead?"

The one I had spoken to was a bald guy, dark skinned. "We responded to a 911 call a couple hours ago from a customer that came into the station and found the clerk unconscious behind the counter. The guy had been smacked around pretty hard. We sent him to the hospital and started looking over the scene, but we didn't find much of anything."

"No forensics?" Kat chimed in, catching the attention of both officers, drawing it away from me. I hated how she could do that, but it was the least of my problems now.

"Nah," Olmstead answered. "The store serves a couple thousand people a day during the summer, more on a weekend like this. There's enough hair and fingerprints in this place to start a new civilization in a petri dish, but nothing we can tie to anybody."

I looked over his shoulder and saw a camera hanging from the awning above the gas pumps. I pointed at it. "What about that?"

"Nothing," he said with a shake of his head. "Perp took the recording and smashed the system. Most of these smaller stations don't bother with off-site data backup because they use the cameras more for people who drive off without paying for their gas."

"Thanks for your help, Officer Olmstead." I smiled at him and he nodded back, slightly tense from what I presumed was being questioned by the FBI. "We'll need the name of the victim and which hospital you sent him to."

"Sure." He pointed to the road we had just been on. "Hospital is that way. We only have one. Follow the signs and you can't miss it. Victim's name is Roger Julian. He was pretty messed up when they carted him away. Couldn't remember a damned thing."

I exchanged a look with Kat. "Nothing?" When I turned back to the officer, he shook his head. "How bad was he hurt?"

"Not bad," Olmstead said. "Scrapes and bruises, lost consciousness for a while. Paramedics said he looked like he'd be just fine, but they wanted to get him an MRI because of the disorientation, the loss of consciousness and the head wound. Thought he might be concussed."

"Uh huh. Thanks for your help, Officer." I nodded at him, and Kat and I walked back to the car. I heard him say something under his breath to the cop that was with him about the FBI recruiting toddlers, but I pretended not to hear it. Once we were in the car, I turned to Kat. "Sounds like this one might have the same issue."

"Yeah." Kat started the car and put it in gear. "I'm not healing this guy unless he's got major problems, but I'll take a look and see how hurt he is. I'm guessing if he can't remember anything about the attack, he's suffering from the same kind of memory loss as the last guy."

"You sure you can't heal him, just to be safe?"

She let out a slow breath. "I don't think so. I don't want to push it. After we get to the hospital, we seriously need to find a place to crash for the night or else you need to take over driving."

I did a little head shake of my own. I couldn't tell if I was sober yet, but I doubted it. "We should just find a hotel. I'm not in any condition to drive yet."

We went a little further down the road, turning when we saw a blue sign with a white H on it. After another mile, the hospital came into view and we parked. It was a predominantly brick building with white trim and an enormous, multi-story octagonal entry. I felt the warmth of the air as I stepped out onto the pavement. I looked into the car before I closed the door; Scott was still passed out in the back, snoring.

I shook my head to clear the cobwebs as I followed Kat across the parking lot and through the sliding doors. The hiss they made as they moved, coupled with the cool air conditioning hitting me in the face, gave me a half-second of disorientation. I'd started sweating, just a little, on the walk from the car. I wished this damned state would come to some sort of happy equilibrium in regards to the weather; but no, she bitterly clung to her extremes.

After inquiring at the check-in desk we were routed up a couple stories to the critical care unit. The tile floor clicked under Kat's heels and I heard the squeak from the soles of my flats as we walked along. She had slowed her pace so that I would trail behind her. The air bore the familiar smell of disinfectants and I heard raised voices ahead of us. We came around a corner and found a nurse's station with three security guards surrounding someone.

"Sir, I'm going to have to ask you to—" One of the security guards stepped forward, blocking my view of the person that the three of them had surrounded. A couple nurses were behind the desk in the station, backing away.

"I don't think you realize the depth of your mistake here." The voice was familiar, but I still couldn't see the speaker.

"Sir, we're going to have to call the police." The lead

guard's hand rested on his holster, and I could see that he was tensing on the grip.

"That's a shame." Cold, bitterly ironic, the speaker didn't sound at all regretful. I couldn't shake the feeling that I knew that voice and I adjusted my position, crossing in front of Kat. I caught a glimpse of him over the security guard's shoulder.

He was in profile to me, looking at the guard closest to him, and didn't see me. His hair was long, brown and hung almost to his shoulder blades. I saw that his face was red, though it was hard to tell through his swarthy skin. I knew his eyes were brown, though I couldn't see them from this distance. I quickened my pace and drew my FBI ID.

"Gentlemen," I said, holding it open. "Sienna Clarke, FBI. This is Agent Ahern." I nodded to Kat. "What's going on here?"

"Ma'am." The lead security guard peered hard at my ID while the other two watched their subject with undistilled suspicion. "This man was trying to access patient rooms long past the end of visiting hours."

I turned to the man they held captive. "Is this true?"

He folded his arms and stared at me with barely disguised disbelief. "I just came here to talk to the guy who got robbed." He nodded at the lead guard. "This clown gave me the party line and I was about to give him the party platter."

Kat squinted. "What...what that does even mean? Is that a threat?"

"Absolutely not," he said. "A party platter filled with meats and cheeses is a generous gift, and he should be damned happy to get it."

"Ma'am?" The head guard got my attention turned back to him. "What is the FBI doing here in the middle of the night, if you don't mind me asking?"

"The same thing your troublemaker is doing," I said. "We need to have a conversation with the patient. He's a witness in a series of robberies that have crossed state lines." I nodded to Kat. "If you could show Agent Ahern to his room while I deal with your interloper..." I gestured with my hand toward the man standing between them all and he rolled his eyes and nodded back, with the greatest reluctance. I locked eyes with Kat. "We'll be outside when you're done."

"Ma'am?" The head security guard spoke up again. "Would you like us to come with you, keep an eye on him?" He said it as the troublemaker walked past me, already on his way back to the elevator.

"Him?" I turned to follow him as he walked past. "If he gives me any problems, I'll just shoot him."

I heard the security guard behind me, a warble of uncertainty as he whispered to his colleagues. I followed the long-haired man back to the elevator, stopping in front of the door after he pressed the down button. "I didn't need your help," he said, stepping into the box.

"Of course you didn't," I said with an easy nod. "You were about to lay waste to three local rent-a-cops and probably a couple nurses because you had it all well under control."

"Damned right." His sullen look finally cracked and I caught the shake of his head that was followed by a grin. "How have you been, Sienna? I haven't seen you in my dreams lately."

I blew air noiselessly between my lips. "Honestly, I've been too busy to think about you, Reed."

"Ouch." He ran a hand through his long hair. "So you're a full-on Directorate agent now, huh?"

"Nah. I work for the FBI. Longer hours, worse pay."

He rolled his eyes. "Sure. Should we play the game of denial about why each of us is here, or can we cut the crap and get right to the truth?"

"I will if you will."

"You're here because of the guy, right?" He stared me down. "The guy going around treating convenience store clerks like he's Chris Brown?"

I started to lie, but he was watching me. I'd known Reed longer than just about anybody, though I hadn't spoken to him in months. "Yeah. We figure this is a new meta, just manifesting, that needs a serious reining in."

"Yeah?" He tugged on the front of his shirt. He was wearing a nice one, a white dress shirt that was untucked, with a suit coat over it and dark jeans. "You talk to the guy in

Owatonna?"

"You mean the guy with a big hole in his memory?"

"He was kind of a dead end, wasn't he?" Reed smiled. "The ones in Wyoming and South Dakota had the exact same problem, oddly enough. How big of a believer are you in coincidence? Because I'm not much of one; and head traumas don't typically cause that much memory loss."

"What kind of meta would be able to do that?" I folded my arms, felt the familiar lump under my left arm as I rested my hand on my pistol.

He shrugged, looking for all the world like he was a man unconcerned with anything. "Well, the beatings could be caused by just about any type...as for the other, there's a few that could cause that, but one in particular I'm thinking of."

I waited a minute for him to answer. "I thought we weren't gonna do the mystery game."

"I said we weren't gonna do the denial game – I never said I was gonna tell you everything I know." He turned and pushed the button to call the elevator and stared at me, puzzlement brewing on his face. "Why Clarke? Why not just go with Nealon?"

I rolled my eyes and lowered my voice. "Because if you're going to commit a felony, it's best not to use your real name, especially if said name is being entered into the FBI database as an agent. That tends to leave a pretty exact record if anything goes wrong."

He frowned. "Well, wouldn't they have had to put a picture of you into the database in a personnel file?"

"I—" I stopped and thought about it. "I don't know. Maybe. I'm not planning on making a major problem of it."

"Huh." He stared back at me with cool amusement. "I might worry about that a little bit if I were you, especially given who you work for."

"Oh yeah?" We both looked up as the elevator dinged. "Care to share what you mean by that?"

He smiled as he stepped into the elevator. "Nope." His hand reached out to hold the door as Kat came up to join us. "What's the word, blondie? Does this guy have a swiss melt for a memory too?"

Kat had the rarest of expressions cross her face, irritation, as she shot me a look, as though she were asking permission before speaking in front of him. I nodded at her. "Yeah," she said. "He's perfectly healthy, his brain is fine, but the memory's just gone, like it never existed."

"Same old story." Reed pulled his hand back and the elevator door started to close. "See you ladies down the road. Oh, and Sienna? You smell like whiskey. Just FYI."

The elevator doors closed before I could snap back a reply. I looked to Kat, who was slightly flushed. "Of course I smell like whiskey," I said. "I've been drinking whiskey." Kat shrugged as I pushed the elevator button to call another one. "Ass," I said, lowering my voice.

"Who was he?" Kat waited until we were walking across the parking lot to ask.

"Him?" I chucked a thumb toward the hospital building. "When Zack and Kurt came to my house for the first time, they ended up drawing guns—"

"What?" She looked at me with incredulity. "Really?"

"Really. I kinda got into a scuffle with them first. Anyway, I ended up running when Kurt started shooting, and Reed was waiting outside and offered me an escape route, so I took him up on it."

"They shot at you?" She stopped and grabbed me by the arm. I felt the strength in her grip; it wasn't quite as much as I could bring to bear, but the girl was no slouch. "With real bullets?"

"Tranquilizer darts. But I didn't know that until later."

"So who is he?" She stared at me evenly, and had the slightest smile. "He's kinda cute, you know."

"I had noticed that, yes." I pulled my arm gently from her grasp. "And if he'd ever stick around for more than five minutes without disappearing, that might matter."

"Oooh," she said in a somewhat high and floating voice. "A man of mystery?"

"The very definition of it." I opened the passenger door to the SUV and climbed in, tossing a glance back to confirm Scott was still snoring softly in the back, head against the window and mouth open wide. "I bet you could do with a

437

little bit more of that in your life right about now."

"Huh?" She cocked her head at me, question written on her face, then swiveled to look when I indicated the backseat. She saw Scott, shook her head and stuck the key in the ignition. "So what did he tell you?"

"Not much. Said he'd interviewed the victims out in Wyoming and South Dakota, that they had the same memory gap as the guy in Owatonna." I leaned back against the headrest. "So now we've got four people who got the holy hell beat out of them and they don't remember a thing about it. We've got no idea where they're going and no clue who's doing it – except..." I frowned.

"What?" She was at rapt attention, looking at me.

"Reed confirmed one thing." I chewed my lip. "He said a meta was definitely causing the memory loss – and I think he knew which kind of meta it was."

Kat looked at me blankly. "So what kind of meta causes memory loss when they attack you?"

I looked out into the black night, and I racked my brain for something, anything, I'd learned in my studies, anything at all about metas that could make memories disappear. Without that clue, we were without anything to do or any lead to investigate until the next call came in. "I don't know," I said. "I just don't know."

9

Someone Else

The heat was near unbearable. Somehow I'd done it again, scored the crappiest possible car I could get my hands on. I'd stopped in some half-assed town called Ellsworth just over the Wisconsin line and stolen an old Dodge that was sitting overnight in a grocery store parking lot. The reeferhead's Honda had started making gawdawful grinding noises in southern Minnesota. I tried to make it last, filled it up in Red Wing, but no, it started going into catastrophic failure mode after I crossed the river. This is what happens when you have to choose between buying weed and performing regularly scheduled maintenance, I suppose.

I thought maybe I'd get lucky this time, but I wasn't. The Dodge was older and the air conditioner didn't work, which might explain why it was left in a parking lot. It was after midnight, and still pretty damned stifling out. I wished for the millionth time that I had made this little trip in winter, then remembered what winters were like in the upper midwest. Spring would have been the time for this. Or fall.

My shirt was dripping with sweat by the time I hit the first exit ramp in Eau Claire, Wisconsin. The home of pretty near nothing, the city of Eau Claire had still somehow managed to attract over sixty thousand people to live within its limits. I'd been here before; I couldn't see the appeal.

The night was dark, but the yellow light of the moon was

in the sky as I rolled through a commercial district. There were a line of little stores and I followed the thoroughfare until I reached Fleet Street, where I turned left. I was going by directions I had memorized before I left Gillette, but they were as fresh in my mind as if I had them with me on a piece of paper. I eased the car down the road, squinting to read the house numbers by the moon and the streetlights.

8453. I stopped when I saw them on the front of a white house, the little bronze numerals barely visible in the dark. I climbed out of the car two blocks down and started to walk back. I felt a grin split my lips and I barely restrained myself from wanting to run.

The house was older, built in the seventies, a little one-floor rambler on a city lot, the grass now overgrown by a week or more, weeds sprouting up all over. The aged wooden siding looked like I'd get splinters just from touching it, and I had a suspicion that the dark lines on the roof meant that this place couldn't hold its water. A red door was the single spot of color on the exterior and a wooden fence higher than my head partitioned the backyard off, hiding it from view.

I cleared the fence with a jump, felt the shock through my knees as I landed and cursed under my breath. I'd been jumping through a lot of hoops the last few days, had been on the receiving end of some rough luck, and whoever crossed my path next was going to be the recipient of all my frustrations for those setbacks and reversals. It was going to be sweet.

I walked slow, letting my eyes make sure the path in front of me was clear. I could see a light on in the back of the house as I came around the corner, crouched in a defensive posture in case someone was waiting for me out back. It never pays to be surprised.

The back of the house was one long, straight line, and I could see a couple people in the kitchen window, having a conversation. Both were men, one older than the other. The younger one looked to be in his late teens, while the older appeared to be in his forties. Looks could be deceiving, though, because I knew he was at least a millennium old if not older. Franklin Beauregard, he was named. He was the reason I was here.

I ducked under the kitchen window and crawled through the grass on my hands and knees. The wet of the dew was the only coolness I had felt since I left the Honda in Ellsworth. I felt it on my knees and the temporary pleasure of the temperature change gave way to annoyance at getting wet – those fellas inside were really gonna suffer for all this crap.

I stood once I was clear of the window and climbed the step to the back door. I braced myself and took a deep breath before lifting my foot and kicking. I hit the door and felt it splinter as my momentum carried me through, breaking it into four pieces. They should have used a steel door; that would have at least slowed me down as I ripped it from the hinges.

I heard raised voices and the young man who I assumed was Franklin's son entered the back hallway first. He uttered a cry of warning when he saw me and whipped a fist through the air. I reached out, caught it and tugged him forward, ramming his head into the wall.

I was past him in a half a heartbeat, looking through the narrow kitchen at Beauregard, a smirk on my face. "Hello, Franklin. What brings Omega to Eau Claire, Wisconsin?"

He clasped one hand over the other at his midsection and I watched his face become calm resignation. "As if you don't know."

"Oh, I know. I just wanted to hear you say it." I took two steps toward him. He didn't move. "Tell me where Site Epsilon is."

His eyes widened and I watched his aged hands turn white as they clenched each other. "How...?" His face went back to relaxed. "You...are batting at shadows."

"Nah, I'm batting at the things that cast shadows." I took another step. "Site Epsilon. Andromeda. Where? Last chance." I angled a hand toward him in warning. "And don't even think about coming at me with those—"

His battered jacket burst open, the ripping of the fabric like a thunderclap in the quiet summer eve. I jumped forward and hit him three times in the face before he landed the first attack, a hard bite on my shoulder. I grunted in pain and slammed his head against the wood floor. Two gargantuan snakes extended from his body, one from behind each of his shoulder blades. I snatched a butcher knife from the block next to the sink and cut into the first as it struck at me, splitting the head from its body. It went limp and dropped, flopping on the floor behind him.

I got to my feet, knife in hand as Beauregard struggled to his knees, the remaining snake head giving him license to do so. It extended five feet from his body, keeping out of range of the knife, hissing and striking every time it got close to me. I feinted toward him and it snapped and came at me. I reached out with my free hand and wrapped my arm around it, trapping it in a headlock as I drove the blade through the top of its skull, slicing the head off. Without so much as another sound, it fell still and quiet, and I turned to Franklin, who was on his knees, both snake bodies limp and hanging from his shoulders.

"Andromeda," I said as I dangled the knife before his eyes. "Would you care to guess what you lose next?"

He bowed his head, and I heard a whisper. "Decorah, Iowa. It's in Decorah."

I knelt and dropped the blade to the ground, clucking my tongue. "Why do you have to lie to me, Franklin? It demeans us both."

"I'm telling the truth." He looked up at me, his fingers resting on the floor as though he were drawing strength from it.

I reached up and my hand wrapped around his neck, applying only the slightest pressure, forcing him to look me in the eye. "Site Epsilon is not in Decorah, and we both know it. You've certainly got an Omega safehouse there, but that ain't where Andromeda is." I smiled at him. "So...the hard way, then."

He gasped as the pain began, my other hand holding him tight on the cheek. "But...you...would have done this anyway..."

"Of course," I said, my hands holding him as he started to

442

grunt, then let out his first scream. "It's not like I trust you." I felt the surge begin as his life, his soul, drained out of him, my hands pressed tightly to his cheeks. His memories flooded into me, into my mind, causing it to swirl, a fresh infusion of life into my brain. I let his body drop to the floor and I stood up, looking down on him in pity. "Now that you're in here," I tapped the side of my head, "you can't lie to me anymore, Franklin."

I heard something move behind me and I turned. His son (I knew because of his memories now in my head) was stirring, moving from where I had put him down against the wall. I walked to the back door and knelt next to him, flipping the boy over. He still looked young, but I'd put a nice gash on his forehead. His eyelids fluttered and he mumbled something. "Shut up," I said. I stared at him for a minute, then shook my head, letting out a sigh of impatience. Too young.

"This is your lucky day," I said as I pressed my hand against his face. Even unconscious, I felt him squirm when the pain started. I held contact for another couple of seconds and then pulled my hand away. I could see the rise and fall of his chest, the regularity of his breathing a sign of the mercy I didn't even know I had in me. "Don't worry," I said. "You won't remember any of this."

10

Sienna Nealon

I awoke to a headache that felt as though a lumberjack had decided to chop down my skull. Light was shining through a window and there was a faint rattling that I was sure was between my ears, the remnants of my brain trying to escape its own stupidity for drinking too much last night. I groaned and realized that the buzzing was not in my head: it was in fact to the left of it, on the nightstand next to the hotel bed I was sleeping in.

I rolled over and grabbed my phone, slapping the talk button without bothering to check the display. I wondered for a half-second if this was what life had been like before Caller ID. "Hello?" My voice was little more than a croak.

"Hey." I heard the quiet voice of Zack on the other end of the line and sat up, far too fast for my own good.

"Owww," I said, my hand rushing to my temple, which felt as though it were about to explode.

"You okay?" Zack sounded a little resigned. Or cautious. Actually, it was hard to tell because the pain in my head was so sharp.

"Yes. Just...have a headache."

"Hm. First night on a mission, away from the Directorate..." He sounded like he was brainstorming. "Let me guess, they gave you cover as an FBI agent, complete with an ID that said you were over twenty-one."

444

"Should I worry that you immediately assume the worst about me?" I tried to cram some reproach into my words, but I'm pretty sure it failed. I dangled my legs over the edge of the bed. Apparently I hadn't managed to shed my suit before I passed out.

"You should assume that I've been a college student at roughly your age. My fake IDs weren't as realistic as what the Directorate can produce. Also, I've been on some of those 'sit around and wait' assignments. They're moments of excitement followed by long stretches of boring nothing."

"That sounds familiar." I stood up and hung my head, because it felt better for some reason. I paused, trying to string together some thoughts. "About last night..."

"It's all right, you don't have to apologize. I know it's been tense for you lately." His voice was soothing.

"Yeah, I...wait, what?" I bristled, every muscle in my body tensing as the meaning behind what he said made it through my fog-addled brain. "What did you just say?"

There was a long pause on the other end of the line. "I...I said..."

"Did you just say '*I* don't have to apologize'?" I felt my jaw clench. "I know damned well I don't have to apologize. I was just minding my own business in my room when you came in and we had a lovely conversation about how you secretly resent the fact that I can't put out, which is something that you've never had the balls to say to my face."

I waited for a response, and when it came, there was a little heat on it. "This isn't the time to have this conversation."

"Really?" I almost yelled at him. "When's a good time to discuss the fact that we've been dating for months and can't touch for more than two seconds per day? Wedding night? Golden Anniversary? When would be the appropriate time to talk about the fact that we can't have sex, Zack? Please, tell me so I can write it into my schedule!"

There was the barest gap of silence on the other side. "Fine, you want to do this now? Yes, it's grating on me, okay? But that doesn't mean—"

"It's grating? Grating?" I let fly with my disbelief. "Just say it, okay? It's frustrating and it's never going to get any better!

Unless you really love the touch of heavy leather gloves, you'll be enjoying a nice embargo of skin-to-skin contact for the rest of your life."

"I – what? Touch of leather gloves? You mean, like—"

"I mean it's never going to get better, Zack." I was firm, final.

"So, what?" He didn't even sound real on the other end of the phone. "You want to be done? Finished with me?"

It felt a little like someone was choking me, and the pain in my head was splintering, telling me to say something I didn't really want to. "I think we've gone as far as you can go with me, Zack. If you ever want to have anything approaching a normal life, yeah...I think we're finished."

There was a smoldering quality about the way he said his next words, like there was a fire underneath every single one of them. "If that's the way you feel—"

"It's not the way I feel, Zack." I should have been on the edge of panic, ending things like this. It's not like I set out to do it the day before, when I was content on the campus, in training, and with my boyfriend. "It's the way it is. You're too big a boy to keep holding back; time to grow up. My life is solitary confinement – it's a prison sentence, and you don't deserve it, even if you do act like an ass sometimes."

"That's it?" I could hear the edge in his voice. "It's over?"

"Yeah." I didn't have an edge in mine. I was just tired. "It's over. Be safe in Michigan." I pushed the end button on my phone without waiting for his reply and sagged back onto the bed, taking a deep breath. I felt a burning at the corner of my eyes, and I couldn't believe what I'd just done.

In a way, I was sorry I hadn't done it sooner. I mean, I kissed another guy at the bar last night, and almost got carried away. That's not the strongest sign that things were going well in my relationship with Zack. In fact, it was probably a sign that there were some deep, serious, underlying problems. Well, one anyway. And just because I had to live the rest of my life to less than the fullest didn't mean he had to.

There was an insistent knocking at my door and I levered myself back up and opened it to find Kat waiting. "Ariadne wants us all on the phone in an hour to make our report."

"Fine." I massaged my temples. "You want to come to my room or what?"

She shrugged. "Sure. I think I can have Scott up and moving by then." She looked down at my attire and made a face. "You might consider showering and changing your clothes. You look—"

I looked down at myself, at what I was wearing. "A little ragged, yeah. I'll do that. See you in an hour."

I shut the door and got to work. I rummaged in my overnight bag and found pain relievers and the other drug I was taking. I popped the acetaminophen, then an equal dose of ibuprofen, then got my syringe ready for my morning injection of chloridamide. The injection was critical because if I didn't take it, the souls of the people I'd absorbed tended to get a little...feisty...in my head. I took a deep breath and plunged the needle into a vein. I was fortunate in that I was a meta; if not for my continuously regenerating vein structure, I'd likely be out of places to inject the drug by now.

The shower brought me back to life, and after I spent a few minutes getting my hair straightened and had changed into a fresh suit, I felt worlds better. The pain was still lingering behind my eyes, but it was in the recesses of my mind rather than front and center. And it didn't hurt to blink.

An hour later, there was a knock on my door and I opened it to find Kat, who was as sunny in her disposition as ever, and Scott, who wore sunglasses and looked as though he'd had an anvil dropped on his head. He grumbled some sort of greeting as he slouched into the room and flopped in a chair at the table. Kat sat across from him, a small smile seeming to be her only defense against laughing at both of us.

When Kat's phone rang, I caught a nearly imperceptible twitch at the edge of Scott's eyebrow. I might not have noticed it but for the fact I felt one myself. "Just a second," Kat said to whoever was on the phone. She pulled it away from her ear and pushed a button. "You're on speaker, Ariadne."

"Get packed and get moving," came Ariadne's voice over

the phone. "Early this morning a car was reported stolen from a parking lot in Ellsworth, Wisconsin, just across the river from you. We flagged it as a suspect vehicle on a hunch and it was found abandoned an hour ago by a police patrol in a neighborhood in Eau Claire, Wisconsin. I'm sending you the address."

"How do we know that the stolen car is linked to our mystery robber?" The question occurred to me even through the haze in my head.

"We don't." Ariadne sounded tense. "But we've got nothing else to go on and car thefts aren't exactly a common occurrence in Ellsworth, where the dairy cows outnumber the people twelve to one. Get moving, all right? I'll check in with you in a few hours; we're managing a crisis with M-Squad so I may not be quite as quick to respond right now. Stay out of trouble." There was a click and the phone shut off.

"Ah, words of confidence and encouragement," I said, lighter than I felt.

We were in the car and moving a few minutes later, leaving the town of Red Wing behind. We rode through downtown, which seemed to be mostly brick buildings, and got on a bridge that stretched across a wide river. On the other side a sign proclaimed that we had entered the state of Wisconsin. If I hadn't been so hungover, I might have rejoiced at crossing my first state line. As it was, I sat in the back and tried to keep my eyes hidden behind my dark sunglasses.

After a few minutes we cleared the low lying river country and found ourselves zipping down a road with farms on either side. Cattle grazed in the pastures as the sun beat down overhead. One cow was lingering so close to the fence I could see her jaw moving while chewing her cud as we passed.

Towns and fields streaked by as I thought about Zack. I closed my eyes and tried to imagine what he was doing right now, facing off against some meta in Detroit. I truly cared for him, which was why I had to let him loose. At least, that's how I justified it as I stared out the window, watching the endless fields of green go by. I felt like a glutton for pain, like

I wanted to clutch the misery close to my heart and let it sit there. It was all for him, I told myself, and somehow that made it hurt all the more.

We took Interstate 94 east to Eau Claire, Kat driving the whole way. She didn't have the siren roaring for this trip, though she did strategically flick it on a few times when we were caught behind slow moving cars on two lane roads. And once for a tractor.

When we got off the freeway, we followed a main thoroughfare into a stretch of commerce, and then turned onto a side street. It was past noon, and the sun was directly overhead, bright and glaring. Kat kept the car under the speed limit as we followed the GPS to the address Ariadne had sent us. There was a car, an old Dodge, parked on the curb. We came to a stop behind it and I looked around. There was no sign of movement, nothing.

I opened my door and stepped out into the boiling midday heat. The humidity once again gave my skin an immediate sensation of moistness and I felt the beads of sweat start to gather on my forehead. "Never thought I'd wish the sun away," I muttered under my breath. I caught a chuckle of appreciation from Kat. Scott just grunted.

The three of us approached the Dodge the way we might have approached a corpse; slow, tentative, and with undue caution. "No one inside," I said. "We'll need to check the trunk." I looked around the street once more. The residents of Eau Claire clearly had enough sense to stay in during this awful weather, though a lawn sprinkler was going off a couple doors down.

"You think there's anything here?" It was Kat that answered. Her blond hair was up in a tight bun today, and her petite frame and dark sunglasses coupled with her black jacket really did make her look like an FBI agent. I felt another tingle of annoyance; the girl could just look good regardless of circumstances.

Scott leaned over the passenger window and reached his hand through. "Glass is broken here." He pushed a button on the dash and I heard the locks disengaging and the trunk springing open.

I walked to the rear of the car, my hand hovering just over my gun. I edged around the trunk lid and sighed when I looked down. "Nothing. A blanket, a spare tire and a jack."

"Sounds like all the ingredients for a redneck first date—" Scott said with a smile that was cut short by a sizzling sound. His body jerked, his face drew tight and his sunglasses flew off as he spasmed, a peculiar blue light dancing over him like little bolts of lightning running across his suit.

"Kat, down!" I shouted and barely had time to hit the pavement before a bolt of electricity shot past me and hit the car. I rolled across the lawn and came up with my pistol, a Sig Sauer P250. I loved my meta powers, but they weren't a hell of a lot of use at range – or against something that shot lightning bolts.

"Too late." The voice was low and gravelly. I saw Kat lying on the street behind the car, splayed out on the ground with three guys in black tactical vests huddled around her and Scott. Two others stood at either bumper of the car, covering me with weapons of their own, big shiny silver ones that reminded me of the kind the Directorate used to bring down stray metas. Their leader was standing over Kat, an assault rifle in his hands and pointed at me. "Now are you gonna give yourself up or are we gonna be leaving your body to go rancid in the heat?"

11

I stared him down, my gun aimed at his comrade who was standing to my right. Assuming they were human, even my meta speed and my skill with the pistol wouldn't be enough to save me from getting blasted by at least one of them. I took a closer look; their vests were bulky, which told me that they were likely kevlar. I considered trying to aim for their heads instead of center mass, but dismissed it as a bad idea. Aiming for a small target in my first combat shoot seemed like a recipe for failure. Besides, even with a vest the bullets would put a full grown man on the ground in a world of hurt.

"So what are you gonna do?" Their leader spoke again, and I saw the others flick their eyes toward him. "Live or die, your choice."

"I'm somewhat attached to the former," I said, keeping my gun trained on the rightmost enemy.

"Then you might wanna put the gun down, real slow." His voice was rough and used to issuing commands. "Otherwise we're gonna have to cut that loose, pretty quick."

On one knee as I was, I couldn't see Scott or Kat, and I wondered if they were still alive. I had seen what hit them, and I hoped that the weapons they'd been shot with were no more fatal than the Directorate equivalent. "All right," I said, not really sure if I was going to follow his command or shoot, but knowing I didn't have much time to make a decision.

"Put the gun on the ground in front of you. Go slow." There was that command again.

I felt my jaw tighten and I started to inch the gun lower, keeping the bearing on my target. I'd be less accurate firing from this position, but I still felt confident I could put him down. The other two...well, that was the problem, wasn't it? That was why I was even considering surrendering. I started to say something but I heard the squeal of tires at the end of the street to my left and it took all my training to keep from jerking my head to look in the direction of the noise.

They were not so well trained, and all three of them turned, giving me an opening. I fired a double tap on my target, two quick shots that sent him over backward, gun skittering away. I changed targets quick, drew a bead on the leader and fired twice more. I knew they were bound to be less accurate than my first shots, and one of them went wide, but the other hit him in shoulder and knocked him over. I started to change targets again to the last guy, but he had heard me firing and had drawn a bead on me. I knew I wouldn't make it in time.

A car slammed into him, bumper smashing him against the stolen car. I watched his body fold at the knees, a scream from him faint in my ears after the echoing of the gunshots nearly deafened me. He was pinned between the cars, legs crushed, and his upper body had fallen into the open trunk. I could hear little cries coming from within; likely the sound of him screaming, but from where I stood it was muffled. I opened my mouth and closed it, trying to restore my hearing after the trauma of firing a gun repeatedly with no ear protection.

I knew there were two more enemies behind the car where I couldn't see them, and I wasn't about to stick my head up to see. I looked at the car that had crashed into the stolen one, but the front window was spider-webbed, the cracked glass obscuring the identity of the driver. I thought I heard the sound of fighting from the other side of the car, where Scott and Kat were laying, but I couldn't be sure through the ringing in my ears. I edged toward the hood, away from the crashed rear, and raised myself up, gun pointed. My eyes

452

widened at what I saw and I hesitated.

"You're just like me; you know how to get yourself in trouble," came the soft voice of the woman standing in front of me, holding the bodies of the two remaining assailants by the back of their collars. Both appeared to be unconscious. She was wearing a red tank top, cut off jeans again, and flip-flops. Her dark hair was hanging around her face and she dropped the bodies to the ground. "What would you have done if I wasn't here to save you?"

"Charlie?" I stared at her in near disbelief. I heard a grunt from the first guy I had shot, laying about a foot to my right, lanced out a foot and kicked him in the head, causing him to go limp. "What are you doing here?"

She shrugged. "I was bored in Minneapolis, so I came looking for you."

I stood slowly, looking around the street, which was quiet save for the ticking sound from the engine of the car that had crashed. "And you decided to go looking on a random street in Eau Claire, Wisconsin?"

She laughed. "No, I absorbed the mind and soul of a tech geek a few years ago. I tracked your cell phone's GPS."

I looked down reflexively at my pocket. "Really?"

"It's not as hard as you'd hope it would be." She shrugged. "Looks like my timing was good. What'd you do to provoke an Omega sweep team?"

"Omega?" I felt a thrill as I made my way around the car to check on Kat and Scott. "These guys are from Omega?"

"Uh huh." She leaned down and grabbed one of them by the chest, ripping open his collar to reveal a small tattoo of the Greek letter Omega. "See?"

"Curiouser and curiouser." I bent over Kat, trying her pulse (not an easy task with leather gloves on). She stirred at my touch, causing me to sigh in relief. I reached out and shook Scott, causing him to groan, his eyes fluttering. "Omega must be tracking our robber, too."

There was a sound from behind me of metal stressing and squealing and I was back to my feet, gun drawn again. The door of the car that had crashed was opening. "I thought you drove that?" I asked over my shoulder to Charlie.

"Nuh-uh," she said without concern. "I parked down the street and hustled up when I saw these guys ambush you. I thought it was one of your guys driving."

"Whoever's in the vehicle, hands up and come out slow," I said. "No sudden moves."

"Uggghhh." The moan was not subtle, and was followed by the sound of a body hitting pavement. I saw the head and shoulders of a man, his long, dark hair tangled around his face. "I save your life and this is the gratitude I get?"

"Reed?" I stared at him before holstering my gun and running to his side. I rolled him over once I reached him; his nose was bloody and he had the start of a bruise forming under his right eye. "What are you doing here?"

He coughed, then grimaced. "There's an Omega safehouse just down the street. I was surveilling it; figured it might be a nice, boring place to keep an eye on while I waited for word on another robbery. Then you and your pals go and get bushwhacked by an Omega sweep team, and suddenly my life gets really interesting."

"Can you walk?" After I said it, I heard Charlie approach behind me, her flip-flops smacking against the pavement. The ringing in my ears had begun to subside.

"I think so." He took my hand and I pulled him to his feet. "We need to get out of here before the law arrives. Doubtful they're gonna ignore a scuffle this big."

"I need to get a look at this Omega safehouse," I said. "Preferably before the cops get here."

Reed waved his hand in the direction that his car had come from. "Down the street. 8453 is the house number." He clutched at his side and his face was a mask of discomfort.

I looked at him, then Charlie in turn. "Can you get Kat and Scott into my car and meet me in front of the safehouse?"

She got a lazy grin on her face. "You just need all kinds of help today."

"Can you do it or not?"

She shrugged. "Sure. Keys?"

"Kat had them last," I said, already turning to run down the street. "Check her pockets – and, Charlie..." She turned and I shook my head at her attire. "Remember to touch them only on the clothing."

"No problem with the blond girl," she called back. "But the boy...I might touch him some other places."

I ignored her and ran down the street at full clip. I saw faces staring out of the windows of houses, saw curtains rustle in others as I passed. I watched the house numbers decrease until I reached 8453, a nondescript single story white house. I decided to avoid the front door and instead jumped over the wooden gate to the backyard. I listened over the slight ringing that persisted in my ears as I came around the corner and saw the back door kicked in.

I drew my gun, changed to a fresh magazine and stepped inside. The door led into a small hallway. I could see a kitchen to my left, along with a body and a lot of blood. Straight ahead was a family room, and off to the right was a hallway leading to several bedrooms. I went into the kitchen first, which had a nasty green tile backsplash over orange countertops and beige linoleum floors. Those were distracting, but the body in the middle of the kitchen was more bizarre than the horrific 70s color scheme.

First of all, it was obviously dead. There was enough blood on the floor to fill three bodies, and his face was frozen in anguish. He was elevated slightly off the floor by something on his back.

Worse than him were the remains of two enormous snakes lying on the kitchen floor. I shuddered. I do not care for snakes. I kicked at one of them to make sure it was dead. It didn't move, but that didn't make me feel much better. While I knew logically that they weren't slimy, I couldn't shake the feeling that if I touched it, it'd be slick and disgusting. I leaned in to look at the dead man, adjusting the body to see what was causing his corpse to incline.

When I lifted him, I almost retched. I saw what was holding him up, and it looked as though the snakes had been growing out of his shoulder blades. I dropped him and stood, stifling an urge to vomit. I kept my gun in hand and stepped over him, coming around the corner of the kitchen into the dining room to find another man on the couch, this one much younger, and with no obvious signs of snakes growing out of him.

He was also quite alive, though he was limp, arm hanging off the edge of the sofa. His chest moved up and down, eyes closed. I heard the faint sound of sirens outside and walked over to him, shaking him with one hand while keeping the pistol pointed at him with the other. He didn't stir, and after two more attempts I left him and took a quick look around the rest of the house. Two bedrooms were pretty simple and a cursory look under the beds and in the closets didn't reveal anything. The third bedroom seemed to be set up as an office, and I grabbed the laptop computer for later analysis by someone who'd know what to do with it.

I started to leave but paused as I headed toward the front door. There had to be a basement, didn't there? I started to set down the laptop when I heard an urgent series of honks from a car horn, just outside. I clutched the laptop tighter and with a last look at the young man unconscious on the couch, I ran out the front door.

The Directorate SUV was next to the curb, and another violent blast from the horn issued forth as I went down the front steps. I saw Charlie in the driver's seat and Reed's long hair through the tinted window in the backseat. I jumped in the passenger side and Charlie gunned the engine, not even waiting for me to shut the door. She slowed the car at the corner, which was fortunate, because two cop cars went shooting by, sirens blaring, and my aunt gave me a grin. She made the car take a leisurely turn to the left, and off we went.

12

"Where to?" Charlie asked as we headed down the road. I saw a couple more sets of cop cars, lights flashing, go past.

"I don't know." I held the laptop tight, almost as if I were afraid to let it go, lest it vanish. "We need to lay low."

"I thought you were with the FBI?" Reed spoke up from the backseat, his voice laced with sarcasm. "Why didn't you just stay on scene?"

"Because while I and my colleagues might well be from the FBI, I'd have had a hell of a time explaining you two." I looked from him to Charlie, who still wore a grin. "If I'd had to, I would have, but let's just say I wanted to make that Plan B."

"That coulda been a lotta fun," Charlie said. I shot her a look of disbelief and she shrugged. "Come on, lying to the cops? Talk about a thrill."

"So is this your aunt?" Reed asked.

Charlie looked back with a faint smile of pleasure. "You know me?"

"Charlene Nealon, A.K.A. Charlie," Reed said. "Didn't know you were still around, but yeah, I've heard of you. I particularly enjoyed reading about your exploits in Nevada."

I saw a subtle change in Charlie's persona then, a subtle clamping of her jaw as her smile disappeared and she turned back around to focus on the road. "That was a while ago. I barely remember Nevada."

I watched Reed, and he smiled. "There's some other

people that could probably say the same."

"How are they doing?" I caught Reed's attention and nodded at Kat and Scott, both unconscious next to him. Scott was leaned up against the window like he had been the night before when he passed out, and Kat was lying gracelessly across his lap. I would have cringed for her, but, frankly, it wasn't as though she'd never been in that position before.

"They're out." Reed illustrated his point by reaching over to give Scott a gentle slap across the face. Scott moaned, but did not wake. "The sweep team hit them with an amped-up version of a taser. No wires needed. I'm told they got the design from the Directorate after you guys left one behind at your house."

"One of those things put Wolfe down on the ground," I said. "I can't imagine it felt very good for either of them." I turned around to talk to him. "Who is Omega?"

He kept a cool dispassion as he stared back. "You don't know?"

"The Directorate knows next to nothing about them." I ran a hand through my hair. "Old Man Winter knows something, but he's...not telling." I frowned. "It's above my pay grade."

Reed shrugged. "I can't help you, then. Sounds like something you'll figure out when your pay grade goes up." He gave me a maliciously self-satisfied smile. "Of course, if you want to leave the Directorate and join me, I could answer your questions instead of keeping you in the dark like they do—"

"Oh, for crying out loud," Charlie said. "They're the gods, okay? The old ones, the ones from the myths, or what's left of them." She turned from driving to focus on me. "The Greek gods, the Roman ones? Persians, Norse, all else? There's a reason there are some commonalities: it's because they were all part of the same group. They ruled the planet for thousands of years, through their intermediaries, and vassals, and kings, and whatnot." She turned back to the windshield as she made a turn, then glanced back at me. "You've gotta at least know that much, right?"

I squinted at her. "You mean...like Zeus and Poseidon and Thor and Odin and all that jazz?"

"Well," she said, "Zeus and Poseidon are good and dead; so's Odin. Not sure about Thor...but anyway...yeah, those guys. What's left of the originals, and quite a few of their descendants. It's kind of a cabal."

I let out a snicker, more from disbelief than anything. "And they're...what? Out to take over the world?"

Charlie shrugged, and I turned to Reed, who rolled his eyes. "Probably not in a literal sense," he said. "Not anymore, at least. But yeah, like she said, they're a cabal, and they have a ruling council and a pretty strong organization. At this point they're collecting metas, building their strength, and...given their history, probably up to no good."

"No, seriously." I let out a short laugh. "What are they up to? What's their objective?"

Reed sighed. "I don't know. No one does. We just know they're making power moves, collecting metas...kinda like the Directorate, but even more shadowy, if that's possible."

"I don't love the sound of that," I said.

"You're telling me." Charlie spoke up, bringing the car to a squealing stop at a red light. "I've tangled with their sweep teams before – they're the ones they send out to bring in metas they want to talk to." She laughed. "They're a fun bunch, but they oughta stick to catching newbies; kids that have just manifested and don't know what they're doing."

I stared at the laptop cradled in my hands. "Why does Omega have a safehouse in Eau Claire?"

"Because the Twin Cities is too hot for them." Reed's answer came with a cringe in his voice. "Minneapolis or St. Paul would be too close to the Directorate. Eau Claire's only an hour away, and a few hours from Chicago, where they have a lot bigger presence."

"But why?" I asked. "Why have a presence up here at all? What are they hoping to accomplish?"

"Tracking metas," Charlie said. "Just like you guys. Track 'em and collar 'em, recruit the ones that seem promising. It's all anybody does nowadays, keep snatching up every unattached meta out there."

"What'd you find in the safehouse?" Reed leaned forward and I felt his hand on the back of my seat.

"A guy with a couple snakes lying on the kitchen floor, dead."

Reed frowned. "The guy or the snakes?"

"All of them," I said. "Looks like the snakes grew from his shoulder blades. Kinda creepy."

"Sounds like a Zahhak," Reed said, exchanging a look with Charlie, who nodded.

"What's a Zahhak?" I wrinkled my forehead.

"Look it up on Wikipedia sometime; it's a pretty scary meta to go up against." He entered a pensive state, his fingers resting over his mouth. "They're pretty rare, but I heard Omega has one – or had one, I suppose."

"Why have they been after me?" I turned to question Reed on this one, and when I looked at him, his expression was suddenly pained, a twisted grimace. "You know, don't you?" He nodded, slow, not looking away. "Why are they after me?"

"They're not after you, specifically." He took a deep breath. "You've never been the end to them, always the means. They're after your mom."

I exchanged a look with Charlie, who seemed surprised. "Why?"

He shrugged. "I don't know for sure, but I think she knows something...something from when she was with the Agency – you know, the government group that was destroyed before the Directorate came onto the scene?" I nodded. I knew Mom had been at the Agency with Old Man Winter before I was born. "Anyway, something happened that has a lot of people scouring for her."

I turned back to Charlie. "Do you know what it is?"

She let out a long cackle. "Your mom and I aren't on what you'd call 'speaking terms'. I haven't talked to her since way before you were born."

"What happened?" I asked.

She turned the steering wheel to bring us into the parking lot of a hotel that was shaped like a giant, round cylinder. "She didn't like the way I did things and I didn't care for the way she told me to run my life." She pulled the car into a parking spot just outside the lobby and gave me another lazy shrug. "So I told her what she could do with her opinions and we didn't really need to talk after that, cuz it'd all been said."

"Can't imagine what she might have taken issue with," Reed said under his breath.

Charlie shot him a searing look and jerked her head toward the lobby. "We should get rooms here for the night, unless you want your friends to continue sleeping in the back of the car." She turned around and saw Kat's head in Scott's lap. "Although she seems comfortable there."

I checked us in to four rooms, using the Directorate credit card for two of them and my personal card for the other two. As I swiped it through their reader, I was reminded that I needed to call Ariadne and make a report, since Scott and Kat were unlikely to do so in the next few hours. Once I was done, I hurried back to the car and Charlie drove us to the outside entrance nearest to the rooms. She and I each grabbed one of the unconscious members of my team and dragged them into the building while Reed walked ahead to make sure we didn't run into anyone. Fortunately, the hotel seemed quiet.

We made it to our rooms without incident, and after depositing Kat and Scott onto the king-sized bed in their room, Charlie grabbed the key for her room and left. Reed lingered, watching the door to the room until it shut. After it did, he remained silent for almost a minute, listening. When I started to say something to him, he held up a finger to his lips and then opened the door, looking up and down the hall. He shut it and walked back to me, stopping only inches from my face. "How well do you know your aunt?" he asked in a low whisper.

"Not well." I looked into his concerned eyes and felt a tremor within. "I met her about six months ago when she tracked me down, and we've been in contact on and off ever since, meeting whenever she's been in town."

"Do you trust her?" He didn't break eye contact.

"Only a little," I said. "I don't exactly know her well."

"She didn't come on the mission with you?"

"No." I shook my head. "She said she tracked my cell phone GPS."

"Uh huh." He licked his lips, thinking. "Sounds a little funny."

"Why so suspicious? You think she has something to do with Omega?" He stared back at me, as though waiting for something. "What? What am I missing?"

He turned a slight smile, and looked at me with expectation. "Come on," he said. "You know."

"Come on, what?" By this point I was just annoyed. Kat and Scott were passed out on the bed behind me and who knew when they'd be coming back to consciousness. I had to report to Ariadne that we'd gotten in a violent clash with Omega forces, ending with two people not associated with the Directorate getting involved to save our bacon, in an incident that would certainly have drawn more than a little attention.

"Nothing," he said. "I'm gonna go...recover for a bit. Let me know if anything major happens."

I shook my head, feeling my annoyance fade at the remembrance that he'd wrecked his car to save me from the Omega sweep team. "Reed..." He looked back over his shoulder, almost out the door. "Thanks."

He nodded, a little smile breaking on his face, and left.

13

I tried to reach Ariadne, but her cell phone went straight to voicemail. I tried her office, but her assistant told me she was out and unable to be reached for several hours. When I asked her to connect me to the Director, she informed me that he, too, was unavailable. I sighed, told her to have them call me urgently, that I had run afoul of Omega, and left it at that.

I stayed in Kat and Scott's room, watching the light fade outside the beige curtains as the day ended. I looked at a clock when the last rays of sunlight were still visible, and it was just after 9 P.M. Neither of them had moved, but their pulse was regular, they reacted to prodding and other stimuli; they just...didn't seem to want to wake up.

There was a knock on my door and when I looked through the peephole, Charlie grinned back at me, her smile overlarge and distorted by the glass as though I were looking at her in a funhouse mirror. Her cutoffs and tank top were gone, replaced by a red dress not unlike the one I had seen her wear when we first met, something with very little length and quite a bit of cleavage exposure. I tried to smile, but inwardly grimaced as I opened the door. "Hey."

"Hay is all around us; this whole damned place is a farm town." She made a slight gyration, as though she were dancing to music only she could hear. "What do you say we go find a couple cowboys to while away the dull hours with between now and morning?"

"Sounds like a great idea," I said. "Because we don't have enough carnage on our hands already without killing a couple of poor locals that are just out for a good time."

"It's not about killing," she said in a soothing voice, "it's about having some fun. Unwinding." Her smile was oddly infectious. "You've been watching these vegetables all day. You need to get out and let loose. Have the other guy watch them for a while." She strolled over to Scott and brushed his cheek with her hand, letting it linger a moment longer than I would have, and a slight shudder ran through her body. "Ooh. Is he a Poseidon type? Tastes like the ocean to me."

"Tastes?" I'm pretty sure my face was locked into disbelief. "You touched him."

"Yeah, it's a sense you start to develop with maturity." I felt a rough swell of annoyance as she walked to the other side of the bed and let her hand drift onto to exposed cheek of Kat. "Mmmm. Persephone type? If you ever get a chance – you know, maybe tangling with one that's a 'bad guy'," she used air quotes, driving my eyebrows up almost to my bangs, "you need to take a drink of a Persephone. They are double yum."

I closed my eyes and felt a throbbing in my temple. "I know you did not just suggest that I drain—"

"A bad one," she said, her voice suddenly higher. "I'm saying that if you run across a bad one cuz I know how focused you are on that sort of thing, catching 'bad guys' – you should definitely drain them dry, because they are all kinds of tasty, let me tell you." She did a pirouette and came around the bed, then brushed my hair out of my eyes, careful not to touch my face. "Come on, get the other guy and get ready. We need to go out, niece."

I sighed. "Go out where?"

She leaned her head in close to me and gave me a mischievous smile. "The bar, here in the hotel."

"I went to a bar last night. It didn't end well. I almost killed some guy."

She raised an eyebrow. "Was he cute?"

I felt a pang as I remembered, not for the first time in the last few hours, that I had broken up with Zack only this morning. And had kissed James last night. "Yes. He very much was."

"Sounds worth it to me." She looked me up and down. "You change and get ready, I'll go knock on the other guy's door and get him to watch the kids." She turned and headed for the door.

"His name is Reed, you know."

She waved a hand carelessly behind her as she walked out. "I've already forgotten it again."

I stood there in the middle of the floor for about ten seconds, pondering my options. I could sit in my room, avoiding the horror that was drunkenness, the searing pain of a hangover and the loss of judgment that resulted from it, or stay here and stare at the walls. I had almost convinced myself that that was the wisest course, the soundest of ideas, when Zack wandered across my mind again, and I realized he'd be doing that for the rest of the night – just like he had been all day – and I'd have only the unconscious bodies of my two colleagues to keep me company.

There was a knock at the door, and when I looked through the peephole, it was Reed, looking a little cross.

"Your aunt just told me to get my ass over here and watch over two sleeping Directorate agents," he said, nonplussed. "You can't be serious."

"I need to get out of here for a while," I said. "We won't be gone long." I started toward the door, my bag on my shoulder, intending to go to my own room, which I hadn't yet seen.

"What am I supposed to do if they wake up?" He looked at me in near astonishment, mouth slightly agape.

"If Kat wakes up first, explain the situation to her," I said. "It's not like you haven't met before."

"And if he wakes up first?"

I shrugged. "I don't know. Get creative."

I closed the door, which muffled his reply. I'm pretty sure it was a curse, and I'm equally sure I didn't care. I went to my room and took a shower, a long one. When I was done, I dressed in a slightly looser suit, the most comfortable one I'd brought with me, straightened my hair and applied some makeup. When I came out of the bathroom, Charlie was waiting, lying on the bed, watching TV. She perked up when she saw me, and I stared at her, question on my face.

"They gave you a spare key," she said. "I pocketed it when you handed me the packets. Figured I might need it later." She smoothed her dress, which didn't show even a sign of wrinkling, and smiled at me. "Ready to have some fun?"

"Sort of."

"But not too much fun, because that's probably against a Directorate rule of some kind."

She dragged a little smile out of me with that one, and we were off. We crossed the lobby, an open air, ornate space with leather couches and decor that looked like it might be just as appropriate in a manor house as it was here. As we walked, I couldn't help but notice heads turn to watch Charlie. Male heads. Lots of them.

We bellied up to the bar, and after I'd shown my ID, the bartender, a skinny guy this time, asked us what we wanted.

"What do you think, daahhhhhling?" Charlie said it with an exaggerated English accent, like she was a duchess or something.

Why break a winning tradition? I only knew one kind of drink, anyway. "Whiskey Sour."

The bartender nodded and Charlie said, "Make it two." He walked off.

"So," I said. "What now?" I swiveled on my stool to take in the whole place. It was Sunday night, and there weren't too many people around. There was a cluster of guys dressed professionally in the corner, ties loosened, sleeves rolled up, lots of laughing going on. I caught a furtive glance from a couple of them at Charlie, who, unlike me, was facing away from the bar and leaning back, her legs crossed and cool indifference beneath her slight smile.

"Now, my dear," she said after a long pause, "we have fun." The bartender set her glass at her elbow and she grabbed it, slow and smooth. "Keep 'em coming." She pressed it against her lips as she stared at the guys in the corner, taking a long, measured drink.

I picked up my whiskey and felt the chill of it in my hand,

then took a sip. It still gave my mouth an involuntary spasm, but not as bad as the night before. I almost enjoyed it this time. It burned, though. I took another, and when I finished, I caught Charlie looking sidelong at me with amusement. "First time?" she asked.

"Second. I did this last night, too."

"Ah." She finished her drink and signaled to the barman. "It's my second time, too." Her eyes fixated on the guys in the corner. "Tell the bartender to send my drink over there." She blinked, then looked at me as though she'd forgotten me somehow. "Actually, just come with me; he'll figure it out."

I looked over at the men she was talking about. Not a one of them was under thirty, and I doubted more than one of them was under forty. "I, uh...think they might be a little out of my age demographic."

"Older men have their advantages. Experience, patience..." She grinned at me wickedly.

I stared back, and I felt the flush come to my cheeks. "How can you...I mean...you could kill someone."

"Pffffft." She waved her hand at me. "First of all, it takes a while for your touch to kill someone; you oughta know that. Second, you just have to be careful, making sure that things are as covered as you can get them...after that, it's all about using strength and muscle control." The bartender set another drink next to her and it was in her hand, then in front of her mouth, hiding her grin. "Just because you're a soul-draining succubus doesn't mean you have to live some kind of virginal life as a nun. I mean, even your mother didn't buy into that idea, and she was the most stiff, serious—"

"Ah, okay." I cringed, interrupting her. "I could have done with a little more exposition and a little less color commentary on that one." I let my expression soften. "But thanks for the info. I was...struggling with some of that."

She pulled the glass from in front of her mouth after taking a long drink. "That's what I'm here for, niece: to teach you all the things that Mommy can't." She giggled. "That's why I'm the coolest aunt. Now, how about we take your newfound knowledge over to the table in the corner and you can find out what I mean?"

I looked back at the guys she was indicating. I felt a reaction, a wave of no, no and hell no. "Um, no. There's not one of them that's my type."

She shrugged, indifferent. "Suit yourself. Sit over here and be a black hole of excitement. In a place like this, you take what you can get. Sometimes it surprises you what you'll find." She stood, draining the last of her drink, and walked over to the table with the guys. When she was a few feet away, they all sat up and took notice of her, especially when she leaned over once she reached the table. I heard her tone, not her words, and it sounded conversational, almost confessional, like she was telling something to an old friend she hadn't seen in a long time. One of them got up and dragged a chair over for her. She sat in it, giving him a smile and running a hand along his exposed forearm, eliciting a shiver from him.

I turned back to the bar and stared at my drink, wondering why I couldn't do what Charlie could. I wasn't that outgoing, that confident, that fearless. Sure, I didn't have any interest in any of those guys because they were way too old for me, but even if they'd been a table full of guys my age, all hot, I still wouldn't have had the guts to do what she did. I turned and watched the easy manner with which she wrapped them all around her finger, with a joke that had them all laughing, with a gentle caress on the back that left the man on the receiving end wanting more.

All I'd had thus far was Zack, and he wasn't exactly wrapped around my finger. I mean, I'd pretty much driven him away because I was afraid I'd hurt him. Even the revelation that Charlie had given me, that there were ways we could be intimate without him getting hurt, sounded awfully risky (not to mention fairly devoid of any romance), maybe moreso to me because I wasn't really sure how it all worked. I mean, I'd only ever kissed him for three to four seconds before I had to stop, and she was talking about protection and muscle control – it was bizarre and exciting and scary as hell all at once, but I didn't know which feeling was heaviest.

Also, I'd let him go. I felt a twinge of guilt and pain, and took a drink to bury that feeling under the rush that the liquor granted, that heady sensation that would be making me drift oh-so-pleasantly in just a few more minutes. Of course the aftereffects would suck, but since when do teenagers worry about consequences? I took another drink, trying to banish that thought. Self-awareness was a curse, a terrible curse. The ice clinked in the bottom of my glass and I realized I had downed the whole thing without noticing.

I started to wave over the barman, but he was already coming with another. His face was almost gaunt, his eyes sunken when he set the Whiskey Sour in front of me. "Here you go," he said.

"Okay, but after this I'm done." I picked up the drink and took a swig.

"And your friend?" He nodded toward Charlie and I turned to see the whole table laughing again, every one of the men paying rapt attention to her, leaning over each other to tell her something, to catch her attention. I watched the way she twirled her hair, the way she laughed at them, smiled. "You gonna keep paying for her?"

I handed him my credit card, the personal one, not the one from the Directorate. "I'm gonna go out on a limb and guess she can probably convince those guys to buy her a round or two, but give her one more on my tab, then close it out."

He smiled at me. "Done deal."

I looked down at my drink, studying the amber liquid in my glass broken by the white of the ice cubes and the red of the maraschino cherry that floated on top. I pulled out the cherry and popped it into my mouth, leaving the stem on the napkin that held my drink. I took another long sip and thought again about Zack. Maybe I'd been hasty. Or maybe I'd been sane. I looked back at Charlie and wondered how she could be so cavalier, so quick with her touch when it could be so harmful, so deadly if she wasn't careful.

"You're prettier than her." There was a voice at my elbow and I looked to see a familiar face. His hair was spiked, and his handsome features looked slightly more rugged tonight, though his shirt was still unbuttoned at the top. James smiled at me, and I couldn't help but smile back. "Don't doubt it for a second; she may have the attention of those geezers, but you're the knockout in this bar."

"James." I said his name with a certain amusement that was probably fueled by the drinks that I was starting to feel the effects of. A little tinkle of suspicion was present too, far back in my mind. I think I might have let slip the barest hint of a smile as I looked back at him again.

"Sienna." He dazzled me with his in return. It started slow, but got pretty powerful pretty quick. I ignored the flutter in my stomach. "Mind if I sit with you?"

I waved a hand vaguely at the stool. "Yesterday you're in Owatonna, today you're in Eau Claire. Are you following me?"

"Can I be honest?" He took off his suit jacket and hung it on the back of the seat before sitting down next to me.

"I'd prefer it, actually. What kind of a girl says, 'No, please lie to me'?" The suspicious part of me was gaining traction.

"A surprising number, actually," he said, keeping it cool. "Though usually not in so many words. Anyway, I'm here because of you."

"Oh?" I took a sip, a very small one, and kept my hand ready in case I had to reach for a weapon. "I have a stalker?"

The bartender set a beer in front of him and he took a long pull. "Nah. I told you I was a recruiter, didn't I?"

"Hmmm." I thought about it. He probably had, but all I remembered was his lips. "I believe you did. So you're here to recruit me?"

"If I can." He had stopped paying attention to the beer.

"You recruit a lot of people away from the FBI?" I turned on my stool to face him, letting my arm rest on the side of the bar.

"No," he said. "But I've recruited a few people away from the Directorate." He kept his body facing toward the bar, but his eyes were on me.

I felt a chill, a little one, and I knew my eyes widened. "How did you find me here?"

He looked away. "Not the hardest thing to do. Go to a town where an Omega safehouse gets hit in the morning, go to all the hotel bars and look for the prettiest succubus around." He looked back at me, and was smiling again.

"You are quite the charmer," I said, vacillating between confusion and feeling flattered. "What will you do if I do say no to your offer?" My hand clenched tighter around my drink, and my breath caught in my chest.

"You haven't heard it yet." His smile took on an otherworldly quality, getting brighter. Or was that the alcohol? "Listen, this is just like Red Rover as a kid. You picked the wrong side and I'm just asking if Sienna can come over."

I looked at him and cocked my head. "Red what?"

"Never mind," he said with a shake of the head. "To answer your question: if you say no, I'll learn to live with my deep, bitter disappointment and hope that you'll still be okay with me trying to seduce you." His smile grew wider, and I found for a flash that I wanted to slap it off him. But just for a second, because damn...he said it with a hell of a lot of charm.

I let go of the breath I had been holding and turned back to the bar, allowing myself just a sip of the whiskey. "You might not be glad if I go along with that. Don't you know what a succubus does to a person?"

He chuckled dryly. "I do. I'm very familiar with it, in fact."

I reached down and pulled off my gloves, slowly, as he watched, then took my drink in my hand and felt the perspiration of the glass mingle with my own and slide down my fingers as I pressed it to my lips and took another swig. "Then are you really sure you want to try that?" I set the glass back on the bar.

He moved fast, faster than I would have given him credit for, probably because I could feel the second whiskey already taking effect. His hand slid across and grabbed one of mine and I felt his skin against mine, slightly warm, mine a little sticky from the light layer of sweat that came from always wearing a glove. I didn't pull away and he cradled my hand in his, bringing his other around, holding it.

"Please," I said after a moment. I started to tug my hand away, but he held onto it, staring into my eyes. I started to count in my head, knowing it wouldn't be long before he'd get weary and pass out. 1...2...

I pulled at it again and he didn't surrender it, instead leaning closer to me. "It'll be all right," he said, bringing my hand to his lips for a gentle kiss. ...3...4...5...6...my eyes widened as he looked back up to me, cradling my hand in his. ...7...8...9...

"You should let go," I said again, more urgently this time, but I didn't pull away. ...10...11...12...

"I don't want to," he breathed, his face next to mine, the smell of his cologne mixed with the beer on his breath in a medley of strong and sweet, and he brought his lips to mine. ...13...14...15...16...17...18...I couldn't remember what came next and it didn't matter: there was just the smell of him, the taste of him...

He pulled away for just a second, looking me full in the eyes. "I'm like you...and you can't hurt me. We...are made for each other, you and me."

I took a breath, a word filling my mind with possibilities, with a legend I'd only heard of and never given much thought to; of a type of meta, my equal and opposite, the only one who could keep my powers at bay. I felt it in my head, in my heart, and on my lips, and it was beautiful; a breath of hope for someone who'd been hopeless for far too long.

"Incubus."

14

He didn't let go of me, not across the lobby, not in the elevator, when the passion was rising and we kissed again, a roaring chorus of excitement building in my head and body. We didn't part when it opened to my floor, nor when we hit the wall of the hallway. I fumbled for my room key as we staggered, blindly, one of us walking backward nearly all the time, to my door. I threw it open and we were in, the lights already on dim, as though they were set in anticipation of our arrival.

My jacket was shed instantly, so seamless I hardly noticed it come off and wondered if it had been he or I that had done it. I tossed my gun and holster onto my open bag, followed by my shoes as I ran a hand over his smooth chest, reveling in the fact that I could touch him without fear. We broke apart, breathing heavy, and he smiled at me as I fumbled to undo the buttons on his shirt. He reciprocated, much more smoothly than I, and we hit the bed, lips once more intertwined.

I felt the weight of him on top of me, his chest pressed against mine, his fingers working on the snap and zipper of my pants. No sooner had he gotten them undone than my jacket began to ring. Loud, musical, the tones a perfect distraction to the symphony of touch and sensation that was going on a few feet away. He caressed me, running a hand along my side, making me shudder while I wished he would finish what he had started and get my pants off. I let the tips of my fingers slide over the smooth skin on his back, holding him in place, pulling him closer to me.

His lips pulled from mine for a second. "Is that your phone ringing?"

I craned my neck to kiss him again. "I don't know, and I don't care." My hands reached up to the back of his neck and pulled him closer. I felt his tongue in my mouth, tasted the beer flavor, and then he pulled away, running gentle kisses onto my chin and then down my neck. I felt his hands as they ran over me, the touches a delight, all different kinds of pleasure running through my skin. The phone had stopped ringing, wherever it was, and I couldn't be happier as I lay there, breathing heavy while he touched me.

The first heavy knock on my door jarred me, causing me to jerk in surprise. I looked at him, locked eyes, and I shook my head. "Just ignore it," I said, running a hand through his hair. A second knock came, louder and more insistent than the first. I leaned back, letting my head fall against the pillow as some of the heat left me. "Oh God, why now?"

He chuckled and lay his head on my belly. "Because it's the worst possible time."

The knocking came again, sustained, persistent and louder. "Sienna?" I heard Kat's voice, then knocking again. "I know you're in there; your phone's GPS is still transmitting."

"Go away!" I cried. "Come back in an hour!"

"I can't!" she shouted back. "Ariadne just called, and we've got things to deal with!"

I felt a kind of surly whine come from my lips as James laughed softly against my stomach. He kissed me on the belly and rolled off me, allowing me to get to my feet and stagger to the door. It took all my restraint, once I had opened it just a crack to see Kat, not to reach out, grab her by the head, and slam it in the door for interrupting my efforts to lose my virginity. "What?" I felt the acid drip from my tongue, looking daggers at the pretty cheerleader who didn't have any problems at all sleeping with her boyfriend.

She looked paler than usual, but then again, she had looked like that a lot on this trip. "Ariadne called."

"Yes, I heard you the first time."

She looked to either side down the hallway, then back at me. "Can I come in so we can talk?"

"No," I said. "You can leave so I can get back to doing what I was doing!"

Her brow crinkled and she looked mildly offended. "What were you doing?"

I let out a heavy exhalation and felt my hand go to my forehead as I bowed my head. "Ugh, never mind. What did Ariadne want?"

"She got your message and was calling you back." Kat looked at me with wide eyes. "Also, leaving us with that Reed guy while you went to the bar? Not cool. You're lucky I woke up first."

I felt a wash of chagrin. "What did Scott say when he woke up?"

"He's still kind of out of it, but he didn't seem too happy." She shook her head and glanced past me, suddenly stiffening. "Is there someone in there with you?"

I opened the door wide enough to show her that I was in my bra with my pants unzipped, then shut it back to only a crack. "Yes," I said with some urgency.

Her eyes widened in alarm. "Won't that...you know," she lowered her voice to a bare whisper, "kill...whoever you're with?"

"Apparently not," I said. "But the mood? The mood is officially dead, thanks to you."

"I'm sorry, but Ariadne wants us on the phone right now." She stared at me, and I knew the firmness in her voice didn't come from her.

"Just give me half an hour," I said, pleading. I started to shut the door.

"Now." She reached out and grasped my wrist, giving it a squeeze, then letting go immediately. "She's in Kansas, and things have gone very, very wrong. She only has a short window to talk to us. She's waiting for you."

I buried my face in my hands and took a deep breath. "I'll be there in a minute."

I closed the door and felt James's hands slide across my hips, teasing and promising more touches, more caresses. He kissed the side of my neck and I squirmed; it hit the right spot. "I have to go," I said, my eyes closed, my words heavy with the regret I felt over every inch of my body – some inches more than others. I slid free of his grasp and turned to kiss him again on the mouth. I broke away after a moment. "I promise I will be right back after this call is over."

I saw his eyes go cool in the half-light. "All right. I can wait." He cracked a smile as his fingers stroked my bare arms and grasped my hands in his. "I think you're probably worth it."

I pulled away, giving him a coy smile before I stooped to pick my blouse off the floor. "Probably?"

He gave me a noncommittal shrug and went back to the bed as I threw my arms through the sleeves of my blouse. "I guess we'll see."

I sat on the edge of the bed and he leaned over my shoulder, kissing the back of my neck as I buttoned my shirt. "You never did tell me who you work for."

"I doubt you'd have heard of us," he said, nuzzling, his tongue on the side of my neck. "But if you're interested, I can give you the whole pitch of why you should join us...after."

I felt a little amusement as I slipped on my shoes. "So recruiting me isn't your first priority anymore?"

"Nuh-uh," he grunted. I gasped as his fingers tweaked me.

I stood and brushed his hands off. "I'll be back as soon as I can." I picked my holster up off my suitcase and put it on, followed by my jacket. I took a last look at him once I was at the door, gave him a weak smile, and closed it behind me.

I leaned against the wall in the hallway, trying to catch my breath. After taking time to compose myself, I walked two doors down and knocked. The door cracked open to admit me and Reed stood there, looking much less beaten up than he had a few hours ago.

"Is that Sienna?" I heard Ariadne's voice crackle from the speaker of the phone sitting on the bed.

"It is," I said. "Sorry for the delay; I was just—"

"It doesn't matter," Ariadne cut me off. "I only have a few

minutes. Our operation in western Kansas has gotten complicated; M-Squad has been ambushed by some heavy-hitting metas, and we've lost half the team from our Texas facility. The Director and I need to manage the fallout from this, but I wanted to get back to all of you first."

"Things have gotten a bit complicated here as well," I said, feeling a little catch in my voice.

"Yes," Ariadne said, "Kat and Scott have explained. We'll have a conversation later about how you've been keeping quiet about your aunt, but for now let's talk about your friend Reed."

I locked eyes with Reed, who looked unconcerned. "You know he's standing right here, don't you?"

"He's offered to help us," she said, "with some additional resources from his organization. He's also shed a little light on what we're dealing with down here in Kansas." I heard the tension in Ariadne's voice. "Omega seems to have chosen this moment to launch a surprise attack against the Directorate. We think they drew M-Squad down here for the express purpose of putting them out of commission." Ariadne's tone was flat. "I'm afraid this little chase we have you on, trying to track down this meta that's robbing convenience stores, is going to have to wait. Reed told me you've captured a laptop from Omega?"

"Yes, I have it right here." I pointed to Kat's overnight bag, prompting a quizzical look from her. I pointed again, and she went over to it, opening it and digging around until she came out with the laptop. "It's password protected, though, and I didn't want to chance digging around in it because...well, because I'm terrible with computers. Figured I'd leave it to the pros."

"I want that computer in the hands of our techies right now," Ariadne said. "How fast can you get it back to the campus?"

I looked to Scott, who cleared his throat. "If we drive fast, with the sirens on, we're a little less than two hours away."

"If there's any hint of what Omega is up to or what their next move might be, we need to know now," Ariadne said. "Get that computer in the hands of our tech support immediately. Do whatever you have to do." She paused. "Reed, is there anything else you can tell us?"

Reed looked like he'd been disturbed from slumber, moving after being still for several minutes. "I can't tell you much about what Omega's up to down there because it's out of my territory, but I can tell you that there's at least one more facility they have here in Wisconsin, something that's a lot more secret than the Eau Claire safehouse. One of our sources called it Site Epsilon, and it was where they were working on something called 'Project Andromeda'. Our agent was tasked to find it and get inside, but they, uh..." He shrugged. "...disappeared."

"Where is this?" Scott asked, his arms folded in front of him.

"Eastern Wisconsin, not far from Eagle River." He shrugged. "I took a preliminary look around after our agent didn't report in, but there was no sign – no trace of his cell phone, nothing. Of course, I'm the only meta my organization has in the upper midwest, and I've got about a million things to do, so it hasn't been something I've been able to get to; Wisconsin's just been too quiet in terms of Omega activity to make it a priority."

"If Omega has a secret facility here in the state that far off the beaten path," Kat was thinking out loud, "that means it's probably something important, right? Something secret?"

"How sure are you about the location, Reed?" Ariadne's voice came off a little tinny, and I heard something in the background over the speaker, some kind of commotion.

"The search radius is about 100 miles," Reed said. "But I have to be honest, we don't know what's waiting, which is another reason I haven't checked it out. I mean, it could just have an Omega sweep team or two, or it could have one of the guys that used to be called a god hanging around, working security."

I heard silence from Ariadne, as though she were spondering her response. "Omega's made a very bold move in their attack on us in Kansas. It's already bad enough that we're not going to be able to keep it quiet from anyone – not the government, not the press and not the public. I doubt they would have made this move if they weren't prepared to follow up with additional attacks, and frankly, we still don't know a damned thing about them.

"We need something, anything. I want one of you three, Kat, Scott or Sienna, to rent a car and get the computer back to Headquarters for analysis. The other two, go with Reed and Sienna's aunt, if she's willing to help, and find that Omega facility, infiltrate it if it looks lightly guarded. If not, put it under surveillance and we'll hit it as soon as we get M-Squad out of this fight in Kansas. We're completely blind here, fighting an enemy we know nothing about."

There was a stark silence broken only by a little static from the phone's speaker. "And if we can't? Can't find anything, I mean?" Kat asked.

"Then we'll need you back at Headquarters as quickly as possible," Ariadne said, voice taut. "Because I think we can safely say that Omega has declared war on the Directorate – and we have no idea where and when they'll strike next."

15

There were a few seconds of quiet after Ariadne had hung up, as the four of us stared around the room at each other. Kat was withdrawn, staring into space, while Reed and Scott were watching each other out of the corners of their eyes, occasionally looking like they were going to throw down right there, glares in the quiet speaking louder than anything else.

"All right," I said. "Who wants to take the computer back to the Directorate?"

"I can do it," Kat said, stirring. "I'm the least useful in a battle anyway, at least from an offense perspective."

"Yeah, but having someone who can heal fatal wounds is sort of a nice card to have in your hand," Scott said.

"I agree with the waterboy on that," Reed said, drawing a scathing look from Scott. "We're going into an uncertain situation against potentially deep odds and gods know what kind of metas."

I put my hand on my head, massaging my temples. An hour ago, I hadn't pictured things going this way. I thought of James, still in my room, and my head spun from the ten thousand questions I had no answers to. I needed to know things, and I needed to know them now. My eyes snapped open and I focused on Reed. "Who are you working for?"

He tensed and a pained expression grew on his face. He nodded slowly, and spoke. "I guess if we're gonna work together, I have to explain a few things, don't I?"

"Yeah, playing the man of mystery isn't gonna do much to endear you to us at this point," Scott said.

Reed seemed to consider that very carefully before he spoke again. "I'll give you some basics. The organization I'm with has one purpose: countering Omega. That's it. We know who the Directorate is because they're a big player in the meta game, but we've got no quarrel with you. The only reason I was after you," he said with a nod toward me, "is because Omega was and we were trying to beat them to you."

"What about a name?" Scott looked at him expectantly.

"I'm Reed, and you?" Reed shot him a smarmy smile, then rolled his eyes when he caught my glare. "Fine, but don't laugh. We call ourselves Alpha."

"And the prize for originality goes to...someone else," Scott said, his lips crooked in amusement.

"I didn't come up with it," Reed said. "Our founders are former Omega, but they got disillusioned with what the old gods had done and decided to band together to stop them. We've been around for a few hundred years, and we've kept them in check during that time."

"Alpha and Omega," I said under my breath. "So, what? They're the end and you're the beginning?" He gave me an oblique nod. "Of what?"

Reed let out a sharp exhalation. "I don't know. I mean, I've seen what Omega does, and it's not been pleasant. This little war they've started with you, it's nothing compared to some of the dirty tricks they've pulled. They've got people working for them that are worse than Wolfe. That should give you an idea of what they're like."

"And what could I tell about you by seeing who you work for?" I stared back at him, watched him stiffen, a resigned look on his face.

"You could see that we've got a common enemy," he said, "and if you keep watching what they do, you'll see why."

"All right," I said. "So what powers do you have?"

His eyes closed and he bowed his head, shaking it like a kid who was asked to give back a toy he really didn't want to let go of. "You're killin' me, Nealon. Can't I keep any secrets?"

"You can keep all the secrets you want," I said, not taking my eyes off him. "You just can't keep them and expect to go into the fight with us at your side."

His eyes came up, burning, finding mine. "Let's get this straight: right now, you need me a lot more than I need you."

"And if we're going into a battle," I said, keeping my tone even, "how are we supposed to work together if I don't know what you bring to the table?"

He squinted, as if he could shut out my damned, unreasonable request, then relaxed and opened his eyes again. "I'm an Aeolus, okay?"

"A what?" Kat asked.

"Like on a breast?" Scott looked at him in confusion. Kat buried her face in one of her hands.

"Like a windkeeper, you jackass." Reed stuck a hand out and I felt the currents of air in the room shift, my clothing starting to flap in a growing breeze. Reed pulled his hand back and the air stopped stirring. "I can control the movement of air, attracting it to me or pushing it away."

"That could be really useful," Scott said, "if we're on a sailboat and the wind dies."

A flash of annoyance crossed Reed's face. "And I'm sure your power is only useful if a small fire breaks out."

"All right, boys, enough of that," I said. "I think we have to send Kat to the Directorate." I looked between the three of them. "We'll need all the offensive power we can get if we're going to assault what could be an Omega base." I looked to her. "But you should get any additional help you can from the Directorate and rendezvous with us as quickly as possible. Depending on how our search goes, you may catch up with us before we even find the enemy."

She nodded. "All right. I'll need a car."

Reed shot her a cool look. "I can help with that."

I took a deep breath and looked to Kat. "Hurry." I shifted my glance to Reed and then Scott. "Bring the car around and meet me outside the lobby in ten minutes." I turned and walked to the door, Kat and Reed a couple steps behind me.

I parted ways with them in the hallway, sliding the card key into my room door. I paused and took a breath before I pulled the handle, wondering if I'd find James still inside.

I did. He was lying on the bed, the covers pulled up to his waist, his shirt still off. He greeted me with a warm smile which I didn't quite match. "I waited," he said in an enticing voice, something that called out to me, urged me on. I wanted to throw off my jacket and blouse and crawl under the sheets with him and stay there for the rest of the night. To hell with the Directorate, Omega, Alpha and all else; forget metas and humans. I wanted them all to go away and just leave me alone with James. Maybe not forever, but at least until morning.

I breathed in deep, and let it out slow. "I'm sorry. I have to go."

He sat up, an awkward discomfort on his face. "What?"

"My office called, and I have to leave on an assignment right now." I tried to convey regret, but I couldn't tell if it was getting across, because his face had gotten red.

"Wow, that's dedication," he said, voice tight. "But you know, there are alternatives." He pulled back the sheet and I looked away. He wasn't wearing anything beneath it, and I was suddenly very uncomfortable. I became even more so when he walked around the bed, rested his hands on my cheeks and gently pulled me in for a kiss.

I returned it, but without the heat, the passion that had consumed us earlier. This one was slow, methodical – enjoyable, sure, but without the possibility of going anywhere. He increased the pressure of the kiss, and I felt the heat from his side, the desire, and broke away, turning from him, groaning as I did so. "I'm sorry, I can't. I have a job to do. I have responsibilities, commitments." I was breathing much harder than I would have thought I would be after one kiss. "I have to go." I looked back at him, and he seemed so solitary, standing naked in the middle of my room. "When I get done with this, I'll call you, I promise. I'm..." I searched for the words. "...I...want this. I wish I could stay right now, but I just can't."

He was silent for a moment, then turned and stooped to pick up his pants. I watched. "Where are you going?" he asked.

"I...can't really get into it. Secrecy and all that."

"I could help, maybe." He stared at me as he put his pants on, then zipped them up. I felt a tremor of regret. Trying to be a responsible adult and do my job really sucked right now.

I sighed. "I don't think so."

"I'm pretty strong," he said with a teasing smile. "You probably know something about that."

"I do know something about that." I tossed the clothes I'd left out into my bag, then pulled my syringe and a vial with my daily dose of psycho-suppressant out.

James's eyes caught the syringe as I injected the vial into my arm. "What's that?"

"That," I said, tossing the empty vial in the trash, "is how I curb the voices in my head." I felt the familiar rush of sleepiness that followed an injection, and shook it off. It barely affected me anymore. "How do you do it?"

"Not like that," he said with some disapproval. "You do it with your mind, not with drugs. If you've got a strong will, you barely feel it with most people, and it gets easier as you learn to control it."

"Ah," I said, slightly sarcastic. "That's where I went wrong. See, when I first absorbed someone, it was a crazed psycho beast who was bent on killing me. I shoulda picked a weaker target I guess, worked my way up to the monstrous, but I didn't really have an option at the time."

"You absorbed Wolfe?" He shook his head and let out a small gasp of amazement. "Wow. I did not know that. I heard you beat him but I assumed you did it some other way." He cringed. "That's a rough way to start out." His face slackened and was overcome with genuine curiosity. "How old were you when that happened?"

"Seventeen," I said. I thought I caught a flash of surprise from him, and I gave him a reassuring smile. "I'm eighteen now. Don't sweat it, okay?"

"Eighteen and headed into trouble," he said. "You sure I can't help?"

"I think my bosses at the Directorate are going to be upset enough with the people I've already dragged into this," I said with a short laugh as I closed my bag and hefted it onto my shoulder. While I did that, I felt his arms wrap around me at my waist, slipping under my untucked blouse and touching my skin, giving me a thrill that ran up my spine.

He kissed my neck again, then whispered, "Surely one more won't matter to them; but I might make all the difference for you if you get in a tight spot."

I pulled away. "Pretty sure it would matter to them." I smoothed the wrinkles in my pants and pulled down my shirt to cover my midriff. I hesitated, staring at him, his muscled chest catching my attention. "I could certainly use some more help, but I can't..." I sighed again. "You seem pretty resourceful, so I'll tell you this much. I'm going east. If you show up, I won't be upset to see you there."

He smiled, a growing, widening one that made me feel a warm flutter. "You might just see me there, then."

I walked toward the door and opened it, casting one last look back. "I kinda hope so."

16

I suspected Reed was stealing a car for Kat to use since there wasn't a rental place I knew of that would be open in the middle of the night, at least not in Eau Claire. I crossed the lobby of the hotel with my bag on my shoulder, heading toward the bar. I hoped that Charlie would still be there; no one had answered her door when I knocked.

The five of them were still clustered around the table, still laughing. I checked the clock on my cell phone; it was close to 3 A.M. One of the guys had passed out, his head down, and another was leaning heavily on his arm, eyes shut, keeping his face propped off the table. "Another round!" one of the two that was still fully upright called out to the bartender, and he stepped into motion behind the bar, his skinny hands grabbing bottles off the shelves.

I made my way through the tables and over to them. My aunt was laughing, hard, when I got there, but I hadn't caught the set-up or the punchline, so I was still serious. She caught my eye as I approached, and stopped laughing when I got close. "This is my sister," she said to the two men who were still awake. They both turned to look at me, and at least one of them came up with an idea that was so obvious it was written all over his sodding-drunk face. His leer made me uneasy, as though I were being undressed by his eyes. "Come on! Drink with us," she said.

Oddly enough, being literally undressed with James, a near-stranger, had been far more comfortable than this.

486

"Hey," I said, leaning over to Charlie. "I have to go."

"Go?" She looked around in confusion and laughed, a deep, drunken laugh. "You just got here!"

"I have to go to Eagle River tonight," I said, keeping my voice low. I heard the men muttering to themselves, something about me that I ignored, otherwise I might have had to smite them. "Will you come with me? I could really use your help."

She met my gaze, her eyes looking into mine, and I caught a fleeting hint of concern that passed in about a second. "I don't think so, sweety." She reached up and patted me on the cheek twice. "I'm not done here yet."

I knelt down next to her. "Charlie," I said, catching her attention again as she was reaching for the glass the bartender had just set in front of her. "I'm serious. This could be really bad and I need all the help I can get."

"I said no." She took a drink, draining half her tallboy glass in one gulp. "God! You're all work and no fun, Sienna."

I felt the sting of her words curiously more given what had happened only minutes before, with James. "All right. I'll leave you be, then." I stood and started to walk out.

"Hey, wait!" She stood, almost turning over the table, and staggered over to me, shaking her head as though she could get rid of the effects of her drunkenness that way. "You're just gonna leave me here? In this town?"

I stared back at her, dully. My aunt, my blood. The person who I thought would be in my corner for sure, especially heading into this mess. "Yeah. You said you didn't want to come with me."

Her head rocked back and she looked offended. "Well, I don't have any money to get home."

I stared at her in disbelief and shook my head before reaching for my wallet. I pulled out five crisp hundreds and handed them to her. She flashed me a bright smile. "Good luck," she said. "I'm sure you'll knock 'em dead, kiddo." She rolled up the bills and slipped them down the front of her dress, then turned and walked back to the table, where she was greeted with laughter and cheers.

I was still feeling burnt as I walked out the doors of the

487

lobby into the stuffy, hot air of outside. The SUV was only a few feet outside the entrance, already running. I walked over to the passenger door and got in, took a quick look to confirm Reed was in the back seat, and nodded at Scott, who put the car in gear.

"I take it your aunt's not coming?" This from Reed, who was bathed in the shadows behind me.

"No," I said, voice tight. "She decided she'd rather drink with her new friends." I rubbed my face, still feeling the effects of the whiskey I'd had earlier in the night. Maybe one of these days I could actually go out and have a couple drinks without it backfiring on me, but apparently now was not the time in my life when I could pull that off.

The road went by, on and on as the GPS guided us onto the freeway and we headed north. My head swam with thoughts of James and Zack, Zack and James. I had been so close with James, so close to something I doubted I'd ever be able to have with Zack. Or anyone, actually. On the other hand, I knew almost nothing about James; in fact, all I knew about him was that he seemed to be the only man I'd met that I could touch without harming.

Plus, I knew how he looked naked. And it was...not bad. Not bad at all.

I cursed my responsibility again, and thought about Charlie, sitting in the bar even now, doing what she wanted to do when she wanted to do it. She blew through town when she felt like it, hung out with me when she wanted to, and, like some kind of idiot, I gave her money pretty much any time I saw her. Maybe I felt guilty because I thought I had it so much better than her, like I'd gotten lucky. Hell, I probably had. But she didn't even seem like she was trying, just doing whatever she wanted.

Meanwhile, I had just put off something I wanted more than almost anything else in favor of doing something I had to do.

I fell asleep sometime after passing a sign that read Chippewa Falls and when I woke up there was light on the horizon. Reed was talking to Scott in a hushed voice, and I heard them both share a chortle. "Where are we?" I asked.

Scott looked over at me. "About five miles from Eagle River. Directorate analysts went over property records in the area and found a few anomalies for us to check out."

"Oh?" I blinked my eyes. "How far behind us is Kat?"

"At least four hours," he said. "She's got some agents with her, and they're going full tilt with the sirens on, but they're just west of Eau Claire now."

"Maybe we'll get lucky and come up empty the first few places," Reed said from behind us. I looked back at him in askance and he shrugged. "It could happen."

We followed the GPS, passing through the town itself and out a side road, stopping at an old building on the outskirts, an aluminum shed that looked a little like a barn. After taking a hard look around inside, we found nothing. The next stop was an abandoned farm on the other side of town. By the time we got out of the car, the sun had been up for a little while and it was already hot. I left my jacket in the car and rolled up my sleeves, shedding my gloves. Reed and Scott shared a look and steered well clear of me as we walked up the dirt road toward the farmhouse.

My holster was solid against my ribs, and, I realized about halfway up the drive, quite visible since my jacket was gone. I felt for my FBI ID and remembered I'd left it and my wallet in the jacket. I shrugged and looked at Scott. "Got your ID?"

"Yep," he said, patting his back pocket.

"Good. I'd hate to get shot by some old farmer because I couldn't properly identify myself."

"As a fake FBI agent, you mean?" Reed cracked a grin when he said it.

We walked up the dusty road, my shoes picking up an accumulation of particles as we went, a fine sheen of light brown earth on the black surface. "How many more of these property anomalies do we have to check?"

"Three more," Scott said as we reached the farmhouse. The screen door was open, hanging off its hinges. The door behind it was cracked and didn't look to be in much better condition. The white paneling that was wrapped around the house was in shambles, and looked like it had been there since the early 1900s, gray in some places, cracked and peeling. The shutters were off all but a few windows and the glass was broken out of those that I could see. "I don't think we're going to have to deal with anyone living here," Scott said in dark amusement.

"I don't know about that," Reed said. "This looks like a fine place for some snakes to nest; or maybe a posse of angry badgers."

I looked at him in confusion. "Badgers form posses?"

"They do in this state."

Scott led the way through the door, his hand extended in case trouble presented itself. He paused and looked at Reed. "You want to check the barn?" Scott turned back to look into the house. "It's not looking like much in here."

"Sure," Reed said, and looked at me. "You?"

"Yeah, I'll go with you," I said.

Scott frowned, looking back over his shoulder at us. "That's okay. I'll just check out this creepy old farmhouse all by my lonesome."

"That's the spirit." I gave him a barehand slap on the back, causing him to jump and then look at me with a stern face. "We'll meet you outside."

Reed and I walked to the barn, an old, decaying structure that looked to be in just about as good a repair as the farmhouse. The silo looked as though it had collapsed years ago, now nothing more than a bed of concrete blocks laid out across an overgrown field, green grass sprouting around the white of the blocks like tombstones in a graveyard.

"You think this is it?" I looked at Reed to see how he was holding up. He looked calm enough.

"Probably not," he said as he opened the barn door wide, letting loose a foul, disgusting smell that caused me to cover my nose and gag.

"What is that?" I asked

"I think something died in here." He tucked his shirt over his nose and walked forward, looking around until he stopped in front of one of the animal stalls. "Yep. Something died here."

"Ugh." I retreated from the barn, moving back to a comfortable distance where the smell started to fade. I could still see him looking around within, but after about a minute he came back to me, popping his head out of his shirt and taking a deep breath. "Why did you think this wasn't the place even before you opened the door?" I asked.

He pointed to the ground in front of the barn. "No sign of vehicle tracks or footprints, here or in the main driveway. I don't think anyone's been here for a long time. Now, it could have been Omega doing a really excellent job of covering things up, but now that I've looked around, I'm inclined to believe it's just an old farmhouse." He wrinkled his nose. "Complete with remains of an old farm animal."

I stared off into the distance, where the sun was up off the horizon, casting its light on the green, rolling fields that surrounded us to the trees that covered the horizon. "We've got a few more to check. I kinda hope the next one is it, though; I'm sick of these dead ends." I turned and started walking back to the farmhouse, where I saw Scott emerging from a side door, brushing his shoulders off with enough emphasis that I suspected spider webs might have entangled him.

"I don't know," Reed said, taking one last look at the barn. "It might be the next one, it might be the one after that, but I kinda hope it's none of them. I know Omega, and I shudder to think about what kind of secrets they're hiding out here." He made a face. "I suspect it'll make us long for an abandoned farmhouse with old rancid animals."

"Maybe," I said. "But whatever they're hiding, I need to find out." I took a deep breath, trying to enjoy for just a moment the feel of the sun's rays beating down on my arms and my hands. I felt like I was soaking them up, taking in the heat. "There's a lot riding on this, a lot we've sacrificed to be at this point, to take the assignment this far." I tried to hold my chin up. "Whatever's waiting for us, we'll find a way past it."

"You sure about that?" He raised an eyebrow at me. "You're talking about the organization that threw both Wolfe and Henderschott at you. I doubt they're gonna just let you waltz into one of their most closely guarded secrets."

"I doubt there'll be much waltzing, at least not until

afterward," I said. "But whatever they're going to throw at us, whatever's waiting, we'll get through it." I smiled. "After all, how bad could it be?"

Reed rolled his eyes at me. "Jinx."

17

Someone Else

It was bad. Worse than I expected. Guards walked the perimeter of their so-called Site Epsilon, black-clad figures that wore tactical vests and hid behind tall chain-link fences with barbed wire stretched across the top. They probably weren't visible to the naked human eye, but a meta would see them if they paid close attention, their black standing out against the green of the woods like tar smudged onto a painting of a summer field.

There was a fairly obvious cluster of them hanging behind the trees just off the driveway, behind the gate. I watched them for a little while, saw them with their underslung submachine guns, and worse, knew they were probably itching for a fight after being stationed out here for so long.

The main gate looked abandoned. I had parked my stolen car a good distance down the road, out of sight. This one had a decent radio but no air conditioning, and I had resolved that the next car I stole would be a new model Mercedes, if possible. The good news was, I had enough money that I didn't have to rob any convenience stores on the way out here. Progress at last.

I took another look at the gate, trying to figure out what their game was. I assumed that they were aiming for the abandoned look, but the gate was too well kept up, without rust. The gatehouse had dark tinted windows, but the paint was peeling. Based on the size, I had to guess there were at least three human guards inside at any given time, plus others lurking nearby. Every last one of them that I could see looked to be geared like a sweep team, not rent-a-cops with batons and pepper spray. Omega was taking their security here very seriously, unlike the safehouse in Eau Claire. They'd even made sure this property was a half-mile off the nearest road.

I slunk through the grass, keeping close to the ground. I hate getting dirty, but this was one case where I had no choice. I had other suspicions about what kind of security I'd find behind the fences; motion and heat sensors, cameras, and a bunch of trigger-happy sweepers who probably had a very aggressive kill order, one that probably transcended attempts to surrender.

I stared at the seemingly impenetrable fortress and it stared back at me. I hoped not literally. If they were watching me already, this was going to be even tougher than I thought.

I was a half-dozen yards off the driveway when I heard the sound of a vehicle. I crouched lower and saw an SUV approaching. I huddled even closer to the ground and tried to hide my face as they passed. They were headed straight for the gatehouse, and I watched as movement started in earnest on the other side of the fence. The squad of guards I'd seen earlier were moving through the underbrush, coming toward the gatehouse. I waited for the SUV to turn around, to throw gravel and spin out, hauling ass out of there, but they didn't. The guards crept closer in position, weapons raised, and I wondered how long it would be before they opened fire.

18

Sienna Nealon

We rolled down the driveway of the next potential base for Omega, this one an old factory. We'd turned off the road almost a half-mile back, and were surrounded by tall trees and heavy underbrush. I was trying to keep an eye out for whatever might cross our path next, but I kept getting distracted by movement in the forest. After the third time, I chalked it up to sunlight coming through the trees in the distance, but I couldn't quite go along with that explanation, not wholeheartedly anyway. We came up on a gatehouse, with a fence that was at least ten feet high and ran as far as I could see in either direction.

"It would appear they're serious about keeping us out," Reed said from the backseat. "Of course, we could almost jump over the fence..."

"I don't know that I could jump that," Scott said, staring straight ahead.

"Well, some of us could jump it," Reed said, prompting Scott to turn and shake his head, amused. "I'm kidding. I could help you clear it."

Scott raised an eyebrow. "And my landing on the other side?"

"As gentle as being tossed over a fence by a tornado."

I watched out the windshield. The gatehouse was in bad shape, looked to have gone years without painting, but the

495

windows were tinted and I couldn't see anything inside. "Something's different about this place."

"It looks pretty abandoned to me," Scott said.

"No, she's right." Reed was leaning between the seats, looking forward. "There are fresh tire tracks leading up the drive, the fence looks like it's in pretty damned good repair, and some parts of that gatehouse look like they've been artificially aged." He pointed at the windows. "Look at those. If the rest of the place is cracked and peeling, why do those windows look new? They're tinted so dark you can't see in them." He squinted. "I think I see some really small security cameras, too. Why wouldn't they remove those if the place is abandoned?"

We had come to a stop about a hundred feet from the gate, just looking. "Well," Scott said, a little tense, "if we want, we can go check it out nice and slow, or we can start our trespassing with a little breaking and entering."

I caught movement off the path behind the gate, but I couldn't tell what, just a black blur. "I think we're gonna need to start with a bang."

Scott looked across at me, then back to the windshield. "Okay. You might wanna brace yourself."

I heard Reed buckle his seatbelt in the back as Scott gunned the engine with his foot still on the brake, the sound of gravel hitting the back of the SUV drowning out any possibility of further conversation. He let loose the brakes and we surged forward, racing toward the gate. I saw it get larger, saw a head peek out of the gatehouse and then dodge back in as we collided with the chain link fencing. I heard the smash of metal on the hood, and the top of the gate whipsawed down and hit the roof of our car with a clash so loud I ducked in fear that it would buckle.

We continued to drive, the gate lodged on our car. I saw men in black uniforms on either side of us, diving for cover. I watched as two of them were hit by the edges of the gate and flew through the air as Scott continued to push the car forward, his teeth gritted and his hands clenching the wheel as he tried to steer.

We came around a bend and I had to catch my breath. At

least a dozen guards were in the road in front of us, but that wasn't what got me. It was one of them, with a long tube slung over his shoulder, down on one knee, the tube being fiddled with by one of the other guards as the man stuffed something onto the tip – a roughly potato-sized object. I watched him start to pull his hand away, his task completed. I yelled and my hand flew to my seatbelt, unfastening it. I could hear Reed in the backseat, already moving, doing the same.

"RPG!" I shouted and reached over to Scott, slapping the release on his seatbelt. "BAIL OUT!" I waited a half-second to see him grab the door handle and start to open it before I did the same. I saw Reed going out the back on the same side I was, and I hit the ground at a roll. There was an explosion as the car was hit with a rocket-propelled grenade as it sped forward, the chain-link gate still on the hood.

The explosion was loud and it felt like my hearing cut out when it happened. I felt the sting of rocks and sticks stabbing through my blouse as I rolled across the dirt sideways, a fern catching me in the face and blinding me. When I came to a stop I spit out leaves and pushed to my feet. The first time I had decided to roll up my sleeves and not wear gloves, I had to bail out of a vehicle into the woods at high speed. Ouch.

"You okay?" I heard Reed's voice and nodded, still trying to get my bearings. We were slightly down from the road and I could hear distant shouting.

"Yeah," I said, ignoring the ringing in my ears, "but we need to get to Scott."

"And cross the open road where the men with guns have a clear line of sight on us?" Reed looked at me in disbelief.

"We'll be careful," I said, moving toward the embankment that led to the road. I bent over and climbed, poking my head up and looking the direction the car had gone. I hoped that it had wiped out the roadblock of guys they'd left for us, but when I looked I realized we weren't that lucky. I saw guys swarming all over the SUV. It was still mostly intact, though it was burning, a small fire on the hood keeping the guards from going into the front seat, which looked to be filled with smoke.

The gate hung off the front about four feet on either side, but it had bent badly upon impact and mangled it further. One of the guards was barking orders at another, but my hearing had suffered from the explosion and my ears were ringing enough that I couldn't tell what he was saying. I watched three of them point in our direction, and I heard the whistle of gunshots over my head.

I reached down and drew my pistol, firing two quick shots, more to discourage them than anything; I wasn't likely to hit them at this range. Something big moved to my left and I realized with a shock it was Scott, running across the road. He jumped, sliding down the embankment next to me and I was following him a second later, running away from the road, Reed just behind me.

By unspoken agreement, we cut a ninety degree path away from the road for a couple hundred yards before halting. None of us were breathing heavy, and I stopped to listen. Behind us, I could hear the shouts of guards; with our superior speed, we had left them behind. Also, I could have sworn there were some coming from our right, toward the perimeter fencing. "We need to head this way," I said, pointing away from the fence.

"You don't think maybe we should get out of here for now?" Reed's head was swiveling around and suddenly his eyes widened. "Never mind, I hear it now. Guard squad coming from that direction."

"Yeah," I said. "If we're gonna escape we'll need to run parallel to the fence for a while. But I don't want to try and get out of here until we know a little more about this place."

"This place has some stiff security," Reed said, pointing back the way we came. "That's not just a sweep team; they don't get armed with rocket launchers. This is a serious installation, and they clearly mean to keep whatever's here protected. We may want to retreat and come back with more forces because with just the three of us, this could get really ugly."

I heard the logic behind his words, knew he had a good point, but I heard Ariadne's words echo in my head, about

Omega and fighting blind, and as I thought about it, something occurred to me. "If M-Squad is stuck down in Kansas, our only backup will be human agents. Not good enough to assault this place without a lot of casualties."

"Yeah," Reed said, "but it would be us plus them. Right now, it's just us."

I thought hard about what he said. "But it's our responsibility."

He let out a long sigh. "I get the feeling you'll be the death of me, Nealon."

"There are worse reasons to go," I said to him with a wink. He grimaced and I shrugged; guess I can't pull it off like Charlie can.

"You got your gun?" I asked Scott, who stood behind me, looking dazed. He nodded, reaching under his jacket to pull out his Beretta. "You might be able to take them out at range with your powers; I can't."

"Gun's gonna be more effective than a blast of water at the range we're dealing with," Scott said. "But they look like they're carrying submachine guns and rifles, so they've got the advantage over us."

"Yes, let's all not get shot," Reed said. "That sounds like a winning strategy."

"I have a backup gun." I looked at Reed. "Do you want it?"

"Nah," he said. "I've never used one; I'd probably end up shooting one of you. Besides, I'm gonna see if I can make things a little more hostile in here for gunplay, maybe level the playing field." He closed his eyes for a moment and the wind picked up around us, howling through the trees. I heard the branches stir and bend, and a strong gale nearly knocked me over. Reed's eyes opened. "Sorry about that," he said to me. "I can control it well enough if I'm paying full attention, but since we're gonna be running, you might get hit by a few unintended breezes."

The wind was roaring now, I heard branches cracking and falling through the forest, and the shouts of the guards were inaudible under the rushing of the tempest. "This way," I said, struggling to be heard as we headed away from the fence. The rattling of the trees and force of the winds blowing past us was an absolute contradiction to the blue, sunny skies above us and the sweltering heat that pressed in as tightly as the countless turtleneck sweaters I'd worn since discovering my powers. It was almost otherworldly, being in the midst of a veritable hurricane in the middle of a hot summer's day.

I could feel the sweat running down to the tip of my nose and rubbed it against my shoulder, trying to dry it. The heat was intense, the humidity drowning me. The beads of salty liquid were springing out on my forehead more from the weather than the exertion. The winds that Reed had stirred were hot, like the breath of hell itself was chasing us through the woods.

The smell of the greenery was carried on the wind. I could taste the salt from the sweat that was dripping onto my lips as we tore through the woods, three metas outpacing the humans that were pursuing us. I hoped that there weren't any of our own kind hunting us; that would suck. A break in the trees ahead of me gave way to a view of a concrete wall. As we emerged from the trees, I saw that the wall was part of a sprawling building in front of us. It was two or three stories tall, though it was hard to tell because there were no windows. There was a loading dock to our left, pavement running all the way around it. To our right, a smooth, empty wall was unbroken by anything but a small, square vent cover.

"There," I said, pointing to the vent cover. "Entry point."

"So in we go?" Scott asked as the wind howled around us. "Maybe we should contact HQ and wait for reinforcements."

"Whatever this Andromeda project is," Reed said, "it's sensitive. Omega will either evacuate it from here or destroy it by the time we get back. Hell, they may already have started to do so." He wore the look of a man doing something he desperately didn't want to. "This is it. We do it now or it'll be gone."

"I guess it's now, then," I said. "But we do this as a team and stick together, coordinating our attacks."

Before they could respond, I heard the squeal of tires and a Jeep came to a halt about a hundred feet away from us, not far from the loading docks. I counted four guys that jumped out, every one of them carrying an AK-47 assault rifle. The winds around us started to whip harder and I looked over at Reed, who was deep in concentration. Rather than powerful, straight line winds, I watched the dust on the pavement begin to swirl in circles, gathering power as it made its way toward the Jeep.

The twisting currents of wind formed a funnel cloud just in front of the Jeep, catching it and swirling it around within. I watched the vehicle buck and twist, hitting two of the men taking cover behind it, hard. One pitched over, blood splattering on the ground next to him. The other went flying, landing on his neck. The other two seemed to be holding onto the sides of the Jeep as it spun into the air, higher and higher, cresting at almost a hundred and fifty feet before the tornado dissipated and the car came crashing to the ground with joint screams from the men holding onto it. I didn't watch.

I looked back to where it had landed and saw red on the pavement, then turned away and started toward the vent. I heard tires squealing in the distance and hesitated.

"Go!" Reed gave me a gentle push. "We're committed now, we can't go back!"

"At some point we have to deal with all this security," I said, my feet pounding against the asphalt. "They're not just gonna assume we left, they're gonna keep looking until they find us."

"Or until we kill every single one of them," Scott said, exchanging a look with Reed. "And it seems like you don't have much problem with that option."

"Omega's at war with you guys," Reed said as we came to a halt in front of the vent, which was a rectangular solid metal panel that fit into the wall flush. "They've been at war with Alpha for years, so I've learned not to show a lot of mercy, because they're not renowned for showing it to us." He held out his hand and the panel started to rattle, then burst from its mounting. "Ladies first," he said with a cocky smile.

"Ass," I said, but didn't argue. "I'll go first because the range of my powers is limited, not because I'm a lady." I bent nearly double and stopped. A long metal duct ran in front of me, and off to my left. I felt a flash of familiarity, looking down the metal tunnel, and my breath caught in my throat. It was like the box.

But it wasn't, not really. I could feel air circulating through, and over it I heard more tires squeal and looked back to see two big trucks full of guards, unloading on the pavement about a hundred feet in front of the panel. "Let's go!" I called to Reed and Scott.

"Shall we hold them off?" Reed said to Scott, who had his gun in one hand and his other fist extended.

Scott fired a couple shots. "Seems the gentlemanly thing to do. Got any ideas for that?"

"Elementally, dear Watson," Reed said, another tornado forming in front of him. "Elementally."

I heard Scott give off a cackle and I started to say something smartass and join them, my gun drawn. I stopped when I saw one of the guards on the truck aim an RPG launcher right at me.

"GO!" Scott shouted, launching himself to the left. I saw Reed go right, leaving the RPG pointed at me. I saw the flare of the tube as I dived into the duct, running as fast as I could whilst bent double.

The RPG exploded behind me, the force of it yanking me off my feet. The ductwork took an abrupt, ninety degree right turn that I couldn't quite make as the explosive force drove me forward into the metal. I burst through the soft aluminum, my head ringing, and realized I was hanging, suspended in mid-air for almost a second before gravity caught me. I fell, dropping, down, down, down into the darkness of the room below me.

19

I hit cold metal, my shoulder landing first, then my torso, and all my breath left me. I gasped, pain shooting through me. I couldn't hear anything but ringing in my ears, again, only worse this time, like someone had set off a fire alarm in my brain, rattling the damned bell so hard I couldn't concentrate on anything else. One by one, little agonies began to work their way into my consciousness; a searing pain in my shoulder, a feeling in my knee like I'd been hit with a hammer, and the taste of blood flowing in my mouth.

I worked my way to my knees and opened my eyes. I'd landed on a metal catwalk and below me was inky blackness. I looked above, to where I'd come from, and far up there I could see a smoking bit of ductwork, mangled by the explosion and my passage through the metal. Tracing it back toward the wall, it was ballooned comically, as though someone had pushed the sides out with all the ease of crumpling tinfoil. I wondered if Scott and Reed were all right, but something told me that even if they were, I wasn't going to be seeing them come down the way I had.

I gripped the railing of the catwalk, trying to force myself to my feet. It seemed to be harder this time than I could recall it being in the past. I had pains everywhere, but after a minute of solid effort I made it to my feet, leaning on the railing for support. I looked both directions the catwalk extended, and decided I needed to pick one. I finally decided on right, not totally at random, but close. Why? Because it was the *right* way. I couldn't bring myself to even chuckle at my horrible pun, such was the pain in my body.

I staggered along, my right leg starting to numb the more I walked. I didn't think it was broken, but I knew I was going to have one bitch of a bruise on it later. I kept my right arm close to my body because the shoulder cried out in anguish anytime I moved it. I had lost my main gun in the explosion and fall, but I had pulled my backup, a much smaller weapon with a smaller magazine, a Walther PPK. Unfortunately, all I had was the seven shots it gave me, and then I'd be out.

My shoes clanked on the catwalk, and I hoped there was no one hiding below that could hear me. It was so dark underneath that it would be near impossible to tell. I took a fragment of duct that had blown loose from the explosion and dropped it over the side of the catwalk. I listened, but either because of the ringing in my ears or the distance it fell, I didn't hear it land.

Ahead I saw the outline of a door, a big, heavy metal one. I urged myself forward, resting more and more weight on my wounded leg. It still stung, but I knew now that nothing was broken, which meant that all I needed to do was fight through the pain. The bad news was, there was quite a bit of it to fight through.

I reached the door and grasped the handle, turning it slowly. I pushed the heavy metal with my shoulder, trying not to rush or fall through. I cracked it and looked inside, finding a concrete room with some lockers along one wall and a set of double doors that went on into the room beyond.

I led with my gun, limping into the room. Some caution signs were posted on the double doors, but they didn't stop me. The doors swung open for me, and I found myself in another room, walking on metal catwalks that led to a center platform with something sunken in the middle. I felt a chill; the room was like nothing I'd seen before in anything other than a movie. Large, cylindrical metal tanks were clustered below in hexagons, ominous chemical configurations written on the sides with warnings not to disturb the contents.

The whole room was cold, bitterly so, as bad as winter, and

I wished for the first time that day that I'd been wearing my gloves and jacket. I felt goosebumps rise on my arms as I approached the center of the room. The catwalk gave way for the circular platform, which looked like it had a segment of metal in the middle that was removable. Exactly what it slid away for, I wasn't sure, but it was obvious that it was patterned differently than the rest of the platform.

"Sienna?" The man's voice caught my attention, turning me around. He was behind me, in front of the doors I had just come through, his face barely visible in the dim light of the room. He was wearing a tight shirt, no buttons, and jeans that would have stirred my imagination even if I hadn't seen him naked the night before.

"James?" I let out a deep breath, all tension. "You found me."

"It wasn't that hard," he said. "There's only one Omega facility in eastern Wisconsin – or anywhere east until New York." He walked down the catwalk, approaching slowly, his hands extended. "God, it looks like they tore you up...what happened?"

I brushed a strand of bloodied hair out of my face. "They fired an RPG into the duct I was using to enter the building." I laughed under my breath, a dark chuckle without any real humor. "I wish I'd stayed in Eau Claire with you. I think it would have been less painful."

"No kidding." He was only a few feet away now, easing closer, when he came to a stop. "I don't mean to be rude, because I know we're in the middle of kind of a hostile place here, but are you gonna keep pointing your gun at me?"

"For now, yes," I said, and the playfulness was out of my voice. "Sorry, James. I don't really know you all that well, do I? You turn up in an Omega base at a convenient moment, and although you may genuinely be here to help me, I can't rule out the possibility that you're working with the enemy."

He flushed but managed to keep his expression under control. "Ouch. So our time together doesn't count for much, does it?"

I stared at him evenly. "Our time together was less than a cumulative hour. So, no...I don't entirely trust you. I'm sorry if that offends you. If you turn out to be on the level, I promise I'll make it up to you in spectacular fashion, but you're going to have to forgive me if I don't trust you with my life yet."

He looked at me in cool amusement, hands at his sides. "You were going to sleep with me not twelve hours ago."

"I was. I might still, depending on how this turns out."

"Do I need to point out how screwed up that is?" he asked.

I cocked my head at him. "I've yet to touch another human being for more than ten seconds without killing them. Just because I wanted you badly doesn't mean I unconditionally trust you. My life is on the line here. Respect that, and we can see what Omega is up to together."

"I'm afraid I can't respect that," he said, one of his hands coming to rest on the railing. His face was calm, still, almost a mask compared to the sly, seductive man that had been unable to keep his hands off me for the last two days. "It hurts, Sienna." He turned his face away, clutching the railing with both hands. "It really hurts." He looked back at me and I caught a glimmer of something that scared me. "But not as much as it's going to hurt you."

The railing snapped off in his hands and he whipped it at me. I fired, missing him twice before the metal rail hit me in the hands, jarring my gun out of them and sending it spiraling away. The end of the rail hit me in the side of the face as I tried to dodge, drawing a cry of pain and causing me to fall down, landing on my back, the metal of the catwalk clattering as I landed.

I felt the pain running down my spine, but I only had a moment to feel it before he was there, grabbing both my arms and forcing me down. He was strong, and his face was twisted with rage. All the handsomeness that I had admired was gone as he put his weight and strength into holding me against the catwalk. He slammed my head into the hard metal and I felt the room spin. "You should have stayed with me in Eau Claire." He was spitting as he said it, little flecks dropping onto my face.

"I can't tell you how glad I am that I didn't," I said as I brought my leg up and hit him on the side of his thigh. I aimed for the groin but he had angled himself so that I couldn't. He grunted and slapped me, hard. I gasped at him in surprise and bucked my entire body, flexing the muscles in my abdomen, bringing my forehead up fast. I felt it make contact with his nose, and I heard the break, felt warm blood wash down my face as he rolled off, shouting and cursing.

"You bitch!" He was clutching his face, a splatter of red smudging his mouth as I struggled to my feet. He rose, a few feet away, glaring at me, his eyes on fire with rage, a world of difference from when he had been kissing and caressing me only the night before.

"So, you're with Omega?" I kept my distance; my right shoulder still in agony, my leg hurt unbelievably and was slowing me down. In addition, I had a host of aches and pains that filled my body, and made me want to just lay down and die. "They sent you to sleep with me?"

"No, they sent me to recruit you," he said, holding his nose with one hand while he watched me. "The sleeping with you would have just been a bonus. I usually don't get to take my time with a woman, you know. They all die so quickly, and it's not much fun then. I mean, don't get me wrong, the rush from the absorption is amazing, it's like a drug, but when that's done they just lie there—"

"You're quite the disgusting pig." I felt a shudder of revulsion run through every part of me. I wished I could parboil my skin off and replace it with a new set. For all I knew, I could and it would just grow back.

"I preferred the sweet nothings you whispered to me last night," he said, jumping at me, swiping out with his hand to grab me. I dodged and maintained my footing, just barely, but my leg screamed in pain. He came at me again, grasping with his hands, and I caught one of them and pulled, taking him off balance. He started to fall and dragged me down with him. Had I been in peak condition, I would have been able to avoid it; as it was, I just tried to land with a knee in his belly. He grunted and slapped me again. I felt a sharp pain and blood started to trickle down my lips as I landed on him.

I tensed my guts, trying to protect myself, and tucked my

elbows close, using my left to hit him across the face. He took another swipe at me but I fended it off, keeping my elbows locked and my hands up, guarding my face. I hit him in the nose twice, causing him to cry out, then his whole body heaved as he bucked and threw me forward. I tried to catch myself and roll out of it but my head hit the metal of the platform and I saw stars. My body came to a landing, pain racing down my back, and while I was trying to shake the colors out of my vision he got on top of me and punched me in the face twice.

I was stunned and he grabbed hold of me by the front of my blouse, holding me up while he hit me again. I heard the cloth tear and felt my head hit the cold metal, a fog surrounding me. "It could have been really nice between us, Sienna, but you just had to go and screw it all up." He was pacing around me now, and I saw him raise a leg and then felt a searing pain in my ribs. "Now you've exposed our location, you've ruined any chance of us having a pleasant evening, and what am I supposed to tell my bosses when I bring you to them? I was supposed to deliver you alive, but honestly, I don't think that's gonna happen now." He kicked me again, and I heard a scream, and it took my sluggish mind a minute to work out that it was my voice doing the screaming.

"I mean, look at this." He grabbed me by the face and shook me, forcing me to look at him. "You broke my nose. Sure, it'll heal, but *nobody* does that. Not to me. Especially not some little teenage bitch that should have been grateful I even took the time to pay attention to her." He punched me in the face again, but I could barely feel it by this point. "I mean, it would have been good between us. Better than you'd ever have again, that's for sure. But you had to go and—"

I had steadily inched my left leg up, resting the bottom of my foot on the ground. I hoped he would just assume I was trying to curl up in the fetal position. I wasn't, although I was sure that'd feel better than the way I was laying presently. My hand reached down, grasping, trying not to be obvious, while he was directing all his hatred at my face. I pulled the knife

Glen Parks had told me to carry as a backup out of its strap. I was grateful, not for the first time in the last few minutes, that James had never gotten me out of my pants, or he would have seen it.

I brought the knife across his face with a blind stroke. I had aimed to land it in his temple, but he moved at the last second and I caught him with a jagged slash just under his left eye and punctured his nose. He let out a cry and screamed as he dropped me, my shoulders hitting the metal catwalk again, but without much pain this time. I rolled to my hands and knees, still clenching the knife. "I had to go and what? Save myself from doing something I'd regret?" I spit blood in his face as I got to my knees. "Thank God. I can't believe I let you touch me, you soulless piece of filth—"

He yelled and jumped from where he lay to come at me, grabbing my hand that was holding the knife before I could attack him with it. He slammed me down again and I struggled, but I felt him reversing the grip. I poured the last of my strength into it, but he was too strong, too vicious. I stared into his scarred face as blood dripped down from his nose onto my forehead, smelled his breath, the foulness of it, all trace of sweetness gone. I felt the very tip of the knife against my belly, felt the first sting of pain as it pierced me, just a centimeter, as I fought to keep him from killing me.

He wore a satisfied leer, and the darkness and shadows made him look demonic. "You could have just had me inside—"

Something hit James in the side of the head with devastating force and he flopped off, unconscious. I was breathing deep, panting, and a gloved hand reached down, offering me help. "I wouldn't worry about it," Charlie said, looking at the little bit of blood running down my belly where he'd stabbed me. "I've been with him; you're not missing anything."

20

"Charlie," I said, breathing the word like it was the sweetest thing I'd ever said. She helped pull me to my feet. "Please tell me you're not with Omega too."

She laughed. "I'm not with Omega. I'm not with anybody."

I found the strength and balance to stand on my own, and she let me go. She was wearing a man's jacket, which she had kept between us while she was helping me up. I saw a watch on her wrist, a shining, gold one that looked like it was at least a couple sizes too big. As I stared closer at it, I realized it was a man's watch. She caught me looking and glanced down. "Oh, yeah, this? From that guy in the bar last night."

"Oh?" I didn't really care. My head was still spinning. "That was nice of him." I looked around and saw a small control panel a few feet away, built into the railing, almost nondescript. "I thought you were gonna stay in Eau Claire?"

She shrugged. "I did, until I got bored. Then I just looked you up through your phone's GPS and headed this way. Things got a little dicey when I found your flamed-out vehicle, but the guards were all pretty distracted by something going on over on the other side of the building. Sounded like a tornado or something."

I hobbled to the nearest railing and leaned against it. "Sounds like Reed. How long ago was that?"

She shrugged again, uncaring. "I dunno. Ten minutes? I came in through one of the unguarded doors while it was going down. Looked around the building until I stumbled in here. Looks like my timing was good. What are you doing here?"

I wondered how long I had been down here. I looked at the panel again, sliding down the railing toward it. "Omega attacked the Directorate. We came to find out what they were hiding here."

"Oh?" She made her way over to me, leaving James unmoving in a pile on the platform. "So what is it?"

"Something called Andromeda."

"Huh," she said, disinterested, as she looked over the edge of the platform. "Sounds boring. And old."

"I don't know what it is, honestly." I stared down at the panel, trying to make sense of it. There was only one button lit up, and it was an option to unlock something, a thought which made me uneasy. I took a deep breath and thought it over. I was here to find out what they were doing, but what if it was a monster of some sort? Between Wolfe, Henderschott and James, Omega certainly loved their monsters. I stared at the unlock button until a finger came down from behind me and pushed it.

I turned and Charlie was there, smiling at me, impish. "No guts, no glory, kiddo."

A slight rumble ran through the room and lights came on, casting it in blue and orange light. There were four different catwalk bridges that led to the central platform we were standing on. Below us, there had to be at least a hundred chemical tanks surrounding an oversized apparatus that was circular, and lined up perfectly so that something could be raised from the top of it into the center circle of the platform.

The control panel lit up, giving me a host of options. I stared at it, trying to take it all in. Charlie peered over my shoulder, her breath heavy and kinda sour. "What's this one do?" She pushed a big red button, and I heard a rumbling from below us as machinery sprang to life. The circular grate in the middle of our platform squeaked and retracted to the side, leaving a hole in the middle of the floor.

"Stop," I said.

"Soooo cautious," she said. "Boring, boring, boring. You

need a little metal in your life, kid, a little action."

I felt the result of all the action I'd experienced today in my bones, in the pains, the aches and blood that still ran freely from different places on my anatomy. "Actually, I could do with a little less action at this point."

"Boooring," she said again. "Why must all you people lead such mundane little lives? I thought maybe you were different than the rest. I thought you were like me."

"Umm." I tried to focus on the panel, tuning out her prattle, ignoring the fact that she sounded almost offended. "I don't know what to tell you. I have a job to do, and it's pretty serious—"

She grabbed me by the shoulders and spun me around, causing my head to wobble, as she slammed my back against the railing. "Hey, kid! Wake the hell up!" She slapped me for good measure, not hard, but enough that I felt it and it pissed me off. I stared back at her, at the intensity in her eyes as she glared at me. "We're at the top of the food chain, darling. Ain't nobody can stop us: not Omega, not the Directorate, nobody. Women want to look like us and men want to grind up against us. You can have anything you want, take what you want, and nobody can stop you, and you're killing time with these white hat Directorate wankers." She let out a sigh of disgust. "Stop wasting your time doing all this crap when you could be having fun."

She slackened her grip on me and started to back off, but I grasped the watch on her wrist and held it tight in front of her. "Ow! What are you doing?"

"What happened to the man who had this on last night?" I twisted her arm to put it right in front of her face. "Where is he now?"

"Who cares?" She said, ripping it out of my grasp. "They're all interchangeable, men. They only last a very short time," she got a wicked grin that I found damned unsettling, "so you have to use them wisely – and I do mean *use*. I keep looking for a man who can last longer, but even he couldn't—" She waved at James. "Though obviously for different reasons, in his case."

I felt a pit of disgust in my stomach. "You're like...you're a serial killer."

"You're so immature." She made a noise of disgust, waving her hand as though she were dismissing me. "We're succubi, Sienna; draining men's souls is what we do. They're there for us; it's why we have the thrall, the dreamwalking, all of it. The world of men is our cup: we're supposed to drink it, and you're afraid to even take a sip." Her face twisted into a humorless smile. "Just like your mom." Her dark hair fell around her shoulders, framing her face in a different light than I'd seen before; she looked almost cronelike, emaciated. "Well, I'll drink enough for all three of us, I don't care. I'm not scared. I'm ready for all of it."

I leaned on the railing for support, trying to edge away from her. "Why?"

"You know. Haven't you ever felt the rush?" She looked at me in disbelief. "I know you've taken souls; haven't you felt it? When you take them, how they scream and rattle in your head at first, how it spins you around? It's the greatest high you'll ever feel, trust me, way better than anything else. I mean, I know it's tough the first few times, like losing your virginity, but it gets so good, so powerful, it feels so right." She let out a little sigh and had her eyes closed. "You have no idea." Her eyes opened and she focused on me.

"I don't want to have any idea what you're talking about," I said. "I'm not a murderer."

"Don't play games with me," Charlie said, a smile on her lips. "I know you've killed."

"Twice," I said. "Once to save my own life with Wolfe and once to save the city of Minneapolis from Gavrikov."

"Oh, right." She pirouetted and sent me a mischievous glance. "Why would you bother doing a thing like that?"

"Because I owed them," I said, trying to catch my breath and push the pain away. "Because it was the right thing to do. I don't kill in cold blood. I might not even have killed Wolfe, but I was so afraid of him I couldn't let him go."

"And what about the other guy? The one you sent for a long fall off the IDS tower?"

"That wasn't me." I grabbed a segment of rail in my hand, wondering if I had the strength to rip it loose and use it as a weapon like James had. I looked around for my knife, but it was far behind Charlie; she'd kill me long before I reached it. "That was Wolfe."

"You're weak," she said, spitting the words at me in disgust. "You're supposed to control them. They're your souls, your puppets, but you can't even keep what you've got in line. No wonder you can't bring yourself to do what's fun, what you should be doing. You're pathetic." She kicked out faster than I could have anticipated and knocked my legs out from under me, sending me to my back. I looked up and saw her face, nothing like the easygoing Charlie I'd seen; her eyes were wide, her mouth twisted in cold disdain. I felt a deep, powerful dose of fear as she said, "You're nothing like me."

"Thank God for that." The voice came from behind her, strong, fearless, and I saw Charlie's eyes widen in fright, her expression chilled as she turned to face the new threat, a woman standing at the edge of the platform, staring her down. Her dark hair was long, but pulled back in a ponytail, and she wore a simple t-shirt and jeans that had some dirt on them, as though she had been crawling around on the ground. "Get away from her, Charlie, or so help me I will crush the very life from your body the way I should have years and years ago."

I felt a swell of emotion deep inside at the sight of her, something I didn't even know I still had in me. Little tears sprang up in the corners of my eyes and I blinked them away, blinked again to be sure what I was seeing was true. It was. She was there. I opened my mouth, and amazingly, a single word fell out.

"Mom?"

21

She attacked Charlie without warning, reminding me of a thousand sparring sessions in the basement. My aunt staggered back under the fury of my mother's assault, kicks and punches blurring through the space between them so fast I couldn't count. I saw Mom jump-kick and catch Charlie underneath the chin, sending her reeling, and followed it up with a flurry of punches that brought my aunt to her knees.

"Wait..." Charlie gasped. "Sierra, wait..." My mother stood above her, hands still raised, ready to rain down a killing strike while looking down at her sister with cold indifference. "I was trying...trying to help her..." Blood ran freely from Charlie's nose, and one of her eyes was already swelling shut. I didn't think she'd even managed to land a blow on my mom.

Mom reached down with a gloved hand and picked Charlie up by the neck, holding her out at a distance, as though she didn't want to get too close. "Help her what? Die?" She threw Charlie to the ground, her face scraping against the grated metal platform as she landed.

Charlie lifted her head and rolled over, holding a hand out as though she could ward off my mother's cold fury with it. "Please...please, Sierra...please!"

My mother halted. "One chance, Charlie. Why should I let you go?"

"Please." Charlie propped herself up, both hands behind

515

her back. "I won't come anywhere near her again, I swear. I swear on my life."

My mother's face twisted in disgust. "You picked the right one to swear on. Heaven knows you've never cared about anyone else's."

"That's not true!" Charlie shook her head, her normally calm or sly expression completely consumed by fear, stricken by the uncertainty of whether she'd live or die in the next moments. "I came to help her, Sierra, I came to teach her because I knew you weren't around! I knew she needed help!"

My mother halted her advance, hovering menacingly over her sister, her face a mask. She stood there, staring down, her expression impenetrable, for a very long moment. "Get out of here," she said, growling. "If you ever come near my daughter again, Charlie, I will kill you. You know I will; and it won't be pretty, or quick."

I saw Charlie slide back, pulling herself to her feet, then turning to see her sister, and she nodded, quickly, all trace of the carefree, cocky woman my aunt had been gone as though she had never existed. "I swear. She'll never see my face again." Charlie turned and began to walk out, down one of the catwalks toward a door on the far side of the room.

"She better not see any of you again, Charlie." My mother's voice was hard, sharp as glass, and unforgiving. "If she sees so much as an eyelash of yours, you won't have time to blink before I drain you into nothingness." Charlie stiffened but did not turn back at my mother's threat.

I watched her leave, the doors swinging shut behind her, and then turned to my mother to find her looking at me, her face the same mask of fearful indifference that she wore when talking to my aunt. "Mom," I croaked. She took a few steps toward me, then stopped at my side. I looked up and saw she was using the console next to me. "Mom?"

"It looks like you haven't been following the rules," she said, voice hollow. "You're not in the house, you're not wearing gloves, a coat." Her gaze hardened on me, leaning against the railing. "Actually, it looks like you're wearing hardly anything." My mouth opened and I tried to say something, but nothing came out. "You're a Directorate Agent now, you're living on your own and you've had a boyfriend." Her eyes narrowed and focused in on mine. "Yeah, I heard about that. You're a big girl, in other words. Big enough to deal with the consequences of your own mistakes."

She knelt next to me, her face hovering a foot away from mine. "You're going to make more mistakes, I know it. But that's your problem." She stood. "Not mine. Not anymore. Time to grow up." She punched a button on the console and a deep rumbling filled the entire room. She turned her back on me and started to walk away.

"Mom, wait!" I tried to use the railing to stand again, pulling myself up. "Wait!" I slumped, putting all my weight on the console as the rumbling noise that filled the room centered on the middle of the platform. A cylinder rose up, sliding through the hole, black, sleek metal that extended six feet above the platform before it stopped moving. "Mom? Help me," I said, my words coming out in a tumble, desperation lacing every one of them. "Help me, please, Mom."

She didn't stop, didn't turn around, didn't even slow her walk as she moved toward the doors I had entered through. "I just did."

The doors swung shut behind her.

22

"God, am I glad she's gone." The voice was solid, strong, and so damned alarming. I turned my head to see James pushing himself up onto all fours. "Both of them, actually." He shook his head as he got to his feet. "Now..." His face was bloody, his nose a shattered mess with a hole in it, crimson running down his cheeks and lips. "Where were we?"

Something clicked in the cylinder in front of me, and a hissing sound came as it seemed to depressurize, fissures appearing in the surface of it. I watched James, whose eyes widened when he saw it, and his face snapped back to me. "Dammit, I guess I'll have to make this quick—"

The cylinder opened, a door sliding back, light shining out of it in a pale yellow across the platform. A face appeared first, followed by the rest of a body. James didn't watch, he didn't delay: he came right at me and I reached out to grab hold of him, struggling as he pushed me to the ground, his hands trying to grip my neck. "Stop fighting me!" he raged, forcing my arms down. "This will all be over in a few seconds."

"That's what you tell all the girls." I rocked my hips to dislodge him, but to no avail. I was too weary, too beaten. Everything hurt, every part of me now, and what didn't hurt just felt weary. All I wanted was to sleep, to not be a big girl, to just be back home with Mom and not have to worry about any of this—

A screech came from behind James and he paused, a look of panic crossing his wrecked face. "Uh oh," was all he had time to say before a woman came out of the cylinder, her eyes tightly shut, a scream on her lips. She was staggering, naked, trying to catch her breath, her dirty brown hair tangled in wet ringlets around her shoulders. Her eyes opened and caught sight of him and me, on the ground, and she screamed again, this time not from fear but rage, and she attacked him, her hand coming down in a hard swipe that caught him by surprise and sent him flying over the edge of the railing, down into the darkness below.

I turned my gaze from where he had fallen to her, glowing brown eyes giving me a sense of deep unease. I had no defense against what she'd done to him; I only hoped that if she sent me over the edge I'd be able to land 1) softly and 2) on him, because I didn't know if I could take any more pummeling.

"Are you okay?" she asked in a throaty voice, a little hoarse, like she hadn't used it in a long time.

I flinched at the sound of her voice, mostly because I was expecting an attack instead. "Do...do I look okay?"

The naked girl studied me, her eyes assessing. "Not really."

I worked my way to sitting again. "Who are you?"

She looked lost in thought, far away, drifting, and I almost thought maybe she'd passed out on her feet, as though the trauma of being released from a big black cylinder was too much for her. She paused, looked across the room, then turned back to me, still almost uncertain. "Andromeda," she said finally. "My name is Andromeda."

I heard voices, raised, from behind me, and crooked my head to look. Andromeda tensed, as though she were ready for battle. The doors on the far end of the room burst open and Reed and Scott came through them, followed by two guys in tactical vests carrying submachine guns. Neither wore masks, and I knew them instantly. One was Kurt, the other was Zack.

"Sienna!" It was Scott who shouted, his hands pointed at Andromeda, who pointed her hands back at him. "We thought you were dead."

Reed matched Scott's position, though his expression was a bit more wary. Both Kurt and Zack had their weapons pointed, and I held up my hand to stop them, and felt myself sag against the railing as they came onto the platform. "Me? Not so much. Everybody calm down," I said. "This is Andromeda." She looked at me, then at them, and began to relax. "Andromeda, this is...everybody."

Scott inched his way around the platform, still keeping his hands up, eyes fixed on her, though they looked down more than once to take in her nakedness. "So Andromeda is not a project...it's a person?"

She cocked her head at him, her pale skin giving off a briny smell, now that she was closer to me. "Perhaps it's both."

"We don't exactly have the perimeter secure here," Kurt said, scanning the room. "We need to find what we're here for and leave."

"She's it, I think." I said this as Zack made his way forward, easing past Andromeda, and grasped me under the arms to help me stand. "She's the reason we're here; though I'm not sure how much she can tell us about Omega."

Her eyes followed mine, and I caught a hint of deep intelligence in them. "Everything," she said. "I can tell you everything about Omega. Who they are, where they started, why they're here and what they're after."

"Then we need to get her out of here," Scott said. "Back the way we came?"

"No," Andromeda said. "This way." She looked at me. "Let me help." She put her hand on me and I started to protest, but something in her eyes silenced me. Her hand was on mine, and a second passed, then five, and nothing happened.

"What...are you?" I asked, staring back at her.

Her eyes glowed and I felt strength course through me as she pulled me along, almost effortless. "Something new. I am a sacrifice made by Omega to bring about change."

"Oh, good, cryptic," Scott murmured from behind me. "You'll get along well with Old Man Winter."

"Are you all right?" Zack whispered next to me, trying to keep up as Andromeda pulled me along. I noticed that all my pain had receded; the wounds were still there, but they seemed not to hurt.

"I think I'll be fine, once I get a day to heal," I said. "Did you drive here from Detroit?"

"All the way through the Upper Peninsula at about a hundred miles an hour." He gave me a tight smile. "Ariadne said you were headed into trouble."

"I was." I tried to smile at him. "I found my way out again, with a little help. What about you?"

His smile disappeared. "We'll talk about it later."

"No, wait," I said. "They sent you after a meta, didn't they?"

"They did."

"So what happened?" I asked.

"Omega jumped ahead of us, bagged 'em." Kurt was the one who answered, and I got a glimpse of him behind me. He had a bandage across the back of his head, and it was bloody. "Happened all across the country last night. The Directorate got a big fat sucker punch to the side of the head."

"Sucker punch?" I shook my head, trying to clear it. "I mean, we heard about Kansas, but you're saying they tried to what? Catch your target before you could?"

"They tried to kill us, Sienna." Zack's eyes were serious. "They damned near did. They've killed a lot of our agents in the last twenty-four hours. Kansas was a war zone; the west half of the state is on fire from the battle."

We made our way down a hallway and through a set of doors to find ourselves in a loading dock. "Your vehicle is just outside," Andromeda said. "It may be a tight fit to get all of us in it."

Kurt looked at her in suspicion. "How did she know that?"

Andromeda's voice dropped to a hushed whisper, and her eyes seemed to focus on something in the distance. "Because I see." They dropped back to looking at Kurt. "It is one of my talents."

Scott rushed forward and hit the loading door, causing it to slowly clank open. Sure enough, when it was up a small SUV was sitting in front of us, the road to the gate visible behind it, complete with the wreckage of the car we drove, gate still mounted on top of it. A few black-clad figures were visible around the yard and I watched Zack and Kurt unload on them at distance, dropping a couple while Reed stirred the winds and sent another tornado toward the largest concentration of Omega agents.

"I think we've worn out our welcome," I said as Andromeda guided me to the car and pushed me into the back seat, squeezing in next to me. Zack and Kurt got in next, firing rounds all the way up until they shut the door. Kurt rolled down his window and pulled a pistol, discharging a half-dozen shots.

Reed slipped in next to Andromeda and Scott piled in after him, slamming the door as Kurt hit the gas. "Might want to call Kat and the others," Zack said as we sped toward the gatehouse. "Warn them off. We can meet them in town and convoy back to the Directorate together."

"Okay," Scott said, already dialing his phone.

"I hope nobody minds if I sit in the hatchback," Reed said. "It's nothing personal; I just feel weird squeezing in this close to a naked girl I don't know." He blushed as he looked at Andromeda, and I realized that I hadn't even noticed that she was still wearing nothing. Of course I also felt very close to passing out now that she had taken her hands off me.

Reed went over the seat into the hatchback, giving Scott and Andromeda a little more room. Scott pulled his phone away from his ear and looked down, messing with the touchscreen. "I can't seem to reach her."

"Think she's out of cell phone service?" Zack said, looking back at him.

"It is a little spotty through here." Scott stared down at his phone. "I'll try again, but take the quickest route back to town. They should be nearly here by now."

Zack turned to talk to me. "What happened in that room?"

I searched my memory and tried to come up with a coherent explanation. "Um, well...one of Omega's lackeys got the better of me after I got blasted through a wall by an RPG. Then I got saved by my aunt—"

"Your aunt?" Zack squinted at me in the backseat.

"Yeah." I nodded. "Then she turned on me when I figured out that she had been killing people just for the rush of absorbing them." I took a breath. "Then my mom saved me from her and unleashed Andromeda."

Zack's jaw dropped. "Your mom?" He looked at me with great uncertainty. "Are you sure you're all right? I mean, no offense, but it kinda sounds like you're hallucinating. Maybe we should call Perugini or Zollers."

I shook my head. "She was real, and she was there."

He got that look on his face that he puts up when he doesn't want to argue. "If you say so."

"What the...?" Kurt slowed the car as we approached the end of the dirt road, ready to turn onto the highway. Off to the side, a car was wrecked against a tree, the hood crumpled, smoke pouring from underneath. "Hope they've got AAA."

"Look further," Andromeda said, "and you will see."

"What's she talking about?" Kurt asked.

"Over there." Zack nodded his head in the opposite direction, where there were two bodies laying on the ground, wearing black suits. "Are those ours?"

He was out of the car, Kurt and Scott a few steps behind him. Scott ran the fastest, pounding across the pavement and off the road. I followed, aided by Andromeda and Reed. When I came up over the edge of the road, I could tell it was definitely Directorate agents, prostrate in the grass, tire marks in the dirt around them. One of them was stirring as Zack slapped him gently across the face.

"Jackson!" Zack shook him, and the agent blinked his eyes a few times. I recognized his face, but didn't know his name. "What happened?"

The agent named Jackson blinked again, staring up at him. "Zack? Where am I? What are you doing here?"

"You were supposed to be backing us up at the Omega site," Scott said. "What happened?"

The agent looked surprised, then pondered that. "I...don't know. I don't remember." He looked around, startled. "I have no idea how I got here."

"Where's Kat?" Scott was looking around, frantic. "Where

is she?" He went back to Agent Jackson. "Where'd Kat go?"

Jackson stared at Scott blankly. "I don't know. Was she with me?"

"Wake the other one," Kurt said.

"It won't do any good," Reed said. "He'll have had his memory drained too."

Something vague and totally improbable caused the wires in my brain to cross. "Just like those convenience store clerks."

Reed raised an eyebrow at me. "Finally getting it now?"

Scott stared back and forth between the two of us, impatience on his face. "So who did it? What kind of meta can steal memories out of someone's head?"

"A succubus or incubus." Reed stared back at me, not breaking eye contact. "But only one that's disciplined enough that they don't want to kill."

I thought about it again, about the whole trail. A willingness not to kill innocent people even when it was inconvenient. Discipline. That ruled out Charlie, and James as well, actually. Only one left. The rest of them were staring at me, but Reed was the only one who did it knowingly.

"Mom."

23

Someone Else

I kept calm all the way out of the room, able to keep myself from looking back at Sienna only through years of ridiculous, rigorous discipline. After I was through the doors, I started to run, making my way through Omega's labyrinthine base. I burst through the exit and smashed the window out of a car that was parked outside. This one looked like something one of the Omega guards might drive, a sedan that didn't look too old. I hotwired it, and it started without a bit of fuss. The engine roared to life, and I paused, taking a breath after what I'd just accomplished.

"Good luck, kiddo," I whispered as I put the car into reverse and made a three point turn, angling it toward the road that would lead me off the premises. "If anyone can do it, you can."

I gunned the engine, scaring the hell out of a few guards. I picked up a few bullet holes on the way out, but nothing too serious, I thought. Then I felt the pain in my shoulder. I looked down, and sure enough, blood was streaming down my arm. Dammit. I hoped my daughter had better luck than I'd had. She should. After all, now she had Andromeda looking out for her.

I swerved as I made my next turn; the wheel was getting harder and harder to control and I felt a little faint. I shook my head, trying to clear the little sparkles of light from my vision. Something was in front of me though, big and black, and very close. I jerked the wheel to the right and my car went off the road. After all this time, I finally had a decent car and I ended up—

I woke up after a few seconds, I thought. I was still bleeding out of my shoulder. I forced the door open and pulled myself out, to my feet. I snuck a quick look in the rearview mirror; at least I didn't look as bad as Sienna had when I left her behind.

I walked across the road in as close to a straight line as I could manage. I recognized the car when I got closer; government plates, men in suits in the driver and passenger sides. The first one was getting out as I got close and I used my meta speed to cut the distance between us, putting my hands on his face. I heard a scream from the back seat, and I could see the other agent pull his gun, aiming it at me, too scared to shoot through his partner. I pulled the pistol out of the holster of the agent I had in my grip and shot the other in the chest, twice, aiming for the kevlar vest I knew he was wearing.

He slammed against the door behind him with each shot, and I let the first agent drop. The door to the backseat of the SUV opened and a blond girl stepped out, flushed and angry. She was tall, willowy, pretty in that annoying kind of way a cheerleader is. I rolled my eyes when I saw her, and she put up her hands, as though she was ready to fight. I grabbed her fist when she threw her first punch, and held onto it until her expression changed.

It was kind of funny to watch. She grunted and strained, and even with my shoulder oozing blood, I still managed to keep a grip on her until her eyes rolled back in her head. I felt good after, which was normal, but when I moved my shoulder, I realized it didn't even hurt. "Persephone," I whispered as she dropped to the ground.

I went to the passenger side and pulled out the agent I'd shot. He was still breathing, so I touched his face, draining him until I was sure he wouldn't remember anything. "Sorry," I said to his unconscious body, "but it's best you don't remember running into me." That done, I pulled the blonde girl into the passenger seat and slid into the driver's seat myself. I started the car and let it run for a second before I put it in gear and pulled back onto the main road.

When I went to make the turn to the right that would take me back to town and eventually an interstate, my eyes caught on the Persephone. I didn't owe her an explanation, not really, especially since she was unconscious, and it was pretty unlikely she would remember. Still, I looked at her, and she reminded me a little of Sienna, mostly in the age, and I told her anyway.

"Sorry, kiddo, but I need you." My eyes traced the lines of her face, the slack, relaxed musculature that reminded me of a little girl who used to be so innocent...but most of that was gone when I'd left her behind just minutes earlier. I wondered when it had gone away, and who had done it. I felt a flash of anger, and knew who to blame. "He doesn't give a damn about human agents, you know, but I bet he'll care about you. That's how he always was. Metas first." I shook my head. "Not that you care, but that's it. That's why I took you with me. You're my insurance, for when we collide...because it's coming soon. I can feel it. Real soon, and after all, I'm just one girl, alone against the whole Directorate. So I'm gonna need some help, and that's you, blondie. You're it. My fulcrum.

"You're my leverage for Erich Winter."

ACKNOWLEDGMENTS

Third time around, and thrice charmed I have been as an author of this particular series. There are again thanks aplenty to be doled out, and here are the responsible parties:

Heather Rodefer, my inestimable Editor-in-Chief (she keeps earning that title) once more deconstructed this manuscript from top to bottom, from left to right. She has my thanks for keeping me between the (electronic) lines.

Shannon Garza gave me feedback on the emotional highs and lows of this piece (in addition to searching tirelessly for all those pesky errors I sneak in to give her something to hunt for) and helped it achieve whatever emotional resonance it may have (for me it held a lot, your mileage may vary).

Debra Wesley once more assisted me in finding errors, eliminating inconsistencies, and picking up little details that I hope my more eagle-eyed readers find (hints for the future, so read close).

Calvin Sams also read over this particular work, giving me some notes on his thoughts, and for that, I thank him.

Robin McDermott also provided a great deal of editorial input, helping to shape the way this manuscript was written, and helped me catch some very important errors.

Wendy Arnburg took time to help me figure out exactly which guns Sienna would find most comfortable. She would want me to tell you that the choice of Sienna's back-up gun (a Walther PPK) was totally the author's choice, and a nod to the world's most famous fiction user of said firearm, and was against her advisement.

Janelle Seinkner took time to answer a few medical questions about things that I wondered about (for Sienna, not for me). That help was much needed, and my thanks go to her for it. Any medical errors that remain are probably there because I should have listened closer to her rather than tried to go with what was best for the story.

The cover was designed by Karri Klawitter (Artbykarri.com).

Exceptional covers, exceptional prices.

Thanks also to Nicholas J. Ambrose, who did the edit and format work here once more. Nick is truly a titan, and one of those most responsible for my work upholding the level of professionalism that it does. During the final phase of publication of this book it was driven home to me in a very obvious fashion how much Nick has contributed to every one of my books, and for that, I thank him.

Sienna Nealon returns in

FAMILY
The Girl in the Box
Book 4

Available now!

Author's Note

Thanks for reading! If you want to know immediately when future books become available, take sixty seconds and sign up for my NEW RELEASE EMAIL ALERTS by visiting my website. I don't sell your information and I only send out emails when I have a new book out. The reason you should sign up for this is because I don't always set release dates, and even if you're following me on Facebook (robertJcrane (Author)) or Twitter (@robertJcrane), it's easy to miss my book announcements because...well, because social media is an imprecise thing.

Come join the discussion on my website:
http://www.robertjcrane.com!

Cheers,
Robert J. Crane

Other Works by Robert J. Crane

The Girl in the Box *and* Out of the Box
Contemporary Urban Fantasy

Alone: The Girl in the Box, Book 1
Untouched: The Girl in the Box, Book 2
Soulless: The Girl in the Box, Book 3
Family: The Girl in the Box, Book 4
Omega: The Girl in the Box, Book 5
Broken: The Girl in the Box, Book 6
Enemies: The Girl in the Box, Book 7
Legacy: The Girl in the Box, Book 8
Destiny: The Girl in the Box, Book 9
Power: The Girl in the Box, Book 10

Limitless: Out of the Box, Book 1
In the Wind: Out of the Box, Book 2
Ruthless: Out of the Box, Book 3
Grounded: Out of the Box, Book 4
Tormented: Out of the Box, Book 5
Vengeful: Out of the Box, Book 6
Sea Change: Out of the Box, Book 7
Painkiller: Out of the Box, Book 8
Masks: Out of the Box, Book 9
Prisoners: Out of the Box, Book 10
Unyielding: Out of the Box, Book 11
Hollow: Out of the Box, Book 12
Toxicity: Out of the Box, Book 13
Small Things: Out of the Box, Book 14
Hunters: Out of the Box, Book 15
Badder: Out of the Box, Book 16
Apex: Out of the Box, Book 18
Time: Out of the Box, Book 19
Driven: Out of the Box, Book 20
Remember: Out of the Box, Book 21
Hero: Out of the Box, Book 22* *(Coming October 2018!)*
Flashback: Out of the Box, Book 23* *(Coming December 2018!)*
Walk Through Fire: Out of the Box, Book 24* *(Coming in 2019!)*

World of Sanctuary
Epic Fantasy

Defender: The Sanctuary Series, Volume One
Avenger: The Sanctuary Series, Volume Two
Champion: The Sanctuary Series, Volume Three
Crusader: The Sanctuary Series, Volume Four
Sanctuary Tales, Volume One - A Short Story Collection
Thy Father's Shadow: The Sanctuary Series, Volume 4.5
Master: The Sanctuary Series, Volume Five
Fated in Darkness: The Sanctuary Series, Volume 5.5
Warlord: The Sanctuary Series, Volume Six
Heretic: The Sanctuary Series, Volume Seven
Legend: The Sanctuary Series, Volume Eight
Ghosts of Sanctuary: The Sanctuary Series, Volume Nine
Call of the Hero: The Sanctuary Series, Volume Ten* *(Coming Late 2018!)*

A Haven in Ash: Ashes of Luukessia, Volume One *(with Michael Winstone)*
A Respite From Storms: Ashes of Luukessia, Volume Two *(with Michael Winstone)*
A Home in the Hills: Ashes of Luukessia, Volume Three* *(with Michael Winstone—Coming Mid to Late 2018!)*

Southern Watch
Contemporary Urban Fantasy

Called: Southern Watch, Book 1
Depths: Southern Watch, Book 2
Corrupted: Southern Watch, Book 3
Unearthed: Southern Watch, Book 4
Legion: Southern Watch, Book 5
Starling: Southern Watch, Book 6
Forsaken: Southern Watch, Book 7
Hallowed: Southern Watch, Book 8* *(Coming Late 2018/Early 2019!)*

The Shattered Dome Series
(with Nicholas J. Ambrose)
Sci-Fi

Voiceless: The Shattered Dome, Book 1
Unspeakable: The Shattered Dome, Book 2* *(Coming 2018!)*

The Mira Brand Adventures
Contemporary Urban Fantasy

The World Beneath: The Mira Brand Adventures, Book 1
The Tide of Ages: The Mira Brand Adventures, Book 2
The City of Lies: The Mira Brand Adventures, Book 3
The King of the Skies: The Mira Brand Adventures, Book 4
The Best of Us: The Mira Brand Adventures, Book 5
We Aimless Few: The Mira Brand Adventures, Book 6* *(Coming 2018!)*

Liars and Vampires
(with Lauren Harper)
Contemporary Urban Fantasy

No One Will Believe You: Liars and Vampires, Book 1
Someone Should Save Her: Liars and Vampires, Book 2
You Can't Go Home Again: Liars and Vampires, Book 3
In The Dark: Liars and Vampires, Book 4
Her Lying Days Are Done: Liars and Vampires, Book 5* *(Coming August 2018!)*
Heir of the Dog: Liars and Vampires, Book 6* *(Coming September 2018!)*
Hit You Where You Live: Liars and Vampires, Book 7* *(Coming October 2018!)*

* Forthcoming, Subject to Change